The Castlefield Collector

FREDA LIGHTFOOT

The Castlefield Collector

CANELO

First published in the United Kingdom in 2004 by Hodder & Stoughton Ltd

This edition published in the United Kingdom in 2020 by

Canelo Digital Publishing Limited
Third Floor, 20 Mortimer Street
London W1T 3JW
United Kingdom
Copyright © Freda Lightfoot, 2004

A CIP catalogue record for this book is available from the British Library.

Print ISBN 978 1 78863 805 0
Ebook ISBN 978 1 78863 667 4

Look for more great books at www.canelo.co

Printed and bound in Great Britain by Clays Ltd, Elcograf S.p.A.

Chapter One

Dolly Tomkins put her arms about her mother's frail shoulders and hugged her tight. 'It'll be all right Mam, you'll see. Dad'll walk through the door any minute with his wage packet in his hand.'

'Aye, course he will, chuck.'

They both knew this to be wishful thinking. When had Calvin Tomkins ever put the needs of his family before a sure-fire certainty? That was how he viewed any bet, whether on the dogs, the horses, or two raindrops running down a windowsill. And since it was a Friday and payday at the mill, his pocket would be full of brass, burning a hole in his pocket. Most women hereabouts would be waiting with their open hand held out to collect wages as each member of the family came home on pay day. Maisie certainly did that with the three children she still had left at home: Willy, Dolly and Aggie, but had learned that it was a pointless occupation to wait for Calvin's pay packet. He wouldn't give a single thought to his long-suffering wife and daughters, not for a moment.

Dolly studied her mother's face more closely as she bent to cut the cardboard to fit, and slid it into the sole of her boot. The lines seemed to be etched deeper than ever. Dark rings lay like purple bruises beneath soft grey eyes, which had once shone with hope and laughter, and her too-thin shoulders were slumped with weariness. She looked what she was, a woman beaten down by life and by a husband who thought nothing of stealing the last halfpenny from her purse in order to feed his habit, his addiction, despite the family already being on the brink of starvation.

Maisie handed the boots to her younger daughter with a rare smile. 'There y'are love, see how that feels.'

Dolly slid her feet inside and agreed they were just fine, making no mention of how the boots pinched her toes since she'd grown quite a lot recently. They'd been Aggie's long before they'd come to her and probably Maisie's before that, and their numerous patches had themselves been patched, over and over again.

Mending her daughters' footwear was a task carried out each and every Friday in order to give the boots a fresh lease of life. Dolly wore clogs throughout the long working week, but in the evenings and at weekends when she wasn't at the mill, she liked to make a show of dressing up. Worse, it'd rained for days and Dolly's small feet were frozen to the marrow. She'd paid a visit to Edna Crawshaw's corner shop and begged a bit of stiff cardboard off her, whole boxes being at a premium. This piece had Brooke Bond Tea stamped all over it but that didn't trouble Dolly; the card was thick and strong and would keep out the wet for a while, which was the only consideration that mattered.

Even so, Dolly longed for a proper pair of shoes instead of this pair of old fashioned button boots; ones with a strap, which would set her off as the modish young woman she so wanted to be. She longed too for a beaded dress with a square neck and no sleeves, the kind with a short skirt that was all the rage at the moment. Perhaps in a deep blue to match her eyes and to set off the shine of her bobbed hair, dark as a blackbird's wing. In all her sixteen years, Dolly had never possessed anything that hadn't been handed down to her from her older sister. She ached for something new, for something entirely her own, instead of having to share everything, even her bed with Aggie.

She never expressed these thoughts out loud, of course, because it would only upset Mam, and where was the point in such dreams anyway? The Tomkins family considered themselves fortunate if they had bread and dripping on the table. Tonight, being payday, Maisie might buy them each a potato pie, and tomorrow be able to afford to add a bit of boiled mutton to the stew pot that sat on the hob day in and day out. Even more exciting, Dolly and Aggie planned to go to the Cromwell Picture House to see Mary Pickford in *Little Annie Roonie*, a rare treat indeed.

'Oh hecky thump, he's here already!' Maisie Tomkins sank to her knees, pulling the two girls down beside her, so that their heads slid down below the windowsill and would not be seen by the man now hammering on their front door. The letterbox flew open and his raucous voice echoed loudly around the small room that served as both kitchen and living room in the back-to-back terraced house.

Dolly felt a surge of resentment that he could see in; that his greedy little eyes could explore their humble home. Though what was there to see? A stone flagged floor, a pegged rug, a black-leaded grate, which combined fireplace, oven and hot water-boiler, and a slop stone where the washing up was done. The only furniture comprised half a dozen bentwood chairs and a deal table where the family ate, (when they were fortunate enough to have food to put on it, that is), or perform any other function that required a flat surface. The table was covered with a dark red chenille cloth with bobbles round the edge, of which Maisie was inordinately proud. This was taken off when the table was used for baking and other messy jobs, or covered with a scrap of scorched cotton for the ironing. Other than the beds upstairs, this was all they possessed in the world, plus what little remained of their pride. No different from anyone else who lived hereabouts, whether in Tully Court or any of the other ginnels, courts and alleyways which led off Potato Wharf.

'I know yer in there Maisie Tomkins, so don't think ye can escape by hiding from me. I'll be back, don't you fear.' Again he applied his fist to the rickety panels of the door, and followed this up with a vicious kick from his booted foot.

Maisie jumped, stifling her own instinctive whimper of fear as she drew her two daughters close and silenced them with a fierce glare. Not that either Aggie or Dolly needed telling to keep their mouths shut and their heads down. They'd been hiding from the talleyman, the rent man, the insurance collector and any one of the many bookies that Calvin got involved with, for as long as they could remember. They'd grown up with these tricks so that even though they were now young women, their one thought was to steer clear of trouble, for their mother's sake. Even Aggie, not known for her patience, was keeping silent, biting down so hard on her lower lip, she was almost sucking off the cheap lipstick she'd so recently applied. Nevertheless, when the knocking finally stopped, Aggie was the first to speak.

'Has the bugger gone?'

'Hush love, I'll have no bad language here. What would yer dad have to say if he heard you?'

'Dad would say nothing against me. It's you what's got us into this mess.' Certain always of her father's uncritical love, Aggie gave a little toss of her head, flicking back her pretty chestnut curls, hazel eyes glinting.

'Eeh, how can you say such a thing?' Maisie heaved a weary sigh and sank further down onto the stone flagged floor, leaning her head against the damp wall. 'Why can you not appreciate that I've done my best to manage but it's not easy? Everyone's suffering with wages being what they are. There's talk of a general strike, of the whole country being brought to a standstill and all workers coming out in sympathy with the miners. Where will we be then, eh? And what has that got to do with me, or yer dad for that matter?'

Despite severe provocation, Maisie had never once blamed her husband for the plight they were in. That would have been far too risky, much safer to blame the bosses, the rich businessmen who cut wages to penurious levels year after year. Dolly understood very little about the economics of an industry which had once been called King Cotton, and in which she'd been employed for the last two years, ever since she'd started work as a doffer in the mill at fourteen. She'd done her job, knocking off the filled bobbins or cops as they were called, and replacing them with empty ones, needing to stand on a stool and use a long stick in order to reach, her being so small. Oh, but she loved it in the mill and was doing well, having achieved her dream to become a spinner. She was proud to walk to work every morning with the tools of her trade clanking in her pinny pocket: including her shears and sharp knife of which she took great care.

Yet she'd never questioned why it was that despite working long hours, she brought home little more than a pittance, a few shillings to give to her mam and only coppers left over for herself, if she was lucky.

According to Maisie, the post-war boom in cotton had lasted barely a couple of years before the bosses, the mill owners, were cutting wages and yet at the same time trying to force up production. The unions, such as existed, had resisted objecting to new technology, to the introduction of ring-spinning and automatic looms which meant fewer operatives would be needed, and in particular to the lower rate paid for piece work. But there was more to the relentless decline of cotton than that, something to do with rigid, outdated systems and of a reduction in demand, with fewer orders coming in from abroad; that mysterious world beyond Manchester and even the shores of England, of which Dolly was largely ignorant, save for the bits of the British Empire marked in red on the map that had adorned her classroom wall as a girl.

Even with her elder brothers having married and left home, with only their Willy, Aggie and herself left to feed, there never seemed to be quite enough to make ends meet. But then Willy was sickly and more out of work than in. She and Aggie brought in next to nothing, as they all knew what Dad did with his money.

There were some weeks when Calvin would be in the pub before six in the morning, tempted in by the ale and a warm fire, and never get into work at all, staying there till closing time, not just drinking but also laying illegal bets with the bookie's runner, celebrating when he won, or drowning his sorrows when he lost. He'd do this day after day for as much as a week, till he was too drunk to get out of bed. Then he'd try and sober up and abstain for a week or two before it started all over again. Somehow or other he always managed to hold on to his job, him being a skilled spinner. Everyone knew his failing and seemed to tolerate it. Unfortunately, much of this betting and drinking was done on tick, or by borrowing money from Nifty Jack, the talleyman, to feed his habit.

Mam too was forced to borrow in order to survive, which left her constantly struggling to catch up with a debt that grew bigger as the months and years slid by, despite the huge sums she poured into Nifty Jack's pocket. Now she was in hock up to her ears and would constantly warn her two daughters to watch for the talleyman. 'He's after more than your money. He'll wring the last drop of life-blood from your veins, if he can.'

As if echoing these thoughts, Maisie said, 'Edna Crawshaw were telling me only this morning how when poor Molly Jenkins died, she were still owing on a blanket she'd been paying off on t'club at threepence a week, and the talleyman came and took it from her starving children, before she was even cold in her coffin.'

Aggie gave a snort of derision. 'Edna Crawshaw's an old gossip. You shouldn't listen to a word she says. What do you think she says about you, about *us* when yer back is turned. I've heard her nattering on about dad an' all, nosy old witch.'

'Nay lass, I don't reckon she says owt that isn't true. Edna's me best mate. She'd say nought against me. Anyroad, she knows how things stand. She understands.'

'Well, *I* don't understand. I wish someone would explain to me how it is we're always on our beam ends despite us all working every God-given hour, and Dad being one of the best spinners in all of Barker's Mill. All right, he falls off the wagon now and then, but what man doesn't round here? If there isn't enough money coming in, why don't *you* get a job, instead of swanning about at home all day.'

'*Swanning about?*' Maisie looked hurt. 'If that's what you think I do, girl, you've a lot to learn. I never had your advantages, reading and writing and such-like. Anyroad, yer Dad will never hear of it. He likes me at home, looking after you lot, and you know very well I help out with the lads' nippers so their wives can work. I've spent all me life looking after childer. What more can I do?'

Maisie also did a good deal of her daughters-in-laws' washing, even now a string of dingy looking nappies hung on the clothes rack above the pitiful fire in a vain attempt to dry them.

Aggie gave a loud sniff, and cast a scathing glance in Dolly's direction. 'You could make her do a few more chores for a start, instead of letting her off just because she's the youngest. It's enough to make a saint swear the way you spoil that girl.'

Maisie looked shocked. 'Now you're blaspheming, our Aggie, and I'll not have it, not in this house.' Her husband might swear and drink like a trouper but Maisie was a devout Methodist and believed in certain standards in a stoic acceptance of whatever life threw at you. She never complained herself, but took her troubles to discuss them with the Good Lord three times every Sunday and refused to tolerate any moaning from other members of her family.

Aggie ignored her. 'I'm stating a simple truth. If you hadn't borrowed so much money we wouldn't be in this pickle, and dad wouldn't feel the need to bury his misery down at the pub, or be putting money he can ill afford on illegal bets.'

'Eeh, Aggie, you can't blame me for that. You can be right nasty at times. You watch yer lip madam, if you please.'

Aggie had no intention of doing anything of the sort. Once having started along this road, her greatest pleasure was to take out on her mother a very real sense of resentment that her life wasn't more comfortable, and nothing Maisie could say would stop her.

'Look at this latest loan you've taken out, just for a frock for our Dolly. What a waste of money when she could have used an old one of mine.'

'I bought a bit of sateen, that's all, and I'm stitching it myself, by hand, for her to wear in the Whit Walks. She wants something new, all of her own, and why shouldn't she have it? She'll look grand in it, a real bobby-dazzler. I never hear you complain when I buy something new for you.'

Feeling guilty that even her own simple dreams had put her mother into further debt, Dolly shut her ears to the quarrel. She'd heard it too often before, in any case. She tried to make herself comfortable on the hard, cold stone flags and mentally switched off; not listening to a word as the two women fell into their usual squabbling, though her heart was burning with hatred for the talleyman. Jack Trafford, or Nifty Jack as he was more familiarly known, had a bag of cold copper coins where his heart should be. It was said that he would take a jam buttie from a baby's fist if its mother was behind with her payments.

Easing herself up a fraction so that she could see over the sill, Dolly peered out into the street, catching a glimpse of his short, stocky figure as he strode away. His walk was unmistakable: feet flung out and with such a swagger and spring to his step you'd think he owned the place, his trademark bowler perched precariously on his round, ugly head. There was a leather bag slung across his hunched shoulders and in one hand he held a notebook, fastened with a piece of black elastic into which he tucked his pencil. He was a couple of doors down now; hammering and shouting for Ma Liversedge, letting the street know her business.

'Open up, you daft old cow,' he shouted. 'You're three weeks behind, so if you don't shape theeself I'll have you thrown in t'workhouse.' He licked the end of his pencil and wrote something in the notebook.

Dolly was familiar even with the style of his writing: small cramped letters in the same dark, purple ink that stained his short, podgy fingers, together with the brown of nicotine from the endless cigarettes he smoked. The nails, surprisingly, were neatly clipped and she'd often seen him fastidiously pick a thread off his jacket, or smooth his stiffly starched collar with the flat of his hand. And his brown shoes were polished as bright as conkers.

Yet for all his dandy ways he was the nastiest, ugliest little man in all of the twin cities of Manchester and Salford put together, certainly in all of Castlefield. Dolly loathed him with a ferocity that ate her up inside. She'd like to see him dropped head first in the River Medlock for all the misery he'd caused their family, positively encouraging her Dad in his daft exploits. And she longed to save her mam from his podgy, grasping fingers. Small as she was, being teasingly referred to by her older brothers as the scrapings up off the mill floor, Dolly had a big heart and wanted nothing more than to see her mam happy again, to see a warm smile light her careworn face.

'I'll go and fetch me dad,' she said, coming to a sudden decision. 'Don't worry I can guess where he is. I'll fetch him home. Strike or no strike we have to eat, and bills have to be paid.'

Maisie put up a hand to stop her but before even she could open her mouth to protest, Dolly was off, knowing she'd find her father in one of his favourite local pubs down by the docks or under the viaduct, no doubt conducting his 'bit of business' as he euphemistically termed his gambling. She'd find him and make him put things right for her mam.

Chapter Two

Dolly ran down Dawson Street, cut across the rickety wooden bridge that spanned the River Medlock, the water beneath black with rubbish and oil. On Potato Wharf she passed carters in their leather jackets, a traction engine bringing bales of cotton to the mills, barges tipping out their cargoes or collecting finished goods to ship to Liverpool and the world beyond. Not lingering to chat to any of the folks she knew, she turned up Elm Street and pushed her way into the Navigation, eyes scanning the crush of men that filled the taproom.

'Have you seen me dad?' she asked of anyone she recognised.

Heads were shaken, bellows of laughter and a few ribald jokes about old Cal having got a boatload on again, meaning he was probably drunk somewhere.

'Take his missus a sweetener till he gets home, chuck,' said one chap, indicating she should buy Maisie a jug of stout.

But she only shook her head and dashed off again. He wasn't in the Queens either, or any of his other usual haunts so, barely pausing for breath she ran the length of Liverpool Road, down Duke Street and round the corner into Bridgewater Street. Neither was he under the viaduct or by the old roman fort, not even by the Rochdale Canal playing pitch and toss, one of his favourite sports. After a few more enquiries she finally learned of a meeting being held on Coal Wharf, something to do with the strike.

It was growing dark by the time she found him and Dolly felt faint with exhaustion, but there he was with a crowd of other textile workers, all shouting their heads off about 'Reds and Bolshies,' which puzzled Dolly since they'd been told in lessons at John Street School that the Russian revolution had been settled long ago, before the end of the Great War. Didn't England rule the waves?

Dolly knew that Prime Minister Stanley Baldwin, who Calvin largely approved of, was in power now and that while his government had tried to lure the miners into accepting a reduction in wages, they'd also urged the owners to make concessions too, to offer better working conditions such as pithead baths and shorter hours. So why didn't the bosses agree to the terms and let them all get back to work? She wished grown-ups wouldn't argue so much.

Her own dad was forever shouting at her mam, who rarely retaliated. Maisie always looked battered and crestfallen, as if she'd fought a battle and lost, when she hadn't even opened her mouth. When he got bored with beating the hell out of her, he'd start on at their Willy for always being poorly, or at Josh, Abel or Eli whenever they came calling with their families, which was less often these days. When the lads had still been at home, there'd been endless scenes of warfare in their house, so was it any wonder.

'It's worse than being back on the Somme,' Josh would say. All four of her older brothers had served in the Great War but only three had come home, Manny having been killed at Ypres. But in Dolly's opinion, a prime minister should surely do better and be able to sort things out good and proper.

From the turmoil she saw unfolding before her eyes, it would seem not. While the miners were yelling 'Not a penny off the pay, not a minute on the day,' many of the textile workers were reminding them that half a loaf was better than no bread and refusing to support them.

'Transport and General have already come out. What are we waiting for?' called one man.

'Aye, and I reckon gas and electricity will be next.'

There was a good deal of booing, bawling and shouting, some men resorting to fisticuffs in an effort to make their point;

much of it, Dolly realised, out of desperation for their own plight. She could see Calvin waving his great fist and shouting louder than the rest.

'Nothing to do wi' us,' he roared. 'Why should we lose our wages for you lot? How will it help if our families starve an' all?'

It shamed her that her own father, a great brawn of a man who'd never lost a day's work through ill health in his life, could have so little sympathy for his fellow men: miners who worked in appalling conditions underground. And he cared even less for his own wife. It was all right him shouting about how his own family would starve if they agreed to the strike, but weren't they close to starvation already? Wasn't he throwing good money down the drain every time he used his hard-earned brass to place a bet?

If she could just reach him before he'd spent it all today, they might get by for another week, although Nifty Jack would take most of what she and Aggie earned. At least they didn't need money to buy coal, since there was none to be had because of the strike. She wished Aggie had come with her, since Dad always listened to her sister. He'd never paid any heed to whatever she had to say, or anything she'd ever done for that matter. Half the time he didn't seem to notice she was around, and when he did it was more often than not to bawl her out or clock her one.

Dolly could still recall with painful clarity the day of the Sunday school party. They were expected to take a penny each in order to pay for it. There was just Willy, Aggie and herself, the others being too old for such things by then. Yet even with only the three of them left to worry about and pay for, he'd forgotten all about her. When Aggie had opened the purse there were only two pennies inside, one for herself and one for Willy. Neither of them were prepared to give up their chance of the party, and if it hadn't been for her friends, Sam Clayton and Matt, who'd begged the Sunday School Superintendent to let

Dolly in for nothing, she would have missed it altogether. It was the most humiliating experience of her young life.

But this didn't stop Dolly from worshipping the ground Calvin walked on, great giant of a man that he was with his broad, square shoulders, pot belly and trousers hanging low from a leather belt she'd felt the weight of more than once across her backside. She always forgave him, as her mother did, for his unfeeling behaviour because that's how he was. He knew no different.

His own parents, who had been so neglectful they'd often forgotten to feed him, or even cut his hair and nails, had shut him in a coalhole for hours on end. Both his brothers had died in infancy and after his father died, the young Calvin had cared for his mother without a word of thanks or sign of gratitude until one day she'd up and left and he'd never clapped eyes on her from that day to this. Consequently, Calvin Tomkins wasn't an easy man to love but he was, nonetheless, Dolly's dad and she lived in hope that he would wake up one day and see that she was only trying to do her best by him and her mam.

Pushing through the crowd, she came up beside him and tugged on his sleeve. 'Dad, are you coming home soon? Mam's waiting for your wages. She's already had the rent man call, put a penny in the gas meter and settled what were on tick. Nifty Jack nearly kicked the door in wanting his whack. He's threatened to come back later.' She relayed this tale in one breathless rush, hoping to impress him with the urgency of the situation.

Calvin shook himself free of her grasp, as if irritated to be reminded of his responsibilities. 'What the bleedin' hell are you doing here? Gerroff home. Can't you see I'm busy and what's going on?'

Dolly realised instantly that she should have taken more care. The minute she'd set eyes on him, she should have known that he was roaring drunk, his great belly in its filthy vest nearly knocking her over as he staggered and rocked, belched and hiccupped.

'Buzz off, you!' he shouted, but Dolly didn't move. She was too used to his raucous behaviour, to his peppering every other sentence with 'bloody' or 'bleeding'. There were times when he used worse epithets to vent his wrath but she didn't mind those either. Not in the least. Far better than the days, weeks even, when he didn't speak to her at all. At least when he was shouting at her he was paying her some attention, and Dolly would persuade herself that this meant he did care for her. Yet he could be so cruel! So unkind! Almost as if he didn't love her at all but then there were times when Dolly wasn't sure that she truly loved him, her own father. Maybe she hated him.

Not that this was the moment to be worrying about all of that, judging by the size of the crowd milling about. She could tell they were growing angrier by the minute. Perhaps Dad was right. She shouldn't be here at all. Dolly gazed up at him out of frightened eyes. 'I can see that Mam's at her wits' end. Give me some money, Dad, and I'll go. Give us yer wage packet. *Please!* That's all me mam wants.'

'Want, want, want! That's all I hear from her these days. What do you think I work for, to see every shilling disappear into Nifty Jack's pocket? Not flaming likely.'

'She doesn't want it wasted on booze and betting, not with the threat of a general strike.'

'This is men's business, gerroff wi' you.' He gave her a hefty shove and Dolly very nearly fell to the ground, might well have done so and been trampled underfoot, save for the press of men who left her barely enough room to stand, let alone fall. A man standing on a wall began ranting on about this not being the moment for revolution, asking who wanted to risk lockouts and starvation? Another responded by saying that if they didn't stand together, they'd all go under.

And then a voice rang out. 'Hey up, rozzers are coming.'

Sure enough, from under the massive dome of railway arches emerged what seemed to Dolly like an army of police, many on horseback, and her heart surged with fear. What would happen now? Would the men fight and her dad get arrested? She saw the horses begin to trot and then break into a gallop, charging towards the raggle-taggle group of men gathered alongside the canal. She heard a crack, like a firework, and it came to her on a fresh beat of alarm that the police were firing over the heads of the crowd. There was mass panic as men started to run this way and that, but, their exit blocked by the canal, many were falling in, others clambering over each other in a desperate bid to escape. Women screamed, batons were swung, clogs thrown, and the ground seemed to be littered with bodies, strewn clothing and abandoned banners.

Calvin stood as if paralysed and once again Dolly shook her father's arm, this time with greater urgency. 'Dad, Dad, come on home with me now. We've got to go quick.'

'I've told you to buzz off.'

This time the flat of his hand caught her smack across the back of her head and Dolly found herself knocked sideways. She was pinioned to the wall, trapped by the crowd, with what seemed like the last of her breath being squeezed out of her by the crush of sweating, frightened men. She felt the weight of a boot come down on her ankle, causing her to scream out loud in agony. Could it be broken? Desperation gave her the strength to hang on, managing not to be dragged to the ground. She became aware of rapidly approaching hoof beats. Utterly convinced she was about to be trampled underfoot by an army of horses, she turned to Calvin for help at exactly the moment her father deserted her. He launched himself into the fleeing crowd, hell-bent on saving his own skin.

He hadn't even noticed her perilous situation, paid no heed to her sobs and cries. Dolly was swept away in a relentless tide of heaving bodies and she knew then that it was useless. Instinct told her that her father was angry because there weren't any wages left for him to hand over. Not a single penny. He'd already lost them in the Navigation or down on the towpath in a betting ring. It was all far too late.

Dolly limped back home to Tully Court empty-handed and Maisie strapped up her ankle which fortunately was only strained and badly bruised, with no bones broken. There was no trip to the pictures that night, and no potato pie supper. They didn't dare risk spending even one of their few remaining pennies. Instead, the three women made do with the watery mess from the stew-pot, although Calvin himself came home roaring drunk around midnight.

–

Ma Liversedge, two doors down from the Tomkins, had another visit from the talleyman later that day, just as she was drinking her milk-less tea out of a jam jar, her only two remaining cups and saucers being kept for best, when he breezed in without even knocking.

'How do, Ma. What've you got fer me then?'

The old woman stared at him grim-faced, the HP sauce buttie in her hand the nearest thing to a meal she'd had all day. 'Nothing.'

'Oh, I think you can do better than that, love. You must have something that you haven't yet pawned. Thirty bob is what you owe me, including rent, and thirty bob is what I intend to have, one way or another.' He smiled at her, his small, weasel eyes glittering with menace.

'I've told ya, I've nothing. Only thing I had left after my George died was the piano, and I pawned that last back end. Everything's gone, even me double bed. But then I never go upstairs. I sleep on this truckle in t'corner to keep warm by t'fire. What else can I give you? Me virginity? Nay, too late.' She cackled with delight. 'Long gone, to a better man than you'll ever be. I can't even give you skin off me rice pudding, cause I've no bloody milk. Nor rice neither.' Enchanted by her own wit, the old woman laughed so much, it set her off coughing.

Ignoring her, Nifty Jack began opening and closing drawers and doors in an ancient cupboard, searching through the detritus of seventy-five long years. He checked the stone shelves in the pantry, finding them largely empty save for stacks of folded newspaper used to cover her kitchen table, and a few jam jars and bottles being saved for the pennies she'd get back on them. He put these into a brown paper carrier bag he'd brought with him. He might as well have them. Every penny helped. Then he rooted under the old brown slopstone sink. 'You must have something to live on besides my generosity, or why aren't you in t'workhouse? Where do you hide it then, your stash? Come on, you old witch, hand it over.'

Her eyes were watchful as he prowled about her kitchen; picked up the empty milk jug, set it down again with a grimace of distaste at the sour stench. She did indeed have a few bob tucked away, sufficient to buy a decent burial and inscribe her name on the headstone of the family grave, but she'd climb into it before she told him where it was. Ma Liversedge folded her arms and her lips, and said nothing.

Then his gaze lighted on the mantelshelf. All the ornaments and bric-a-brac, which had once adorned its surface, were long gone, including the gold-plated clock her late husband had been presented with for his years in the mill. It had paid for his funeral expenses when he died of byssinosis a year or two back, the result of cotton dust in his lungs. Nifty ran his hand under the pristine clean lace cover, then noting the fineness of the fabric carefully folded it and slid it in the carrier bag with the jam jars.

The old woman flinched, her mouth trembling with distress. 'That were me mother's.'

'And now it's mine.' He glowered at her for a moment longer then smiled. 'It's the perfect solution. You've not pawned your wedding ring.'

Ma Liversedge was utterly startled, and she cupped her right hand over her left, covering the plain gold band to cradle it against her breast. 'Nay, lad, my George give me that near fifty year ago. Tha'd not take an old woman's wedding ring.'

It took him a long time to get it off, and a good deal of soap to ease it's path but as he worked it over the bent, swollen knuckles he paid no heed to the old woman's protests, her shouts and curses, and finally her tearful pleading to spare her this most treasured possession. When he finally succeeded, he slipped it into his pocket with a flourish of triumph and strode away, leaving her slumped in her chair in a state of shock.

But it was the last money he ever got out of her. Poor Ma Liversedge joined her poor late husband, George, before the week was out.

Two days later the call came. 'Everyone out!' Aggie and Dolly, along with the rest of the women, shut down their spinning frames, flung their shawls over their heads and had no option but to walk out of the mill and join the strike.

Chapter Three

'Why shouldn't I have a smoking suit if I want one? They are all the rage. Quite the latest thing, don't you know? I shall have one made in gold satin, trimmed with burgundy and finished with a matching sash, scarf and turban. Don't you think that would be too divine? I do believe that I'm sufficiently svelte to have the trousers quite wide, don't you?' Evie ran a delicate white hand over one slim hip, while holding a glass of Tio Pepe with the other.

Nathan Barker raised his eyes from his copy of *The Times*, a mere shadow of its former self due to the strike, consisting as it did of a single folded sheet, to scowl at his daughter. 'You don't smoke, Evelyn, and I have no intention of allowing you to start such an unpleasant habit, no matter how fashionable, so you will have no requirement for a smoking suit.'

'Oh, fizz, what an absolute bore you are, Pops. Where is the harm? You're far too serious for words, isn't he Mummy? You'd have no objection to my having one, would you darling, and a divinely long cigarette holder to hold my Turkish. What do you think, Mumsie sweet?'

Clara Barker cast a quick glance in her husband's direction and assured her darling child that she would look utterly sparkling and scintillating in a coarse linen sheet, should she choose to wear one.

'Don't be silly, Mumsie, but you have no objection to my smoking, have you? And if I do, I must wear the proper outfit, must I not?'

Clara gave a sigh of resignation but chose not to answer her daughter's enquiry, rather she turned away from nineteen-year-old Evie, who looked on the verge of one of her tantrums to quietly address her husband, a slight frown marring her usually smooth brow. 'Is it true that the strike is going ahead?'

'According to *The Times* there's been a complete walk-out, although apparently the Stock Exchange remains calm. I've never known it so quiet. Eerily so, as if it were a Sunday and not a working day. Not a soul to be seen out on the streets. The mill fires are damped down so there's no smoke from the chimneys, no trams or buses running, no mail being delivered. Just a few young lads selling these newssheets. I will say there's little sign of disorder, no lawlessness but then there are soldiers posted around the city. Police on patrol. They at least have no option but to work.'

'But how will it affect us?'

'It could go on too long, quite badly. We're suffering enough at present, what with foreign imports and the whole way the industry is set up.' Nathan tossed the paper aside, his florid face filled with irritation as it always was when he expounded on his favourite hobby horse. 'The fact that we have separate organisations for weaving, another for spinning, one for dying and finishing, merchanting and so on is creating a constraint to the development of the industry. Why can't anyone see that this may have worked well before the war, but not now, not any more. How can we move forward when we still have one foot planted so firmly in the past?'

'But don't you think the strike is justified? Or do you believe the Earl of Balfour is correct when he says that no revolution in Britain is going to diminish foreign competition?'

Nathan gave his wife a sharp look. It always surprised him how interested she was in politics, and how much of a radical she was. Yet on this matter they were, for once, in agreement. 'I'm sure that is absolutely true, dear, but, like it or not, the strikers do have a point. Much as I am compelled to comply with the practice, I am aware that constantly cutting wages is not a long-term solution. The principle is unsound. How can we possibly reduce them sufficiently to match those in India? Even if we did, how would that increase productivity? If I've said so once when we've discussed this at the Exchange, I've said it a dozen times, we need to put a stop to this business of protective tariffs and level the playing-field.'

He was on his feet now, stalking back and forth, stabbing the air with an urgent finger, as was his wont. 'More importantly, we need to restructure the entire industry, to get all sections to pull together in order to eliminate waste and properly use spare capacity. We'll never deal effectively with our competitors if we're too busy squabbling amongst ourselves. If the industry is to survive, we *have* to make it more efficient and less of a blundering albatross.'

'Excuse me,' Evie interrupted, rather peevishly. 'I believe we were discussing my new wardrobe and forthcoming engagement to Freddie, not the *strike*, nor the *mill*.' She pronounced the word as if it offended her, stamping one small foot in order to gain her parents' attention, although taking care not to spill her drink as she did so.

'Can't you ever think of anyone other than yourself, child?' Nathan said, losing patience with her sulks, as usual. 'It may surprise you to learn that while we sip our aperitifs before dinner, some people can't afford to put bread on their table, let alone purchase ridiculous costumes they don't need.'

'Now you're just being unkind.' Evie let out a heartrending sob.

Setting down her glass of fine sherry, Clara rose elegantly from the sofa and hurried across to put her arms about her daughter and pat her gently on the shoulder. Flushed quite pink in the cheeks, if there was one thing Evie hated, it was to be ignored. 'Darling, you should remember that there will be no wardrobe, or lovely wedding for that matter, if the mill doesn't survive.

'I'm trying to make you understand that smoking suits and engagement parties are not the be all and end all in life,' her father snapped. 'Not when folk are starving and many mills in danger of going bump.'

Evie's wide, expressive mouth quivered and her eyes filled with tears. 'Oh Pops, how can you be so cruel? It's not *my* fault they are starving, so why take it out on me? You always have to spoil everything. I simply want things to be *nice*. It's not every day a girl gets engaged, and I have to start thinking about my trousseau, or it will never be ready in time for the wedding. What is so wrong in that?'

'Nothing at all, darling,' Clara soothed. If challenged, she would freely admit to having spoiled Evie. Hadn't Nathan told her so a hundred times? But after losing her first three babies, and with a largely absent husband, was it any wonder? 'It's just that Papa has other priorities and worries on his mind at the present time. You should try to see his point of view, at least a little, my sweet.'

Evie set down her glass with a snap, almost breaking the stem. 'Why should I? I think this strike business is absolute tosh. I cannot see what the working classes hope to achieve by it. They should be thankful they have employment at all.'

'By our grace and favour, I suppose,' commented Nathan drily.

'Quite! And if you think I intend to sacrifice *my* wedding for the cause of the Great Unwashed, you are utterly mistaken.' Evie's shrill voice rose on a note of near hysteria.

Clara shook her head in despair. 'Oh, Evie darling, no one is asking you to. In any case, I'm sure this threat of a national strike will all blow over and soon be resolved. Then we can get back to choosing delicious things like bridesmaid's dresses, the cake, and what sort of wine we should serve.'

'*Champagne* of course!' Evie screamed. 'Don't you know *anything*?' And in a frenzy of temper and tears, she fled to her room.

'Oh dear, this is all very bad timing for the poor girl.' Clara put a hand to her heart and cast an anxious glance at her husband. He rarely had much patience where Evie was concerned. The pair seemed to rub each other up the wrong way. But how handsome he still looked with his tall, imposing stature and not an ounce of excess fat, for all he was forty-nine. Apart from his hair, which had gone prematurely grey from all the worry of the mill, he seemed not to have aged at all. His face was square, the features seeming to comprise a series of horizontals. The mouth was still firm, even if the eyebrows were more often than not drawn into a constant frown these days, the blue-grey eyes frequently narrowed as he shrewdly assessed the situation.

Clara was flattered by his taking the time to explain things to her. He rarely shared his worries over the business, shouldering any difficulties without complaint, feeling the responsibility to be entirely his. On the whole, he'd been a tolerant and generous husband, if somewhat neglectful at times as he spent most of his waking hours at the mill.

But then Clara knew that she'd been a disappointment to him, failing to provide him with the son and heir he'd so badly needed. They managed well enough, she supposed, carrying out their respective duties and living quite comfortable, if largely separate lives, as most couples did. She with her painting and her poetry, and he with his club, his 'good works', and of course his cronies at the Cotton Exchange.

'The mill is safe, isn't it, my dear?' Clara asked, needing reassurance that her allowance was in no danger of diminishing. 'I'm filled with admiration for what you've achieved without a scrap of help from anyone. Your father would have been so proud of you, but I'm also aware that there have been immense difficulties, and still are.'

Nathan gave a grunt of annoyance which might pass for agreement. Somehow he felt as if he was losing his edge; his ability to cope with these latest troubles. 'If we don't win back some pretty big contracts soon to replace those we've lost, this strike could indeed break us. The situation is immensely worrying.'

Clara went to kiss him on the forehead. 'I'm quite sure that whatever the problem is, you will solve it. I trust your judgement implicitly. In the meantime, I must go and soothe away those hysterics, or Evie will be in a sulk for days, and I really don't have the energy to endure one of her moods at present, not on top of everything else.'

Nathan gave an unsympathetic grunt, experiencing the usual surge of irritation that Clara should offer to smooth matters over. It was so typical of her to imagine that any problem could be resolved with a pat or a kiss, an indulgent smile or perhaps some inconsequential gift. But that was how she operated. His wife was far too indulgent of Evie, and of himself, of which, God help him, he took ruthless advantage, suffering only occasional bouts of guilt.

He'd not been a particularly loyal or faithful husband but had built up a good business to provide them with the security they needed and all for nothing, it seemed, since the mill would probably die with him, if not before, with no son to follow on. Nathan could sense he was growing increasingly bitter over this fact and hated himself for it; almost hated Clara for being the cause of his disappointment. Which was unfair, because aside from failing to provide an heir, she'd been a good wife to him, a trifle vague perhaps, rather a homebody spending far too much time with her pots of paint and shunning public functions where she might have been more use to him. Without doubt, he would have preferred a more outgoing wife, one with a little more passion in her soul.

Evie, of course, was another matter. Utterly hedonistic and passionate about everything, she was always off to some party or other that demanded yet another new gown. The girl was a constant thorn in his side. The sooner he got her married off, the better, so long as she didn't bankrupt him in the process.

Yet how could he blame Clara for fussing over the child. Who else did she have in her life to swamp with love and affection?

He kissed his wife lightly on her brow and tenderly patted her shoulder, his temper easing a little as his sense of justice reminded him that he'd got away with a good deal over the years because of her vagueness and the fact she never questioned or challenged him about anything. 'Tell her she can have a pair of Turkish trousers, but absolutely no smoking suit. Not at any price. Tolerant as I am of our darling daughter's whims and fancies, I must draw the line somewhere. And if this strike goes on for too long, even dear, selfish Evie will be forced to curtail her extravagancies.'

'Then let's hope to God that it doesn't,' Clara said with feeling. 'I doubt I could live with such dreadful consequences.'

–

As the strike progressed, Evie made certain that it did not interfere with her own plans. She continued to play tennis at the club, took tea with her friends, dined and danced each evening, if only to records on her dinky new gramophone. The fact there were no trains or buses running didn't trouble her in the slightest since she had her own motor and never used them anyway. On the contrary, Evie found there were distinct advantages to the strike. The roads might be busier but the pavements were less congested with no workers clattering along in their noisy clogs, and the air was cleaner since no soot fell from the factory chimneys, so her fashionably pale gowns stayed pristine longer.

There were one or two minor irritations such as the theatres being closed when Freddie had promised to take her to see HMS *Pinafore* with dinner afterwards at the Midland Hotel. Instead, they had to make do with singing *Poor Little Buttercup* together as they enjoyed a May picnic by the banks of the Irwell. Worst of all, the shops were closed. Really, one would have thought that Kendals at least might have had the decency to stay open.

What irked her the most was that her father still saw her as some sort of peevish child. She adored him, but he always seemed to see the worst in her, accusing her of having no sensitivity. Absolute tosh!

Four days into the strike Evie had one of her grand ideas. She would prove that she was sympathetic to the workers' cause, whatever that might be. She quite understood that there were people less fortunate than herself, those who were forced to use trams, for instance. And since there weren't any running and she had her own private mode of transport it occurred to her that she could do her bit by offering joy rides. Absolutely free of charge. What could be more thoughtful or generous? That would show Pops, and Mumsie, that she too could do her bit.

Decking herself out in a suitably natty costume with a simple cloche hat, not even sporting a feather, and her best tan leather gloves, of course, she set out in her smart little Morris motor and drove straight to Albert Square. Here she wrote a notice: *Volunteer driver will take you anywhere you wish to go.* And another comment, which said: *No fares. Come for the joy of the ride.*

Evie drove her motor up and down the streets of Manchester offering these less fortunate souls a lift; perhaps to visit relatives, go to the doctor or to attend hospital, or even to watch a football match, without asking a penny in payment. It was all such a lark! Really quite jolly. Nor was she the only one. She spotted Johnny Warbeck and his brother Tommy driving an omnibus of all things, looking very dashing in their plus-fours and check caps. Quite the ticket!

Sometimes she would ask her grateful passengers if they were enjoying their 'unexpected little holiday', although she did get some funny looks by way of response. Absolutely no sense of humour these people.

One morning, she spotted a young woman standing forlornly outside London Road Station, loaded down with boxes and a tribe of children clinging to her grubby skirts. She gratefully accepted Evie's offer of a lift and then confessed that she'd been recently widowed and was moving in with her sister who lived down by the basin, close to Potato Wharf.

'Tisn't no place for the likes of you, ma'am.'

'Nonsense. Climb aboard. I'll have you there in a jiffy.' Evie loaded the woman's many boxes into the boot and didn't even blench or utter a word of complaint when her brats put their filthy boots all over the smart leather upholstery of the rumble seat.

The woman directed her under the railway arches and along a maze of streets, past warehouses, deserted mills, empty wharfs and rough looking rows of houses the like of which Evie had never seen in her life before. In Evie's opinion, the fact that her family owned one of the largest cotton mills in the district did not in any way oblige her to take an interest in the operatives, or visit the dreadful slums in which they chose to reside. She had always kept well away from such unpleasantness.

Now she was confronted with children playing barefoot among the rubbish, horse dung and other unspeakable filth that littered these godforsaken streets. She saw one child swerve slightly to avoid a dead cat as she played a game of tag. A group of young girls were swinging on a rope from a lamp post, skirts flying out to reveal they weren't even wearing underwear. Women stood gossiping in doorways, arms folded, apparently with no work to do on this bright May morning. Men in slouch caps hovered at street corners, Thankfully the pubs seemed to be closed so they appeared to be quite sober. Even so, their very presence was disturbing. They watched her drive by with dark envy on their angry faces and Evie realised she'd ventured into territory that was quite beyond the pale.

'Here it is, love. Corner of Medlock Street will be grand. Eeh, I'm right grateful.'

A group of rough-looking men edged closer for a better look at the car. Hurrying now, and anxious to be out of this grim neighbourhood, Evie jumped down from the driving seat and began to fling boxes out onto the pavement. The children were making no effort at all to disembark, being too engrossed scrapping and fighting each other, pulling hair and climbing all over the leather seats like a tribe of wild monkeys.

The woman was hammering on a nearby door, evidently in an effort to alert her sister of her arrival. The door remained obstinately closed and yet the men drew ever nearer. It was then that the engine cut out.

'Drat!' Evie had quite a high opinion of herself as a chauffeuse, nevertheless this wasn't exactly the moment she would choose to encounter mechanical problems. Grabbing the handle she started to crank it, silently praying the engine would burst into life as it should. Unfortunately, this was one of those days when it chose to be temperamental. The engine groaned and clanked while a great puff of smoke bellied out all around. Evie's heart sank to her boots.

'Having trouble, love?'

'You should happen have taken a tram instead of bringing out yer fancy motor.'

'Nay, tha couldn't, could you? Seeing as how there's none running.'

'Did you not notice there were a strike on?'

They were gathered all around her. Filthy, desperate-looking men, dressed in fustian suits and mufflers, slouch caps pulled down over faces pitted with grime, hands in pockets, shoulders hunched, glowering as if the strike were all some fault of hers. There was no sign of her passenger now, nor her rapscallion children, and other than this group of ruffians Evie realised, to her horror, that the street was deserted. Every doorstep was now mystifyingly empty of their curious occupants. She felt her heart beat a little faster and applied yet more elbow to the recalcitrant engine.

'I'm surprised a young lass such as yourself dare venture round these parts.'

'Has yer mam given you a permission note?'

'Where's your chaperone then?'

The taunts came thick and fast and Evie felt her strength ebb away and her knees weaken, as she grew more confused and afraid. She could smell the sweat of their filthy bodies as they pressed ever closer and fear curdled in her stomach. She remembered her father's comments only this morning at breakfast. All about how we might have won the war, but had still not made this a country fit for heroes; and how *The Times* had predicted a genuine concern that a national strike could well turn nasty. 'Blood could be spilled before we're done,' he'd read. And right at this moment it seemed as if that blood might be Evie's own.

One of the men snatched at the fabric of her silk motoring coat, rubbing it between his dirty fingers and thumb. 'This isn't cotton. I reckon it cost a bob or two.'

Evie emitted a tiny whimper and tried to back away but saw that she was hemmed in on all sides. She couldn't even reach the driving seat.

Her grand idea no longer seemed quite such a lark. She felt something strike her on the cheek, then another blow to her shoulder. With a squeak of terror, Evie realised they were throwing stones at her. The missiles were raining on her thick and fast, showering her with a hail of muck and filth they'd plucked out of the gutter.

'Take that, you bloody blackleg!'

'Would yer steal food from t'mouths of us own childer?'

'Get back home!'

'Aye, be off with you, back where you belong. Bloody toff!'

Evie was almost fainting with fear, gagging with terror, desperately attempting to protect herself from the worst of the onslaught when somewhere amongst the din she heard a voice ring out. 'What the hell are you lot doing?'

A pair of hands grasped her, a girl's urgent voice in her ear. 'What were you thinking of, coming round here in yer fancy motor? There'll be blue murder done if they get their hands on you.'

'I'm trying to do my bit. I didn't mean to give offence.'

'And you do that by strike-breaking, do you? No wonder they're accusing you of stealing their bread. You must have a death wish to come round these streets in that motor.'

'Oh dear, I never meant…'

'Never mind what you meant, not right now. I'll get you out safe and well, don't you fret.'

The two girls pushed their way through the gathering crowd who shrank back a little, some still grumbling and shaking a fist at Evie, others looking shamefaced as Dolly Tomkins bravely confronted them, hands on hips. 'Could one of you not think to give the lass a helping hand?'

Irritated as she was with the girl, that didn't stop Dolly from taking to task the crowd of grumbling men. 'You ought to be ashamed of yourselves, you great useless lumps. And you can wipe that smile off your face, Sam Clayton, you've done nothing clever.' Dolly was desperately disappointed to see Sam there. 'What were you thinking of?' she challenged him. 'It's not like you to start bullying folk. Is it that Davey Lee egging you on, or Matt Thornton?'

'It weren't my idea, Dolly,' Davey said, always happy to shift the blame on to someone else.

Matt looked wounded by the accusation, as well he might. He was not known as a rabble-rouser, more as a shy sort with a stubborn streak. He didn't seem to be doing anything much, just standing watching events with his quiet, brown eyes. 'I've done nothing, Dolly.'

'Mebbe not, but you've done nothing to stop 'em neither.'

His neck reddened and knowing that she'd embarrassed him, that the lad always went tongue-tied for some reason whenever she spoke to him, she turned back to Sam.

Dolly had adored Sam Clayton for as long as she could remember. He was a skinny lad with too many brains for his station in life. In Dolly's opinion he shouldn't be working in the mill, by rights he should train to be a teacher or something equally grand, were that possible.

He had fair hair cut into a fringe above peaked brows and soft brown eyes which seemed to view the world with a sparkling mischief, as if everything about life was good. He showed a great pride in his appearance, which Dolly admired, was always neat and tidy, even to his ears which lay curled and flat against the side of his head. But then he was a good-looking lad was Sam, few better in all of Castlefield. And if he thought well of himself because of it, who could blame him? He set many a girl's heart pounding, including Dolly's own. She was most fascinated by his mouth, full and soft and pouting, one that she'd be happy to kiss, given half the chance. Sadly, although they'd been friends for as long as she could remember, as she had with Matt and Davey, Sam had never thought of her in that way. To him she was simply the younger sister of the glorious Aggie who he'd been sweet on ever since they'd been in the same class together at John Street School. Dolly herself was stuck with the quietly adoring, boring Matt. Just her luck!

'It were her own fault for being so daft as to come down these streets in the first place. Daft lummock!' Sam was saying. 'She shouldn't even be here. She's not one of us, Dolly, she's one o' them lot. One of the toffs. Gaffer's daughter. She's lucky not to be lynched.'

'She's a human being what fetched Maggie's sister home, so the least you can do is to give her a shove to get her out of here.' Dolly turned to Evie who was busily brushing clods of earth and worse off the silk coat, dabbing at the blood on her cheek with a lace handkerchief. 'Are you all right, love? Not seriously hurt?'

Evie managed a little shake of her head, which no longer wore a cloche hat, with or without a feather. 'I do believe I'll live,' she said, although the tremor in her voice expressed doubt on the matter.

'Right, let's get you on your way then. Come on, you lot, shoulders to the wheel. Let's help this young lady, who I reckon has learned a lesson or two about life this morning, back home to her good folks. What do you say, lads? We haven't lost our manners entirely in Castlefield, I hope.'

For one dreadful moment, Evie thought they might be about to refuse and that the girl's forthright manner would incite them to further violence. She was possessed with an urgent desire to turn tail and run and might well have done so had she not been transfixed by the way her rescuer, this young girl as small and perky as a sparrow, stood her ground and outfaced the men, not all as pliant as these three so-called friends of hers. Yet even that rabble seemed to be held in thrall by the very effrontery of her courage until finally, shamed into action, the men shuffled behind the motor.

The girl grinned good-naturedly at Evie, giving a huge wink, which made her whole face light up so that she looked surprisingly pretty, despite the lankness of her bobbed hair and her grubby cheeks. Not that Evie was in any position to criticise her on that score. Her own cheeks were streaked with oil following her efforts with the crank-shaft, in addition to the spilled blood. Evie held a secret fear that her face might well have been scarred for life.

'That's more like it,' Dolly cried. 'One, two, three, push! Nay, shove a bit harder, Sam.' Turning to the now shaking Evie, she continued, 'Right then, hop aboard. We'll have you out of here in two shakes of a rat's tail though I wouldn't recommend you returning in quite such a hurry as you came in.'

'Oh, no indeed, I'm sorry I intruded. I was only trying to help.'

'Course you were. Come on you lot, Matt, Sam, Davey, get stuck in.'

Clambering aboard and grasping tight hold of the steering wheel, only just remembering in time to release the hand brake, Evie breathed a sigh of relief as the motor began to edge forward under the driving force of many hands from behind, willing or otherwise. A few yards further along the street the engine coughed and spluttered, belching out yet more smoke, jumped and jerked a bit before purring smoothly into life.

'Thank God!' Evie soared off on a cloud of smoke and dust without a backward glance, without even calling out her thanks, nor even a cheery wave for the girl who stood in the middle of the road, watching her go with an expression of stunned disbelief on her face.

'No, don't mention it. Glad to be of service,' said Dolly, shaking her head in despair over the young woman's rudeness. Some folk really didn't know when they were well off.

Chapter Four

After five days with the country at a standstill, the General Strike was declared illegal and Union Leaders were warned that they might be liable for damages caused by the dispute. By the end of eight days it was called off, cited as a failure. Trains and trams were running once more, post was being delivered, everyone was back at work, including the operatives at Barker's Mill, everyone, that is, save for the miners. Baldwin was being sited as 'the man who kept his head.' He certainly kept a tight hold of his cherry wood pipe.

The Tomkins family, having lost a couple of week's wages, were in a worse situation than before since rent, insurance and other expenses still had to be paid. If Maisie had been afraid before the strike, she was even more so following it. Nifty Jack, sporting a new pair of two-tone shoes, was back on her doorstep, demanding his pound of flesh like some sort of modern-day Shylock, and she didn't have a penny left in her purse to give him, nor any food in her larder to feed her starving family. There was no help for it, she'd have to ask him for another loan, just to tide her over.

Dolly stood at her frame, concentrating on the task of winding yarn from hundreds of spindle bobbins on to the larger cones. She was skilled at her job after two long years but it still required concentration to control the speed and make any necessary adjustments, if breakages were to be kept to a minimum. She was hot and tired and ringing wet, the air full of cotton dust, the atmosphere uncomfortably humid from the steaming water sprayed between the rows of frames to keep the cotton damp and pliable. A constant working temperature of seventy degrees or more was necessary as otherwise the cotton threads would tighten and break, which meant that time, and therefore money, was lost.

For Dolly it had been a long and difficult morning, trying to avoid putting too much pressure on her strained ankle and worrying over the situation at home. Even so, she loved her work and enjoyed a bit of a laugh with her mates. Not that many of them were laughing today, the first day back following the disastrous strike. Tempers were short and morale low, and no one was saying much to anyone, with only the singing of the spinning frames to be heard.

On top of everything, her cotton this morning was of a poor quality, filthy with fleas and, as the yarn twisted and drew out, these were caught up in the slender rope of parallel fibres which was the roving, and wound onto the cones. Later, they would be woven into the fabric and finally dissolved and got rid of in the bleaching process but she hated the feel of them on her fingers. The older women, Dolly had noticed, were adept at feeling the cotton and choosing the best quality for themselves, probably because they were more dependant upon the wages than young girls such as herself.

Except that in Dolly's case this wasn't true at all. The Tomkins family needed every penny it could get, since most of it ended up in the bookie's pocket. Only when they were free of debt to the talleyman would she be happy.

She'd seen Nifty Jack standing at the door deep in conversation with Mam, handing over more money and a new card, indicating that this strike had cost them dear. And poor Ma Liversedge was to be buried on Wednesday, her unexpected death coming so close after Nifty's last visit it made Dolly shiver.

Striving to keep her mind on the task in hand, yet a part of it began to turn over the possibility of finding a second job, in the hope of bringing in more wages. Perhaps working in the taproom at the Navigation or some other local pub. Then again, her mam had never let her do that. Happen she could find work on Campfield Market of a Saturday afternoon after she'd finished her morning shift at the mill.

Dolly's attention was brought sharply back to the job in hand as a thread broke, by no means the first that morning and, irritated with herself, she quickly pieced it together to get the yarn running smoothly again. She must get it right or she'd be up in front of the gaffer for bad work; the waste she'd produced carefully weighed, to check there wasn't too much. Mr Barker was a stickler for watching every penny.

The machine was stopped only once a day, for cleaning, for which no more than five or six minutes was allowed. If she needed a pee she had to get Aggie or one of the other girls to mind it for her while she dashed to the smelly lavatory in the mill yard. Since it was a long way, and with only three between sixty or seventy women, she'd learned quite early on that it was better to exercise control. Nor were the girls permitted to stop production in order to have a brew of tea, or go home for their dinner. They would take it in turns to fetch hot water from the factory steam boiler to wet the tea leaves in their brew can, which they drank from the lid while standing at their frame. They brought their dinner in a pot with a plate on top, identifying it with a label, or cloth wrapped around it. If they were lucky, they'd find room to put it, along with all the rest, in an old oven set on top of the big coal-fired boiler that ran the mill engine, and by dinner time it would be heated up nicely.

They took it in turns to eat. One girl would mind her mate's frame while the other ran down to collect and eat her dinner either in the boiler room, called 'the snap hole,' or out in the mill yard. Dolly preferred the latter, since she found the air in the engine room almost too hot to breathe with its blazing fire and massive engine capable of generating unlimited amounts of power. Or she would take her dinner back upstairs and eat it with her back propped against an empty skip, right by her frame. This meant that not a penny was lost in wages, or a cone in lost production.

On this occasion Aggie had gone first, as usual, and Dolly, bursting to go to the lavvy, waited impatiently for her return. She was starving hungry, there having been no breakfast that morning, as was too often the case these days, so she was relieved when Aggie finally appeared, indicating it was her turn to take a break.

'Happen I'll get to be first for me dinner one day, eh?' she commented drily as Aggie sauntered back to her frame, swinging her hips from side to side in that showy way she had when she imagined all eyes were upon her. 'That's a full forty minutes you've taken. Who've you been gossiping with, that Davey Lee?' Aggie was a shocking flirt and always managed to find time to chat up the lads.

Her sister patted her chestnut curls as if to reassure herself of her own prettiness, while utterly destroying the effect by scowling. 'As if I'd waste time on that useless lump. I'm looking for someone with a bit of class.'

'Bit of brass more like.'

'Aye, that too! How else will I ever escape the horrors of living in a house within sniffing distance of the canal, the abattoir and the hide and skin market?'

'Well you won't find him in this hole.'

'Oh, I wouldn't be too sure about that.' She gave a little smirk as she cast a sideways glance across the room but Dolly couldn't quite make out who she was smiling at, and was far too desperate to escape, to care.

'I'm off, an' I'll have me full thirty minutes today, at least.'

'Don't run.' Aggie yelled after her, as Dolly set off at a lick across the greasy wood floor.

–

Because she was so late the boiler room was empty, with not even old Ned, the engine-tenter, who minded the big steam engine present. Dolly decided he must have slipped out for a quick game of footie with the lads in the mill yard, since everything was running smoothly. Most of her mates were back at their frames, apart from those who'd sneaked off home for a quick bite. Juices running at the prospect of the leftover stew Maisie had put up for her, Dolly was shocked to find the shelves empty, with no sign of her dinner. She stared into the little old oven dumbfounded, looked all about the boiler room, in case someone had taken it out by mistake and forgotten to put it back. But it was quite clear that her dinner had gone. Someone had stolen it.

'The rotten thieves! Why would anyone steal my dinner?'

Everyone knew which was hers, as she always wrapped it in the same blue checked cloth. Again Dolly searched the boiler room, more frantically this time as the thought of the rest of the day stretched ahead of her with no food in her belly to ease the cramps of hunger, and the tiredness. She found the blue cloth, tossed in a corner among the oily dust and filth, but not a sign of the two plates containing her dinner. 'Mam'll kill me for losing them plates.' More urgently, Dolly had not a penny in her pocket even to buy herself a pie from the cook shop. A great lump came to her throat and her eyes filled with tears. She couldn't help herself. It had been one of those mornings what with the fleas, and the yarn breaking every five minutes, Aggie taking too long over her dinner, and now no dinner. She sank on to old Ned's stool and began quietly to weep.

'What's this? Little Polly Flinders?'

She turned on the stool and lifted her wet face to see who it was that addressed her thus, a sharp rejoinder already forming on her tongue. But the boiler room door was flung open and framed within it stood Nathan Barker, the gaffer himself, staring at her with a startled expression on his face.

She leapt to her feet. 'I'm so sorry, I was just going.'

'Don't go on my account. You've come for your dinner, I expect.' Nathan looked down at her and felt something stir within. It caught him so unawares that it quite took his breath away. Whoever the girl was, she was a right bonny lass. He never paid too much attention to the young girls who worked for him as they were generally a rough, brassy bunch. But this girl was different. The smooth, delicate skin, the swing of glossy raven hair framing the perfect oval of her pale face, the soft rosy lips and her lovely blue eyes moist with tears, reminding him for a brief second of his own darling mama; a recollection so strong he could almost smell his mother's lily-of-the valley perfume. No, perhaps it wasn't his mother she reminded him of but someone else entirely. He'd always had an eye for a pretty woman, same as the next man, had strayed more than once over the years, though always taken great care not to cause any scandal. He'd become quite skilled at covering his tracks. He struggled to put a name to the face, but gave up and Dolly became once again an ill-dressed mill girl, a scruffy child. He must be growing senile, seeing fanciful visions. 'Have you been crying?'

Dolly dithered before him, uncertain what to do, whether to push past him and make a dash for it, or ask his permission to leave. But this show of sympathy was too much and the tears started again, running unchecked down her flushed cheeks. 'Somebody's pinched me dinner.'

'Oh dear.'

'Bloody mean, I call it.'

He gave a quiet smile. 'Quite so! Bloody mean.'

'I'm glad you find it funny. I can't say I'm laughing much.'

'No, of course you aren't. I beg your pardon.' He handed her a clean white linen handkerchief, wanting her to leave and yet seeming to encourage her to stay. 'It could simply be a careless mistake on someone's part. It always amazes me that so many dinners do manage to find their rightful owners.'

Dolly began to use the handkerchief to mop up her tears, embarrassed suddenly for making such an exhibition of herself in front of the boss. 'I doubt it. They took the plates and everything, 'cept the cloth.' She indicated the blue check napkin still lying on the floor, then blew her nose loudly on the linen handkerchief.

'I see.' He was frowning again. 'You'll have to nip out and get yourself something else then. Go on, you'll have time, if you're quick.'

Dolly shook her head, started to hand him back the handkerchief, and then realising she'd used it, changed her mind. 'Sorry, me mam'll wash it for you. I'll fetch it back in a day or two.' She tucked it into her pinny pocket amongst her tools and cast him a nervous, sideways glance.

What was she doing standing in the boiler room talking to the owner of the mill, to Mr Nathan Barker himself? She could hardly believe it. She'd only ever seen him from a distance before, walking through the place at a great lick, nodding to right and left as he went by, pausing only to have a few words with Harold Entwistle, the overlooker on their floor. It made her feel awkward. 'I'd best be getting back to me frame,' she managed at last, hoping he'd take the hint and shift himself.

But he didn't move, just stood there looking at her in a funny sort of way which made her go all hot and uncomfortable. It seemed to take forever before he responded though it was probably only seconds, almost as if he were returning from some far distant place and had to drag himself back to the present by sheer physical force. 'It's Milly, isn't it?' The Barkers liked to imagine they knew their operatives, each and every one.

'Dolly.'

'Ah yes, of course. Dolly. I remember.' He cleared his throat and for a brief second she thought he was about to reach out and pat her on the head, but then he put his hand in his pocket instead. 'Do you have enough time left of your dinner break to nip to the cook shop, Dolly, or do you need a note from me to say it's all right? I wouldn't want you to get into trouble with Harold, if you were late back at your machine.'

Dolly was startled, and surprised that he should be so considerate. To be fair he didn't look in the least bit stuck-up, as folk claimed the Barkers were and he wasn't bad looking, considering he was so old. His face bore a quiet, thoughtful expression, and the blue-grey eyes steady upon hers with a trace of curiosity in them. Even so, she reminded herself sternly, what did he know of hunger? No doubt his table was groaning with food every flipping night of the week.

'I've plenty of time, just no money,' she commented. The words had popped out unbidden and she followed this unhappy confession with a bitter little laugh for she might well have added: how could I have on the wages you pay me, and with a dad who drinks and bets away every penny he can get hold of? But pride held the words in check. Besides, he'd been kind and this wasn't the moment to complain about poor wages. Dolly offered a watery smile instead and tried to slip past him, to make her escape through the open door. He put out a hand to stop her leaving, grabbing her elbow and then just as quickly let go, as if the very touch of her offended him. Probably thought he'd catch something nasty. But again his words surprised her.

'Nay lass, you can't possibly return to your work with no food inside you.'

'Don't worry, I allus give value for money and get the right number of yards spun, empty belly or no.'

Dolly got little satisfaction from this burst of insolence for the next instant he was holding out a shilling, bright and shining, between finger and thumb. His hands were clean; the skin soft and pink, nails neatly clipped with long, tapering fingers, very much the hands of a gentleman.

She was shocked by the gesture. 'I can't take yer money. I couldn't do that.'

'Why can't you?'

'Well, because…' Dolly couldn't think of a single reason, and standing so close to him in the doorway, not knowing which direction to move to avoid him, she felt trapped, and furious with herself for feeling so small and inferior. She didn't normally get into a state just because someone was better off than she was. Dolly believed all men were born equal, it was just that some were more equal than others, as the saying went, and she certainly had no intention of being bought off by someone as condescending and full of himself as Nathan Barker, gaffer or no gaffer. If his conscience was troubling him over the state of his workers then that was his problem. 'It wouldn't be right, not the done thing at all,' she tartly informed him.

'You could call it an advance on your wages, if that would help?'

'An advance?' She looked at him askance. 'It's well near a third of what I earn in a week.' The expression of surprise on his face was such that Dolly let out a harsh little laugh. 'You've no idea how much I earn, have you?'

'Not the slightest,' he admitted, and the guilt etched on his face somehow made him seem younger, more vulnerable. Not that she allowed this to influence her attitude one iota, and Dolly quickly thrust aside the slight flicker of pity she felt for him.

'Three bob.'

'Three shillings, is that all?' He saw that she was regarding him now with almost mischievous amusement, as if she knew more about his own mill than he did. Which may well be the case on issues of this nature. He remembered his most recent, and difficult, negotiations with the unions: how he'd insisted upon a reduction as the only means of survival, ruthlessly over-riding their objections. 'Ah yes, of course, three shillings would be about right for someone as young and inexperienced as yourself.'

'Inexperienced after two years? It's a flipping scandal, that's what it is. I should be earning two or three times that sum, the union says. Plenty are in this town.'

'You have to appreciate how fortunate you are that I allow unions to exist in my factory at all. Many of my colleagues won't tolerate such anarchy.'

Nathan was annoyed with himself for opening up this whole sensitive issue of pay. Why on earth was he arguing the case with a twopenny-halfpenny mill girl? Yet he sensed that he'd insulted her in some odd way by offering her any money at all. Perhaps sixpence or a threepenny bit would have been better, a more realistic sum for her to accept without injuring her working class pride. Nevertheless, he couldn't back down now. He felt lost for words, his charm, even his common sense having deserted him. He had nothing but admiration for the way she was so bravely standing up to him. Was it any wonder he'd seen his mother in her, for hadn't Mama possessed just such courage, and those eyes; a deep and glorious blue that blazed with pride and beauty. Then again, the differences between this child and his scented, gracious, sainted mother were manifest; the one so richly blessed, while the other...

Just for a second another face blurred before his eyes, one he had once known well, too well. He blinked and it was gone and Nathan stoutly turned away from the memory, not wishing to examine it too closely. Yet it left a sense of guilt gnawing at him for he knew that from this moment on, he'd never get the sight of this child's achingly sad and hungry little face out of his mind. Nathan Barker also experienced an uncharacteristic surge of protectiveness, as if he could change the way the world turned, if only to see her lovely little face light up with happiness and look upon him more kindly. 'Here, take the money anyway. Call it a bonus, or compensation for your stolen dinner.'

Dolly stared at the coin with longing in her heart as she thought what it would buy. She could get herself a threepenny pie from the cook shop. And the balance would buy her a good dinner for the rest of the week, or she could save it up towards a pair of new boots. 'No thanks. Wouldn't be right. I'll not take brass I've not earned. Not with the strike and everything.' And pushing past him, chin held obstinately high, she went out the door and set off down the corridor.

Secretly, Dolly rather hoped that he might chase after her, offer her sixpence instead, or say he'd take her to the pub himself and treat her to a slap up meal, but of course he did nothing of the sort. He simply watched her walk away in silence. That's bosses for you, she thought, all talk and no action. For no reason she could think of, since it wasn't his fault that her dinner had been stolen, Dolly felt irritated that he'd given up so easily and not insisted she take the shilling. Perhaps that was why she paused at the foot of the stairs and, seeing that he was still watching her, couldn't resist having the last word.

'Course, if you provided a decent place for folk to eat: some-where clean with tables and chairs, instead of a filthy, smoky, hot old boiler room, this sort of thing might never happen. Not to mention how much easier life would be if we were paid decent wages in the first place.'

Nathan Barker's jaw went slack and his mouth fell open. Dolly allowed herself a small, superior smile as she stalked off upstairs, back to her machine, with at least her pride intact as she strove to ignore the noisy rumblings of her stomach. Obviously he wasn't used to his operatives giving as good as they got, and her parting words had hit home. Serve him right! That'll teach him a sharp lesson for attempting to patronise Dolly Tomkins.

–

It was as she was crossing the floor that it happened. Paying no heed to her sister's warning to tread carefully, since Dolly never did anything slowly, and perhaps because her mind was still on the conversation with Nathan Barker and the loss of her dinner, she wasn't paying proper attention as she hurried back to her frame. But then something struck her on the back of her ankles and she went sprawling, face down on the oily, wet floor. It seemed to be her week for falling.

'That'll teach you for favouring blacklegs.'

To her horror, Dolly realised she'd been felled by a large spindle, rolled right under her feet from the hand of Betty Deurden, a buxom wench twice Dolly's size. She was not one of her favourite people at the best of times. Hot with fury and without pause for thought, Dolly gave a blood-curdling roar and launched herself at her assailant. Catching Betty off guard as she stood laughing at the result of her clever trick, Dolly wrapped her arms about the girl's plump waist and brought her down. Within seconds the pair were grappling and rolling about the floor, spinning and sliding in the muck and oil, arms flailing as they aimed and dodged blows, tore at each other's hair and attempted to scratch whatever came within clawing distance.

'I'll flay you alive,' Dolly yelled.

'You asked fer it, helping that hoity-toity little madam take work from our lads, and bread from our mouths.'

Gasping for breath, Dolly saw the uselessness of argument even as she yelled, 'She were only doing her bit...' and Betty's fist connected with her jaw. Why do I bother? she wondered in a haze of pain. What's it to me? I don't even know the girl in the fancy motor, and had accused her of the self-same thing. Except that Dolly had seen how relieved Maggie's widowed sister was to arrive safely, having surely suffered enough troubles recently, so recognised that toffee-nosed though she might well be, the girl had meant well in her clumsy way. Besides, Dolly always liked to give people the benefit of the doubt, particularly when they were helping others.

And then the spindle struck her again, this time on the back of her head, felling her with a single blow. That made her see red, and stars too.

Despite feeling dazed, she was on her feet in seconds, as feisty as a terrier: blood up, fists flying and temper running hot and high. My God but she'd make Betty Deurden sorry for that one. But before Dolly had time to catch her breath let alone consider just where on Betty's plump form she should place the next blow, a hand grasped her by the collar and lifted her bodily off the ground. This was not difficult for anyone to do, since Dolly was aptly named and her size diminutive. The hand belonged to that of the overlooker, Harold Entwistle, who did not suffer fools gladly.

'Right, Miss, I've had enough of you and your trouble-making.'

'What, me? What've I done?'

'What have you *not* done? I still remember the time you climbed out the mill window and got yourself locked out. Made me look a proper Charlie in front of the gaffer.'

Dolly was outraged. 'That was only because it was hot and I needed a bit of fresh air. Why take it out on me now? Anyroad, it weren't my fault someone closed the window, and this isn't my fault neither.'

'I've been patient with you, Dolly Tomkins, let you try jobs you weren't really up to, put up with that sharp wit of yours, said nothing when you shinned down the drain pipe after the Christmas party. Didn't even dock your pay when you were late in to work and—'

'That were only because I were looking for me dad.'

'Nevertheless, fighting on the mill floor is one step too far for me to turn a blind eye to, so is arguing with your betters. So you can pick up your cards and go.'

'But it were Betty what started it.'

'I don't care who started it, I'm finishing it.'

Aggie was beside her in an instant, pointing out to Harold that he was being unfair, but he would have none of it. 'Nay, I'm sorry Aggie. I'll not have no bother, not on my shift. They can both go. Betty *and* your Dolly, and that's my last word on the subject, or else it'll be my neck on the block.'

'You rotten coward,' Aggie cried, driven to defend her sister since she'd seen exactly what had taken place.

Harold flushed scarlet. 'Are you wanting to join her on t'dole? Because I'll take no lip from you neither.'

Aggie at once began to cry, weeping copious tears into her grubby hanky.

'Nay, Aggie lass, don't take on. She's brought it on herself.' Stricken by his apparent cruelty, Harold turned on Dolly. 'Look what you've done now, Dolly Tomkins, upsetting your Aggie. I've heard of your latest exploits, about you helping a blackleg. You're a liability, that's what you are, and we don't want your sort in this mill. You should take a leaf out of your sister's book and be more ladylike. Next time you consider doing a bit of strike-breaking, Dolly Tomkins, you'll happen remember this episode and think better of it. Meanwhile, you can pick up what's due to you, and get off home.'

'What's going on here?'

Dolly's heart sank even further, if that were possible, as she recognised the bulky shape of her father approaching, his face like thunder.

Chapter Five

Someone had evidently told Calvin that his two lasses were in a bit of bother and here he was, bearing down upon them, eyes almost popping out of his big, round head, great fists clenched, his whole, bulging body swollen with rage. And Dolly knew, she just knew, that he wouldn't take her part in the dispute. Not for a second would he see her as the victim in all of this, but would be sure to put the blame squarely on to her shoulders. What her mam would say when she learned she'd lost her job, Dolly didn't dare to think. 'It weren't my fault,' she said, before ever he'd reached her.

Aggie chimed up. 'Aw Dad, she's been sacked, me an' all.'

'Na then,' said Harold in his most conciliatory tones. 'Don't start something you might regret, Calvin. Thy lass is only getting what she deserves. And I didn't mean it about your Aggie. She's a good worker and can stop on, but Dolly goes.'

Calvin wasn't even listening. The moment he'd drawn level with Aggie, seen how his precious daughter wept and taken note of her disastrous news, he turned to Dolly and landed her one with the flat of his hand, right across her face, sending her sprawling. 'So you've lost us your wages now, have you? You great gormless lump.'

Holding her stinging cheek, Dolly decided that she'd stay where she was on the floor. If she risked getting up he might only knock her down again. Besides, she couldn't seem to move a muscle. Her head was spinning and tears of agony were running down her flushed face.

'Here, hold on,' Harold put in, finding himself in the peculiar position of defending the very person he'd just sacked. 'There's no need to get nasty. We've had enough fisticuffs for one morning.'

'And you can mind your own business.' So saying, Calvin threw a punch right at the poor man's face. Fortunately, Harold Entwistle spent his spare time in the boxing ring, a useful skill he'd always thought, in his line of work. Being in charge of any group of workers was a hazardous task at the best of times, let alone during a period of strife. A bit of fancy footwork had often stood him in good stead. On this occasion he neatly evaded the blow with a swift sideways motion, so that it did not connect. Unfortunately, the force of his punch carried Calvin relentlessly onward and his heel caught on the very same spindle that had felled Dolly. His feet skidded like pistons beneath him, arms winding round and round like the sails on a windmill as he strove to keep his balance. It might almost have been funny had he not grabbed hold of the long rope which hung from the enormous fly wheel and drove the great engine that operated the spinning frames. Somehow he got himself tangled up in it and Dolly knew that as long as she lived, she would never forget the surprised expression on her father's face as the giant pulley lifted him high up into the roof, carrying him effortlessly the length of the room where finally it crushed him like an ant.

–

'Are you trying to put the blame on to me? How on earth can I be responsible for some girl being given the sack, and her father killed?'

'It was the very same girl who helped you get the car going that day. They blamed her for strike-breaking; called her a blackleg, like you, and the whole episode led to a terrible accident.'

Nathan thought of the girl's lovely face and felt again that stab of guilt. Was he to blame for her suffering? He'd always believed in taking responsibility for his own life, and assuming others would do likewise. Seeing that young girl with the desperation of hunger in her haunted gaze, pinching her cheeks to hollow shells, he'd been moved to pity. A reaction, which had unnerved him, since he'd never seen himself as the over-sensitive sort. And his daughter was even less so.

Evie tossed her head, buttering her breakfast roll with a studied grace, as if this were of no concern to her at all. 'Utter tosh! When Mumsie comes down, I shall tell her that you're being unkind to me again.'

'Oh, for pity's sake, Evie, stand on your own two feet for once and leave your mother out of this. You know it only upsets her.'

'I know that *you* are upsetting *me*. I was only doing my bit to help. And the woman I gave the lift too was glad enough to have it. You should have seen how her brats crawled all over my lovely leather seats in their filthy boots. Really, these people can't have it both ways.' She bit delicately into her roll, taking the smallest nibble, and then thought better of it and set it back on her plate. If she didn't start eating a little less, she'd never squeeze into the divine wedding gown being made for her.

'I can't imagine what you were thinking of to drive your car into the midst of those streets.' Nathan was well aware that the mill-operatives called him a 'careful' man, the sort who would cut an apple in half to make it go further. And what was so wrong in that? As a non-conformist he didn't care to be 'showy'. He was reasonably content with his lot, believed in living well but lording his good fortune over his workers could prove a risky operation as they might then start pressing for higher wages. Most mornings he would walk to work rather than take his car, using his Rolls Royce only on a Sunday. Sadly, Evie never showed the same restraint.

Utterly spoiled and selfish, she was quite incapable of grasping the difficulties faced by anyone, let alone those less fortunate than herself. 'A man was killed, Evie.'

Tears clouded her lovely pale blue eyes. 'You can't blame me for that. You are being deliberately cruel, Pops.'

'Of course I'm not being cruel, you silly girl. It was a dreadful accident. Most unfortunate.' Irritated that he seemed to have been put in the wrong, Nathan crisply folded his paper and, pushing back his chair, abruptly left the table. He'd had enough of female tantrums and was anxious to get back to the mill and blessed reality. Even so, he wagged the folded paper at her, determined to make his point. 'This isn't some sort of game, Evie. We've lost money through that damned strike, and now one of my operatives, so don't try to wash your hands of responsibility altogether. All I'm trying to do is point out that occasionally you should consider the possible consequences of your actions.'

'Oh, for goodness sake, Johnny and Tommy Warbeck were driving an omnibus, so why shouldn't I do something too? What's the difference? And don't give me that "because you're a woman" nonsense.'

Nathan snorted his derision since a less likely candidate for a campaigner for women's rights would be hard to find. Evie had never shown the least interest in being a suffragette, of learning about the mill and her inheritance, nor in taking up any other sort of employment or useful occupation whatsoever. Perhaps he would've liked and admired her more if she had. But then, perhaps it was his fault for pandering to her whims too much. He gave her shingled hair an awkward pat, recalling with nostalgic affection how he might once have tugged at soft curls, but that was when he'd still nursed hopes of a son to follow this delightful little girl. As a child, he'd found it quite impossible to be cross with her for long, however naughty. Now, a distance had grown between them, one he couldn't quite bridge. 'A woman alone in those streets is asking for trouble. You put yourself in danger, and others too.'

'Rubbish, and there have been no *consequences*. I won't accept that I am responsible for some petty quarrel between two silly girls on the mill floor, nor that terrible accident.'

Nathan growled his displeasure. 'For once in your idle life, Evie, think of others before yourself. A man is dead because two girls were fighting over *you*. He leaves a wife and family. What is it you want me to do, ignore that tragic fact? Pretend it never happened? I can't do that. I take my responsibilities to my workforce seriously, and give them the respect they deserve if only because it is politic to do so.' He turned to leave but at the door, swivelled on his heel for one parting comment.

'And I certainly cannot condone a big wedding, not now, not when half the district is in mourning for Calvin Tomkins. He might've had his faults, but he didn't deserve to end his life like this, and we must pay all due respect, otherwise, I'll have his family and half the workforce back out on strike. It's only good manners, common humanity, for you to scale things down to more manageable proportions.'

'*What?*' Evie gave a screech of temper. 'So that's what this is all about! Nothing whatsoever to do with common humanity and absolutely everything to do with you being mean; as parsimonious and penny-pinching as ever. If you simply want to make my life a complete misery, I won't allow it, do you hear? Freddie's people are expecting a monumental thrash with copious amounts of top-notch champagne, and I intend to give them one. Is that clear?' she screamed.

'Not if I have to pay for it,' Nathan calmly remarked, in his darkest, most damning tones. 'There's nothing to suggest that this strike is over yet. The miners are still out, and the rest could easily down tools and come out again in sympathy, for longer next time. How can I explain things to you, Evie, in words that you might possibly understand? Apart from the sensitivities surrounding this tragedy, I really cannot afford, right now, to pay for a big wedding. Scale it down or postpone it for a year.'

He walked from the breakfast room without waiting to witness her response to his decision, though by the hysterical screaming which followed him, he really didn't need to.

'I hope you realise what you've done, Dolly. You've ruined, no – destroyed us, and our poor dad is dead.' Aggie flung the accusation at her sister then let out a great wail of distress, wanting to be fussed over by any or all of the various members of the Tomkins family who had gathered to see her father properly dispatched. No one rushed to do so.

'Put a sock in it, Aggie, you're not helping with your cater-wauling,' grumbled Abel, the eldest of the brothers and most like his father in temperament. 'We all know our Dolly's to blame, point is, where do we go from here? I can't help. I've enough on my plate.'

Eli, in his quiet, authoritative tones, told his brother to leave Dolly alone. Always her most stalwart supporter, he'd been the one to stand up to their father, the only one Calvin hadn't ever clobbered. Willy said nothing, as was his way, yet still Aggie glared at him, just as if he had.

'Aye, give it a rest,' agreed Josh. 'There's nothing worse than a wailing woman.'

Aggie was outraged. 'Why do you all defend *her*, and not me? The nasty little cow nearly got me sacked.'

'I bet your tongue's glad when you're asleep and can have a rest for a change. Put a clip on it for pity's sake.' Josh preferred his women silent and obedient, which his wife had learned to her cost, and he'd certainly no intention of making a big thing of this accident, tragic as it was, or he'd end up having to support his mother as well as a wife and four kids. Nor would he grieve for a father who'd leathered him as often as Calvin had. He'd got his just desserts in Josh's opinion, and the sooner this day was over and done with, the better. He'd neither time nor patience for weeping and wailing. 'I've lost a day's pay for this funeral, so shurrup, will you. Just be glad you're weren't the one who was sacked, after all.'

'Nor the one who's dead,' added Maisie in her quiet voice. 'So you can all guard your tongues. I'll have no family feuds today, ta very much.'

Her husband's body had lain like a wax effigy in the front parlour for the required number of days, pennies covering his eyes, blinds drawn, mirrors draped, even the big mantel clock stopped, and today he'd finally been put to rest in the cemetery. She'd been worried how she was going to manage, there being no compensation forthcoming from the mill. Fortunately, the Rechabites had helped out with the cost of the funeral, although if they'd realised Calvin Tomkins didn't go in for temperance quite as his wife did, they might have thought twice. Well, he'll sup no more now, that's for sure, Maisie thought. It had given her quite a lift, in that sad moment of farewell, to consider the benefits of Calvin's demise. No more roaring rows, no more drunken rages, no more beatings.

But the family squabbles were clearly due to continue unabated.

There seemed to be kids everywhere, like a party, not a wake, and Maisie had already been given instructions on her next child-minding dates, plus a bag of washing dumped in the corner for her to 'just rinse through later'. Funeral or no funeral, nothing changed.

Now they were partaking of the customary ham, washed down by copious amounts of tea while the deceased's life was scrutinised in fine detail and the repercussions of his shocking death considered. Having quietly reminded them that quarrelling amongst themselves wasn't appropriate in the circumstances they'd fallen into a grudging silence. There was nothing more to be said, no will to worry about since Calvin hadn't possessed a penny to his name, and not one of her sons asked how she would go about settling his debts.

Maisie was thankful when the family finally left, hurrying back to their own lives, duty done, all save for the two girls and Willy. She put the washing to soak then brewed yet more tea, the age-old remedy for disaster. Aggie returned to the lament which had occupied her all day, still complaining that it was all Dolly's fault.

'Who else can you blame? Our Dolly *is* a blackleg. As much of a strike breaker as that daft cluck what ventured down these streets in her fancy jalopy. If she hadn't got involved with that stupid girl in the first place, this would never have happened. We'd all still be in work, and Dad still alive. So whose fault is it, if not hers?'

Her daughter's distress was genuine, the tears still rolling down Aggie's cheeks so Maisie's reply was gentle, even as she made a very fair point. 'Our Dolly didn't know it'd end up like this when she went to that girl's aid, now did she?'

Maisie couldn't help thinking that if her hot blooded husband hadn't shoved his oar in, Aggie might well have been able to wheedle the overlooker into letting Dolly off, and Calvin might indeed still be alive. Being the youngest and the last in line for everything, Dolly could be fierce when it came to sticking up for herself but Aggie could wind a chap round her little finger with a smile and a flutter of her eyelashes, if she put her mind to it, as easily as yarn on a cop. Tragically, she'd never got the chance, all due to a bit of fancy footwork on Harold's behalf. Matters had taken a nasty turn for the worse and Calvin had come off the loser.

The police had been called, naturally, but after due investigation and numerous interviews of witnesses to the scene, the authorities had decided there were no charges to answer. Everyone agreed that Calvin never actually touched Harold Entwistle, though there was an altercation between them, following the scrap involving the two girls. The mill management did not feel inclined to have Dolly continue in their employ and she was banished to join the ranks of the unemployed. Betty Deurden and Aggie, were both reinstated.

Even so, Aggie was determined to lay the blame on someone for the loss of her beloved father. 'She shouldn't have gone to her aid. She should have thought of the consequences. Now my wages, and our Willy's, are all you'll have coming in now. We're done for, and all thanks to that silly cow. If you hadn't spoiled her so much, she might have shown more sense. You're useless, you, both as a mother and at managing a house.' Aggie's voice was again rising to a shriek and not even gentle Willy was able to calm her. 'You were *lousy* to me dad, a rotten wife. He told me so a dozen times.'

'If I was as useless as you say, happen the way he treated me had something to do with that.' Thin as a drink of water, Maisie Tomkins had learned to be circumspect in her dealings with her drunkard husband. Least said, soonest mended had always been her motto. That way you lived longer and didn't carry so many bruises. It hadn't taken much to offend Calvin, or bring about a violent response and Maisie had spent her entire life walking on egg-shells, always taking the easy option, and the line of least resistance. The memory of when he'd once broken two of her ribs was still branded on her soul. Had that been because she was a bad wife? Happen so on that occasion, since she'd been guilty of the worst sin in the book. She'd taken her punishment without complaint or shedding a single tear, nor cried since. Where was the point? She'd been caught, like a rabbit in a trap, with nowhere else to run.

Now she was free at last, and had no intention of being bullied by her own daughter. 'If our Dolly did something she shouldn't, it were only because she were afeared for that lass's life. What would you expect her to do, walk on by as if she'd seen nothing and let them chaps beat the poor girl to a pulp?'

'Why not? It generally pays to keep your nose out of other folk's business,' Aggie said, tossing her curls in that flighty way she had.

Willy gave a philosophical smile. 'Nay, that's our Dolly all over, allus one for getting steamed up.'

'I didn't get steamed up. It was Betty Deurden who felled me with her spindle. I'll get another job, I *will*, I swear it. We'll not starve.'

'Course we won't starve,' her loyal mother agreed. 'So leave her be, Aggie, why don't you?' Maisie couldn't seem able to stop herself from over-protecting this youngest child of hers; the one who had always landed her in the most trouble throughout a long trial of a marriage. Largely, Calvin had ignored her, almost as if she were invisible or didn't exist, favouring Aggie and calling her 'his precious girl', as if he didn't have another. Maisie had understood his attitude but as Dolly had grown, she'd been relieved to note that she became her own person, despite her father's blatant neglect. Perhaps because Eli and her lovely Manny, at least, had petted and spoiled her while they'd still lived at home, which had provided her with the love and attention she craved and given a much needed boost to her confidence. And Willy adored her, of course.

Not that they didn't all have their faults, with a great deal of rivalry, and backbiting always going on between them. Much as Maisie adored her sons, they were, to a man, utterly wrapped up in themselves and their own concerns; each wanting to be the best; each needing to outdo the other, just like their father before them. Abel and Josh, and even the quiet Eli couldn't be described as saints or the most charitable of souls, despite their biblical names. They generally put their own interests first, even, in some cases, before that of their long-suffering wives.

Dolly was quite the opposite, entirely different from the rest of the Tomkins brood. Small in stature yet she was ever ready to stand up for the underdog. Where she got that from Maisie couldn't imagine, certainly not from her. Even as a child she'd collected a veritable tribe of lame ducks, the kind of friends no one else would look twice at.

'I understand that you're grieving, Aggie, but I'll not have you blaming your sister, or taking your nasty temper out on her. Our Dolly is special. Happen one day she might escape this hole and make something of her life. She certainly has it in her to do so, which is more than you have, selfish madam that you are. But then she's worth more than the lot of you put together.'

Maisie saw at once that she'd gone too far. She could tell by the way Aggie bridled and puffed herself out, looking so much like her father in that moment it brought a prickle of ice to her spine.

Ignoring her mother and Willy completely, Aggie stuck her face so close to Dolly's, the spittle from her foaming mouth flicked across her sister's cheeks, making her flinch. 'Mam might think the sun shines out of you, girl, but I know the truth, because Dad told me. I asked him, straight out, why you looked so different from the rest of us, and if you were one of his by-blows. He thought that was funny but was far enough gone in the drink to admit that you weren't his at all. Wrong side of the blanket just the same, so it's no skin off my nose if you can't get work and are forced to go out on t'streets. Earn your living same way as our precious mother earned hers, why don't you, and spare us all the bother of putting up with you. It'll be one less mouth to feed, at least.'

Dolly was gazing at her sister dumbfounded, her mind a whirl of confusion. Something wasn't quite right. Her sister's venomous tirade was now being drowned out by the sound of her own heart like a heavy drumbeat in her ears, and she couldn't quite take anything in. Glancing across at Maisie she saw that her mother had gone death pale, her hand across her mouth. Dolly cleared her throat and tried out her voice. It was a bit croaky but she got the words out somehow.

'I didn't quite catch what you said. What was that about blankets and earning a living like me mam? What did you mean by that, Aggie? What was it Dad said, exactly?'

A finger wagged furiously in her face. 'Don't you even call him by that name. Haven't I just explained, he wasn't *your* Dad, he was *mine*!'

Somewhere in the dim recesses of her consciousness, in the part of her skull that wasn't crying in agony, Dolly thought she heard Maisie give a low groan that turned into a sob. Yet she calmly felt the need to ask. 'Then who is my dad?'

Aggie laughed, a sound to chill the stoutest heart. 'That's a good question. Could be the milkman for all I know. Ask your bloody mother.'

Chapter Six

'I need to know, Mam. It's no good you sitting there stony-faced telling me it's nothing to do with me. It's everything to do with me. He wasn't my dad, was he? That's why he never liked me. Why would our Aggie say such a thing otherwise?'

'Because she's hurting, and wants you to hurt too.'

'Are you saying she lied?'

The pause this time was longer and more painful. Having delivered this damning piece of information, Aggie had been packed off to bed, much against her will, Maisie insisting she needed to talk to Dolly alone. Willy had also made himself scarce, as was his wont in times of crisis. Fresh tea had been brewed and here they both were, facing some uncomfortable truths.

'No, it's true enough, and yes, it does concern you. I was just hoping that you'd never find out, that's all. Now that you have, I suppose you might as well hear the whole sorry tale.' Maisie could feel a panic welling up inside her. What on earth could she say? Not the truth, the whole truth and nothing but the truth that was for sure. She decided to start at the beginning, to give herself time to think.

'When Calvin and me first got married I were already carrying our Abel. The babbies seemed to come thick and fast after that, one year for four years. Then I lost a couple. Weren't meself for a time, grieving for me lost babbies, and run ragged with them that I had, so there was a bigger gap before I had our Willy. Seven years later our Aggie come as a bit of a shock like. I was thirty-four by then and reckoned I were finished like.

And Calvin were showing less interest, if you take my meaning. After Aggie was born I were thankful to keep it that way, cause I didn't want no more childer. Except that he got obsessed with the booze and the horses instead, which didn't help one bit, and I had to keep borrowing more and more money to keep us afloat.

'Then I just clicked with this other chap. He were good to me and we had a bit of a fling like. It all started off very innocent, but things weren't going quite right for him and he was lonely. I felt the same, so, well, you know how it is.'

'No, I don't. Who was he?'

'You don't want to know.'

'I do. I want to know everything. This man was my father. Who is he?'

'No one you know.'

'I don't believe you. For God's sake, Mam, *tell me*! Surely I deserve that, at least.'

Maisie could feel her heart pounding. She'd sworn to keep his name secret, yet she must say something. Hadn't her lass suffered enough? 'It were a chap from t'chapel but, like I say, no one you know. That's all I'm saying.'

'Who from the chapel? Not the superintendent?'

'Goodness me, not Mr Baxton? Not flippin' likely.'

'Who then?'

Maisie avoided her daughter's fiercely probing gaze, desperately searching for some way to put her off the scent, but Dolly was tenacious, as always.

'Let's see, what were you involved with at the time? The Mother's Bright Hour. Playing the piano for the Sunday School. The choir. You once told me you were in the choir. Good lord, not Cyril Duckett?'

Maisie was stunned by her daughter's perspicuity. It brought a shiver to her spine, considering the circumstances. 'What made you think of Cyril?'

'I remember you once saying that he'd been sweet on you when you were a girl, before you married Dad.'

'Oh aye, that's true, he was.'

'But he's... *old.*'

'Cyril is a nice man. He's eleven years older than me. A safe, solid sort and we have a lot in common.'

'What, singing the 'Messiah' together at the chapel?' Dolly might have giggled, had it not all been so dreadfully serious and her mother's face a picture of misery.

Maisie's response was sharp. 'Don't take that tone with me, young lady. I wasn't always like this, this lank, mousy woman with no shine to her. Once I had something special. Chaps very often took a fancy to me, as they will to you, all in good time. And it felt good to be noticed again. Anyroad, what if it were Cyril? I'm not saying it is, mind, but he wasn't always old. He was quite good-looking in his day, and very much the man–about–town. I should happen have accepted his proposal. Anyroad, if we made each other happy for a while, what would be so wrong in that?' My goodness, Maisie thought, I've dropped meself in it good and proper now. And Cyril too!

'You were already married, Mam, that's what's wrong with it. Oh, I'm not meaning to accuse you or anything, but it's all come as a bit of a shock.'

'Course it has. Well, it's all water under the bridge now, so best to forget about it.' Maisie knew that she should have denied it was Cyril. Why hadn't she? He was a good man. He didn't deserve to be dragged into this mess. She'd need to have a quiet word with him, ask him to stand by her. She was quite certain that he would, as he had done in the past, so what harm could it do as long as Dolly was happy and never discovered the truth? Cyril would understand, and Maisie had no intention of breaking her silence, her promise. Far too dangerous for everyone concerned! 'I don't want no gossip, my private business is my own, not to be talked about the length of Castlefield.'

Dolly looked shocked. 'What do you think I am?'

Maisie got to her feet, and collecting both mugs went to wash them in the sink. 'Well I hope you're satisfied, though what good knowing all this will do, I can't think. Best to put it out of your mind and forget all about it. No matter what our Aggie claims, Calvin fetched you up as his own without too much complaint over the years.'

'How can you say that?' Dolly's blue eyes stretched wide in disbelief. 'He ignored me all my life, probably from the day I was born. Are you saying he didn't object to your sleeping with another man?'

Maisie flushed bright pink and began fussing over refilling the kettle, lighting the gas, even though she was sick of tea and had no wish to drink another. This discussion was the last thing she'd wanted on this night of all nights, and it had gone far enough, too far in her opinion. She'd very much like to put a stop to it right now, take back every word. But it was as if she was on a roller coaster that she couldn't get off till she'd hit the bumpers at the end of the ride. 'No, I couldn't rightly say that.'

'What did he do to you then?'

'No more'n you'd expect.'

'Tell me, Mam. He belted you, didn't he? How did he find out? Did he hurt you badly? What did he do?'

Maisie turned off the gas under the kettle and let out a great shuddering sigh, as if remembering this painful time was all too much for her. Dolly went and put an arm about her shaking shoulders, drew her back to the table and sat stroking her arm. 'Come on, Mam, tell me everything, and I won't interrupt.'

–

Hard as it was to relate this part of the story, Maisie felt calmer now, her panic subsiding a little, for with this bit, there need be no lies. 'I told him myself. Not that he needed no telling. He knew, soon as he found out I were pregnant. We hadn't – you know – slept together for a long while. Not in that way, as a married couple. Just sharing the same bed like, so I told him I'd had an affair, and that I were leaving him. And yes, he thumped me, broke two of my ribs as a matter of fact, even though I was carrying you. I left him and moved in with Cyril Duckett. Eeh, it was a revelation. We were happy as a pair of larks.'

Maisie's face lit up at the memory, and for an instant Dolly caught a glimpse of the pretty young woman she'd once been. 'He was so good to me were Cyril, a grand chap. Made me laugh and fussed over me, fetched me a cup of tea in bed every morning. I thought I'd landed in heaven.' Then her face darkened, as if a cloud had blotted out the sun. 'But it couldn't last. I knew, deep in me heart that it never could've lasted.'

'Why, what happened?' Enthralled by this apparently tender love story, Dolly had tears in her eyes at the thought of these two lovers being parted, of her mam, always so downtrodden and browbeaten, finally finding happiness and then losing it.

'I had my baby. You. And you were all right, not hurt in any way by him belting me, though I'd feared you might be. But I had to go back because of the other childer. They needed me, I was missing them badly, and Calvin wouldn't let me see them otherwise. Our Aggie was only two when you were born, our Willy nine and badly with his chest even then. The youngest of the other lads was our Eli at thirteen, about to start work and needing his mam. But all the others were still at home too, even our Abel who was sixteen at the time. I had to go back. They weren't coping without me.' She gave a hollow laugh. 'You couldn't see your dad – Calvin – doing the washing and mending and cooking, could you? So I decided to call it a day and go back home.'

'You mean you and Cyril agreed to part?'

Maisie flushed. 'Aye, you could say that. I didn't want to go, not after all those months of peace and quiet. And he'd become very special to me, had Cyril.' If not in the way you might imagine, Maisie thought, but as a friend she'd turned to in her hour of need. Every fibre of her being still ached for the man she really loved, whose name she never would mention till her dying day. That way there would be no more hurt, to his family or her own. 'I've no regrets. If I couldn't have the man I loved, then at least I could have me kids about me. You're the ones who matter most.'

Following this heartbreaking confession there followed a long silence as two tears ran unchecked down Maisie's cheeks. Dolly leaned over and wrapped her arms about her, understanding, perhaps for the first time, the true nature of a mother's unselfish love.

'You'll always have me, Mam. Always!'

Maisie patted her arm. 'Aye, I know that love, and I wouldn't be without you, for all the bother you caused by just getting born. But if I'd accepted Cyril's offer of marriage all those years ago, when I were nobbut a daft young lass, it might all have been so different. I might never have strayed from the paths of righteousness, eh? But there we are, we make our bed and have to lie in it.' She smiled over-brightly at Dolly, and unable to think of any words of comfort to offer, since the day of Calvin's funeral didn't seem quite the moment to say she was almost glad that he was dead, Dolly smiled bleakly back.

–

Evie continued to rail about the loss to her wedding plans but in spite of enlisting her mother's support in an effort to change her father's mind, Nathan remained adamant. His decision, he said, was final. She could have a smaller wedding, or postpone it for a while.

'Feel free to discuss the matter with Freddie and his parents. I'm sure they will understand and see that a decent period of mourning should be acknowledged.'

In the end, against all her better judgement, Evie had no alternative but to explain the delicate situation to her future in-laws since plans were at an advanced stage and must be brought to a halt. But Freddie's people, Mr and Mrs Fitzgerald, were not in the least little bit understanding. They sat in their crimson and gold Edwardian parlour and declared themselves appalled by the idea of both postponement and a scaling down. Mrs

Fitzgerald wailed on and on about how the outfit she had bought, particularly the hat, would be quite out of fashion a year from now.

Mr Fitzgerald grumbled over the cost of buying a new morning suit while pointing out how you couldn't hope to get decent champagne if you went in for unnatural penny-pinching. 'That's the problem with the sons of self-made men. Taught to watch the pennies too closely and far too left wing, don't you know. That dratted father of yours will have us all eating pie and peas and drinking stout at some common hostelry, if we don't watch out.'

Whereupon, his wife nearly fainted on the spot and was forced to resort to a hefty dose of *Sal Volatile* to help her to recover.

And then there was the matter of their friends and social standing. 'They'll think we're destitute or about to go bankrupt,' Mrs Fitzgerald complained. 'As if we can't afford to see our son properly launched into the world.'

'Dash it, Mama, you make me sound like some sort of cruise liner.'

'Don't be facetious, Freddie.'

No matter how much Evie attempted to explain, they failed to see the problem. But then neither could she. The whole problem had grown quite out of all proportion. After a half hour's discussion, which grew increasingly heated and desperate, even Freddie turned on her, condemning her for recklessly endangering her life by driving about Salford and Castlefield without even a chaperone. 'Not at all the kind of behaviour one expects from a future wife. Not the done thing, old fruit.'

Evie looked quite taken aback by these censorious remarks from such an unexpected quarter. Surely he wasn't going to take his mother's side against her? 'How dare you call me that? I'm not an *old fruit*! And what sort of wife do you expect me to be? One who does only what her lord and master tells her to?'

'That is the usual way, dear,' put in his over-helpful mother.

'Why cannot anyone see that I was only trying to help?' Evie cried, driven to beating her fists on the arms of her chair in frustration.

'Of course you were, dear, but Freddie is absolutely correct,' Mrs Fitzgerald interjected, smiling fondly at her son as she attempted to placate his overwrought fiancée. 'There are standards to be kept, a right and proper way of going about things from someone who hopes to be our future daughter-in-law. I freely confess that I have, on occasions, entertained grave doubts about the appropriateness of your behaviour, your equilibrium shall we say? But then I blame your upbringing. With a bohemian mother, and that father of yours being far too democratic for words, is it any wonder? Marriage with my darling Freddie will calm you down considerably, I should think.'

'I have no wish to calm down,' screamed Evie, but then, to her credit, did just that, drawing in a deep, cooling breath. In truth, she felt this to be one snide remark too many. However irritating her father might be at times, keeping her on a tight reign and constantly picking at her over the slightest thing, she couldn't bear to hear someone else being rude about him. As his daughter, *she* had the right to quarrel with him and make his life as difficult as possible, but what right did *they* have? And Mumsie may well spend every waking moment writing romantic poetry or painting dreadful arty pictures; admire the works of Elinor Glyn and think that Mrs Baldwin wears dreadful hats, but she was an absolute darling. In Evie's view, no one had the right to criticise her family but herself. As for her own behaviour, she would tolerate disapproval from no one, certainly not from this silly woman and her sycophantic son.

The silly woman in question was still ranting on. 'May I remind you, young lady, that the Fitzgeralds have enjoyed a position in society and considerable status for generations, not a mere decade or two, as your own have.'

Evie was incensed by this criticism. 'I'll have you know my grandfather made the family fortune a good fifty years ago, and my father has added to it. Ah, but you're no longer wealthy, are you?' The look she gave her future mother-in-law could only be described as imperious. 'I've always been of the opinion that you'd happily give your right arm to be linked in marriage with the Barker family, mad though you may claim us to be. The moment you saw Freddie and I were hitting it off, you were like a cat who'd swallowed the cream. Isn't that the truth of it?'

'Well, upon my word! Freddie, are you going to stand there and allow her to speak to me like this?'

Freddie half-heartedly attempted to interject. 'I say old sport, you're cutting it a bit sharp, don't you think?'

Evie was on her feet, standing full-square before them on their faded Aubusson rug, screaming like a fishwife. 'Oh, shut up, you stupid nincompoop! Who do you think you are? I'll do as I damned well please, drat it.'

Mrs Fitzgerald gasped. 'I know you are upset but please do not take your ill temper out on my dear boy. He's a perfect darling, and really doesn't deserve to be treated so ill.'

'I'll take it out on whosoever I please, and behave as I think fit. I've certainly no intention of *ever* kowtowing to a man, particularly not a husband, and certainly not your perfect, darling son. The real reason why you want a big wedding is so that you can show off to all your silly, snobby friends. Maybe Pops is right and my efforts to help in the strike were misguided, but I'll not stand here and be taken to task by *you*, nor have my family maligned.'

Whereupon, before she'd had time to consider the consequences of her action, Evie ripped the sparkling diamond from the third finger of her left hand and flung it at Freddie.

A third alternative had apparently been found to the dilemma of what was or was not appropriate behaviour following Calvin Tomkins's demise. The wedding had been called off.

Chapter Seven

In the days following, Dolly suffered a strange reaction. She saw Calvin now in an entirely different light. She realised that all her life she'd been struggling to love him as a good daughter should. Now she didn't have to pretend any more. He hadn't been her father, was no relation at all, and it suddenly felt such a huge relief. Her feelings towards her mother were mixed. A part of her understood and sympathised for no one in their right minds could call him an easy husband to please. On the other hand, Dolly resented the fact that she'd been kept in the dark all these long years. Why had Mam never told her? Why keep it such a secret? It seemed so cruel, particularly when it was obvious that Calvin hadn't treated her right. Dolly spent many sleepless nights worrying about that.

The result was that she thought of yet more questions, which needed answering.

She wanted to know everything about Cyril Duckett, whom she'd deduced to be her true father. She'd seen him often enough at the chapel, of course, but not to speak to. He was the choirmaster, a distant, exalted figure. Now she wanted to talk to him face to face. She wanted to understand what sort of person he was, what his reaction had been when he'd learned that Maisie was pregnant; why he'd never shown any interest in herself, his own child.

Dolly asked her mother these questions, and any number of others, including how she'd managed to see him constantly at the chapel, week after week, and not be tempted to go to him again, particularly once the lads had left home. Maisie refused to answer any of them, or discuss the matter any further.

'It's private. I've said all I've got to say on the subject. Leave well alone, lass.'

But Dolly wanted to know if he liked walking over the moors, as she did. Was he fond of cheese and hated fish, and impulsive with a quick temper? Did she get this passionate sense of independence from him, since she'd seen little evidence of it in her mother? And did she look anything like him? Had his hair once been black before it went grey? Did he have eyebrows that winged upwards; a mouth that was always saying the wrong thing and earning rebukes for impertinence? Did he talk to himself as she did all the time? On a more practical level she needed to ask if he'd ever remarried; whether he had any more children who would be half brothers and sisters to her.

Oh, there was so much to learn about him; her father, her real dad.

The tragic accident had come about because of a terrible chain of events and Dolly began to worry that it might make things worse between herself and Aggie. Never particularly close, yet Dolly had always been fond of her pretty sister, admiring her tall elegance and easy confidence, and although Aggie could be unkind, she'd always been there for her when needed. Even in the middle of that fracas at the mill, her sister had come to her aid, speaking up for her to the overlooker.

For several days nothing was said, not a word between them, as if an odd sort of reticence to mention the subject was growing in both their minds. Aggie went back to work and carried on as usual, if rather more self-righteous and full of herself than ever. One night, Dolly could take no more, and, as she climbed into the bed they shared, finally plucked up the courage to broach the subject.

'I want you to know that I don't bear any grudge over what you revealed. Where's the point? You were upset at losing Dad – *your* dad, that is – which I can understand.'

'I'm sorry I had to be the one to tell you,' Aggie said, offering token sympathy although Dolly could see that she didn't look sorry at all. She was almost hugging herself with glee as she sat at the end of the bed, rolling her hair into curling rags.

Aggie had always been a bit jealous of her, though why that should be, Dolly had never been able to work out. She claimed that Dolly was always given an easy time of it because she was the youngest, which wasn't true at all. While some of her older brothers might pet and spoil her, they could also be merciless in their teasing, as only brothers can, playing practical jokes on her like putting frogs down her neck and spiders in her school lunch box. Dolly had been forced to learn to stand up for herself from quite an early age. Otherwise they'd have made her life impossible, as well as have her fetching and carrying for them like some sort of obedient puppy.

'It's amazing really that you ever imagined he could be your proper father,' Aggie said, pouting as she began to smear cream all over her face. 'It's quite clear he always liked me best, and is it any wonder? Anyone can see what an ugly little sparrow you are, with your skinny legs, pale skin and pointed chin. Quite different from me! You have those unnatural blue eyes and, apart from Mam's, which are a wishy-washy grey, everyone else has brown, green or hazel. And you have black hair, when the rest of our family have brown, although mine is a beautiful chestnut, of course. So I always knew there was something funny about you. That's why he told me, because I wanted to know why you looked so different.'

It was true, Dolly thought, watching her sister's protracted beauty preparations which she devotedly carried out night after night. She'd often felt herself to be the odd one out. And no wonder Aggie had always been Calvin's favourite. She could understand it all now.

At long last, Aggie turned off the gas lamp and bounced into bed. 'Sam Clayton won't ever fancy you now,' she said, her light voice tinged with malicious pleasure.

'Why won't he?'

'Because you're one of them – you know.' She dipped her voice to tragically low tones.

'One of what?'

'A *bastard*!'

Dolly felt herself go rigid with horror beneath the cold sheets. 'I am *not*! My dad, Calvin that is, was my stepfather, that's all. That doesn't mean I'm a – what you said. Don't be so nasty, our Aggie.'

Aggie turned her back on Dolly, wiggling her shoulders in self-righteous indignation. 'I wasn't being nasty, I was only warning you that whether you are – one of them – or not, Sam isn't going to like it. I know you fancy him rotten but he won't want to get himself hooked up with someone like that. It isn't moral, is it? Not proper. I always knew our mam had done something to hurt Dad and when I asked him what it was, he told me. No wonder the poor soul spent all his time in the Navigation.'

'How can you say such things? Implying Mam isn't moral, that I'm not what I should be. As if I were *abnormal* in some way. I'm still *me*! I'm still *your* sister, same as I was yesterday. Nothing has happened to change the person I am inside. And Sam Clayton might be nuts about you right now, Aggie, but he won't always be, not when he realises what a nasty cow you really are.'

–

Dolly didn't have much time to feel sorry for herself over the next few days as she devoted much of her time to trudging around all the other local mills, looking for work. It came as no surprise that there was none to be found. Work was scarce in any case but the tale of the fight had got about, so what mill manager would be keen to take on the girl who had sparked off such a row, let alone caused the demise of her own father?

She could have said that Calvin had brought about his own end, through a typical fit of rage and violence but she was determined to think kindly of him, as Mam had asked. You shouldn't speak ill of the dead. After all, he'd taken on another man's child, had not thrown his wife out onto the streets however selfish his reasons, yet hadn't been able to help being what he was, a big bully. The marriage must have been little more than a sham from the start; otherwise Mam would never have gone with Cyril Duckett in the first place. Dolly had used to think that her mam and dad had a lot of children because they loved each other. How utterly naïve she'd been. Oh, what a muddle life was. How confusing. Her life had been turned upside down, everything changed and now she didn't know who she was; who her parents were or even whether her friends would still speak to her.

Dolly sat on the wall at the end of Potato Wharf and gave the situation deep thought. Men were working, trundling boxes, timber and bales of cotton down to the canal basin. She could hear their voices, calling and joking with each other; see the bulkheads of the ships docked, smell tar on the wind, sawdust and soot. It was a perfectly ordinary scene in Castlefield, a day as normal as any other. Except that, for her, nothing would ever be normal again.

Dolly wasn't generally one for moping and had no intention of starting now. She couldn't pretend to mourn for a father who'd either ignored or bullied her for most of her life. Maisie didn't seem to be mourning much either. Only this morning she'd taken charge of Abel's tribe, as usual, because his wife did have work, unlike herself. When Dolly had left this morning, the place had already been taken over by wailing kids and wet nappies.

'He pays me a bit for helping out, and we need the brass, love,' Maisie had argued, when Dolly had remonstrated with her, saying she needed time to recover from the tragedy.

So Dolly was determined to be equally practical and look on the bright side. At least Calvin couldn't bully her mam any more either. Hard as life was going to be in the future, particularly if she failed to find a job, they were, at least, both free. If she'd never had a normal father to love and care for her, if Aggie was in a huff and hardly speaking to her, then she did at least have her lovely mother and Willy, her other brothers and sisters-in-law, and her nieces and nephews. She still had a family. And she still had her friends. Or did she?

A picture of Sam Clayton popped, unbidden, into her mind and Dolly smiled, her natural optimism reasserting itself. Even at nine years old she'd vied with Aggie for his attention, actually fighting over him on one occasion. But then they were forever falling out over something or other. Not that their squabbles greatly concerned Sam, flattering as that might be. His great strength was his innate confidence and unflappability. Nothing ever troubled him. He was the easiest person to get along with, and always good for a laugh and a bit of fun.

He and Dolly, together with Matt and Davey, and Aggie of course, used to ride their bogey carts, nothing more than a pair of old pram wheels and a plank of wood with a bit of rope to steer it with, and bounce over the setts. They'd play ticky round the railway goods yard, and in the summer when the street was running with tar, they'd get all grubby making tar babies and Sam would tease her by sticking it in her hair. Mam would go mad over the mess.

Sometimes they'd all go off to the Corporation Baths together on New Quay Street and Sam would peep at the girls through the windows on the roof. Davey would be right beside him, of course, though denying it, and soft Matt would blush at the very idea. All five of them had sworn to be friends for life, so how could it be true what Aggie had said? Why would Sam or any of them turn away from her if they discovered the truth about her birth? It wasn't Dolly's fault, after all, what her mam had done all those years ago. Why should Sam hate her because of that? She felt quite certain that he wouldn't see her as the least little bit immoral.

Oh, but she couldn't bear it if he did. It would leave her with nothing. No, she wouldn't believe it, not for a second. Sam was a bit misguided perhaps at present, so far as his affections were concerned but Dolly hadn't given up hope, not by a long chalk. Once he realised just how nasty-minded her sister could be, that Aggie intended to set her cap at someone with a bit more brass than he'd ever have, Sam would surely stop pining over her. Dolly's fantasy was that he'd then see herself in an entirely different light, discover that she wasn't stuck-up like Aggie, and that he'd liked her best all along. He might even ask her out on a proper date and make her his girl.

The power of youth exploded within her, glorying in the mysteries of feminine power, the knowledge of all those long, lovely years ahead still to be lived, with ample time to set things right and make a good life for herself. Dolly was perfectly certain that if she could only get him to see how things really were, it would all work out grand.

—

Sam looked at her, nonplussed. 'What are you saying, Dolly? I'm not sure I'm properly understanding you.'

Dolly sighed, though she wasn't surprised. She'd waited for him to come home from the mill and they were both now sitting on the wall at the end of Potato Wharf. She'd gone round and round in circles trying to broach the subject and yet not reveal too much, but had rather lost track herself. 'I was only wondering that if you discovered something – different – about me, whether it would change your attitude towards me? Spoil our friendship like.'

'Spoil our what?' Sam looked puzzled, fidgeted a little on the wall, as if all this personal stuff bothered him.

'Spoil our friendship,' Dolly repeated, irritated by his apparent slowness. She was quite sure that he put on this act of being slow-witted to make the point that discussions of a personal nature were beneath his contempt; that he could have his pick of any girl, if he so wished. There were certainly any number of girls lining up in the hope of catching his eye, so she must take care not to scare him off. 'I wouldn't want anything to spoil our friendship,' she continued. 'We've known each other a long time, Sam Clayton, and you reckon you know everything about me. Well, what if you were wrong and there was something you didn't know. What then?'

'Oh, I see.' It was clear that he didn't see at all, that he was only being polite in a bored sort of way. 'Depends what it was. I mean, what sort of thing? Eeh, Dolly, you're processes are so convoluted a bloke can get lost in them.'

Dolly had no real wish to explain, or reveal the extent of her shame, so she remained obstinately vague. 'What if it was something in my background, say?'

Sam chewed on his lip while he considered. 'Happen if you did your Aggie in as well as your dad, I reckon that might change our friendship. But then they'd lock you up in Strangeways then hang you for murder.' He made a strangling sound deep in his throat then laughed at his own joke.

'What a thing to say! Hang me for murder indeed. You're not taking this seriously.'

'Dolly, I'm completely baffled. I haven't the first idea what you're talking about.'

'Anyroad, I thought you liked our Aggie.'

'Course I like her, but she drives a bloke barmy blowing hot and cold all the time. One minute all over you, the next giving you the cold-shoulder as she does it to you an' all, I can tell.'

'Oh, well that's true enough, I know she's a pain but that's our Aggie all over, doesn't know what she wants half the time. But it's your own fault if you let her lead you a merry dance. You don't have to put up with her, as I do.'

Sam grinned. 'I rather like women who are unpredictable. Makes for a bit more excitement in life.'

Dolly felt her heart sink. No one, she thought, could be more predictable, boring or unexciting than herself. 'So you still fancy your chances with her then?' She said this in a teasing way, her heart nearly stopping as she waited for his answer.

'I'll have to think about that one, Dolly.' Sam lifted those enigmatically peaked brows right up to the ragged line of his fringe and gazed wide-eyed at nothing in particular, as if weighing up all possible implications.

Dolly would have given anything on earth to read those secret thoughts which must be whirling around his head, but all she could do was gaze at his deliciously wide and sensual mouth, and wait for what seemed like eternity. She didn't even know why she liked him so much. He *did* used to make a mess of her hair with that tar, *and* was cheeky enough once to ask to see her knickers, though she'd been only nine or ten at the time. On another occasion when they'd all gone on a Sunday School trip to Fleetwood and played stalking games among the sand dunes, he'd even tried to kiss her. Stupidly, Dolly had been too shy to let him and he'd laughed and called her a curiosity. The name had stuck ever since.

Sam Clayton was certainly no innocent, and his opinion of women was of a traditional nature, because of an ineffectual mother who could never make up her mind about anything, not even what to make for tea. He frequently complained that Dolly asked too many questions, as if he resented her natural curiosity and independence, her ability to think for herself. It was his only flaw, in Dolly's humble opinion, and one she could tolerate because he was so handsome, so *exciting*! And he would never hit her, as Calvin had done. Despite his laid-back approach to life, Dolly was quite sure that Sam Clayton was far more intelligent than he let on. She'd even seen him surreptitiously trying to read books and magazines while working on his frame. When she'd asked him what they were, he'd laughed and said they were a foreign language so far as she was concerned.

'Why, are they French? Why would you need to learn French?' she'd asked.

'You never know what skills you might need in life, eh?'

'Can I learn? Are those pictures of French ladies then?'

'These magazines aren't for your eyes, my sweet, innocent Dolly.'

She'd wanted to challenge him, to say she could learn French too, but he'd locked them away in his lunch box. He was a right card was Sam. An answer for everything, except today apparently.

He stirred himself at last and gave her a sideways smile. 'This inquisition you're putting me through, Dolly. This isn't because you fancy me yourself, is it?'

Dolly did her utmost to appear shocked at the very idea. '*Me?* Fancy *you?* Lord, no. Whatever put such a daft notion into your head?'

Sam grinned and thumped his chest a few times with the flat of his hand, as if able to breathe again. 'By heck, that's a relief, 'cause that certainly would spoil our friendship, don't you reckon, if we got into all of that love stuff?'

A slight pause while she digested this remark, not sure of the best way to answer. In the end, Dolly opted for caution. 'Of course it would. Don't you worry your head about that, Sam Clayton. You'd have to be the last bloke left in the world before I looked in your direction.'

He sauntered off for his tea then, hands in pockets, claiming he'd promised to meet up with Aggie later. Dolly was left to walk home alone. Outside her front door she found Matt Thornton waiting, as he so often was, and sighed with weary resignation. 'Hello Matt, at a loose end again, are you?'

'I thought happen you might feel like a bike ride after tea, Dolly?'

Poor old Matt, she thought, still thinking they were kids to play out on their bikes. Still, he was harmless enough. She glanced back over her shoulder to make sure there was no chance Sam might change his mind and come dashing back to ask her out instead, but no, the street was empty. 'All right,' she agreed. Why not?'

It was a day or two later when Maisie asked Cyril if she could have a quick word with him, standing on this doorstep and shuffling her feet with embarrassment. She hated coming to his house, had been avoiding him this last week or two at the chapel, though perhaps a quiet word with him in the vestry after the service would have been better. Yet if she was any judge, Dolly had no intention of waiting another day, let alone another week till Sunday came round again, before she came looking for him. 'Is it all right if I come in, Cyril? I'd just like a quick word.'

Cyril looked surprised but pushed wide the door and invited her inside. 'You are always welcome here Maisie, you surely know that.'

He took her no further than the front parlour, the back kitchen being far too intimate a place for them both. He rarely used this room, musty and gloomy though it was with its green paper blind, and heavy Victorian furniture, but it felt more like neutral territory.

They sat facing each other in the wing chairs at either side of the fireplace. The grate was empty save for a neatly pleated paper fan, and a pale shaft of early summer sunlight slanted across the room, showing up a trail of dust motes in its path. The ornaments on the dresser didn't look as if they'd been dusted for a long time either: a stuffed bird under a glass case, a loudly ticking clock, a slender girl in an Alice blue gown and a small boy in baggy breeches. All looking dull and neglected with pockets of grime filling the pottery folds, and even from where she was sitting, Maisie could see that the mantles in the gas lamps were broken.

It hadn't always been that way. This little parlour had once glowed with polish and pride, showing itself off as the fine house it truly was: not your common back-to-back but a double-fronted, corner terrace on Gartside Street. And it could all have been hers for the asking, if she'd taken on its owner all those years ago. Would that have saved her from making her Big Mistake, stopped her loving the wrong man? How could she be sure? It was too late to worry about that.

Cyril was thinking almost the same thing, wondering how he'd managed to let this lovely woman slip through his fingers. Why things never turned out the way he hoped. Women always wanted something better beyond their reach. He'd have given anything in the whole world to win her. He thought he'd almost won her once, but it had all fallen apart.

There came the clatter of clogs as someone hurried by, stirring them from their nostalgic reverie and it was Cyril who broke the silence by clearing his throat. 'What am I thinking of? Where are my manners? Can I get you a cup of tea, Maisie? Kettle's on.'

'No, don't bother. I mustn't stop long having things to do. I just wanted a quick word.'

Cyril was offering his condolences, making the usual noises but Maisie interrupted him. 'I've not come about my late husband, but to warn you that you'll be getting a visitor.'

'A visitor?' Cyril frowned, looking puzzled, as well he might. Maisie knew he didn't get many of those nowadays, not since his mother had passed away a year or two back.

'Our Dolly has taken it into her head to pay you a call.'

'Your Dolly is coming to see me? Why would she do that?' His face seemed to change suddenly, to go all pale and stiff, then flush with crimson. 'Oh, bless my soul, no, not after all this time. You haven't gone and told her? Nay, what a burden to place on a child, as if you haven't enough troubles right now.'

'She's not a child any longer, Cyril, and I told her nothing. It were our Aggie's doing. She apparently got the whole story out of Calvin, or as much of it as he knew. After that, well, our Dolly isn't one to sit silently by and say nothing. She had to pester me for the whole sorry tale and when I wouldn't explain, started making guesses of her own.'

Maisie seemed to be fidgeting with her gloves, drawing them off, not quite meeting his gaze. 'We got to talking about the

80

chapel and, well, she mentioned your name. I didn't disagree with her assumptions. I couldn't. If she comes, I wondered if… Well, all you have to do is listen and go along with whatever she says. Will you do that for me, Cyril?'

'I'd do anything for you Maisie, you know I would.'

She looked at him fully then, meeting his gaze at last, and her cheeks pinked with embarrassment or else over the naked adoration in his eyes. 'I'm grateful, only sorry you're involved in all of this muddle yet again.'

'Don't you trust me, Maisie?'

'With my life, Cyril, but I made promises I must keep, as you know.'

'And so did I. You can rely on me to be discreet. As ever.'

They sat for a moment in silence, their business concluded satisfactorily yet apparently neither anxious to put an end to these few moments of peace and this quiet understanding between them. Two sad people disappointed by life, sitting with their heads bowed deep in their own private thoughts, saying nothing. Again Cyril offered tea but she was on her feet in a second.

'No thanks, I'd best be off. I've said what I came to say.' Still she hesitated, applying herself to pulling her gloves back on. 'I'll see you on Sunday then, as usual.'

'Aye, Maisie, you will. I thought we'd do 'Crimmond' this week, in respect for Calvin. One of your favourites, eh?'

She gave a soft smile. 'That'd be grand, Cyril. And you'll think on about our Dolly.'

'I will. Your secret is safe with me, as it ever was.'

Hovering on the doorstep, Maisie glanced up and down the street before stepping out, just to be on the safe side. Gossip about her comings and goings was the last thing she needed. Fortunately it was quite empty, with not a soul in sight. Not until the echo of her hurrying footstep had died away did a figure once more emerge from a nearby ginnel, and he was smiling.

Nifty Jack had been hanging around at the end of the street, leaning casually against a lamp post while he waited to do his bit of business. He'd watched Maisie Tomkins enter Cyril Duckett's house and was filled with curiosity. This widow visiting a bachelor, having recently buried her husband, was the last thing he'd expected to see. A man had come clattering by in his noisy clogs, two children skipping along beside him but nobody was paying Nifty Jack the slightest attention, avoiding him, as was generally the case.

He'd edged further down the street and walked stealthily past the window, trying to peep in although he could see little beneath the half-drawn blind. He'd hovered close for a few moments, hoping to hear something of the conversation within, but the mill stone grit walls of the terraced houses were too thick. He needed to know what she was up to. Recently widowed, she still owed him a deal of money. He slipped into the small vestibule between the open front door and the glass inner door, which shielded the parlour from draughts and found he could hear every word, clear as a bell. Even better, he'd put his eye to the keyhole and watched the entire scene. Then when he heard her coming out, he'd quickly escaped. Eeh, but what he heard was most interesting.

There was more to Cyril Duckett than one might imagine, as well as Maisie Tomkins. Yet they were a dull, restrained pair. With her old man dead, why didn't she dash upstairs and leap into bed with her lover? Why didn't Cyril rip off her clothes and ravage her there and then on the rug? Nifty felt a swelling in his groin at the very thought of it. He would certainly have done so in the past.

It amused him to think of Maisie as someone who'd play the dirty on her husband, not that Calvin was ever in a position to complain about that, not being the most faithful of spouses himself. What would he have said if he'd been here? Nifty chuckled, knowing full well. It had always been easy to get

Calvin riled up, but less so to control that temper once it was roused. Nifty had always taken great care not to upset him. Calvin Tomkins had been a big man with a powerful punch. Did he know that his wife had betrayed him? Nifty wondered. Then he recalled a snippet of conversation he'd once had with his erstwhile friend. As he swaggered off down the street in the direction of his favourite watering hole, it all came back to him, clear as day.

It must have been around the time that Maisie had left home and there'd been quite a bit of gossip. Calvin was drowning his sorrows in the Donkey, after having followed her and spotted her entering Duckett's house. With a few pints inside him he was all fired up, ready to take on the world. 'I'm going to go round there and clock him one, or chop off his nuts.'

Nifty had attempted to calm him down.

'How can you talk about being calm when me wife's making a flaming fool of me? By God, I'll make her sorry, I will an' all, and make her rue the day she ever betrayed me. Bloody tart. I'll give her a right pasting when I get her home.'

Nifty had sunk his nose into his pint, so that Calvin couldn't see the sharpening of interest. 'You should keep her under better control, lad. Letting a wife run wild is allus dangerous.'

'I don't let her run wild but by heck, I never thought our Maisie would put it about, and with him of all people. I saw him as some sort of Nancy-boy singing in the choir, being a sidesman at the chapel. I mean, how did she ever persuade him to… you know…?'

Nifty had done some fast thinking, wanting to know as much as possible. 'I'll admit he's a whey-faced git but you can't judge a book by its cover, isn't that what they say? So are you saying that Cyril Duckett's her bit on the side, eh?' The question was asked in tones of pseudo-sympathy but it always paid to know which women might prove pliant and biddable.

'Aye, so far as I can make out. We had a right barney about it the other week. I thought I'd made my position clear, made sure she'd not see him again in a hurry. Now she seemingly has, bloody tart. I'll flaming kill her.'

Calvin's nostrils flared so wide Nifty had half expected flames to appear out of him.

Now he struggled to remember what had happened next. Calvin had sunk several more pints to console himself, or fuel his anger. He'd then spoken of an unexpected pregnancy. Given a big wink as he tapped the side of his nose, he said, 'Don't let on I've told you! It's all hush-hush. I don't want it getting about that I were cuckolded by the likes of Duckett.' And he'd fallen back in his seat and belched loudly.

'How can you be sure it's Cyril? If your Maisie is putting it about, it could be with anyone, couldn't it?'

He remembered Calvin looking startled, struggling to focus and think it through. 'Nay, that's all I need for me wife to be servicing the whole blasted neighbourhood.'

Nifty had made the right sort of sympathetic noises since it suited him to lead this stupid man by the nose, as his wife could well be doing, at least till he had the information he needed and his pound of flesh.

Following that interesting discussion and judging his moment, he'd made his approaches or so he'd thought. Except that Maisie hadn't been as biddable as he'd hoped, nearly cracking his head open with the frying pan when he'd suggested she repay her debt in kind. She'd made a fool of him because she was still spreading her favours, even now years later, after poor old Calvin was dead.

But she had another daughter. Dolly Tomkins was as tasty a piece of fruit as her mother before her and Nifty had a healthy appetite for sweet things, especially young ones ripe for the picking. Any hold he could find over Maisie Tomkins might help him to tighten the screws on her pretty daughter. Information he'd learned over the years resulted in power, very much to his advantage.

Chapter Eight

It was payday and Aggie was waiting anxiously for the man to come round with his polished wooden box. She could see him at Betty Deurden's frame, handing over shillings the girl had no right to be getting, in Aggie's view, considering the trouble she'd caused. The mahogany box held rows of little numbered cups and her own money would be in one of them. He thought he was ever so important and would no doubt take the opportunity to ask her out again since he seemed to have taken quite a shine to her. But he was only a wages clerk, nowhere near good enough for Aggie.

He was standing before her now, his piggy eyes fixed on her bosom. 'Here y'are Aggie! Don't spend it all at once.' This was his weekly joke and Aggie managed a faint smile as he counted the shillings into her hand, half her mind working out how many she could slip into her pocket and keep for herself before handing the rest over to her mother. 'I wondered if you'd happen care to come with me to the pictures tonight.'

Aggie smiled coolly and sadly shook her head. 'I'm afraid I've already made arrangements. Some other time perhaps.'

'Nay, lass, don't be unkind.' He edged closer, and began to tell her how well suited they were; how he'd fancied her for as long as he could remember. He was panting hard, his breath reeking of picked onions and under cover of the box balanced on one arm, he gave her breast a quick squeeze. Aggie began to panic. She could see Harold Entwistle approaching. If he got wind they were wasting time, or worse, thought they were doing a bit of canoodling, as some of the operatives did when his back was turned, she'd be out on her ear again, probably for good this time.

'Anything wrong here?' Harold was coming swiftly towards them along the row between the frames, his face wreathed in a scowl, and Aggie was desperately trying to loosen the grip the clerk now had on her wrist.

'Get off me,' she hissed. 'You'll get me sacked.'

'Say you'll come out with me then.'

With no release from his hold and the sound of the over-looker's boots ringing in her ears, Aggie took the only option open to her. She fainted. It wasn't uncommon for girls to come over all funny and swoon, what with the heat and the humidity, not to mention the constant hunger. She'd never suffered from such weak afflictions herself despite good cause, but this wasn't the moment for pride. She rolled back her eyes, let her head and shoulders slump and, sending up a silent prayer that she didn't bang her head on the machine, or get her hair trapped and be scalped as a girl did only a month or two back, she slid gently to the floor.

Aggie judged it prudent to open her eyes and feign recovery reasonably quickly, not wishing to make too much of the faint or she'd have her pay docked. She found that the wages clerk had been sent packing and it was Harold Entwistle himself who cradled her in his arms, patting her cheeks with a gentle hand. When she looked up at him from beneath her lashes, his response was all she could have wished for. It gave her quite a start of surprise and a warm glow of satisfaction to see the extent of her power. She hadn't lost any of the progress she'd made after weeks of careful flattery, despite her daft sister's bit of bother. Which was just as well, as that would have been truly annoying. An overlooker was much more promising meat than either a wages clerk or Sam Clayton.

–

Nifty Jack was waiting at the gate when the mill loosed, as he always was on a Friday. He questioned several of the operatives, and took a portion of their wages appropriated before ever they left the premises. Some even queued to willingly hand over a shilling or two, perhaps in the hope of keeping him off their backs for another week. Betty Deurden, was one such.

'I'll give you sixpence on account,' she said, fluttering her eyelashes at him and trying not to snort with laughter at the jeering pantomime her mates were making behind his back.

'You'll give me a shilling Betty, plus twopence interest, as is my due.'

'I can't afford this week, Nifty, not after having me pay docked for smoking in the lavvy. Anyroad, me mam's not well.'

'That's your problem, not mine. This is the third week in a row you've not paid the right amount, and before that a couple when you paid nothing at all.'

'But that was because of the strike.'

He gave her a smile that would chill any heart, even Betty's. 'I don't like being let down. I don't like it one little bit.' His eyes glittered and he lowered his voice as he bent his mouth to the curl of her ear and slid one hand to cup her plump breast. 'But don't worry about it just now, Betty love. I'll see you later tonight, shall I? You can settle up with me then, one way or another.'

Betty shoved him away and fled to join her giggling mates. 'No fear, leave me alone, you nasty-minded old git!' And she flounced off, arm in arm with her best friends.

It was a mistake. Not that Betty thought so at the time, not until later that evening when, on her way home from the dance hall and having said goodnight to her friends, Nifty Jack stepped out right in front of her just as she'd taken a short cut down a ginnel. She saw her mistake then clear enough, and couldn't help but give a little squeal of terror, which made him laugh out loud. Betty cursed herself for not even noticing that he must have been following her for some times. Now she could do nothing to protect herself. She was quite alone.

'Pity about this habit of yours of wriggling out of paying what you owe me, Betty, but then happen not. There's more than one way of cracking a nut than stamping on it, wouldn't you say?'

Poor Betty wasn't nearly so brave now as when she'd brought Dolly tumbling with the spindle. She was trembling as he drew closer, whimpering with distress as he unfastened her coat, crying and begging for mercy as he dragged her down onto the cold hard cobbles, and by the time his dry, rough little hands had tugged off her knickers, tossing them aside in the mud so he could satisfy his lust on her, she opened her mouth and screamed, very loud. Not that there was anyone to hear, and even if they had, they'd shut their doors and pretend they hadn't heard, or even noticed his squat, bowler-hatted figure sneak by. It didn't pay to interfere in Nifty Jack's business or stop him from getting what he wanted. Betty learned that simple fact tonight, the hard way.

–

It was Dolly's turn to sit in Cyril's front parlour, fidgeting her bare legs on the rough fabric of the old chairs, eyes fixed on Alice blue gown and her adoring swain. Her gaze was caught by a picture of Daniel in the Lion's Den, which brought a slight smile to her lips. Right now she felt rather as Daniel must have done. Following her failure to find work, Aggie's unfriendly attitude and the confused conversation with Sam, she'd made up her mind to follow her first instinct and meet with Cyril Duckett. No matter what the consequences, or how difficult and painful it might be, she must find out what sort of person he was, and what sort of person that made her. Maybe then she could deal with things better.

But what could she say that wouldn't sound rude, or too abrupt? She couldn't just come right out with it: I believe you're my dad. But what could she say? Did you have an affair with my mother? Dolly inwardly cringed. Neither sounded in the least bit polite.

Cyril, unable to bear her obvious embarrassment, or the silence, any longer, cleared his throat and saved her from her dilemma. 'I know why you've come, lass. Your mam explained everything.'

'Did she?' Dolly was surprised. This was the last thing she'd expected. 'So, it's true then, what our Aggie said?'

Cyril cleared his throat again, which seemed to be causing him some problems. 'You could say so, in a manner of speaking.'

Now what was that supposed to mean? Dolly felt in need of confirmation. She drew in a deep breath. 'You and Mam, you were fond of her.'

'Very fond.' Cyril met her gaze unflinching and she knew he spoke the truth.

'Did she tell you she was pregnant with me?'

'She did.'

Dolly sighed. A man of few words obviously. It was no easier getting information out of him than it had been from Maisie herself. He was a small, faded little man, his head bald save for a fringe of grey around the sides. He wore glasses, was dressed in fustian trousers and a grey cardigan that had seen better days. Everything about him was grey. His clothes, his hair, his eyes, even the skin of his face an odd sort of putty colour. Where was the vibrancy that marked her colouring? To say that she was disappointed in his appearance, was putting it mildly. Not at all the sort of man anyone would choose for a father. Dolly let out a small, philosophical sigh. 'So what did you do when you heard? Did you offer to stand by her?'

'I offered her a home. There wasn't much more I could do. She already had a husband, remember.'

'But you wanted to marry her once.'

'I did, no question about that. I did what I could. She was upset and in a terrible state, needing someone to take care of her, you understand? There was no one else as...' Then he clamped his thin lips shut, as if he'd said too much. To Dolly's mind he hadn't said nearly enough.

'Were you married too?'

'No. I was a widower.'

'Have you remarried since? Any more children?'

He shook his head, gave a little smile. 'None that I know of.'

'If you knew all along that you were my father, why did you never take an interest in me?'

Cyril looked nonplussed, as if she'd caught him on the hop, which, in a way, she had. Questions about his love for Maisie he could deal with, about fathers was another matter altogether. He'd practised what he wanted to say, had the whole tale off pat following his discussion with Maisie, but he'd given no thought to this more personal side, and the question threw him off-balance. He frowned, attempting to give it due consideration now. 'Why should I? You had a father already. You had Calvin. He was your mam's husband and it was only right and proper that I stayed out of the picture, once she was well again, that is and had made a full recovery. That was the decision she made and I feel sure it was the right one.'

'So I got Calvin as a dad – instead of you.'

'You could never have me. I wasn't – wasn't married to your mam.'

'I know that, but – did you never wonder? Didn't you ever want to know how I was? If I minded not having you as a father?'

Cyril felt lost, the whole thing suddenly quite beyond him, and he stood up abruptly. 'I don't think it'll do either of us any good to rake over matters long dead. Best let sleeping dogs lie and all that.' He walked briskly to the door, indicating that the interview, since that was what it felt like, was over.

Dolly stood up too, her face serious, her voice calm as she went to stand before him. 'You've admitted you were fond of her but just tell me this. Did you love her? Did you love my mam?'

'Aye, I did,' Cyril said without pausing for a single heartbeat. 'I loved her very much.' He looked as if he might be about to say more, but then thought better of it and pressed his thin lips tightly together.

'And if things had been different, would you have accepted me then?'

'Eeh lass, I'd've been proud to have had a fine daughter such as yourself, given half a chance.'

'Would you be now, if I asked you to?' Some instinct made her reach out a hand to him but Cyril stiffened and, backing hastily away he flung open the door. 'I'm not sure what it is you want from me, lass, but I can't give it. I'm sorry but there it is. You have to understand that I couldn't interfere. It's all in the past, over and done with.'

'But D— Calvin's dead. I don't have anyone. Nor does Mam, not now. If you and she were in love, involved in this eternal triangle, you can finally get together now, can't you?'

'It's not quite so simple as it may appear.'

'Why isn't it?'

He was growing confused. It was all far too complicated, and not his place to explain. An eternal triangle indeed, but not the one this child imagined. 'It wouldn't be right for me to say anything more. I'd need to speak to Maisie, your mam before I... You were Calvin's daughter, born in wedlock, no matter what happened since, or how you came about in the first place. Best leave it at that, eh?' Then he almost shoved her out into the street and shut fast the door.

–

Heart sore and bitterly disappointed, Dolly wept silent tears as she trudged wearily away down Gartside Street and on through Byrom Street towards Liverpool Road, the walk home seeming twice as long as when she'd come in the opposite direction. But what else had she expected? That he'd throw wide his arms and clutch her to his breast, like in some silly, silent movie? Dolly didn't truly know but somehow she hadn't expected this. It felt as if he had rejected her a second time, as if, despite his words and the very real love he obviously felt for her mother, he didn't want the trouble of admitting that she was his daughter, that he held any responsibility for her.

I'm not sure what it is you want, he'd said, but I can't provide it.

So, what did she want?

Did she want a father who truly cared and loved her?

Dolly thought about Calvin, the only father she'd ever known, and of how his first instinct had always been to hit out first and ask questions afterwards, sometimes not even then. That was because he'd never really loved her. But then why should he? She wasn't his child.

Footsteps behind her, the click of toe caps on cobbles, a familiar voice, warm with feeling. 'You all right, Dolly?'

She slowed her pace to allow Matt to catch up, quickly wiping the tears from her cheeks and fixing a bright smile to her face. 'I'm fine, why would I not be?'

He regarded her shrewdly with his soft, brown eyed gaze. 'You don't look fine to me.'

He wasn't an easy chap to fool, was Matt Thornton, and he looked so kind and sympathetic that she felt oddly comforted, just by his being there, walking quietly beside her, matching his pace to hers. 'To be honest, I was feeling a bit sorry for myself. Not having a job and after everything that's happened. And I was thinking, why did Mam put up with him all those years?'

Matt didn't ask whom she meant. He'd known the family too long. 'I don't suppose either of you had any choice. The alternative would be starvation on the streets or else incarceration in the workhouse.'

It was true. Alternatively, Maisie would have had to risk losing her children if she'd shacked up with Cyril Duckett. Not a happy set of options.

'And what choices do I have, now?' she went on. 'No job, no father – or rather my bully of a stepfather dead, and my real father…' Dolly paused, not wanting to mention Cyril and then changed her mind. If she didn't tell someone, she'd burst, and surely she could trust Matt, one of her oldest friends, less of a tease than the other lads. 'Cyril Duckett, my mother's fancy man, doesn't want to know me apparently, so what do I do about that, eh?'

Matt cast a sideways glance at her averted face. 'Do you reckon that's him, your father?'

'I believe so, but I don't know for certain, do I?'

'Forget him then. What does it matter who your father is?'

'It matters to me.'

'No it doesn't. You can look after yourself, Dolly Tomkins. I've always admired you for that. Though you're only the size of twopennorth of copper, you've never allowed yourself to be bullied by anyone.'

'Anyone but Calvin, but who will now?'

Matt shrugged and grinned shyly at her. 'You'll cope Dolly. You're the sort who can do anything you set your mind to. Seems so to me anyway.'

Dolly glanced up at him, great lanky lad that he was, at his soft brown eyes and self-deprecating smile and found herself offering a shy smile in return. He was right. She could indeed look after herself, no doubt about that. She'd made up her mind long since never to let anyone, after Calvin, lay a finger on her. And nothing lasted forever, not even bad things. She would find a job in the end, maybe be given her old job back, just as Calvin had after one of his drinking binges. 'I never knew you were such a thinking chap, Matt Thornton.'

'There's a lot you don't know about me, Dolly.'

'Well, you're right on this score, I will get another job or die in the attempt. I'll make a start tomorrow by going to speak to Mr Nathan Barker himself. It's not as if we're strangers. We had quite a chat once, in the boiler room. If anyone can help me, he can.'

'That's the ticket, Dolly. Never say die. Come on, I'll buy you a bag of chips to celebrate.'

So what if Cyril Duckett didn't want to publicly acknowledge her as his daughter? He wasn't a bad chap, even if he was a bit grey looking and dull.

'Just think,' Dolly said later, as they strolled along, companionably eating chips with their fingers out of vinegar drenched newspaper, 'things could've been much worse. What if my real father had turned out to be Nifty Jack, for instance? Lord, I'd've slit me own throat.' No, things were nowhere near as bad as they might be.

–

Evie was in despair. She lay on the sofa in the drawing room, as she did most afternoons after lunch, with a cold compress on her head. Ever since that dreadful confrontation with the Fitzgeralds she'd been plagued with headaches. She hadn't set foot out of the door in days – weeks for all she knew – since she'd quite lost track of time. Not that she wanted to see anyone. Evie felt utterly devastated; rejected, cast out, unwanted: by Freddie, by his family, by her father, by everyone. Even Mumsie had been less than sympathetic.

'But darling,' she'd said. 'Daddy and I didn't go in for all that fandango of a fancy wedding. We eloped to the Riviera; much more fun. Why don't you and Freddie do the same? You'd be the talk of the town.'

'I have no wish to elope.'

'But it's so romantic, darling.'

'Not to me it isn't. It smacks of failure. I want a proper wedding with six bridesmaids and that wonderful gown I've had designed specially.' Her eyes filled with tears at the thought of her loss. The dress would never get made now. Strangely, she'd thought very little about Freddie since the wedding had been called off, but she was simply haunted by the memory of that beautiful dress with its handkerchief hemline, silver tissue sleeves and veil. 'I deserve a proper wedding, and Pops is utterly heartless to refuse to give me one just because some man at the mill got himself killed. For God's sake, why should I be held responsible for these people?'

'Papa simply wants to do the right thing, sweetie. What about Italy then? You and Freddie could travel on the Orient Express.'

At which point, Evie had stormed out of the room, since everyone refused to see her point of view.

Now, as she heard the front doorbell ring, she didn't even consider getting up to answer it. There were maids, and her mother to do that, for heaven's sake. When it rang a second time, she remembered that it was the maid's afternoon off and Mumsie would be up in the loft dabbling with her paints, as usual. Sighing with irritation and feeling harangued on all sides, Evie got swiftly to her feet, crossed the hall in three strides and flung it open. 'Yes?'

'Oh! Good afternoon, I was wondering if I might speak to Mr Barker. Mr Nathan Barker.'

'I know who you mean. My father isn't at home,' Evie snapped.

'I rather hoped he might, it being a Saturday and the mill closed. I'm so sorry to have disturbed you. When would be an appropriate time to call again, do you reckon?' Dolly was doing her best to curb the roughness of her accent and to be as polite as possible. Her future may depend upon it. Since the girl holding the door didn't respond, she cleared her throat and tried again. 'Would tomorrow be convenient, after chapel perhaps?'

Evie's gaze was fixed upon the caller. At length she frowned and said, 'Don't I know you? Haven't we met somewhere? Silly me, we couldn't possibly have.' Thinking, where on earth would I meet such a person? And then just as Dolly turned to go, it came to her. 'Oh, I remember. You were the girl who saved me from that angry mob.'

'Aye, that's right. I was wondering if it would come to you.'

Evie dithered. A part of her knew that she should ask the girl in. It was only good manners after what she'd done, but another part rebelled at the very idea of inviting this person, from such a dreadful neighbourhood to even set foot over the threshold. 'Well, I'm sorry but my father is out. Probably playing golf, or at his club. May I take a message?'

Dolly didn't know what to do. Should she take the risk? It was so important to get it right, and yet time was of the essence. She couldn't afford to be out of work for too long. 'Perhaps you could say that Dolly Tomkins called, and she asked to beg leave to have a word with him. I'll call tomorrow, after chapel, just in case he's free.'

–

Dolly was even more nervous the following day, as if the wait had played upon her nerves. Yet was it any wonder with Mr Barker's Rolls Royce parked out in the street? He never failed to drive to chapel of a Sunday, though there was little need for him to prove how important a figure he was, mill money largely being what kept the chapel going. They certainly couldn't depend on the annual sale of work. But should she tackle him here, in the porch after the service perhaps, or wait till he got home? Just trying to make this simple decision caused her to go all wobbly inside. So much so that Sam remarked upon it as she handed out hymn-books and kept dropping them, seeing as how she was all fingers and thumbs.

'What's up, Dolly?' he whispered. 'You look like you've lost a pound and found sixpence. Or have you been at your dad's whisky?'

She gave him a fierce glare, not in the mood for his silly jokes, but readily accepted his invitation to sit with him, thankful to escape being in the family pew with her mam and Willy. Dolly wondered why Aggie wasn't beside Sam as she so often was, but didn't like to ask. While the congregation sang 'All Hail the Power', Dolly took the opportunity to tell him, in low whispers, all about her intention to ask for her job back.

'I need to explain properly how it all came about. I'm sure that once he understands, it can all be put right. All, that is, apart from me dad – Calvin. We can't bring him back.' She really must learn not to call him 'Dad' any more.

Sam was staring at her, wide eyed. 'You're going to go to the gaffer's house? Walk up to his door, bold as brass, and ask for your job back?'

'I've already done it once, yesterday, but he wasn't in. I'm scared he might not agree to see me now he's been warned, so I thought I'd try and catch him after chapel. But if I don't manage to catch him, I'll have to.'

Sam was filled with admiration, yet he could see the fear in her eyes, the way her small mouth trembled. It had ever been so with little Dolly. She'd sound as fierce as a lion but inside she'd be quaking. He could always tell, had been obliged to step in and protect her from her own recklessness on a number of occasions in the past. He supposed she was the nearest he had to a sister, them being neighbours and growing up together, so he felt responsible for her.

Aggie was his girl, of course, or he used to think so. She'd been acting a bit cool lately, and he couldn't quite make out why. But then it wasn't difficult to offend Aggie. One day she'd cut him dead and the next be sweet as pie and all over him again. Today he'd intended to walk her home, the long way via the canal, but since she'd turned up her nose about sitting with him during the service, opting to stay with her family for once, he thought a bit of jealousy might do her good. 'I'll walk round there with you, if you like,' he said to Dolly.

'What? Oh no, Sam, there's no need for you to get involved. I don't want you in lumber too.'

'Don't worry, I won't interfere. I'm not taking any risks with me own job but I'll be on hand, should you need a shoulder to cry on, if it all goes wrong like.'

Dolly was filled with gratitude. 'Oh, thank you Sam. Thank you so much. What a friend you are.'

Sam looked into her shining blue eyes and felt himself swell with self-importance and an odd sort of protective warmth. It felt good to be of use. And Dolly looked different somehow, not half as small and funny-looking as she used to be. She turned away to speak to someone and he caught a sideways view of her profile. Flipping heck, he thought, she's even getting breasts, quite pert and firm they are. Dolly Tomkins was growing up, looking almost pretty. Happen he'd been messing about with the wrong sister.

As she turned back to him with a grateful smile, Sam cleared his throat, which seemed to have gone dry. 'Aye, well, it's no skin off my nose. Anyroad, yer not so bad.'

Chapter Nine

The service seemed to go on interminably with the minister prattling on about the grand total of the collections from last year's *Messiah* Sunday, in comparison with other chapels in the neighbourhood, and how he hoped for them to do even better this time around. And there was Cyril Duckett leading the choir as usual, looking remarkably pleased with himself. Dolly stared at him for a long time and felt nothing, except that he looked faintly ridiculous flinging his arms about as they sang 'Fling Wide the Gates'. Surely if he really was her father she'd feel some sort of kinship with him, some emotion?

When it was finally over, Mr Barker spent a long time talking to the chapel superintendent and she didn't dare to interrupt. And then without warning, he climbed into his Rolls Royce and drove away, every eye following him, caps being touched in deference.

'I'm going to his house now,' Dolly said, a grim note in her voice.

'And I'm coming with you.'

They walked together, not exactly hand in hand or arm in arm, but Dolly was acutely aware of Sam's presence by her side, the warmth from his body as he swung along beside her. Aggie's face had been a picture as they'd left the chapel, and was it any wonder? He looked so handsome, and so smart in his best Sunday suit that it filled Dolly with pride just to be seen out walking with him. She wished it was more than that, that they were actually 'walking-out' or 'doing a bit of courtin'' as her mam would say. Still, who knew what might happen later?

Mr Barker did agree to see her and she was led down a gloomy passage into the depths of the house by a sour-faced maid. The interview wasn't an easy one, taking place in his book-lined study with him seated behind a big mahogany desk and Dolly hovering on the rug in front of it, like a naughty schoolgirl. He wouldn't look at her properly, keeping his gaze fixed on his steepled hands, as if she were nought but an interruption.

She took a deep breath and told her tale, the whole sorry story of the thrown spindle and the accident from start to finish and he sat listening to her without interrupting, impassive throughout. Dolly interpreted this as genuine interest.

'So you see, it wasn't really my fault. I can understand how it must have looked that way, but it was all Betty Deurden's doing. I reckon that if she can be reinstated, even though she was the one what flung that spindle at me, then I could be an' all. We need the money, d'you see? Me mam does, anyroad. Our Willy isn't well, and with me dad gone and no compensation for the accident...'

He did glance at her then, surprise registering on his face. 'Compensation? You surely didn't expect any? Not after your father was the one who first took a pop at Harold. He brought about his own end, by his own foul temper.'

This momentarily silenced Dolly and she swallowed hard. 'I'm not defending him. I'd be the last to do that, I promise you. And I didn't mean to imply that you, or Harold, was to blame. Only, as he never actually touched Harold – it being just an unfortunate set of circumstances – I did hope that happen you'd see your way to letting me have my old job back, for Mam's sake if nothing else.' By the time she was finished, Dolly had quite run out of breath.

He was on his feet, moving away from the desk, away from her. 'And what sort of an example would that set to the rest of the workforce? Shall I tell you? They would imagine that they could do whatsoever they pleased to the overlooker as they'd be forgiven, with no punishment of any kind. I'm sorry Dolly, but I can't possibly reinstate you. I'm surprised you even ask. That decision has been made, so best let it lie. Find yourself a job elsewhere.'

'I've tried but no one will take me on, not after what happened, and without a reference.' She could hear the desperation in her own voice. 'Can you not give me one of those at least?'

He was holding open the door, his face rigid and Dolly experienced a pang of bitter disappointment. Despite him being so grand and proper, she'd thought that he quite liked her, following that meeting in the boiler room when he'd been so kind. Now she saw that he was as unfair and pig-headed as all the other mill owners. He was addressing the air somewhere above her head. 'Cotton operatives flit from mill to mill, as you well know, largely without troubling about such things as references. If your reputation has gone before you and no one will take you on, that has nothing to do with me.'

Disappointment turned to hot fury that surged through her veins. 'How can you stand there and tell me it's nothing to do with you? If you offered decent wages and proper facilities folk wouldn't be so desperate, then these things might not happen. And if by some misfortune they did, you could at least treat everyone the same instead of picking on me, particularly since *I* was the one attacked. Beside which, it was *your* daughter I saved that day during the strike. Have you thought about that?'

A flush of crimson crept up his throat but Barker stood his ground. '*I* am not responsible for Evie's foolishness, although I thank you for your actions on her behalf. However, that does not influence my decision in the slightest. She has been punished too. The decision has been made and must stand.'

'So you are not a man with a heart, after all.'

He looked wounded by this charge. 'However much I might sympathise with the fact it was your own father and you are suffering a double blow, if I went against Harold's judgement

I'd weaken my position. I'd be considered easy meat in future and who knows where that might lead? It could well result in further strike action. I'm sorry, I can't take the risk.'

'I'll never forgive you for this, never! Not as long as I live and breathe.'

The fierceness of her passion left him momentarily stunned. 'I'm sorry, Dolly, but there's nothing I can do. I must sacrifice you rather than lose the stability of the entire workforce.'

Hunching her shoulders and biting down tightly on her lower lip, chin tucked well in as she struggled not to shame herself by crying, Dolly strode from the room, mouth pressed into a grim line,. It had been a dreadful interview, a complete and utter failure. She'd got absolutely nowhere, gained nothing and even lost the last remnants of her pride. All she wanted now was to escape this dreadful house, go home and let out all this painful emotion in a good cry.

As if all of that wasn't bad enough, when she reached the hall and did finally look up, there, lounging in the doorway, chatting to Evie Barker with that unmistakeable predatory glint in his eye, was Sam. Dolly knew at once that he was pouring out all his charm, and Evie was lapping it up.

He leapt to attention the minute he saw her, but Dolly marched straight past him out into the street, head held high. Not for a minute would she let him see that she cared one jot. Men! You could keep 'em.

–

Dolly spent the following days and weeks going around the very same mills over and over again. Tight-lipped and filled with a choking fear, she barely spent a minute in the house, returning home only to eat and sleep, even then avoiding both Aggie and her mother. Maisie, because she couldn't bear the look of agony and fear in her eyes as she worried over what lay ahead with so little money coming in, and Aggie because she never seemed to be in the house much at all. More often than not she would be off to the pictures or strolling by the canal with Harold Entwistle, the overlooker, no less. Apparently he'd taken quite a shine to her and it was generally assumed that they were walking-out. Aggie was certainly behaving as if she hadn't a care in the world.

'Some good has come out of this mess,' she commented in silky, self-satisfied tones. 'He's very nicely placed is Harold. Most eligible husband material, I'd say.'

'But he's too old!'

Aggie tossed her head. 'Nonsense, he's thirty-one, only twelve years older than me.'

'Thirteen. And what about Sam? I thought you and he were walking out?'

'Whoever told you that?' Aggie picked up her brush and began to tease her chestnut curls.

'I rather assumed that you and he—'

'Don't you dare assume anything about me, madam. You can have him, if you want him,' she said, as if he were one of her leftover frocks that she was done with.

Dolly thought about the way Sam had looked when he was chatting up Evie Barker, all glittery eyed and alive. 'Why would *I* want him?' Oh, but she ached for him, with every fibre of her being.

Aggie was riffling through her wardrobe for something half decent to wear for her latest date with Harold that evening but glanced up in surprise at this comment. 'Ah, learning a bit of sense at last, are we? Sam's all right, in his way, but he's going nowhere. He might have good looks and reasonable intelligence, all of that and more, but he lacks ambition and thinks far too much of himself. Imagines he can have any girl he chooses, well he can't have me. I want much more in a man than anything he can offer.'

'You only say that because he's stopped making a fuss of you. No doubt he's getting to know your nasty, underhand little ways. He told me he was fed up with you blowing all hot and cold. He meant to dump you. Maybe he already has.'

'He has not! Sam Clayton is nothing to me and never was.' Aggie went quite pink cheeked, though whether that was because Dolly had hit on the truth, or she was simply having trouble getting into her dress, it was hard to say. 'I can twist Sam Clayton round my little finger any time I choose,' she said, coming up for air. 'I just don't want to, thanks all the same. He'll never make any brass, not enough for my needs; certainly not to get me out of this flaming hole. Whereas Harold has already made his mark in the world.'

She fluffed out her curls, smoothed down the short skirt and smiled at her reflection in the tiny mirror on the washstand, giving her hips a little shimmy.

'Harold is taking me out tonight for the third time this week, would you believe? I've said it before, our Dolly, and it bears repeating, the answer to this dire situation we find ourselves in, is to make a good marriage.'

–

Aggie was well pleased with herself. There were some who might not see Harold as quite such a great catch. He wasn't the most handsome man on God's earth, his face being round and his pale blue eyes often holding the expression of a startled rabbit behind the steel-rimmed spectacles that he wore, particularly when she let him kiss her, which was happening quite often these days. Although his lips, she was sorry to say, were rather thin. Some might claim that his recessive chin with its slight cleft indicated weakness, but Aggie thought it rather cute. Such hair as he did have, which admittedly wasn't as much as one would expect for a man of his age, was of an indeterminate brown. And his clothes, she thought now, as they settled themselves in the back row up in the 'gods' at the Salford Palace, had a tendency to always look slightly stained and creased. But then he was in need of a good woman to look after him. He'd said as much himself a dozen times, which was encouraging.

He was certainly free with his money. Admittedly the Palace was a bit of a fleapit and she preferred the Oxford Picture House or the Winter Gardens but this was only a Thursday, and Aggie didn't expect the best every night. At least he'd driven her there in his Ford motor, and there weren't many of those around, not even among overlookers. She was also aware that Harold Entwistle had a bit put by, left to him by his long dead parents. A most satisfactory state of affairs!

On a Saturday afternoon, after the mill closed for the week, he'd take her round the market and buy her little trinkets and ribbons. There'd be tea and cakes at Lyons Tea Shop which stood on the corner of Princess Street, next to Albert Square. Later, she'd put on her glad rags and set her hair into waves with sugar and water, and he'd take her dancing at Dyson's Dance hall on Devonshire Street. He wasn't much of a dancer himself, being a big man, but he did his best, for her sake. He even had a go at the Charleston and the Black Bottom, though he wasn't quite nimble enough to do them properly. Aggie was having a wonderful time, the best fun she'd ever had in her life. And it didn't cost her a penny.

Tonight, he'd treated her not only to a good dinner of steak, chips and peas, but this trip to the pictures as well. He had his arm about her shoulders already, and his heavy body felt a bit hot and sweaty next to hers, not that she minded. Sex, so far as Aggie was concerned, was a means to an end. If you were attractive, why not use it to your advantage? The fingers of his other hand were sliding beneath her stocking tops to caress her bare thighs under cover of darkness, before slipping up to more private parts. Aggie didn't object to his fumbling, not one little bit. In fact, it got her quite excited. She liked to hear his breath coming in little rapid gasps of pleasure. But she really did wish that she could have a pair of proper cami-knickers in crepe de Chine. These serviceable flannels bought at the Flat Iron Market, made her feel cheap and Aggie felt she deserved better.

After a while she pushed his hand away and feigned modesty, crossing her legs. 'Ooh Harold, what will you think of me. What sort of girl do you take me for?' Aggie was wishing she had a pair of silk stockings like the ones Vilma Banky was wearing on the screen in front of her, instead of these boring lysle full of darns.

'I thought you were my sort of girl, aren't you Aggie? Aren't you my sort of girl?' Harold was furtively doing up his flies which he'd optimistically unbuttoned.

'Well, I wouldn't want you getting the wrong idea. Anyway, someone might see us.'

He thought about this for a moment, then leaning closer, whispered against her ear. 'You could always come round to mine on Sunday, for your tea?'

Aggie looked at him askance, her heart beating with excitement. Did this mean what she thought it meant? A chap didn't ask you round for tea unless he was serious. And Harold had such a nice house on Quay Street. She wasn't against having a look inside. More importantly, nor would she be against the idea of taking up permanent residence there, but if she was to achieve that end, she had to play her cards right. 'And would there be anyone else present, Harold?' she coyly enquired. 'Because if not, I'm afraid I must decline. I'm a bit surprised you'd ask, if that should be the case.'

A woman from behind shushed her, and Aggie dropped her voice to a soft murmur while hammering home her point. 'Like I say, I'm a decent, respectable girl and I'm shocked if you should think otherwise. Perhaps we'd best stop seeing each for a while. Till you've calmed down a bit.'

Harold suddenly saw his heart's desire begin to slip away from him. He didn't wish to calm down. Not at all! He wanted Aggie Tomkins stripped off and in his bed. And he'd do whatever was necessary to get her there. 'Nay Aggie,' he murmured, stroking her knee consolingly before giving her ear a little nibble, thrilled when it made her giggle. 'I'd never suggest any such thing. You know how I feel about you.'

'Do I, Harold?' Aggie uncrossed her legs. Harold did not miss the implication and his heart leapt.

'Aye, course you do, Aggie.' His hand slid a little further under her skirt and her elbow didn't come jabbing down. He was making progress.

'Perhaps you should tell me just how you do feel. Happen we should talk about it, you and me. Then I'd properly understand, and be more – shall we say – obliging.'

Harold felt his heart start to pound. What was she suggesting? What was she promising? Perhaps he wasn't behaving quite as a gentleman should but he couldn't seem to help himself. Perhaps they ought to put things on a more formal footing. Once this notion had occurred to him, he began to warm to the idea. 'Aye, you come round to mine and we'll talk about things, eh? There might well be something I want to ask you.'

He could sense the moist heat of her as he neared the top of her leg and he went all hot under the collar, knew his armpits were sweating unpleasantly. He'd offer her anything, anything at all.

She glanced sideways at him, saw the excited glitter in his eyes. 'And what might that be, Harold? What might you want to ask me?' She moved slightly against his hand and heard him groan with pleasure. She was winning. A little more daring and he'd be putty in her hands. She egged him on a little further, let his fingers slide beneath the elastic once more, and then with a little gasp, she pushed the hand away.

'Ooh, you naughty boy.' He always loved it when she called him a boy, or young man.

He sank back in his seat like a pricked balloon, took off his spectacles and began to polish them furiously on his handkerchief. Aggie smiled to herself, well pleased, but when he made no further move towards her, she began to worry that she might have put him off. She hugged his arm and gave it a little squeeze. 'It's all very confusing for a girl. Hard to know how to respond, and I worry what you might think of me, if I let you go too far.' She managed a little sob of anguish.

'Eeh Aggie, I'd never think anything bad about you.' He could barely restrain himself from grabbing her delicate white hand and shoving it down his trousers, his agony was so intense.

'And you're making me curious. I don't think I can wait till Sunday. Why don't you ask me now, whatever it is?' She giggled entrancingly, and Harold was lost.

Drawing in a deep breath and puffing out his chest he said, 'Aggie, I'm that taken with you...' but he could go no further. The words wouldn't come. He was too aware of the woman behind listening to every word. 'This isn't the place. Come on Sunday. Say you will. I want to do right by you, Aggie.'

She turned her head to meet his wide, yearning gaze. 'In that case, Harold, shall we say four o'clock?'

–

Dolly wished she could view life with her sister's assured complaisance. But then, she didn't have the overlooker panting after her, did she? In any case, she had no wish to talk to anyone about her problems, certainly not her mam. Dolly's feelings towards Maisie were strangely ambiguous. She was still concerned for her mother, still wanted to put things right, to wave a magic wand and pay off all those burdensome debts but at the same time she couldn't quite forgive Maisie for lying to her all these years. Dolly had always believed that she and her mother were close, so why had she never told her about this great love of her life, and the identity of her true father?

It made her feel as if there was no one left whom she could trust. Not her mother, certainly not her jealous sister, nor even Sam, her best friend. It hurt her still to think of him. He'd offered to come along with her to the Barker's house and give his support, and the minute her back was turned there he was chatting up another girl. Perhaps Aggie had a point. He was a bit too full of himself. But then weren't all men? Wasn't that part of their charm?

Of course, as Sam had frequently reminded her, there was none of that love-stuff between the two of them. They'd never been anything other than friends. Nevertheless, it still hurt. Aggie had rejected him and still he didn't look her way. What was so wrong with her, that he never could see her as someone he might fancy? And the fact that it was Evie he was fawning over, the very girl he and his daft mates had threatened when they'd first come across her in that fancy jalopy, made it ten times worse. Now she too, the girl whom Dolly had saved and was the cause of all this mess, was also against her. Oh, it was too much.

Dolly's one desire was to prove to everyone that she could manage on her own. She would trust no one, never again, and make her own way in the world. All she had to do was to find herself a job, then a place of her own to live and she'd be nice as ninepence. She wouldn't need anyone. Oh, but she'd still see that her mam was all right. Once she'd got on her feet, she'd settle that flipping debt, then Maisie could be free of Nifty Jack too.

But how? She'd been all round the problem and was right back where she'd started. There was no denying the facts. They couldn't all live on Willy and Aggie's pay. Once they'd paid the rent; the Prudential burial fund; saved a few pennies for the gas and paid a sizeable portion to Edna Crawshaw at the corner shop off the growing list of items on tick, whatever was left went straight into the talleyman's pocket, and the next week, with interest added, the debt would be as big as ever.

'Watch for the talleyman,' her mam would endlessly cry.

They would watch for him every Friday night, but no matter if they locked the door, drew the curtains and hid, he would come again on Monday, on Tuesday, every day of the week until he caught them in. The three women spent hours hiding from him, fearing being caught for they knew that they had no money to pay him. But surely Mam was wrong. He might be a nasty piece of work, but he'd never do anything to really hurt them, would he? He just wanted the money owed to him, which was surely fair enough.

–

Nifty Jack was making money hand over fist, puffed up by his own arrogance as a result. He didn't like to think anyone could get the better of him, whether it was a debt or a slight of some kind. Today he was calling on Betty Deurden's ma, a sad old lady who, like her daughter, what she lacked in common sense she made up for by complaining. He could see her now peeping from behind her filthy net curtains. 'I know you're in there, Mrs Deurden, are you going to open this door,' he bawled, 'Or do I have to break it down?'

The bolt slid back and Nifty swaggered inside. 'According to my reckoning, you still owe me two pounds, fifteen shillings and threepence, plus this week's rent of seven and sixpence.'

Predictably, Mrs Deurden protested that she had no money, none at all. 'I'm not so good on me pins, as you know. And our Betty hasn't been so well lately and has had to take a lot of time off work. She's not herself at all. Something happened to her one night and it right upset her. She came home covered in bruises but she won't say who gave them to her.'

Nifty Jack tut-tutted in sympathy. 'Dear me, I'm sorry to hear it. However, that's none of my concern. You must have some money somewhere. A bit put by like, for a rainy day?'

Mrs Deurden was a widow who had seen better times but was fading fast. Being too rheumatic to work herself, she depended entirely upon her only daughter, who was a bit of a disappointment to her in many ways. 'Only what my Joe left me, enough to keep the wolf from the door in lean times, like now, and what I shall need to pay the undertaker when I'm gone. I've got it in the Post Office Savings Bank.'

'Ah, the very thing! How much?'

'Only a few quid, nine or ten pounds, not much more.'

'It's enough. Get your coat on.'

'What?'

'Don't stand about wasting my time. You wouldn't want anything more to happen to your Betty, now would you?'

Mrs Deurden looked confused for a moment then dumbly shook her head.

'Course you wouldn't. It'd be a crying shame. Right then, let's be having you. Grab your shawl, woman, and we'll take a nice little stroll down to the Post Office and settle your account. You can manage to walk that far, I trust, with a bit of help. And think what a relief it'll be to have matters all settled between us.' He smiled grimly at her, showing all the gums above his false teeth.

Later that day, when Betty forced herself to stagger downstairs, knowing she should be at work but too afraid to even step outside her own front door since the attack, she asked her mother if she'd been out and managed to get them something to eat.

Mrs Deurden shook her head, her eyes glazed as if she weren't quite seeing clearly. 'No love, I've never moved from this chair all morning. What we'll have for us tea, I can't think. That cupboard was bare last time I looked.'

'We're going to have to draw a bit more money out of the Post Office then,' Betty said. 'Till I'm on me feet again.'

Her mother said nothing. Betty would find out soon enough that the talleyman had not only taken the money they owed him, but the rest of their savings as well.

Chapter Ten

It came to Evie one day, quite out of the blue, or rather out of a rain-filled Manchester sky, that apart from the loss of the bridal gown and the fancy reception, she'd really lost nothing by calling off the wedding. On the contrary, she had gained a great deal. She found to her surprise, that she didn't mind in the least being free of Freddie. He was really becoming something of a bore, and it was a positive relief to be rid of his dreadful mother.

She'd been quite taken by that very nice young man who'd come to the house with that pushy girl, Dolly or Polly or some such dreadful name. He was quite a dish, and wouldn't it serve Pops right if she opted for him instead of dear, safe Freddie. She'd slipped a piece of paper with her telephone number into his jacket pocket before he left, hoping he'd ring. Sadly, he never had. Probably had never used a telephone in his life, poor soul. The next day, feeling at a loose end, Evie brazenly waited for him outside her father's mill. She was wearing a new little number in jade green, and there he was looking all grubby and careworn, twice as handsome and deliciously scrummy.

He was more startled than pleased to see her, his first reaction being to ask what she was doing there.

Evie offered her most entrancing smile, eyes glimmering. 'Why else but to see you, sweetie? Couldn't resist.' Pops would hate it if he knew she was 'making herself cheap' by meeting one of his workers. It almost made her laugh out loud to imagine his shocked expression. Evie half hoped he might walk through the mill gates any minute and catch her. Oh, sweet revenge. But then he should have given her the lovely wedding she deserved. 'Thought you could buy me a drink, a coffee, or a cup of tea. Whatever it is you working men have at this time of day.' And she gave a little shrug, as if it were all some jolly jape.

Sam stared at her, perplexed, then grabbing her arm dragged her down an alleyway, out of sight of his mates. He'd never hear the last of it, if they spotted him with this girl, the gaffer's daughter. 'Have you lost your marbles? Haven't you caused enough bother by driving round our streets? What is it you're after this time?'

Evie leaned against him, smelling the oil on his clothes, rubbing the prickles on his unshaven chin with the back of her hand, loving the rough maleness of him. 'Nothing, I've come to see you, darling. Aren't you pleased?'

Her mouth was a glistening scarlet, held temptingly close to his own, the smell of her perfume, something flowery and fresh, made his head spin. She looked marvellous, so clean, so feminine and fashionable, soft and desirable that Sam could have taken her there and then up against the dirty wall. 'This isn't the moment. I have a job to do.' She was twining her fingers in his hair, pressing her ripe breasts hard against his chest, which was doing terrible things to his self-control.

He'd almost made up his mind to kiss her when she tilted her head away from him, smiling coquettishly from under her lashes. 'What sort of job? I thought you'd finished work for the day.' She pretended to sulk, certain of her charms, that it was only a matter of time before he succumbed. Where was Pops? Why didn't he come?

'I've finished at the mill, only I'm going round to help a mate. He's building a hen cote and I said I'd give him a hand.' He felt breathless with need, knew he was babbling, but couldn't seem to catch his breath.

She lifted rosy red lips to his. 'Can't it wait? My car is parked just a discreet distance away. We could drive somewhere quiet, and have a little chat. What do you say?' If her father wasn't going to show up, she could have some fun at least.

'I'd say, I'll see you safely back home.' Sam told himself to breathe slowly, breathe in and breathe out. That's it. He was feeling better already. He escorted her safely back to her Morris motor, parked beneath a railway arch. She still had hold of his hand, and before he'd given the matter any sensible thought, she was pulling him into the back of it with her. She offered him a strange smelling cigarette, which she called a Turkish. It tasted odd, not like his usual brand.

When he began to cough, she put back her head and screeched with laughter. Sam noticed how the line of her white throat arched deliciously, like an elegant swan.

'I think you're in need of a little education, my boy.'

'Don't call me that. I'm a man.'

'Are you? Prove it.' She lifted his hand and began to nibble each fingertip. 'Ooh, what a funny taste. What is it?'

He pulled his hand away, embarrassed. 'Muck from t'mill.' And she trilled with laughter.

'*Muck?* What a lovely word.'

She was slipping out of the beautiful silk frock she was wearing under the fur coat, revealing something lacy over her breasts, a pair of cami-knickers, and not much else. Sam was stunned, could feel himself hardening. He could imagine those long legs wrapped about his waist, those luscious, slender curves all his for the taking. The blood was pounding in his head, in his loins. Dear God, she made it difficult for a man to remember his manners. He pulled her to him, made a clumsy attempt at a kiss but she pushed him brusquely away, still chuckling.

'What's the hurry, sweetie? Why don't you just watch first? She look off the lacy top, and then the stockings, peeling them down over those endless legs one by one. Sam was beside himself with need, groaning in his agony, which made her chirrup with glee. The light from the street lamp illuminated the velvet globes of her breasts. Sam thought he had never seen anything more beautiful in all his life.

'Let me touch you Evie, please.'

'Oh very well,' she said, pale blue eyes glistening provocatively, scarlet lips pouting. 'You can touch me here, and here.' She pointed to parts of her anatomy that had him salivating with anticipation. 'Now you can kiss me... hard... harder... no, not on my lips, you'll spoil my lipstick. Here and here.' She was panting now, tugging at his shirt and dragging her long fingernails over his back, seeking the buttons on his trousers. 'Pull me under you. That's it, and if you're suitably *impatient*, who knows what might happen next? You and I could be such *good* friends and have *delicious* fun.'

For no reason he could fathom, an unwelcome image of Dolly popped into his head, quite without warning. Perhaps because of this girl, she was out of work. Sam pushed the thought aside. This wasn't the moment to think of Dolly and her problems. She was nothing to him, not his responsibility. He was a normal, red-blooded male, free to do as he pleased, with any woman he chose. And Evie Barker wasn't the sort of woman a man would easily say no to.

But Evie hadn't missed his momentary lack of attention. She was slapping his hands away, pulling the fur coat back around her half naked body. If a man wasn't begging for her, where was the fun in getting herself messed up for nothing? She visibly cooled and turned away to find her stockings. 'That's enough for today. Perhaps I'll be more generous next time. We'll see. But you'll certainly have to pay better attention.'

Sam was mortified. He'd ruined everything. Or rather Dolly had, damn her. 'I am paying attention. I haven't been able to get you out of my head, Evie. I want you. God, how much I want you.' But his words rang hollow, even to his own ears. Somehow the urge had left him.

She was pulling on the lacy top, scrabbling about the back seat in search of the silk dress. Heartsore, Sam helped her.

'Who were you thinking of, if not me?'

'I was thinking of Dolly.' Lord, why had he said that?

'What, that girl, Dolly Tomkins? I don't believe it. You really don't deserve me to be so generous to you.'

'I do, I do, it's just that she's in a right pickle is poor Dolly. Lost her job because of that accident, which would never have happened if...' He stopped, appalled by what he'd been about to say.

'I hardly think *I* had anything to do with it. Not my responsibility. Get out of my car. Get out now, if you please.'

'No, no, I didn't mean that.'

'*Get out!*'

She drove away, leaving him standing on the pavement, not even daring to call after her to say he'd left his cap on the back seat, because he felt such a complete fool.

–

It was one evening when Dolly was alone, that there came the familiar hammering on the door. Maisie was round at Edna's, Willy was asleep upstairs and Aggie was out with Harold, goodness knows where, up to goodness knows what.

'I know you're in, so open this door. It's you I want to talk to, lass. I've a proposition to put to you that'll happen get your mam off the hook.'

Dolly dithered. 'What could he mean? What sort of proposition? Well, she'd never know if she didn't open the door, would she?' She glanced up the stairs, taking some comfort from the sound of her brother's peaceful snores. She could always give their Willy a shout, if Nifty Jack got difficult. Dolly slid back the bolt and let him in.

Nifty set his bowler hat on a corner of the table and demanded a mug of tea, since robbing people blind was apparently thirsty work. Dolly made him one, albeit grudgingly, setting it before him with the comment that they'd no milk and no money to buy any.

'Aye, I know things are tight, that's why I'm here.' He let his gaze travel over the starkness of the back kitchen, not even a comfy chair or the usual horse-hair sofa to rest in after a long day's work, nothing save the table and hard kitchen chairs so no wonder Calvin had spent all his time in the pub. The only sign of cheer in the gloomy kitchen, since Dolly still hadn't lit the gas lamp, was a picture on the wall entitled: *Moses in the Bullrushes*. It seemed to be a pair to the one of Daniel in Cyril Duckett's front parlour.

Watching this careful assessment, Dolly clasped her hands tightly together to stop them from punching him. 'We've nothing left to sell.'

'I can see that. There'd be some insurance though, no doubt? Enough perhaps, to pay off a tidy bit from what's owing?'

'Not enough to even cover the cost of his funeral,' Dolly drily commented. 'So don't stand there slavering with greed, you'll get nothing off us, because we've nothing left.'

'I'm sorry to see you brought so low,' he smoothly remarked.

Dolly gritted her teeth. 'So, what's this proposition then?'

Nifty hid a half smile in the mug as he noisily slurped up the tea. Then he set it down with care, smoothed a hand over his baldpate and turned to Dolly, still with that chill smile in place. 'I've heard you're having problems finding work, that no one will take a chance on you. Word will have gone around about that bit of bother at Barkers and that you were responsible. No, don't deny it, because it doesn't really matter whether you were or not. They think you were. So I'm here to offer you an alternative.'

'I'm waiting.' Dolly sat very still, feeling confused, nervous. But what he had to say was the last thing she expected.

'I'm in need of a housekeeper. I've no wife or family, so I could do with someone to mind me house and look after me. I'd like to come home to a hot meal on the table, to find the place clean and tidy, beds made, washing and ironing done. How does that appeal?'

'Is this some sort of joke?'

'No joke, and I don't reckon you're in a position to refuse.' His hard little eyes were fixed on her face, bringing a shiver to her spine.

'Do you not indeed?'

'There'd be no wages, of course, not till all debts were settled, but you'd have a room of your own, and I keep a good table.'

Dolly felt sick at the thought of living in the same house as Nifty Jack. The very idea turned her stomach. 'I'd rather go on the streets than pander to you, you're no better than pig-muck.'

Nifty sucked in his breath and attempted to look shocked. 'Dear me, I don't like to hear such foul language from the mouth of such a pretty young lass. I think you should at least consider the idea.'

'I wouldn't work for you if I were at death's door.'

'Happen you're nearer to that sad state of affairs than you might imagine. Remember your mam could end up in prison, if she doesn't pay something soon. Besides which, she might also be interested to learn that I've bought this place from the landlord. He was one of my clients too, and had got quite a bit behind with his payments, so we came to a deal.'

Dolly listened open-mouthed to this latest piece of disastrous news. They already owed Nifty Jack a small fortune trying to keep their heads above water, not to mention paying off Calvin's gambling debts, now they'd owe him rent as well. It felt as if he owned them, lock, stock and barrel.

'Think on that,' he said, tapping one nicotine-stained finger on the table top, his nasty little eyes flicking over her. 'If you worked the debt off, it would at least be one less mouth for your mam to feed. And once it's settled, I'd pay the going rate for the job. I can't say fairer than that, now can I?'

Dolly's mind was whirling as she thought through the implications. Had she been a touch hasty? Might there be advantages in the proposition after all? It was certainly true that having one less mouth to feed would be an enormous help, and then there was the enticing prospect of helping to pay off the debt. How else could they achieve that? And once it was done, Mam truly would be free, and so would she. Even so, could she bear to work for this man? Dolly felt she could hardly bear to have him in the same room.

'I'll think about it.'

He stood up, replaced the bowler hat square on his head. 'Don't take too long. My patience is short and this offer won't last for ever. Don't bother getting up. I'll see myself out.' And he did so, just as if he owned the place.

—

Dolly went straight round to each of her brothers in turn, told them about the offer and asked for their help to avoid taking it up. But when she added how much money they needed to pay off the loan, nearly fifty pounds, they laughed. Not at *her* exactly, more at the idea that she'd ever imagined they might have a fraction of such a sum. Eli gave her what he could, Josh offered his sympathy but said he was stony broke and his missus was pregnant again. Abel told her she wasn't in a position to refuse. It was a job, after all, and that was the end of it. They had their own families to feed. Money was tight.

But Dolly dreaded the thought of accepting Nifty Jack's offer. 'Don't worry, I'll think of something,' she brightly informed them. Two weeks later she still didn't have a job. Despite her best efforts and a fierce determination to succeed, no matter how many doors she knocked on, she always got the same response. 'Tomkins? Aren't you the troublemaker from Barkers? We've nothing for your sort here.'

In desperation, she started trying for other kinds of jobs but Dolly had no experience for anything except spinning and whenever anyone asked why she'd left the mill, she never seemed to have a satisfactory answer. People would eye her suspiciously, say they'd no vacancies and shut the door in her face. She'd need to go much further afield where she wasn't known, but she'd no wish to do that, not only because it would mean leaving her lovely mam but also she wouldn't ever be able to see Sam, which didn't bear thinking of.

For a while she got a job sorting rags, the lowest of the low so far as Dolly was concerned, but at least she drew some money at the end of the week. And then her mam found out and that was the end of that.

'I'll not have a daughter of mine working in a midden,' Maisie declared. 'I'd throw myself in the canal sooner. Have you no pride? That's the one thing we do still have, our pride, since it costs nothing. Don't you dare lose that, madam, or we're done for, finished.'

'You think I'm not already? You think I didn't lose my pride knowing I'm not who I thought I was?'

'Oh lass, don't say such things. It's cruel hard. I've done me best to be a good mother to you. Don't I love the bones of you but we all make mistakes. I'm human. I'm a woman with a heart that beats fast when a man touches me. You'll learn that yourself one day.'

For supper that night, Maisie produced one piece of cod between the four of them, a small dish of peas and not even a bag of chips to share. Willy, who rarely said boo to a goose, remarked, 'Nay, Mam, it's our stomach what holds our back up. How can we work on this?'

Maisie ran from the room in tears.

The next night they had some sort of stew made from rancid bacon and what looked like potato peelings. Maisie didn't eat a scrap. Aggie screwed up her nose but was too hungry to refuse it, and Willy said not a word.

When the usual knock came to the door at the end of the week, this time Dolly let him in, ready to give her answer. She gazed at Nifty Jack, sitting ramrod straight in the upright chair, his bowler hat placed carefully beside him on the table and his bald head glistening with sweat. He was just a sad old man with surely nothing to fear about him at all. As he'd carefully explained, she'd have her own room and even the run of the house for much of the time while he was out and about on his calls. It surely couldn't be any worse than enduring Aggie's spiteful jealousy, or watching her mother's daily decline into depression and starvation.

'All right,' she bluntly informed him, having come to a decision. 'I'll do it.'

–

Aggie couldn't make up her mind what to wear. Not because she was spoiled for choice. Rather the reverse. She really didn't think she possessed anything quite suitable for a Sunday tea that could well lead to a proposal. In the end, there was no alternative but the dress she always wore on a Sunday for chapel. It was a dull navy blue serge with a crochet collar and unfashionably long, being a full inch past the knee. She decided at least to shorten it, trimmed the hemline with a little rick-rack braid, pinned a bunch of violets on to the dropped waistband and wished she had a full length mirror to admire herself in it. She also made sure that she had on clean underwear, even if it was her tried and tested flannel drawers. Just in case. She didn't even possess one of the new brassieres although fortunately her breasts were small enough to be entirely in fashion, with no need for flattening.

Harold had laid tea on a little folding table before a bright coal fire in the front parlour. The teapot, milk jug and sugar bowl, Aggie noticed, were best silver plate; the cups and saucers prettily painted with maroon flowers. All of which seemed to indicate affluence. The room, however, was disappointingly gloomy and old fashioned, painted in a dull brown and still with Victorian gas brackets no different from their own and not the modern electric light she had hoped for. The furniture too was of that era: too big and heavy for the small parlour, every surface covered in crocheted mats and antimacassars, with even the table legs draped in swathes of velveteen, in case their provocative shape might bring the subject of sex to mind. Sex was certainly on Aggie's mind. She had no objection to a man older than herself, so long as he was experienced and exciting.

Harold was bringing food from the back kitchen including soft white buttered slices of bread and strawberry jam. He'd bought cream cakes from Bradburn's and there was a fruit loaf to cut. Aggie's mouth started to water the moment she set eyes on the feast, reminding her just how hungry she was. No rancid bacon and leftovers here.

'Sit yourself down, Aggie. I want you to feel at home.'

Harold poured the tea, handed her the bread, and strawberry jam, pressed her to take a second cake, waiting on her every whim. Aggie forgot all about proposals and dreams of silk cami-knickers, and stuffed her face with food. Only when she was quite replete and satisfied, did she sit back with a contented sigh and turn her attention to the matter in hand. She asked if she might powder her nose and was directed, not to a shared privy, as it was in Tully Court, but upstairs to a small, private closet in which was a flush lavatory and a wash basin with running water. Aggie had never seen such luxury. There was even a mirror on the wall, which enabled her to tidy her hair and put on some of the lipstick she'd brought with her.

Back downstairs, Harold leapt to his feet as she entered and she could tell that he was nervous as tiny rivers of sweat were running down his round cheeks into his collar. Aggie cast him what she hoped was a shy smile of encouragement and settled herself daintily on the sofa, as directed.

He'd removed the table and cleared away the cups and saucers while she was absent, which seemed to prove that he was handy about the house, and now they sat side by side, stiffly to attention like soldiers waiting to be court marshalled. Aggie experienced an almost uncontrollable desire to giggle but then Harold cleared his throat and slipped an arm about her waist, giving it a little squeeze. That's better. He was starting to relax.

'I'm that glad you came, Aggie. I can't tell you how pleased I am. I wanted everything to be perfect for you. I hope you enjoyed your tea.'

'I certainly did. It was a proper treat, Harold. Lovely.'

Again an awkward silence fell between them: Aggie hoping the hand resting heavily upon her waist would do something more exciting soon and Harold allowing himself a small sigh of relief that she was pleased, privately hoping that the large sum the shop delicacies had cost him would prove to be a worthwhile investment. Harold enjoyed his food but, if all went well, he'd have home baked cakes in future, which would be even better and far cheaper.

He couldn't quite make up his mind whether to try and kiss her or go down on one knee and get the proposal out of the way first. He'd never got this far with a woman before, always feeling rather shy and awkward with them. But Aggie was different. And if he didn't get her up them wooden stairs and into his bed pretty damn quick, he'd die of apoplexy. He could barely sleep at night for thinking about her and when he finally did, from sheer exhaustion, his dreams were lurid to the point of erotic. He'd wake up drenched in sweat and other unmentionable fluids, and he'd have to change the sheets. It was all most embarrassing.

Aggie decided that she'd waited long enough through this long, agonisingly thoughtful silence and gave him a gentle prompt. 'Was there something you wanted to say to me, Harold? The reason you asked me here.'

'Oh, yes, Aggie, you know there was.'

She blinked at him and waited hopefully. 'Well?'

Harold drew in a sharp breath. It was almost as if, in his nervousness, he'd quite forgotten what it was. But he knew that he must get it right. If he said the wrong thing, which he was quite capable of doing, he might never get another chance. Aggie Tomkins had any number of admirers and he could hardly believe she was sitting here, in his front room, on his sofa, letting him hold her hand and put his arm about her. But how to get started, that was the puzzle!

Aggie cast him a sideways glance and pressed her lips into a mischievous smile. 'I'm beginning to think you just want your wicked way with me, Harold.'

'Oh, I do want that an' all. I do, Aggie.' Realising what he'd said, he flushed scarlet and looked at her, appalled. Now he really had blown it. Trust him. Now she'd be off out of here faster than a bullet shot from a rifle. But then he saw to his great amazement that she was laughing. She had her hand in front of mouth and was chortling with glee.

'Harold Entwistle, what a thing to say! What would the mill operatives think if they could see you here with me, like this, and hear you saying such things?'

Her giggles were infectious and he found himself chuckling too. 'Ooh, Aggie, you're a good sort, you are really.'

'You haven't gone off me then? You still fancy me?'

'Like crazy!'

'Well, why don't you put that spare hand of yours wherever it fancies, give us a kiss and see where that takes us. Then you might remember what it was you wanted to ask me.' Whereupon, she removed his spectacles and planted a warm, moist kiss full on his eager mouth.

After that it was what Harold would describe as plain sailing. Not only did she let him kiss her, but made no objection when he began to fondle her breasts, albeit on the outside of the navy serge dress. He did consider asking her to remove it but decided that prudence was the better part of valour. The last thing he wanted was to risk losing her. But yet again she startled him out of his indecision.

'Since we're now betokened, as it were, soon to be engaged, Harold Entwistle, we could go a bit further. So long as we stayed above the waist, that is.'

The prospect of seeing those pert breasts, of rubbing his hands over the rosy nipples, brought him out in such a sweat that although he had no recollection of actually popping the question and asking her to be his wife, or fiancée, he was more than delighted to go along with the plan. He had that dreadful frock pulled down to her waist in no time, even found no difficulty with the mysteries of her camisole top and when she was finally in his arms, semi-naked, she was everything he'd ever dreamed of. For a long moment he gazed at her in reverent awe, and it was Aggie again who urged him to 'Get on with it and do something for God's sake, before I die of pneumonia.'

Oh, and he did get on with it. He did indeed. He kissed and fondled her till his head was spinning with desire, and most delicious it was too. Aggie Tomkins was proving to be quite a revelation, spicing up his life and enlivening his education no end. But then he made the mistake of touching her knee and she very swiftly called a halt. Harold thought he might go crazy he was that worked up, though perhaps it was just as well. A proper spectacle he was making of himself.

'Aggie love, the sooner we call the banns the better,' he gasped, his body giving a telling little shudder.

'Ooh, Harold, what can I say but yes!'

Chapter Eleven

Wasting no time, as she didn't want to take the risk that he might go off her, Aggie introduced her 'intended' to her surprised family the very next week.

'While I've no wish to cause offence by robbing you of your usual rights,' Harold told her astonished mother, 'I shall be more than happy to pay for this wedding.'

'And I'll be more than willing to let you, lad' said Maisie, wondering if she should feel insulted that the man involved in her husband's final moments, was about to become her son-in-law. Or was she relieved that she'd soon have Aggie off her hands?

Within days he'd bought a ring, small admittedly, but with a dear little sapphire heart set in a cluster of tiny diamonds. Riches indeed. Before the week was out, he'd posted the banns at the chapel and Aggie was planning her wedding frock. It would be cream crepe de Chine, with pink rosebuds all around on the hem, cut to precisely on the knee. She'd seen a picture of such a gown in a magazine. All she had to do was persuade her mother to make it for her. She meant to fashion the satin headdress herself, and purchase cream satin shoes to match. The reception was to be held at the Co-operative rooms and afterwards Harold had promised to take her to Lytham St Annes for their honeymoon. Aggie felt quite sick with excitement.

'Now if there's anything you don't like about my little house, you only have to say the word, Aggie love, and it can be changed.'

'I will admit, Harold, that it does look a bit old fashioned.'

Harold glanced about his family home, the house where he was born and had lived all his life, in some surprise. Blinking behind his spectacles, he saw it with new eyes. My word, of course it was old fashioned. Nothing had been changed since his parents had died years ago, and probably since his grandparent's day. 'Then we must have new,' he decided. 'We can start afresh. I'll get rid of all this lot and you can go round to the Co-op on Saturday, Aggie, and choose whatever you fancy, the very latest in house furnishings.'

'Ooh, Harold, can I really?' She fell into his arms and began to kiss him wildly, so that Harold's head started to spin and he felt that familiar, pleasantly painful movement in his trousers. 'Aye, why not? They'll fetch it round in the van next week and we can start our married life with new stuff, with whatever your heart desires, my little love.' And as Harold gave himself up to Aggie's frantic kisses, he was mentally struggling to recall the exact sum in his savings account.

But Aggie was deeply content. Everything was progressing exactly as planned. She had big plans to put new life into that old fashioned house, and her own future. It was all most satisfying. Her only moment of doubt came when she was on her way home from work one day and chanced upon Sam and Matt leaning on the wall by the wharf.

The moment he spotted her, Sam broke away from Matt and came over. 'Hey, it's our blushing bride. Is it true that you're to wed Harold Entwistle?'

'What if it is?'

'By heck, Aggie Tomkins, you give a chap a hard time. Is this some ploy to make *me* pop the question, because if it is...'

She didn't even let him finish but tossed her curls and stuck her nose in the air. 'You can be absolutely certain that marriage to you is the last thing on my mind, Sam Clayton. Why would I live in a shabby old court with you, when I can have a fine house on Quay Street, with all new furniture?'

Sam raised his eyebrows in mock surprise and considered her for a moment before smiling his wide, crooked smile. 'I can see that a fancy house and such fol-de-rols will make you very happy, Aggie, but does *he* make you happy?'

'Course he does.'

'So you no longer fancy me then?'

'I certainly don't.'

'Are you sure? Can you be absolutely certain?' Taking hold of her, he drew her into his arms and kissed her, pushing open her eager mouth with his tongue.

Aggie couldn't help herself as she melted against him. Everything she'd ever learned about sex, she'd learned here, in Sam's arms. Oh, and with those lips, and those strong muscles holding her tight, what a fine teacher he was. She felt quite unable to control the surge of excitement that jolted through her as his tongue caressed and circled her own. She was whimpering with need when he released her, quite abruptly. Aggie staggered a little, so dazed with longing she almost lost her balance.

Laughing softly, he turned his back on her and began to stroll away. 'Just as well I no longer fancy you then, isn't it? Happen I should give your Dolly a chance, instead.'

Aggie flounced off in high dudgeon, swinging her hips provocatively, as if hoping to remind Sam that he would miss her. Frowning, he watched her go, wondering if he would.

'You must be disappointed,' Matt said, coming to join him. 'You and Aggie have been together for years.'

'There are other fish in the sea.'

A small silence, and then, 'You didn't mean it about her sister, did you? Dolly isn't your sort at all.'

'Whose sort is she then? Yours? Don't make me laugh. You couldn't catch a woman in a million years, not even Dolly.'

'You're probably right,' Matt conceded. 'But I think Dolly is cute.'

'You always were smitten, but she'll never look your way.'

Matt was frowning, not liking where this conversation was leading. 'That doesn't mean she'd look at you any more favourably.'

'Oh, aye, she would. She's been hankering after me for years. If I put my mind to it, I could have her easy-peasy. But you're probably right. I don't reckon she'd be worth the candle. Bit too complicated, our Dolly, and there are better prospects on the horizon.'

'What sort of prospects?'

'Never you mind. Meanwhile, let's see what talent there is in the crown.'

Matt fell into step beside his best mate, and breathed a quiet sigh of relief.

–

Dolly was determined to make the best of things. It would all be worth it in the end when the debt was settled. The good thing about her new role as housekeeper was that Nifty had kept his word, she was well fed and did indeed have a lovely room for herself. It worried her slightly that there was no lock on the door and each night she would jam a chair under the handle. So far he'd given her no reason to be alarmed and she was growing used to the routine and her new life.

Most of the day and often well into the evening, Nifty would be out collecting, or off down the pub and so, in a way, the worst aspect of this job was the loneliness. Dolly missed her mates at the mill, the routine and feel of the cotton in her hands. Whenever she called at Tully Court, as she often did to see her mam, she felt quite jealous of Aggie's ability to carry on working at Barkers, found herself desperate for any bit of mill gossip, even about the hated Betty Deurden, who had apparently been attacked while walking home one night. No one knew who did it, though gossip pointed the finger at one of her no-good boyfriends. Betty wasn't saying. She hadn't been to work since and rumour had it that she was pregnant.

The good news was that the Tomkins family was speaking to each other again and Dolly's relations with her mother were almost back to normal, so long as she restrained from asking any questions about her father.

Whenever Dolly popped in, Maisie would brew a pot of tea and they'd sit and drink it together, mother and daughter, quite like old times.

Maisie was surprisingly perky these days, partly due to the fact that she didn't have to worry about the talleyman any more, and she'd taken to going out, something she hadn't been able to do in years. Dolly presumed she was off out with her friend Edna, or with other choir members from the chapel but when she asked her mam about it, she found she was wrong.

'Edna Crawshaw, nay, I haven't seen her in ages. As a matter of fact I've been seeing Cyril. We don't do anything special, just go for walks, drink cups of tea and have a bit of a crack.' Maisie's cheeks flushed pink and Dolly had to laugh.

'You old dark horse, are you and Cyril doing a bit of courting then?'

The cheeks fired to scarlet. 'Eeh, our Dolly, what a thing to say! As if we would. We're far too old for such nonsense.'

'You're not old at all. And if he's my dad, then it keeps it in the family, doesn't it?'

Dolly wondered how she would feel about a possible marriage between these two, and couldn't quite make up her mind. Cyril Duckett didn't feel like her father, even if he was, not after having rejected her. She felt no kinship with him at all, which was a bitter disappointment. Even so, Dolly wouldn't deny her mother a little bit of happiness. Didn't she deserve it after all those years with Calvin?

'Cyril's good company and allus was easy to talk to. Things are looking up grand, what with our Aggie getting wed and Nifty Jack not bothering me no more. It's such a weight off me mind I feel like a new woman. Yer a grand lass doing this for your mam, so how are you finding it, chuck? How much do you reckon you've paid off so far, by working for him?'

Dolly shrugged her shoulders, trying not to show her concern. 'I don't know. He never says. I asked him to keep tally and he's said that he will.' Dolly was acutely aware that she'd no control over his promise to subtract the wages she should be earning from the debt. She could only hope that he would keep his word. Changing the subject, she asked her mother for tips on how to make a good rice pudding, which Nifty Jack had requested. Maisie dug into her memory to the days when she'd once possessed the wherewithal to make such treats, recollecting the correct quantities, cooking times and temperature.

'And don't forget to sprinkle a bit of nutmeg on top for a nice tasty skin. So how are you at cleaning windows? I noticed they were looking a bit streaky the other day when I walked by. Tea leaves, left to stand for a bit first, do the job best.'

All manner of useful tips and wrinkles Dolly learned from her mam and yet still she found the work hard, and so boring, with precious little in the way of fun. She polished and scrubbed, washed and ironed, cooked and baked, cleaned and swept and shopped and all the other mundane tasks that make up a woman's day. Dolly felt at times as if she was actually turning into her mother, old before her time, except that she didn't have to endure a husband who belted her if she got the least little thing wrong, so perhaps she should be thankful for small mercies.

And then one night, Nifty came home drunk.

He came rolling into the back kitchen, eyes glazed, with that studied quality to his speech which indicated he'd taken a skinful, his bowler hat lop-sided on his bald pate. Nifty he might be at relieving folk of their money, but not on his feet, not on this occasion. He lurched across the room and collapsed into a chair.

Dolly had been raking the ashes and riddling the fire, preparatory to going to bed. She'd spent a lonely evening mending his socks, feeling more than ever like an old woman and wondering what on earth she was doing with her life. She was pleased to be helping her mam, oh, but this job was hard going and half the time she was bored to tears.

When she'd finished the socks, she'd read for a while and then fallen asleep in the chair, waking to find the fire almost out and the clock striking midnight. She should have been in bed long since and her heart had plummeted when she'd heard his key in the door. What a stupid thing to do! Now she'd have to make him a bit of supper as he was often hungry when he came home from the pub and she wouldn't get to bed for ages.

She was right, the moment he walked he started issuing orders.

'Pull me boots off, girl. Don't just stand there looking gormless.'

Dolly bent to the task, trying to stay upwind of the stink from his breath. She was worn out and anxious to get some rest, kicking herself for falling asleep in the chair instead of making her escape while she had the chance. She hung up his jacket, folded the tie he'd just taken off and offered to put on the kettle and make him a cuppa.

'Nay, I don't want owt to drink. I've supped enough.'

'I can tell.'

'Don't look so po-faced. A chap deserves his pleasures.'

'I'll say goodnight then.' She made a move to the stairs door but he caught her by the wrist.

'Nay lass, would it split yer face to give me a smile, or a wee kiss? Or even to sit and talk to me for a while, instead of allus looking so uppity. You surely owe me a few home comforts in return for what I've done for you.'

'I know it's only the drink talking but I'd be obliged if you'd take your hands off me. This minute, if you please.' Since he made no move to do so, simply continued to leer up at her out of half-closed eyes, Dolly shook him off and took a step back, out of his reach. 'You've given me a job, for which I'm grateful. But may I remind you that I don't get a penny in my pocket other than something going off my mother's debt each week, or rather, Calvin's debt. Whatever we owe, and I know it's a great deal of money I'm working as hard as I can to pay it off.

I owe you nothing more and I've no intention of staying here forever. Once it's settled, I'm off.'

'I'm not talking about money, lass. I'm talking about something far more precious.'

Dolly frowned. 'And what would that be, exactly? What could possibly mean more to you than hard brass?'

'You. We're getting on fine, you and me, don't you reckon? We'll be nice as ninepence together.'

Dolly froze. What was he suggesting? Hadn't she heard enough tales from the girls in the mill about men who took advantage of a situation for their own gratification? Look at what had happened to Betty Deurden. Arch enemy or no, Dolly wouldn't have wished such ill fortune upon her. And she knew from experience how drink could affect a man, making him unnaturally quarrelsome, which could easily turn to violence. She'd rather die than submit to Nifty Jack's fumblings.

'If you're looking for a bit of how's-yer-father, you've come to the wrong shop.' Dolly couldn't believe how calm she sounded when really she was shaking inside, backing away, anxious to escape upstairs without upsetting him. Tomorrow, she'd go to the ironmongers and buy a bolt for her bedroom door. Why hadn't she thought to do that before?

'I'm very fond of you, Dolly. And you could be of me, I'm sure.'

His words struck a new fear in her heart. 'You're not going to ask me to wed you, are you?'

All he did was laugh, as if she'd said something funny. 'Nay lass, the thought had never occurred to me, though now you suggest it, I'll give it due consideration. I know all about your dodgy birth but I'll not hold it against you. Not many would have owt to do with a bastard, but I can overlook it, since I was one meself. Some might say I still am.' He laughed more than ever at this, enjoying the joke. 'So you can't afford to be too choosy. No knight on a white charger is going to come looking for you.' Dolly simply stared at him, transfixed.

'That's why I asked you to come here. I thought the best way to settle this enormous sum of money what your mam owes, was for us to get to know each other a bit better, then we could come to a friendly arrangement like. It'll take you half a lifetime to pay it off just by washing my socks. So why not offer a few extra services. What's wrong with that? Isn't that a grand notion? So don't get uppity with me. I know about your mam's dallyings with Cyril Duckett and all her other men friends.'

'What are you suggesting? Mam's dallied with no one but Cyril. They love each other, always have.'

He snorted with derision. 'Oh aye? Pull the other leg and see if that's got bells on it. She were a right looker in her day, was Maisie. Had all the chaps panting after her, even the maister at the mill, at one time. Who knows how far she spread her favours? Calvin told me all about her once, in t'pub.'

It was as if she were spinning through space, as if she were falling downwards into a dark pit where there was no sound, no light, no sensation of any kind and she was suffocating, quite unable to breathe or think or move a muscle. And while all sensible consciousness oozed out of her in the depth of this black hole, Nifty pulled her into a clumsy embrace. Whether it was because she instantly resisted, or because he was so stewed, he lost his balance, toppled over and they both fell to the ground, sending the coal bucket and fire irons flying.

Dolly desperately struggled to push him away and escape his clutches but she seemed to have no strength in her limbs and in seconds he'd rolled on top of her, the weight of him pressing down upon her, squashing all breath from Dolly's small body. He stroked her hair, her cheek, her throat; his ale-soaked breath almost making her gag.

'Nay, lass, stay calm. Don't get all het up now. I know a young lass such as yerself doesn't care to imagine her own mother doing *IT* – you know – what comes naturally, let alone with every Tom, Dick and Harry. But it happens more than you might think.'

'I don't believe you. *She didn't, she didn't!*' Somehow her skirt had got rucked up in the tussle and Dolly could feel the pressure of his fingers pulling it up still further, rubbing up and down her bare thigh, patting and fondling her bottom. Up and down, up and down.

'I'll not hurt you, or belt you one, as Calvin used to. I'll take good care of you lass, with lots of treats and petting.' He kissed her softly on one cheek, then on the other, and finally on her mouth, allowing his tongue to flicker lightly over her tightly closed lips. 'So long as you're generous with me, I'll see you right.'

Nifty felt a surge of power. He'd taken over ownership of the Tomkins's house to put himself in a position of strength. He didn't like folk getting away with not paying what they owed, particularly if there was a juicy morsel of female flesh to be enjoyed. He'd planned to have a bit of fun for a while then pack her off back to her mam but he'd found himself captivated by her, enjoyed listening to her humming or talking to herself as she polished and swept. He decided that he wanted to keep her around, might indeed agree to marry her one day and make an honest woman of her. He could do worse and a wife was cheaper to keep than a mistress, and far less trouble. Not that he expected her to come easy. She was a mettlesome little madam, in need of a bit of taming. But he was certainly the man for the task.

Dolly was staring up at him out of eyes glazed with terror, scrubbing frantically at her mouth as she strived to eradicate all taste of him, whimpering softly in fear.

'Hush, lass. Hush! And keep still, fer God's sake, or I'll forget me promise not to land you one. I'm easy to please. Good plain food and a clean house is all I require. Oh, and a bit of a kiss and a cuddle now and then, eh? Just to help you pay off that debt a bit quicker.' He sniggered, then launching himself upon her once more, started to lick and suck at her throat, slobbering all over her.

Dolly cried out, striving to shove him off, pushing and slapping at him, beating him about the head. '*Get off me! Get off. Get off. Get off!*' She tried to shove a thumb in his eye but he stopped that with a simple twist of her wrist, making her cry out in pain. 'I swear I'll kill you!'

This seemed to amuse him and he laughed in that unpleasant, sarcastic way he had, still sticking to her like glue as if he had a dozen hands, with arms and legs everywhere.

'Temper, temper! Don't you fly into one of your paddies with me, girl, or you'll be the loser.' He stroked her hair, slick with sweat and spoke to her in soft, chilling tones. 'All I want is to check out the merchandise. Nothing wrong with that, is there? Come on girl,' he crooned. 'Relax, why don't you? Your mother was always so generous-hearted with her many lovers, though I wasn't good enough apparently. She owes me this, a taste of her precious little girl. I could eat you all up, I could really.' He was tugging at the buttons on the front of her frock and Dolly heard the tearing of thin cotton as he grabbed and clawed at her breasts. 'Come on girl, show a bit of gratitude.' He winked roguishly at her and kissed her, swamping her small mouth with his great wet one.

Dolly made a choking sound deep in her throat, tasting the acrid burn of bile in her throat, which the minute the kiss ended she vomited all down the front of his clean waistcoat. Nifty looked down at it with sad disinterest.

'Nay, you could've given me fair warning. But I'll not chastise you for it. Tis only nerves, I imagine.'

The air in the small, stuffy room now reeked of vomit in addition to the stink of his sweat, and the beer and nicotine on his breath. This man, this *odious, evil man* had called her a bastard, accused her mam of being a woman of easy virtue, and believed he could do with her as he pleased. '*Damn you, get off! Get off me this minute.*'

He laughed.

Even as she fought with all her strength, Dolly knew it was useless. There was no one to hear, or come running to her aid.

The neighbours would be fast asleep, perhaps also well soaked in beer or gin. She felt dazed with fear, close to exhaustion, couldn't seem to get her thoughts together. She was losing the strength to fight. It was slipping away from her.

Having successfully reached bare skin, Nifty clamped one hand on her breast and Dolly screamed. Somehow the sound of her own voice brought her back to life, sent a surge of renewed energy flowing through her frozen limbs.

Her fingers scrabbled frantically among the coals that had spilled from the bucket when they'd fallen, searching for something, *anything*, to use as a weapon. They closed around the handle of the poker and Dolly brought it down with a violent crack on to the back of his head. He gave scarcely a whimper as he slumped against her, but there was a great deal of blood. It went all over Dolly too until she finally managed to pull herself free of him, scrambling free in desperation and terror.

She wasted no time in weeping or mentally going over what had happened. Time enough for that later when she was free and clear of this place. She paused only long enough to grab her few belongings, then ran straight home to her mam's house.

–

'Lord above, what's wrong now?' Maisie had her lank, mousy hair done up in plaits, since she'd been fast asleep when Dolly had hammered on the door. Now she rubbed the sleep from her eyes and reached for the kettle, recognising trouble when she saw it.

'Nifty Jack went for me, so I clocked him one.'

Maisie gave a sharp, bitter laugh. 'Serve him right, the nasty old goat.' She slid the kettle on to the hob but the fire had been banked down and there was no flame to warm it, so she began to prod the fire with the poker, hoping to encourage a bit of life to it. 'It'll be a while, love. Sit down and take weight off your feet. You can have your old bed back tonight. Now, tell me what happened.'

Dolly had already sunk on to one of the hard kitchen chairs. 'I hit him because of what he said about you, not just what he tried on with me.'

It all came out then, in a breathless rush: how he'd accused Maisie of 'putting it about', of betraying her husband with more than one man.

'He said you were a looker in your time, implied that you had loose morals and had spread your favours wide, even with the gaffer, Nathan Barker himself. Have you ever heard anything more...' Dolly's words stuttered to a halt as she saw the change come over her mother's face. 'What is it? What have I said?'

'Nathan Barker? What did he say about – about the master?'

'He said— Mam, why are you looking like that? Your face has gone all grey, like putty and... Oh, God, it's true, isn't it? You did sleep with other men, not just Cyril. Nathan Barker, and who else? How could you lie to me again? How could you?'

'You'd believe that nasty tyke rather than your own mother, would you?'

'Well, tell me the truth.'

'I don't want to talk about it.'

'You must talk about it. I need to know.'

'There are some things best not spoken of. I can't tell you, love. There are other people involved.'

'Why do you always have to *lie*? Why can't you *ever* tell me the truth?' The pain in Dolly's chest felt as if her heart would burst in two at any minute. Who could she trust, if not her own mother? Who was her father? Cyril? Nathan Barker? Or some other unknown man, as Nifty had hinted. At least it couldn't be Nifty himself, him having tried to assault her. *Unless he didn't know for sure either!* 'How many other lies have you told me? How many more men did you sleep with? Who were they? I want all their names.'

'Oh, Dolly.'

'How many? It wasn't just Cyril, was it? If he really is my dad, say so now. *Say it!*'

But even as Dolly waited impatiently for an answer, she knew one wouldn't be forthcoming. Her mother sat unmoving, the silence seeming to develop a life of it's own, reverberating around the small kitchen that smelled of coal dust and carbolic soap, and the stuff she put down every night to kill the cockroaches. The expression on her mother's face was enough. No words were needed.

Dolly was on her feet, words spilling out of her mouth faster than she could think. 'I don't suppose you even know who my father is, do you? It could've been anyone, half the chaps in Castlefield. What our Aggie has always said about you is right, isn't it?'

Maisie had sunk onto a chair one hand to her mouth as tears spilled and her nose ran. But even if she had been able to speak, Dolly was no longer listening. She turned on her heels and ran from the house. She didn't look back, not even when she heard her mother cry out her name.

Chapter Twelve

Dolly soon learned that it was one thing to say that she could look after herself but quite another to actually go ahead and do it. The streets of Salford were not at all a safe place for a sixteen-year-old girl to be. Sleeping in doorways and living on charity might sound perfectly feasible, and although the prospect of being free and independent had seemed like an answer, the reality was entirely different.

She'd taken with her a heel of bread and a small chunk of cheese but that didn't last her any time at all. In her purse she had one shilling and sixpence which she didn't dare touch, resolving to save it for when she found a room. Dolly soon discovered, however, that a bed for the night cost five whole pennies, unless she shared it with a stranger, which halved the price. On that first night, it being well past midnight and being near exhausted, she'd shared one with a fat old woman who snored loudly and stank of gin.

There were five other beds in the room, set only inches apart along walls streaming with water, caked in grime and unidentifiable clumps of fungus, and no doubt infested with cockroaches. Dolly didn't care to investigate too closely. Each iron bedstead held a stained, blue striped mattress and a single blanket. Nothing more, not even a pillow. One bed was occupied by a man who'd shaved off his hair, his bald head covered by strange, red scabs. Dolly kept well away from him. Another seemed to house an entire family: man, wife and five children all rolled up together in a tight, stinking ball. They carefully explained to Dolly how they'd fallen onto hard times when the husband had lost his job.

'We borrowed off Nifty Jack,' he explained. 'Have you heard of him?'

She agreed that she had, without giving any more information.

'Promised to allow us time to pay but his interest rates were exorbitant and we couldn't keep it up, so he just turned up one day with his henchmen and chucked us out onto the street. And we've ended up like this, no better than beggars.'

The woman said, 'Once these last few shillings are gone, it will be the workhouse for us, but for now at least we can spend these last few days, and nights, together.' And they clung together weeping, so that Dolly had to turn away, unable to witness their misery.

As for the rest, there seemed to be a shifting movement of ever-changing occupants throughout that long, endless night. Dolly didn't sleep a wink. The stench of the airless room made her gag, and the threat of a cockroach creeping into her bed kept her wide awake, let alone the unappetising grunts and snores and other unseemly noises that occur when people are trying to sleep. She lay staring up at bits of plaster hanging from a ceiling coated in soot, trying not to think about Nifty Jack.

It was then, during that long, dreadful night, that the fear came. What if he didn't wake up with a thick head the next morning? What if she'd done for him? She was already indirectly responsible for one death, now it looked as if she might have caused another. What would happen to her? She'd be caught and hanged, that's what. Dolly broke out into a cold sweat at the very thought and began to shake with terror. Oh, why did she have such a temper?

But what else could she have done? She had to save herself or he'd have ravished her.

And then she thought about her mam, and that brief, but so telling, exchange. Her silence had said everything. She'd lied again, hadn't she? Said there was only one man, the love of her life, but that wasn't true. And if there were two men, why not three, or four or… Dolly put her head in her hands and felt the tears spill between her fingers. It was all too awful to think about. What sort of a mother was she? If even Nitty Jack knew all of this, who else knew? Was her mam common gossip? Did everyone know that Dolly hadn't the first idea who her father was, that perhaps even her mother didn't know? 'Oh God, how do I begin to live with that?' Dolly squirmed with embarrassment, wishing she could die in this awful stinking bed here and now. 'No, that's wicked. I don't mean it.' And she buried her face into the fetid mattress and sobbed silent, heartbroken tears.

The next night Dolly wrapped herself in her shawl and slept in the Co-op doorway but was moved on at dawn by a police constable when he came on duty. Summer was drawing to a close and the nights already bore the cool bite of autumn. How she would endure a winter on the streets if she didn't find a place to stay, she didn't dare to think.

By the third day with no bread and cheese left, hunger drove her to use one penny to buy a tin of soup, which she asked the shopkeeper to open for her, and drank cold from the tin.

That left her with one shilling. At this rate, she'd survive only two more days. Then what? And would anyone care if she didn't?

–

How long she'd been on the streets, living from hand to mouth, raiding dustbins and the leftovers from market stalls, Dolly couldn't rightly remember. She knew only that she'd been wandering in a part of the city she didn't know for weeks but then she'd spent her entire sixteen years moving only between the mill and her home, and around the canal basin. She found herself now in a veritable maze of streets with courts leading off; dark cobbled ginnels and back-to-back houses each with a short row of three or four privies, which by the stink of them must serve the entire street and were never emptied.

Desperate to relieve herself she pushed open the door of one and found the floor flooded with urine and other ordure. She couldn't even consider going inside so lifted her skirts and used the corner of a back alley instead. At least the decaying vegetable matter and excrement that lay about here, had stood outdoors which had muted the smell somewhat. She'd thought Tully Court was bad, but this was ten times worse.

She must be in the heart of Salford somewhere, though where exactly, she couldn't make out. Occasionally her glazed eyes would focus on a street name: Calhoun Street, Cook Street, Market Street. Each and every corner thick with its quota of layabouts and drunkards, and often the scene of fisticuffs or a brawl of some sort. Dolly would hurry on, not daring to so much as glance their way. Dazed with hunger and weak with tiredness she could scarcely find the energy to place one foot in front of the other and deep inside was the dawning realisation that the longer she stayed out on these streets, the less likely she was to be able to find work. What respectable employer would take her on after this? She would look what she had become: a beggar.

Yet she daren't go back home and face being charged with murder, sent to prison and hear the judge declare that she would be hanged by the neck until dead. Every time she saw a policeman, she'd hide in a doorway or behind a dustbin, heart beating with fear, quite certain he must be looking for her.

On one corner she saw two girls fighting, sprawling on the cold, hard pavement, which brought back the memory of her own fight with Betty Deurden: the one that had led to her discovering all these unsavoury facts about herself; the horrors of her own birth. But how far would she have to run in order to escape?

'What else could I have done? I had to protect myself and not just let him have his wicked way. Why did he have to spoil everything?'

'Because isn't that the way of the world, love? Certainly the way of men.'

Dolly hadn't realised she'd spoken these words out loud, for all it was a common fault of hers. She spun about to find an old woman, thin as a linnet, with a face as wrinkled as an old prune. A scrag of hair was wound up into a knot on top of her tiny head, with trails of greasy locks escaping all around, and her dark, boot button eyes were piercing, seeming to read Dolly's past, present and future in one swift, assessing glance. She was dressed in an unfashionably long black skirt and a green coat that buttoned up to her chin. She wore no shawl but a large straw hat with a cluster of imitation fruit that might be berries since they were certainly red and shiny; almost good enough to eat so far as Dolly was concerned. Around her neck was tied a filthy scarf, although Dolly noticed that it was made of silk, not cotton. The woman had very few teeth and seemed to be missing one eye since one appeared white and glassy. Dolly couldn't restrain a shudder as a kindly hand reached out to touch her arm.

'Poor love, you look fair starved with cold, and hungry too, I shouldn't wonder. Come with me, lass, I'll give you a good hot meal that'll set you up grand. Lily Martin is the name, though most folk round here call me Cabbage Lil, 'cause that's where I were born, on a pile of cabbages in Smithfield Market. It was a handy place to live for a while, but I've moved on and doing nicely now, as you can see.

Dolly didn't see at all. The woman looked like a pauper, albeit one without that pinched, starved look all too familiar in these parts. But for this reason alone the offer was too tempting to resist. 'Thank you, that's very kind.'

'Tis only Christian! And you can meet the rest of my little family. My girls.'

144

One glance at the 'girls' in question revealed, even to Dolly's unpractised eye, that they were not family or related in any way to Cabbage Lil, except by profession. She saw at once what she had got herself into. A harlot's nest in a house of ill repute, a brothel no less.

Their ages varied from around fourteen to forty, perhaps older. Several lounged on a sofa, others on one of the numerous chairs that cluttered the dingy room, looking rather as if they were waiting to be called into the dentist's surgery, except they seemed perfectly happy about it, some of them actually laughing and playing a game of cards while they passed the time, hoping for clients. On the table stood a large bottle of dark liquid, spirits of some sort, she guessed, from which the girls would refill their glasses from time to time. Two were seated on the lap of one huge fat man in a big chair in the corner and Dolly had to quickly avert her eyes from whatever activity he was engaged in. Nifty Jack's fumblings seemed tame by comparison.

Cabbage Lil proceeded to introduce them, as if they were all at a party. 'This 'ere is Gladys, she comes from Deansgate, or Devil's Gate as we like to call it.' Chuckling softly. 'And here's our lovely Joan who's very popular with the swells from the country, being so young and pure like.'

Dolly didn't think she had ever set eyes on a girl less fitting that description. Joan looked not a day under thirty-five, old by Dolly's standards. She had brightly rouged cheeks, black eyes and resembled a scarecrow brassily attired in bright colours, feathers and probably every piece of trashy jewellery she possessed. Her face looked as if someone had walked on it and flattened it into a pancake.

Dolly caught up with what Cabbage Lil was saying. 'Them two in the corner are Sylvie and Fran, each seduced by the overlooker at Ordsall, though not at the same time you under-stand. But they both ended up here, where at least they get paid for it, and their shared experience has given them a bond.' She went on in this fashion for some time, introducing more girls but Dolly stopped listening, having quite lost track. In fact, the oppressive heat in the over-crowded room that reeked of human sweat and something Dolly couldn't put a name to, was beginning to make her come over all queer.

'Hey up, what am I thinking of? Gladys, fetch this child some nosh. Don't you fret, my lovely! Food is all I'm offering today and no payment required. So make yourself comfortable lass, and sup up.'

Dolly was quickly seated at a table, a heaped plate set before her and she did just that, tucking into a plump steak and kidney pudding that ran with hot gravy the minute she slid her knife into the crust. Oh, and it was so delicious she didn't once lift her eyes from her plate, not till she'd eaten every morsel and it was quite empty.

'Why don't you lick it clean, love?'

Dolly laughed shyly, feeling a flush of embarrassment join the heated glow produced by the excellent food. But then she glanced about her again. The chair in the corner was empty now, and only Gladys remained on the old couch, scowling and looking cross, perhaps at being left behind. At that moment a young man staggered in. Waving a bottle about he grabbed one of the girls and the pair of them went off upstairs, giggling, with their arms wrapped about each other. It was all somewhat sobering, reminding Dolly that this was a place of business, not homely charity. 'I can't pay you,' she said.

Cabbage Lil, rocking in her chair whilst keeping one beady eye on events, gave a hearty chuckle. 'You're not big on trust then, little un? I thought we'd agreed that no payment was required. Not at present, anyroad.' A girl came up to her, handed over a few coins, which Lil swiftly pocketed, slipping one back into the girl's outstretched hand. 'Should things change, or you find yourself in a position to pay later, that's different. We can always talk terms.' She fixed Dolly with a steely glare. 'I can promise you that you'd earn a good income and be quite safe and taken proper care of here. Ask any of my girls. They've no complaints.'

Dolly stared at her, fully understanding the implications of the carefully worded offer but not quite knowing how to respond. Yet she was in no position to quibble about the methods these girls had chosen to earn a living. Hadn't she come to see over these last weeks how very difficult life was when you couldn't find honest employment, and how quickly you could reach starvation point and death's door, of which she'd once spoken so lightly.

Now that Dolly was fed and sipping a mug of hot, sweet tea, the whole world had taken on a rosier glow. She felt half inclined to stay and join them, as Lil was suggesting.

Is this where I really belong?

Surely, going with a sailor or some fancy swell from the country, couldn't be any worse than being beaten by Calvin, or interfered with by Nifty Jack. She'd no idea who her real father was, and what's more, she no longer wanted to know. Much as she hated what her mother had apparently done, happen no better than these girls here, she was still her lovely mam and Dolly still felt responsible for her. She regretted walking out so abruptly. It was the shock of her not denying Nifty's accusation. But once she'd had time to get used to the idea and was settled some place, she'd write to her. Maybe she'd be able to understand and forgive her one day, but not just yet. It was all a bit too much to take in.

Oh Mam, what am I doing here? And who am I?

All the women looked well and almost happy. They weren't finely attired, most of them being barely more than half-dressed, but then they were working girls, ladies of the night. Perhaps they were indeed properly cared for by Cabbage Lil, their madam. Could it be so bad to eat like this every day, as rich as a queen! It might even be fun. And think of the money she'd earn? She could pay Nifty off in no time and be free of him for life, Mam too. But had she been a bit hasty, condemning her mother in that way?

Even Cabbage Lil looked different somehow. Removing the musty, green coat had revealed that the black gown was crusted in lace, if slightly tired looking, and with tiny teardrop pearls all around the high collar and forming a vee down the front of the bodice to a tiny, fitted waist. For that reason alone, and despite the lacy shawl she draped over her shoulders, the style seemed dated, probably pre-war, but clearly expensive. And having taken off the tatty hat, her hair turned out to be a burnished copper, glowing in the light from the fire. Yet her profession told in every line of her bony face. She was not beautiful, even had she been in full possession of both eyes. Dolly wondered how she'd come to lose it and if it was painful to wear a glass one.

Perhaps Lil noticed her scrutiny because as if reading her mind, or needing to deal with a question she was often asked from the start, she gave a wry smile and commented, 'A client got a bit too handy with his knife, love, but don't worry, it takes more than a drunken sailor to finish off Cabbage Lil. Nay, don't take on. Eeh, I shouldn't have spoke so carelessly. Gladys, come quick, this child has turned ash white and she's going to… eeh, catch her quick, she's keeling over.'

–

When she came round, Dolly was full of apologies. 'I don't know what came over me. I'm not usually so soft.' Mortified by her ill manners, she offered to clean up the kitchen now that the 'girls' had all finally retired or gone about their business. 'I want to help pay my whack,' Dolly said. 'I don't want to be no burden.'

'Not tonight, lovey, you look done in, but happen if you offer again, I'll take you up on it. I'm not a natural housekeeper, nor is anyone else round here.'

From that day on, Dolly made it her business to keep the place looking neat and tidy, exactly as she'd done for Nifty, only with a greater show of gratitude.

'Smart as a new pin, we are these days,' Cabbage Lil would gloat. 'We'll have to be putting up our prices if we get much posher.'

Dolly would giggle but then took over the cooking as well. She made the girls hotpot and steak and kidney pie, tasty stews and heart-warming puddings. She loved to see them cleaning up their plates and asking for more. She enjoyed going round the market with her basket and a purse full of money, which Cabbage Lil had given her to buy whatever food took her fancy. She'd buy fillets of plaice, or a whole box of mackerel; the leanest meat she could find instead of the fatty leftovers at the end of the day, and any amount of fresh fruit.

'Only the best for my girls! Chaps like a nice bit of flesh.'

Even Joan began to put on weight and was soon showing off her 'good figure', and pushing her breasts high in the trashy dresses she wore, to display her new cleavage.

And if one of the girls had a torn blouse or a loose hem, Dolly would mend it for them. She would sew on buttons, replace tatty ribbons with new ones she'd found on the market, add pieces of lace or braid to liven up a tired outfit, and let out seams, should this prove to be necessary on occasion. It became accepted practise that if one of the girls had a problem with an article of clothing, Dolly was the one to fix it.

'You're more than earning your keep, girl,' Cabbage Lil told her. 'You're a vital part of the team.'

'Why shouldn't I pull my weight? You've given me a home. Saved my life in a way. I want you to know how much that means to me.'

Cabbage Lil put back her head and laughed till her sides ached. 'I never thought I'd see the day when someone was actually grateful for being taken in by a tart, let alone be happy to call a brothel her home. You're a right card, you are, Dolly Tomkins.'

Dolly gave a shy grin. 'I know how to make the best of things, and which side my bread is buttered, if you catch my drift.'

Cabbage Lil's gaze grew quite shrewd, as she looked Dolly over, taking in her shining bob of raven hair, her glowing skin and sweet smile. 'And how much further will you go, I wonder, little one, to express this gratitude of yours? No, don't decide now. But you have a charm I could market, no doubt about that. No doubt at all.'

–

Dolly's first client was due in less than a half-hour and she was nervous. The other girls, whom she'd come to know and like over the weeks she'd been staying here, were all outrageously vain with a fondness for wearing anything a bit showy. Dolly had objected when Cabbage Lil had offered her a tangerine frock with frills and tassels, declaring she could never wear such a thing. But Lil had insisted that her task was to please the customer, not herself. Gladys had put rouge on her cheeks, painted her lips and nails red, and put something dark on her lashes and eyebrows. Joan even loaned her one of her feathers to stick in a band that she fastened around Dolly's forehead. Dolly felt like a circus clown and wanted to hide away, not parade herself before strange men.

What was she doing here? Whatever had given her the daft notion that she could carry this off? All right, Lil had provided her with a warm bed these last weeks and Dolly had paid for her keep by helping with the chores, doing the cleaning and washing and providing meals for the girls at all sorts of odd hours. Nothing else had been required of her.

Even today, Cabbage Lil had placed no pressure on her to do this. She'd declared herself quite happy with the way things were, so Dolly had only herself to blame. The decision had been entirely hers, the only way she could think of to make sufficient money to start again.

And if her mother did it, it couldn't be too bad, could it?

She had only to listen to the tales told by Sylvie and Fran of their own unfortunate experience with the overlooker, to understand their decision. Was her situation so very different? All right, Nifty hadn't exactly *done the deed*, but then Fran and Sylvie hadn't clobbered their assailant and done him in, as she had with Nifty. Dolly had scoured the papers for weeks afterwards, quite convinced he was dead. She'd also been responsible for the accident, which had led to Calvin's death. Oh, she was in right lumber she was. Dolly looked at what was left of her wrecked life and closed her mind upon it all. It was far too horrible to contemplate. So why not make some real money for a change?

Both Sylvie and Fran had secretly admitted to not relishing the life, but having no choice in the matter. Neither did she have any choice, so Dolly had made up her mind to lie back and think of the money. That's what the other girls did, and that's what she would do.

Lil had chosen what she termed 'a nice gent' for her first. He was a real swell who worked as a clerk in a warehouse and was not known to be violent. 'Once you've clocked him, girl, you'll be raring to go with the next.'

Is this how you started, Mam? Dolly wondered. Like mother, like daughter. Well, why the hell not?

–

Dolly struggled with the buttons on the tangerine frock, keeping a professional smile pinned on her face, as instructed by Cabbage Lil. Meanwhile, Bernard – that was his name, or at least the one he'd instructed her to use – sat on the bed and watched. His piggy eyes in the round fat face were dark with lust, the full mouth moist and quivering. Dolly was all fingers and thumbs, the tiny pearl buttons refusing to do her bidding and she could see he was growing impatient. Then he suddenly got up from the bed, came over to her and ripped the buttons apart.

'Take it off, for God's sake. I haven't got all day.'

The frock dropped to the floor, forming a puddle of silk around her feet and Dolly stood before him now in her knee-length Princess petticoat, shaking with fear.

He gave her a leering grin and took a long swig of beer from the pint glass he'd brought up with him. Dolly wished she'd accepted the shot of gin which Gladys had offered her, but she'd been taught at Sunday School to tread the paths of temperance, had even signed the pledge and couldn't quite bring herself to break it. As if that mattered now when she was about to do something far worse: turn herself into a woman of shame.

'Come on lass, get them togs off, or have I to help you with the rest an' all?'

'No, no, you enjoy the show.' Saying what she'd been told, and at least managing a sickly smile, Dolly kicked off the petticoat. Now clad only in silk cami-knickers and a lace trimmed, broché bodice with long suspenders attached that held up a pair of white silk stockings, more likely artificial silk but they certainly felt glamorous. Dolly rested one foot on the edge of the bed, unpinned one stocking and started to roll it down, taking as long as possible over the task, and not simply from a fear of laddering it. Undressing in front of this slavering stranger was bad enough. But when that was done, actually getting into bed with him would be far worse. Beyond her comprehension!

She started on the next stocking, mouth dry as sawdust and could actually see her leg physically shaking. If she put it next to the other, they'd knock out a tune. Dolly turned her attention to the bodice, searching for straps and fasteners with trembling fingers. There was only this and the cami-knickers left. What then? Dolly wasn't letting herself think any further, was keeping her mind firmly closed on what would happen next.

Bernard was kneeling up on the bed, his eyes out on stalks. He'd taken off his trousers and was, by this time, clad only in the grubby striped shirt he wore to work, the lap of it hanging over his fat backside while he was doing something nasty with his hand at the front, jerking in a funny sort of way and making loud grunting noises. Dolly took one look, gave a great sob of revulsion and that was enough. She fled. She didn't care that she was half naked as she ran along the landing in front of several gawping men on their way to and from various bedrooms. She didn't stop running until she reached the sanctuary of her own room up in the attic, the one she shared with Fran and Sylvie. Flinging herself down upon the flea-bitten blankets on her bed, she sobbed as if her heart would break.

Chapter Thirteen

Having discovered she was pregnant Betty Deurden hanged herself from the banister with her own dressing gown cord. Her poor mam was taken off to the asylum with dementia. Friends and neighbours said she'd never be right again. Word was now being put about that Nifty was the one who attacked Betty, though no one could prove it.

The gossips were also saying that Dolly Tomkins had simply vanished off the face of the earth. Sam was bewildered. What was going on? When Aggie had first told him, he'd thought she was spinning him some daft yarn by accusing him of running off with her sister. Then Dolly's mam came and asked the three of them, Matt, Davey and himself, if they'd seen her. Maisie it was who told them that Nifty Jack had attacked her and ended up in hospital as a result. The three lads realised then that the situation was serious. Matt was beside himself, hopping about from foot to foot as if he wanted to chase off that very minute, soft fool that he was.

'We don't want what happened to Betty to happen to Dolly,' he said.

'By heck, you're right,' Sam agreed. 'If that gobshite has hurt her, I'll finish the job Dolly started with me own bare hands.' It briefly crossed his mind that if he spent his free time searching for Aggie's daft sister, there'd be precious little left to spend with the captivating Evie. But then he'd waited night after night for her at the mill gates, and there was still no sign.

Maisie put a kindly hand to Sam's cheek. 'Nay, lad, I know you're fond of her, and she's fair taken with you, but revenge won't do no good to anyone. That Nifty Jack won't be going anywhere in a hurry, mark my words. What we have to do is to find my lass. Daft lump must have got some idea fixed in her head and has done a runner.'

Matt frowned. 'What sort of idea, Mrs Tomkins? Does she imagine that she's killed him, do you reckon?'

Maisie snatched at the suggestion since it neatly avoided any further explanations, and it may well be true. 'Aye, very likely that's it. But she can't be far away now can she, or come to much harm?'

The desperate appeal in her eyes left all three young men lost for words. What possible comfort could they offer? The twin cities of Manchester and Salford had more than a sufficient number of dark alleys, courts and ginnels, cellars, empty ware-houses and old mill buildings, some of them far from salubrious, in which one young girl could hide away for a long time, perhaps indefinitely. And they knew from personal experience what evils lurked in the shadows.

Matt put his arm about the woman's shoulders, giving her a little squeeze. 'She'll probably walk through that door any minute, Maisie.'

'Aye, course she will, lad. She's had a hard time of it lately, but she'll be back, like you say.'

'She'll turn up like the proverbial bad penny, grinning sheepishly and asking for a cuddle from her mam, like she allus did when she got up to mischief. Remember the time she got lost on Dawneys Hill that day we went flying kites and had a picnic?'

'Eeh, she must have walked for miles, poor love, then caught a bus all by herself and fetched up at home hours later, no bother at all. And she were only four.' Maisie's eyes were bright with tears at the memory of that worrying day. 'What a trouble that lass has been to me all her life.' She half turned away but then added, just for good measure, 'To be on the safe side like, will you all keep a look-out? Keep an eye open for her?'

Matt looked at her unsmiling, brown eyes glittering with a strange light. 'Aye, Maisie, don't you fret. We'll do all we can.'

'Course we will. We'll find her,' Sam put in, not wanting to be sidelined by Matt's more sympathetic style. Besides, helping to search for Dolly would offer him the opportunity to keep in touch with Aggie, to check out that she was serious over this engagement of hers. 'We'll make it our first priority. I'll be round to yours first thing after work tomorrow, Maisie, right? You know you can rely on me.'

–

Evie discovered that she quite enjoyed being footloose and fancy-free. Just nineteen years old with money in her purse, free to please herself what she did, and felt desperate for fun!

She did not return to the mill, or seek out Sam Clayton. Evie wasn't one to waste her time on those who didn't properly appreciate her. All too boring! Besides, she'd thought of another grand idea. She decided it was time that she saw something of the world and broadened her experiences a little. Where was the point in having money if you didn't spend it? Travel, that was the thing, and with winter approaching she made plans to visit the continent, the Riviera, Italy, Rome.

Mumsie was against the idea at first, not unnaturally, but once the notion came to her that she could accompany her daughter, as chaperone, her entire view changed. 'How delightful. I've always had a fancy to visit the Portuguese Riviera, much quieter and an excellent winter climate, I believe. I could bring my watercolours. You wouldn't object to a little company, would you darling? I really don't think it quite proper for you to go alone. We could perhaps hire a villa for a few weeks. I believe they are quite cheap.' This comment was for the benefit of her husband, who was frowning upon them both. 'You wouldn't object to my taking a short vacation, would you darling?'

'Apart from the fact that there's been a further fall in demand for cotton products, and in commodity prices, plus Japan is now developing its own textile industry and could finish us with lower prices, no, I see no reason why you shouldn't go on a continental spree and spend every last penny that I own.'

'Oh Pops, don't be such an old misery boots.' Evie was not against being accompanied by her mother, not in the slightest. They got along well enough and Clara was good company. Better still, once engaged upon her painting, she was quite easy to shake off, which would leave her free to do exactly as she pleased.

'We could have marvellous fun,' Evie agreed, giving her darling mama a hug, then went to kiss her father on his frowning brow, thinking she'd best try harder to win him round. 'Do let us go, Pops. At least you don't have to pay for a wedding.'

And feeling guilty that he was spoiling his only daughter's continental trip as well as her wedding, Nathan growled something to the effect that he'd be glad to be rid of the pair of them and have some peace for a while.

–

It took no more than four days for Evie and Clara to reach Lisbon. They'd travelled by liner, a 'floating palace', and the sea had been like a millpond, even round the Bay of Biscay. From here they took a train to their hotel at Mont Estoril and were utterly delighted as it was run on English lines with every comfort so there was no difficulty with the food, or the language, since the proprietors spoke it fluently.

They settled in quite comfortably, soon making the acquaintance of the other guests, and the climate was indeed most clement, with balmy breezes wafting in from the sea. So content were they that they decided not to go home for Christmas. Following this decision, Nathan wrote to remind his wife and daughter that money was tight and his bank account not a bottomless pit.

'Why does Pops have to be such a wet blanket?' Evie complained, making Clara laugh.

The letter was little more than a lecture on thrift, including a lot of boring stuff about the bank manager having to increase his overdraft, and the state of the country going from bad to worse, despite appearances to the contrary. Even the miners had now been forced back to work, largely because it was harder to live on homegrown vegetables and little else in winter time. Nathan was also having trouble with his colleagues in the cotton industry and told some convoluted tale of a member of the Federation of Master Cotton Spinners not being prepared to attend a dinner that included merchants, whom the man saw as his natural enemies. *Lot of damned nonsense!*

Evie sighed, and skimmed over that bit. He went on to ask if they remembered the girl who had saved Evie from the mob during the strike.

> *She seems to be missing. Has simply vanished and nobody knows where she is. Her mother is quite demented with worry, I believe. She appears to have had some sort of altercation with Jack Trafford, the talleyman, for whom she was working as a housekeeper. He has ended up in hospital with a cracked head and she has gone they know not where.*

His letter was so depressing that it had quite the opposite effect to Nathan's intended purpose and decided them to stay well into the new year. Why should they return home to the gloom of a cotton slump when they were perfectly comfortable here?

Clara would sit happily for hours on her balcony, painting pictures of the prettily coloured villas that fringed the coast, occupied by the Lisboan aristocracy. She would doze in the sun, gaze out over the Atlantic, or read endless romantic novels. Sometimes she might chivvy Evie into joining her for a stroll along the shore as far as the Bocca da Inferno. It was always spectacular on a windy day to see the waves smashing into the cliffs, carving out little caves and hollows in the rock. On quieter days they would bathe in the sun-warmed sea and feel wickedly daring.

Evie was never still for a moment. There was always something going on: a cocktail party, soirèe or dinner to attend; people to meet, and best of all – men to flirt with. Any number of men in fact who came and went over the course of that winter, many of them well-heeled and some seriously rich.

The best place to come across them was at the casino. Every night, Evie dressed as imaginatively and glamorously as she dared, always choosing bright colours to suit her mood: tango, cerise, burnt sienna and her particular favourite, mauve tulle. She had her hair cut into an Eton crop, wore nail varnish and took up smoking, since Pops wasn't around to stop her. She drank copious amounts of champagne but only ever picked at her food, determined to stay reed slim. To own a bust was so declassée and she hated all those contraptions of canvas and elastic. So restricting. Soft flesh was much more exciting for a man to feel.

Not that she was concerned in the slightest about finding a suitable husband. Should one present himself, Evie would certainly not be against the idea but she no longer ached to walk down the aisle. She might even try a 'companionate marriage' which were all the rage and had no formal ties at all, so that if the latest beau started to bore her, or, more important, ran out of money, she could move on to the next delicious man. She was having far too good a time, at the moment, even for that, and the parties were growing ever more wild. These were often themed by style of dress: Romans, circus, gypsies, pyjama, even a baby party once when they all went along wearing nappies and little smocks, carrying cardboard dummies. What a hoot!

She saw herself as a gad-about-girl, thoroughly relishing being free and single. And a healthy sex-life was essential for her mental well-being, Evie decided.

The first time she went to bed with a man wasn't particularly successful. She'd imbibed a little too much champagne, had agreed to take a midnight stroll with Archie or Thomas or whatever his name happened to be, and it had all been over before ever she realised what was happening. Rather a let down without the slightest jolt of excitement. She had an uneasy feeling that, like Sam, or whatever he was called, in the back of her motor, his attention had been elsewhere.

The next occasion had been far more pleasurable. He was called Antonio, and worked at the hotel as a waiter. He was an absolute darling with mysterious dark eyes and glossy black hair. Evie couldn't take him up to her own room, as Mumsie was there, and a light sleeper, so she accompanied him to the servant's quarters. This was a rather small room in the attics that smelt of garlic but gave the whole adventure an interesting little fillip, that essential spark of danger. And she certainly knew what was happening this time. Antonio took great care that she did.

But when he wished to repeat the exercise the following evening, she pretended not to understand and went off with a Polish Count, who was less amorous, admittedly, but reasonably good-looking and quite revoltingly rich.

After him came an Italian opera singer, a Belgium millionaire with a penchant for playing Mah Jong in the raw and more recently, a rich American who told her amusing tales of his several divorces. She was part of quite a marvellous little circle, constantly changing as they came and went to the hotel, and they were all having ripping fun. On one occasion they played a wonderful little game where everyone was given a number. You spun a dice and went off with whoever you got. The challenge was to find somewhere completely outrageous to do *IT*. Evie and her partner, she couldn't quite recall his name, did it twice, once on the back of a tram, secretly hoping the conductor might turn round and spot them, though unfortunately he didn't. And once among the rubbish bins behind a restaurant between courses, what delicious fun that was!

Oh, yes indeed, Evie thought, the little episode at the mill, which had seemed to cost her dear by losing her a husband, had now achieved quite the reverse. Life had taken a surprising turn for the better.

And who knew what might happen next? The Polish Count or an Italian millionaire could propose to her at any moment. It was all most satisfying.

–

Aggie was busily planning her wedding, which was to take place in the spring. May, she decided, would be an ideal month. There was to be a maypole and a May Queen set up on the wharf, a band concert and the usual jollities that heralded the start of a new season, so it somehow seemed to be an ideal time for a wedding. She was loving the attention and all the excitement of buying new things; had gone a bit mad ordering not only new furniture for the parlour such as a three piece suit in Rexine, but also for their bedroom. She hadn't wanted to sleep in Harold's old bed so had bought a new one, together with a matching, solid oak bedroom suite that had cost nineteen pounds. And the new gas cooker she'd ordered for the back kitchen was the very latest in modern appliances.

The only irritation was that her sister would clearly not be available as a bridesmaid. How selfish of Dolly to disappear and not let anyone know where she was; to think only of herself and not of others.

Worse, those three lads always seemed to be hanging around the house. Aggie particularly objected to Sam. It was most disturbing having him around on a daily basis, being reminded of what she'd given up. Matt and Davey would go off searching for Dolly while Sam remained, a constant presence in their kitchen at Tully Court, worrying over the situation with her mother. Not only was he a thorn in her side, but all this fuss about Dolly detracted Maisie's attention from the wedding, upon which she should more properly be concentrated; making Aggie's dress for one thing.

Not that she let Sam see how he affected her. She made it very clear by her constant references to Harold and the wedding plans, her hopes for the future, including a family, that their own little relationship was well and truly over. There was no question but that she'd been potty about Sam Clayton at one time and if he'd come up to scratch financially, she'd have chosen him for a husband like a shot. But she'd opted for Harold instead, since he was so nicely placed, and had no wish to make comparisons between the two men.

Even so, each and every night when she got home from the mill, Sam would be there, a map spread out on the kitchen table, going over with Maisie where they should search next. He was planning it like a military campaign, as if he were a sergeant sending his men out on patrol. Tonight, he was off to Smithfield Market, not for the first time but he was explaining that it was worth trying again as folk came there from all over Manchester.

'Get on your way then,' Aggie curtly instructed him.

'Nay, let the lad finish his tea first.' Maisie had even taken to feeding him and since his own feckless mother was a terrible cook, Sam wasn't likely to refuse.

'Why doesn't he stay away?' Aggie grumbled to her mother, when he'd finally gone.

Maisie looked at her askance. 'Sam and his mates are doing a grand job looking for our Dolly. Who else is taking the trouble? Not you, lady. Nobody else seems to care but them and me, Sam in particular, I'd say, judging by the number of times he's round here. So I hope you're happy about giving him up. He seems to have changed his allegiance.'

Aggie thought he might have a different motivation, still angling for her to have a change of heart and go back to him, but she flicked back her chestnut curls and pretended she didn't understand what her mother meant. 'Then I wish he'd hurry up and find that stupid sister of mine, preferably in time for my wedding. Have you started on my dress yet, Mam? You'd best hurry up and get on with it. Make one for our Dolly too, just in case.'

'And how will I find the cash to buy the material?'

'Don't worry about that. Harold will pay.'

'He has bottomless pockets, has he?'

'Deep enough for a decent wedding so stop worrying about money the whole time. Harold wants only the best for me. *He* adores me.' Raising her eyebrows questioningly, as if to imply that her own mother didn't.

'It may surprise you to know, Aggie love, that there are more important things for me to worry over than your wedding.'

'Isn't that typical of you, always putting our Dolly first.'

'Perhaps that's because she needs more help than you do, even if she doesn't realise it.'

'Well, she obviously doesn't care about us any more. Not a word since she left.'

'I'm sure she's just confused, that's all. Apart from losing her dad in that terrible accident, which affected us all, it was a shocking thing for her to find out about herself, and not in a nice way either. You'd no right to drop it on her like that. It wouldn't do any harm for you to be a bit more generous-hearted, girl.'

Aggie stretched wide her lovely hazel eyes. 'Generous to you, my immoral mother who betrayed my poor father and would probably sleep with anything in trousers? I don't think so. Personally, I'll be right glad to get out of this godforsaken hole myself. It can't happen soon enough for me.' And having said her piece, Aggie flounced out of the house leaving Maisie in tears.

–

Following the debacle with her first client, Dolly didn't intend to hang around and repeat the occurrence. She wasted no time in packing her bag, although not the tangerine frock, only her own things that she had arrived with. She thanked Cabbage Lil, offering profound apologies for the trouble she'd caused and admitted that it simply wasn't in her to do what was required.

'I expect I owe you a deal of money, for me food and keep. Once I get a proper job, I'll send it on to you.' All she ever seemed to achieve was more debt.

But kind-hearted Lil wouldn't hear of it. 'Nay lass, don't worry none about that. I were never certain that you had it in you to be a shameless hussy.' Lil chuckled and then allowed the smile to fade into a frown. 'You should go home to that lovely mam of yours what you're always talking about, and be respectable. You never did say why you left in the first place.'

And because Lil had been so kind to her, Dolly finally told her everything. The woman listened carefully, head on one side like an attentive sparrow, without interrupting once. When she was done, Lil quietly asked: 'But how do you know that he's dead, this talleyman? How can you be sure? Because if he isn't, then there's no reason why you shouldn't go home to your mam, at least to give yerself time to find a proper job and a place of yer own, happen get yerself a nice young man.'

'If only I could be sure.'

'I'll find out for you. It can't be too difficult. Murder might be reasonably common in these parts but it still excites gossip. I can ask around. Nifty Jack, you say?'

Within twenty-four hours she had the answer that he was perfectly fit and well. Dolly marvelled at her own stupidity at not mentioning it sooner, which would have saved her all this worry. Consumed by guilt, she supposed.

'They say he spent a few days in hospital, and several more in recuperation, so you obviously gave him a real clout with that poker, though it didn't knock any sense into his head, apparently. He's back to his old tricks, pushing folk into borrowing more than they need by promising them extra time to pay it off, and then changing his mind and putting the thumbscrews on. There are too many suffering at his hand, or so I'm reliably informed.'

Dolly thought of the couple with the five children whom she'd met on that first night, all sleeping in one bed and knowing that they faced the workhouse because Nifty Jack had evicted them from their home. She wondered about Betty Deurden. She knew Betty's mam wasn't well and couldn't work. Had it been Nifty who'd attacked her, just as he'd done to herself? And what of old Ma Liversedge, who had suddenly turned up her toes for no apparent reason, only hours after he'd called? What a callous-hearted, nasty little man he was. Oh, but despite the misery he caused, her heart lifted with happiness and new hope. If he wasn't dead, then she wasn't going to be locked up, or hanged. She could go home to her mam.

Dolly began to cry from sheer relief. 'Oh, Lil, I'm that grateful for your help.'

'Here, don't cry, I've another bit of good news for you. I've fetched someone back with me. That nice young man you were telling me about. Found him wandering the streets looking for you. He's been asking after you on Smithfield Market where they do know me. "Ask Cabbage Lil, she knows everyone," they said, so he came down here.'

And there he was, standing in the doorway grinning at her.

'Sam!' Dolly flung herself into his arms, so delighted was she to see someone from home.

There was no time to talk, as Lil was suddenly very anxious to get Dolly out of the house and on her way. 'Here, I've fetched yer bag. It's all packed. Now get off home with you lass, and don't let me see you back here in a hurry.'

Sam took the bag from Lil, equally eager to be off. 'By heck, but I can't wait to see your mam's face. She'll be made up to see you.'

As Dolly moved to follow him out the door, Lil whispered quickly in her ear. 'I haven't told him. He doesn't know what this house is, or what I am, or what you nearly were. And I'd advise you not to tell him neither. Men can be a bit two-faced when it comes to sex. Least said, soonest mended.'

'Eeh Dolly, I can't believe I've actually found you at last.'
They were walking along Liverpool Road in Castlefield, nearly
home, and they'd hardly stopped talking the whole way. Sam
had described to her how and where he'd searched, day after
day, and how her mother had wept.

'I bet our Aggie hasn't shed many tears.'

Sam chuckled. 'Aye, you might be right there.' Sam had
pretty well given up all hope of recapturing Aggie's fickle affections. She was clearly besotted with Harold Entwistle, or with
his money at least. And the more he'd thought about Dolly
and searched for her, the more he'd needed to find her. He
stopped walking to look down at her, his gaze unwavering,
steady on hers. '*I've* missed you Dolly. Never thought I would,
but I couldn't get you out of my mind.'

Dolly stared up at him, her heart giving strange little flutters.
He seemed taller than she remembered, bigger, stronger, and
even better looking, if that were possible. 'Could you not?' she
asked, in her softest voice.

He shook his head, then before she guessed what he was
about to do, he'd dropped her bag, pulled her into his arms
and was kissing her. It was the softest, warmest, most exciting
kiss she'd ever experienced, and seemed to go on forever. Not
that she'd had many to compare it with, and most of those had
been rushed and stolen in the schoolyard, behind the bike shed.
Now she melted against him, felt his arms go tight about her,
half lifting her off her feet, and Dolly thought she must be in
heaven. When the kiss finally ended she felt giddy with delight,
all light-headed and dazed with wonder.

'By heck,' she joked, not wanting him to see how much he'd
affected her. 'If I'd known you were missing me that much, I'd
've come home sooner.'

'Where have you been, Dolly, all this time? Who was that
woman, that Cabbage Lil?'

'Just someone who gave me a helping hand when I needed it. Nobody you need worry about. Do you want to kiss me again, Sam Clayton?'

He grinned at her. 'Fast piece.'

Dolly knew she was being forward, but she was desperate to get the conversation off Cabbage Lil. 'I'm making up for all these missing weeks. Hey, this offer doesn't last forever. Do you or don't you?'

'Don't mind if I do.' And he gathered her to him and kissed her again, finding it really quite pleasant. Dolly put her arms about his neck and kissed him back for all she was worth.

–

The reunion between mother and daughter was difficult. Certainly Maisie wrapped her arms around Dolly and gave her a big hug, tears of relief rolling down her cheeks, but there was a slight awkwardness between them, despite her mother's welcome. 'Poor love, I expect you thought you'd killed that rogue.'

'I did, Mam. I thought they'd lock me up if I ever came home.'

'I'm sorry to say he's alive and well and going about his business as nasty as ever, so don't you fret none about him. Sit yourself down and get some food inside you. You must be starving.'

Dolly didn't like to say that she'd been better fed these last months than ever before in her life. Nor did she explain where she'd been exactly, or what had happened to her. Least said, soonest mended. Wasn't that Cabbage Lil's advice? One she would most certainly heed, particularly where Maisie was concerned.

Somehow, neither woman felt able to broach the real reason for her hasty departure, that of Dolly's need for an explanation about her father, and so it continued to fester between them, like a sore, with no healing words or explanation forthcoming on Maisie's part, and no offer of trust or forgiveness on Dolly's. It wasn't that she wanted to believe her mother was a whore, just like Sylvie and Fran, Gladys and all the rest, but what alternative did she have?

Chapter Fourteen

Aggie's wedding was to go ahead as planned. The girls at the mill had had their bit of fun, decorating her frame with chamber pots and a frilly nightdress. They'd even had a collection and bought her a baking bowl and rolling pin for her new kitchen. 'Or belt him with one when he comes home late,' suggested one.

Mr Barker walked through the mill specially to give her half a crown, as a token of his good wishes. Aggie very nearly dropped a curtsey she was so thrilled, but then remembered to tell him that she might be leaving. 'I'll be giving my job up once I'm wed.'

He gave a sarcastic little laugh. 'I doubt you can afford to do that. You'll need the money even more now. What about that sister of yours, Dolly. Has she come home yet?'

Aggie was stunned, not simply that he should imagine Harold couldn't afford to keep her, but that he should be aware Dolly was even missing. 'Yes, Sam Clayton found her.'

He smiled. 'I'm glad to hear it. No harm done then.' And he continued on his way, with a good deal of whispering and mee-mawing from her work mates as he walked slowly down the alley between the frames.

'Stop gawping,' Aggie snapped, annoyed her resignation had gone so badly. 'It was good of him to think of me, and I shall put the money in a special box and never spend it.'

Aggie felt proud to have been given the half crown, though it had spoiled the moment somewhat that he should mention Dolly in the same breath. But at least her sister would be present after all in the bridesmaid frock that Maisie had sat up all night to finish.

That night the two sisters tried on their finery and yet again Aggie pumped Dolly for information, curious to discover what she'd been up to all these long months. She'd said infuriatingly little about it and even now studiously avoided answering. Dolly seemed more interested in Aggie's own plans.

'I can't believe you're going through with this wedding. *You*, marrying Harold Entwistle, the overlooker, I can't quite believe it.'

'And why shouldn't I? He's a good man, and he'll make a kind and generous husband.'

Dolly chuckled. 'Don't think because he's been splashing his money about while he courted you and generously paid for a grand wedding, that it will carry on that way. He might be well placed, but he's not made of brass. Harsh reality will soon strike home once the honeymoon is over. You'll be back in the mill trying to make one shilling do the work of two, same as always.'

Aggie twitched the skirt of her wedding gown, cream lace with a handkerchief hem, just as she'd wanted, positively weighed down with beads; and a veil trimmed with a wreath of tiny rosebuds. She'd changed her mind about letting her mother make it, leaving Dolly to wear something homemade, while she'd bought her own gown from Kendals department store instead. Aggie felt as grand as the Duchess of York had looked at her own wedding just a few years back, and she certainly had no intention of taking advice from a sister who'd been up to goodness what in the back streets of Salford.

'If it has anything to do with you, Dolly, which it hasn't, I'll have you know that you've got it all wrong. Harold has let me buy all new for the house, and I'm going to give up work and look after it. So what about you? Are you going to tell me what you've been up to? Don't you realise Mam's been worried sick. We all have,' she added, thinking it politic to include herself in the general anxiety.

'Come off it. I don't believe *you've* given me a second thought.'

'Well, all right, not me perhaps. But everyone else, all your friends and family have never stopped talking and worrying about you. Look at those three lads, Sam, Matt and Davey, wearing their shoe leather out walking the streets looking for you.'

'I know Sam has.' Moved to tears by this image, and melting inside at the memory of his kisses, Dolly couldn't help but soften, suddenly feeling a great urge to share this exciting secret with her sister.

'He told me all about that. Oh Aggie, then he kissed me, would you believe? He told me how much he's missed me, and that he wants me to be his girl.'

Aggie looked stunned, as well she might. This was the last thing she'd expected. Hadn't she spent her entire life keeping the pair apart? Being married to Harold and living on Quay Street suddenly didn't seem half so much fun any more, not if Dolly was going out with Sam Clayton.

Having revealed this precious secret, Dolly felt anxious to share the rest and get it all off her chest. She sank on to the bed she shared with Aggie, dark blue eyes filling with tears and let it all pour out. 'Oh Aggie, it's been awful, it really has. You wouldn't believe what I've seen, what I've been through. The first lodgings I stayed in were alive with fleas and cockroaches, full of desperate folk who had no home to go to. After the money ran out I stayed out on the streets but the privies were overflowing, I had to sleep in doorways and eat whatever I could find that had fallen off market stalls.'

Aggie was gazing at her open-mouthed with horror. 'I hope you won't tell Mam any of this. She'd have a fit.'

Dolly frantically shook her head. 'I didn't tell her anything. Nor about Cabbage Lil.'

'Cabbage Lil? And who's she when she's at home?' Sensing something sinister, Aggie strived to repress a shiver as she sat down on the bed beside her sister. 'Don't stop now. Who is she?'

'More to the point, *what* is she?'

Seeing Dolly's expression, Aggie's eyes widened in horror. 'No, she wasn't a madam, was she? Oh, Dolly, what have you been up to?'

'Nothing! Not me, I couldn't,' Dolly giggled, feeling suddenly relieved to have it all out in the open, but just as quickly sobered. 'I nearly did, but he was so fat, so horrible with his trousers round his ankles, it makes me sick even now just to think of him. I just couldn't do it, so I ran. Even so, Cabbage Lil was good to me. She looked after me when I was on the brink of starvation and at me wits' end.'

There was a telling silence while Aggie digested this shocking news. It took some getting used to that her own sister, *their Dolly*, had stayed in a brothel and seen a man – *naked*! It didn't bear thinking about. 'And what do you reckon Sam will say when he finds out?'

'Sam?' It was at this point that Dolly realised she should have kept this piece of information to herself, a carefully guarded secret. Not shared it with her tittle-tattle, holier-than-thou, know-it-all sister. 'Why would Sam find out?'

'It kills me to say this, but I reckon Sam Clayton might be in love with you, girl. Why else would he run himself ragged all over Salford for weeks on end looking for you. And you've just confessed that he's kissed you and asked you to be his girl. If that's true, you've no choice but to tell him, have you? Before somebody else does.'

–

The wedding was nowhere near as grand as Aggie had hoped for, but at least the salmon tea at the Co-operative rooms was tasty, there were no fights or fallings-out among the family, and her brothers didn't get too drunk. Harold provided them with no less than two cars to ferry bride, bridesmaid, best man and all her brothers and their families to church. Backwards and forwards they went for hour upon hour, having all the neighbours agog, never having seen such a thing in all their lives, not in Tully Court. But then Harold had promised her the best, so it felt good to show off in front of them all. He even provided a lovely sparkling wine that tickled Aggie's nose, and the wedding cake was a splendid two-tier affair.

Maisie gave her a telling wink. 'We'll only cut the bottom part today. You can seal that top bit in a tin for the first christening, eh love?'

'For goodness sake Mam, why do you always have to embarrass me?'

Harold didn't seem to have any family at all, save for one maiden aunt who sent a small cheque but chose not to attend the wedding due to ill health.

The girls from the mill: Myra and Lizzie, Annie and the rest, had a high old time, enjoying themselves hugely at Harold's expense. So much so that he declared himself relieved when the time came for himself and his bride to depart for their honeymoon. He'd had quite enough of their prattling, not to mention the tin cans and old boots they tied on the back of the hired motor. Fortunately it didn't have to travel more than a few hundred yards but everyone ran after it as far as Liverpool Road Station so they could liberally sprinkle the newly weds with confetti and see them onto the train which was already standing in the station.

'Are you happy, love?' Harold asked, as they leaned out of the carriage window to wave goodbye to friends and family gathered on the platform.

'Ooh, course I am. How could I not be?'

'It was certainly a good do, don't you think? Although it should be, it cost enough.' The bill from the Co-op alone had made him blench. He dreaded to think what the motor hire would come to. And then there were the flowers, and that dress. Lovely as it was, it had cost three times Aggie's original estimate.

And of course he'd had to pay for a photographer to record this important moment in their lives.

'Now you aren't going to go all penny-pinching on me, are you Harold? Not on our honeymoon?'

'I wouldn't do that, love. Time enough to tighten the belts when we get home, eh?'

'Ooh Harold, you will have your little joke,' Aggie said, squeezing his arm and giving a little giggle. 'I never know what you'll say next.'

The train had departed, taking the newly weds with it and the wedding party prepared to disperse. 'Can I walk you home, Dolly?' Matt offered. He looked unusually smart in the dark blue suit he'd worn for the wedding, even if the legs of his trousers did stop short of the ankle and the sleeves reveal rather too much of his bony wrists.

'Sam's already offered, thanks anyway,' Dolly said with a vague smile, her gaze sweeping the gathered assembly on the platform, seeking him out. He hadn't said anything of the sort but Dolly had made up her mind that he would. He'd kissed her on that day he'd brought her home and although she hadn't seen him since, chiefly because of all the fuss over Aggie's wedding, he'd surely be desperate to walk her home so he could kiss her again. He seemed to be talking to that gaggle of girls from the mill and Dolly felt a familiar stab of jealousy.

She ran over to him and linked her arm in his. 'I'm ready to go now, Sam.'

He looked down at her in surprise for a moment, then flicked back his fringe and grinned. 'All right, if you say so! Bye girls, it was good chatting to you.' And he gave his bevy of admirers a cheery wave, making Dolly almost breathless with pride as he strolled away with her arm tucked into his, just as she'd once dreamed of doing.

It was as they walked home that Dolly hoped to broach the subject, which had obsessed her ever since Aggie had mentioned it. How to explain to Sam in the most tactful way what she'd been involved with over these last months. It would not be easy.

'You remember us once talking about how it might affect our friendship if something changed between us?'

Sam groaned. 'Not that again, Dolly! I don't think I could take it, not after everything. But if you're worrying about what your Aggie told you, about you not being Calvin's daughter, well I know all about that, and about Cyril Duckett. Maisie explained it all to us when you were missing, and how much it had upset you. It doesn't bother me in the slightest, so stop fretting. You're my girl, that's all that matters now.'

Dolly felt tears prick the backs of her eyes. Hadn't she been right all along? Hadn't she known that he would stand by her? If Sam knew all about the scandal of her birth and still wanted her, there was nothing left to fear. It hadn't bothered Matt either, but then she wasn't Matt's girl, so he wasn't so important. Dolly guessed that her mother wouldn't have mentioned Nifty Jack's claim that she'd put it about all over Castlefield, and, as a consequence, the identity of Dolly's father was not quite so certain as one might imagine. But that didn't mean she had to keep quiet about her own misdemeanours. Dolly didn't believe it would be a good thing to start their life together on a lie. But how to do it right, that was the question.

'Our Aggie said you wouldn't want to know, not with me being a — a bastard.'

Sam's face darkened with anger. 'Don't say that word. You're not — one of them. I won't have anyone say that about my girl. And what docs Aggie know? Take no notice of her. She's never happier than when she's causing trouble.'

'Oh, Sam, you're so understanding.' Dolly snuggled closer. 'And I do like being your girl, I do.' She very nearly said that she loved him, but stopped herself just in time. That would have been far too forward at this stage.

He grinned down at her, tilted her chin and dropped a kiss lightly on her upturned nose. 'That's good, because happen we should start thinking about our own wedding. Your Aggie isn't the only one who can get wed, eh?'

He was still smarting from his recent encounter with Aggie. She'd cornered him on the stairs in the Co-op, teasing him by lifting her fancy skirts to reveal a captivating length of leg and a lacy blue garter. 'Something borrowed, something blue,' she'd said. 'Thought you might like to see you what you've lost.'

'I've lost nothing,' he'd said, his eyes riveted to the glimpse of lacy cami-knickers he could see just above the said garter. She'd noticed the direction of his fascinated gaze, dropped her skirt and gone off laughing. By heck, but he'd show her that he didn't give a monkeys what she did.

Dolly had stopped walking and was gazing up at him, open-mouthed with shock. 'What did you just say?'

Sam drew in a breath. Marrying her sister would be the perfect revenge! Anyroad, Dolly was quite a nice handful nowadays, with a fetching prettiness to that funny little face of hers. He grinned down at her. 'I said, time we happen thought of getting wed.'

'If this is one of your daft jokes, Sam Clayton, it's not funny and I'm not laughing.'

'I don't want you to laugh. I want you to say yes.'

'But...'

'But what? You aren't going to turn me down, Dolly Tomkins? Not after chasing after me all these years?'

'I didn't chase after you.'

'Then why did you only catch me when I stopped running?'

She had to laugh then because he was so funny. The next minute that lovely sensuous mouth of his was pressed upon hers and she couldn't seem to think clearly at all. There were strange things happening to her insides, and she came over all giddy.

'You don't even know what happened to me these weeks,' she said at last, when they finally came up for air. 'Where I went, or what I did.'

'No, and I don't want to know. You're back safe and sound, which is all that matters.' And to prove it, he kissed her again, good and hard.

When she'd caught her breath a second time, Dolly asked, 'But what if there was something – something you *should* know, something I should explain, in case it changed things between us?' She was trying to test what his reaction might be, her mind racing, although the carefully prepared words had gone from her mind in the excitement of his proposal and those knee-weakening kisses.

He groaned. 'Not again, Dolly. I don't think I can cope with one of your convoluted arguments right now.' He pushed open the neck of her pretty pink bridesmaid's dress so he could kiss the pulse beat at her throat.

Dolly gasped, struggled to concentrate. 'I'm not saying there is, I'm saying *what if*?'

'Let's not worry about "what if"'s. What if I laid you down on this pavement and ravished you in the middle of Liverpool Road, what would the neighbours say? And you look that tasty, I just might.'

Dolly giggled, trying to slap his hand away, which was doing wicked things she didn't care to think about. 'Stop being daft and listen. And I don't want an argument, I'm just saying that if—'

He heaved a great sigh. 'Your mind is so complicated, Dolly, it'll tie you in knots one day and strangle you.' He stopped kissing her, took a step back, and she felt the loss of his closeness acutely. 'Maybe things did happen to you that weren't too pleasant. Things happened to me too. But they're best forgotten. Why drag up the past? Let things lie, eh?' Sam was anxious to get off this subject. The last thing he wanted was Dolly's heart to heart where he might be driven to confess that little episode with Evie in the back seat of her motor. That wouldn't do at all. 'So you can take that enticing little pout off your face and stop looking so woebegone and tempting, or I will have me wicked way with you right here and now.'

'What are you waiting for?' she teased.

'That bit of paper which says I can. In the meantime, I'll make do with what I can get.' And so the moment passed and Dolly lost her nerve, or was too much engaged with enjoying more of his kisses.

–

Maisie was astonished to learn that there was to be another wedding in the family, and so soon. 'I'll be bankrupted by the pair of you,' she said, seeming to forget that Harold had borne the cost of Aggie's wedding. Dolly and Sam carefully explained that theirs would be a very small affair, with no bridesmaids and no fancy reception at the Co-operative rooms, and they'd pay for it themselves, somehow or other.

'The only thing is, we've nowhere to live, so can we move in here? Sam can help with the rent.'

'He's more than welcome, with or without the rent. I hope you'll be right happy, love.'

Dolly thought she certainly should be happy. Wasn't this what she'd dreamed of all her life, to be loved by Sam Clayton?

Matt was even more shocked by the news. 'You're going to wed Sam Clayton? Have you taken leave of your senses?'

Dolly bridled at his tone. The group of friends had all gathered to celebrate at the Crown. Having made the announcement, Sam was at the bar, buying drinks all round, while Dolly happily accepted everyone's congratulations, except there were none forthcoming from Matt. 'Why should I have? Sam's mad about me. Says he can't think what's kept us apart all these years.'

'You know what kept you apart. Your Aggie.'

'Well, she can't keep us apart now she's wed to Harold, can she?'

'I never took you for a fool, Dolly, but if you think he's over her, you're most certainly fooling yourself.'

Dolly flushed bright pink. 'That's the unkindest thing anyone has ever said to me. How could you, Matt Thornton, after we've been friends all these years?'

'It's because we've been friends all these years that I can. I generally like to keep my nose out of other folk's affairs but in your case I can't. Happen I should've spoken up sooner when I first saw him looking your way. Unfortunately, I didn't think even Sam could be so cruel as to take advantage of someone as nice as you, Dolly. Obviously I was wrong.'

'He is not "taking advantage of me" as you quaintly describe it. For goodness' sake this isn't one of those soppy movies where the sheik carries the girl off into his tent and ravishes her. Sam has been the perfect gentleman.'

'So far, maybe, but he won't make you happy, Dolly. He'll lead you a right merry dance. You deserve better.'

Dolly was feeling all hot and bothered, the flush on her cheeks turning to angry flags of bright crimson. 'I believe I should be the best judge of who or what will make me happy, and it certainly wouldn't be someone as bossy and nasty minded as you clearly are. Why I ever imagined you to be the quiet, inoffensive sort, I cannot imagine but I'd be obliged if you would take your prying nose out of my affairs, as you claim you'd prefer to do.'

Davey bounced over at just that moment and lifting her up in his arms, exuberantly swung her high in the air, teasing her about soon having a clutch of children at her knee and needing to keep her new husband on a short lead.

'So, are you going to wish me well, or what?' Dolly challenged Matt, when she was back on her feet again.

'Of course.' He gave her a peck on the cheek but his face was strangely pale and he remained cool and aloof for the rest of the evening, both with herself and with Sam. Dolly put it down to the fact that Matt had always been a shy boy and a bit of a worrier. Also, those two men hadn't been getting along well in recent months.

Aggie came home from honeymoon and settled into her new home, looking very content and matronly. She expressed herself flabbergasted to hear Dolly's news. 'You're marrying Sam Clayton? By heck, you've kept that quiet. You must be mad to even think of getting wed at your age. You're only seventeen.'

'Can't you just be pleased for me? Anyroad, we're not getting married till I'm eighteen, which will give us a few months to save up.'

'Have you got a job then?'

'No, but I'll find something soon, I'm sure.' Dolly frowned. 'Have you any suggestions where I might try next? Do you know of any place taking operatives on?'

'There are no vacancies at Barkers.' To Aggie's great surprise, Harold had taken it for granted that she would return to her job at the mill, so it was just as well, as it turned out, that Mr Barker hadn't accepted her resignation. She was now earning nine shillings and sixpence a week and Harold expected her to use that for the housekeeping money as well as put a bit by for a rainy day. This had been something of a blow, as she'd pictured herself swanning about the house all day with nothing more taxing to do than a bit of washing and ironing, putting up lace curtains, shopping with money in her purse for a change, and making delicious little suppers for the two of them.

But Harold had promised her that if they both worked hard for a year or two, and held back on starting a family, they could afford a place in the suburbs; somewhere a bit more upmarket like Rusholme, Didsbury or Wythenshawe. So it pleased her to see Dolly was still struggling, and she sincerely hoped that even if Sam was better looking than dear Harold, he was less of a provider. She didn't want her younger sister getting above herself, or worse still, becoming better off than herself.

'So when are you going to tell him about – you know?'

'Cabbage Lil said that I mustn't, that men were a bit two-faced about sex and didn't want to know anything – unpleasant

– about their girl. Sam said he didn't need to know all the details, so why should I tell him?'

'You know that he'll find out anyway. *Someone* will tell him, even if you don't.'

Dolly stared at her sister, wide-eyed, and drew in a shaky breath. 'You wouldn't!'

Aggie merely flickered her eyebrows and shrugged her shoulders in a non-committal gesture as she gave her full attention to polishing her new sideboard. She wasn't in a particularly good mood today since Harold, having promised her a new summer frock, had gone back on his word, claiming money was a bit tight at present, what with the wedding and honeymoon and all, so would she mind making over last year's instead? Would she mind? Of course she flipping well would. So she certainly had no patience for Dolly's self imposed little problems, particularly when they involved Sam Clayton. Serve her right for running away in the first place. 'All I'm saying is, don't leave it too long.'

'I won't, so you'd best not poke your nose in where it's not wanted. I'll know who's spilled the beans if he ever did get wind of it. I'll tell him myself, thanks very much, in my own good time, and I don't expect there to be a problem. He'll understand and be fine about it, I'm sure. You were wrong about him before. Sam doesn't mind in the least my being a bastard, if that's what I am, so there.'

'He'll not be so generous about this other business,' Aggie warned.

Dolly was less sure of her ground than she had made out, guessing Aggie was probably right. Now that Sam had actually gone so far as to ask her to marry him, she really should tell him the full tale, whatever the risks. How could she live with herself otherwise?

Even if Dolly never set eyes on Cabbage Lil ever again, the fact that Aggie, her spiteful sister, knew her secret and held it as a threat over her, was something she really couldn't live with.

She'd be in a constant state of fear, a bag of nerves that Aggie might spill the beans, should it take her fancy, and Sam would learn the truth in the worst possible way, just as she had over her own birth.

But what if he didn't believe in her innocence and thought she'd actually done *it* with that horrible chap? What then? She might lose him.

Dolly thought of her own reactions when she'd learned of her own mother's failings. How she'd run from the house, unable to face the truth that despite all her chapel-going, and her preaching to be good and moral, her mam was a woman of easy virtue, just as Aggie had always claimed. Even now, the subject was too painful to be mentioned between them.

What if Sam didn't believe in her innocence either?

Oh, it was all too dreadful to contemplate. Surely, it was best not to rake up the past, but to plan for the future? Sam loved her and they were saving up to get married. She couldn't be happier. It was more important to find work, so she too could save up. Dolly decided to put the matter of Cabbage Lil right out of her mind and deal with it at some point in the future. Aggie wouldn't do anything in a hurry. Even her selfish sister couldn't be so cruel.

Chapter Fifteen

Evie saw herself as a sort of female Prince of Wales. That's not to say she thought of herself as a princess, since ladies of the royal household seemed to have restricted lives, confined by protocol and tradition, whereas the men were largely free to come and go as they pleased. Or so it appeared from all the gossip columns that she read. And while the prince danced with every pretty girl from Newfoundland to Canberra, New York to Paris, Evie did the same with every eligible bachelor, and quite a few married gentlemen in between.

She tried her hand, or rather her toes, at the 'Twinkle', the 'Jog Trot', 'Missouri Walk', 'Black Bottom' and her favourite, the 'Shimmy'. Of the 'Charleston' she considered herself an expert. Her one criterion for her choice of partner, as with the prince, was that they should be good-looking, and preferably very rich.

Dearest Mumsie returned home to Salford at the end of spring 1927 because she missed her darling husband, leaving Evie in the charge of Miss Howell, a companion. Naturally, she didn't stay with her but picked up a few nondescripts and gigolos along the way and moved on to Spain. Then to Rome where she encountered Paolo at the top of the Campanile di Giotto in Florence, not too satisfactory since he became angry with her when she discovered she had no head for heights and was therefore nowhere near as athletic as he would have liked.

She moved on to Paris and met sexy Philippe who brought her breakfast in bed in their little pension on the Montmartre before climbing in beside her to help her eat it, largely by decorating her breasts with strawberries and licking the cream from her nipples. Bliss! Ah, what a delightful spring that had been. Recalling the places she had visited was the only way she could remember the names of her many lovers.

There was one awkward moment when she'd found herself 'up the spout' but a short visit to a certain address on the left bank had put that right. This woman had been clean, if expensive, even so the bleeding had taken weeks to stop. The pain was excruciating – a dreadful bore – which meant that in the end she had to be taken into hospital. The doctor had gently informed her that she would be unable to bear another child as her womb had been punctured. He did not ask how that terrible thing had come about and Evie didn't trouble to explain. They both pretended that it was some unforeseen accident, so that no charges could be brought. Evie shed not a single tear, felt only an unspeakable relief, as she never had been able to imagine herself with children, dealing with sticky fingers and tantrums, and happily left the hospital that day.

Enjoying herself in this hedonistic fashion was an excellent revenge against her father's petty meanness and the humiliation he'd heaped upon her by ruining her wedding. Best of all, was to deny him the possibility of a grandson. Serve him right. She smoked her head off, not knowing what kind of cigarette it was exactly that she fixed in her long, tortoiseshell holder. She would drink tea out of a brandy glass, put up her hair in a fish net and daub jam on her bread with a spoon if she felt like it and not care a jot. Most vital of all, she mixed with the right sort of people in various countries and then with actors, artists, dancers and musicians. She became, in short, a bright young thing and continued in this fashion for some time.

But ultimately grew bored. Proposals had become less common, and there no longer seemed to be the enticing choice of escorts she had once enjoyed. Paris, she decided, was overcrowded, and rented a 'studio' in Mayfair and became Bohemian, as dearest Mumsie had done before her. Except, of course, Clara was a proper artist and had actually sold several of her paintings to various hotel guests, friends and acquaintances they'd made along the way. Evie, on the other hand, only dabbled.

And then her regular sum of money was stopped.

Her father finally called a halt to her profligate ways and, no matter how much she protested, he remained adamant that he would finance her excesses no longer. Evie wrote him any number of persuasive letters, some attempting to be humorous and jokey, others making promises she had no intention of keeping. When those didn't work, she became maudlin and self-pitying, making sure she smudged the ink with her tears. Not even these sentimental little notes had the desired effect and, as a last resort, she was forced to drive her car all the way to Manchester and beg him to relent.

'Absolutely not! Enough is enough. I have watched your progress with an increasing loss of patience, Evie, and it is time for this hedonistic lifestyle to end. The moment has come for you to do something useful with your life, perhaps even to find employment,' her father firmly stated.

'You expect me to *work*?' Evie made the mistake of bursting out laughing.

Had she not done so, Nathan might well have backed down, but enraged by the bills that had flowed in from every corner of the continent and worried over the failing fortunes of the mill, her casual attitude was too much to bear. 'You will indeed find yourself some useful employment, or I will put you to work in the mill. Do I make myself clear?' Daughters, he decided, were the very devil.

Evie, of course, did nothing of the sort and, within a month punctuated with many similar arguments and despite her vigorous protests, sulks and near hysterics, he carried out his threat. She wept and sobbed, pleaded and argued but Nathan remained adamant. He would fund her irresponsible lifestyle no longer. 'You must stand on your own two feet from now on.'

'How can you do this to your daughter?' Clara protested.

'Because it might teach her some proper values if she encounters real people in the world! We've protected and indulged her for far too long, and this is the result.'

'We've given her the love she deserves.'

'As well as nannies and governesses, fancy schools and expensive clothes, holidays and parties. If she asked for something, we gave it to her – anything rather than sit down and talk to her, or spend time with our daughter. Because you resent my apparent neglect and became entirely engrossed in those dratted pictures, you churn out by the score. Me, because I had to somehow earn the money to fund all of this! But now I'm calling a halt. Enough is enough. It's time for her to grow up. With the best will in the world I cannot sustain her in the manner to which she has become accustomed. If she wishes to continue in this heedless fashion, she must find herself a rich husband who can accommodate her. Otherwise she must work for a living like the rest of us.'

Clara went ash pale. 'You would abandon darling Evie, because she isn't the son you craved?'

'Because she's a *liability*!' he roared. 'And a lazy, selfish little madam.'

–

Much to the surprise of the girls at the mill, a new member came to join them. They gathered around to take a closer look, plucking at the skirt of her fashionable frock, touching her hair, remarking on her scarlet lipstick. Her whole appearance was entirely inappropriate for working in a mill.

'By heck,' said one. 'This is a turn up for the book. The boss's daughter gracing us with her presence, so do you want to borrow me pinny, love? You mustn't get that fancy frock mucky?'

Evie shuddered with distaste. 'I don't think so.'

Harold hurried over. 'Don't you cause no trouble, you lot. Get back to work. I'll find Miss Barker an overall.'

'Ooh, *Miss* Barker, is it? Well I'm *Miss* Crabtree then,' said another, a red-headed girl called Elsie who seemed to have quickly stepped into Betty Deurden's shoes and set herself up as ringleader. 'If she's to get special treatment we want the same, or we might object, mightn't we girls?'

There were murmurs of assent from the gathered group and Harold began to feel a bit hot around the collar. The last thing he needed was any more trouble. He thought Nathan Barker must have taken leave of his senses to put his daughter to work in the spinning room with this lot.

Aggie pushed herself forward to offer her support. 'Maybe it's a good thing she's come. Happen things will start to improve round here. Better manners for a start.'

'Don't think I'm staying,' Evie said. 'This is purely a temporary arrangement, I do assure you.'

'Temporary or not, you'll get stuck in and work like the rest of us,' ordered Harold, reasserting his authority. 'Now then, Aggie, you can show Miss er um… what's what.'

'I'd be glad to,' Aggie said, preening herself for being chosen, as she naturally should be, being the wife of the overlooker.

Elsie Crabtree sneered as the pair walked away. 'I must make sure I'm around when our *Miss* Barker comes face to face with the lavvies in the mill yard for the first time. That could be most entertaining.'

–

In the months leading up to her wedding, Dolly got by on odd jobs, taking work wherever she could find it. The best one was packing the finished cones ready for the weaving shed. A menial task but she was delighted simply to be back in a mill, until the firm went bust and she was back looking for work again. After that she got a part-time job in a warehouse, packing knitting bobbins, and another finishing the seams on overalls, but neither lasted very long. Sometimes she would stand in for Edna Crawshaw at the corner shop, whenever the older woman needed a break. She even did a paper round on a borrowed bike for a while. But no matter how tough the work was, or how little she got paid, she saved every penny she could.

But Dolly was worried about how much interest might have been added to the debt they still owed, now that she'd left Nifty Jack's employ. The first time he'd appeared on the door step, she was nervous of even speaking to him.

'You showed yourself to be handy with that shovel then,' he drily remarked, a sly grin on his moonlike face.

'I know how to put one to good use when needed.'

'Well, I'm not one to bear a grudge.'

'You'd pinch the flea off a dog if you thought you could make money out of making it dance.'

'Less of your sharp wit, Dolly, or you'll cut yourself with it one day. Though we do still have a score to settle, you and me, eh?'

'I've no regular work and no money to pay you any extra, so you'll just have to be patient.'

'Nay lass, that won't do. You'll have to try harder. I'm not the patient sort.'

Pride kept her from calling on Nathan Barker to ask a second time to be reinstated. Dolly even avoided going to chapel in case she should see him, which was unfortunate as that was often the best place to hear of any work going. And the flighty ones would turn up in their best bib and tucker, catch the boss's eye and he'd think of them warmly the next time they came asking for employment. But Dolly wasn't the flighty type and had no wish to beg.

Deep down, she knew she was avoiding chapel and Nathan Barker because she couldn't quite summon up the courage to confront him. She longed to ask if it was true about him and her mam but what if he said yes, that they had slept together? What would be the next question after that? Dolly quailed at the thought. It was one she didn't dare to consider. There was no way she could go around asking all the men in Castlefield if they were her father, let alone the gaffer, the master of Barker's Mill. She didn't have the nerve. Besides, it was more than likely she was the daughter of the milkman, or the rag and bone man.

Dolly begged her mother on several occasions to reveal the truth, but she absolutely refused to do so. Maisie insisted the past was over and done with, that other people were involved and it wasn't her place to name names.

'So you won't tell me who my father is?'

'No, Calvin brought you up, no matter what his failings. Let that be an end to the matter. There's nothing to be gained by stirring things up again.'

'But people will talk. They'll say you were – are – a loose woman.'

'Let them talk.'

So Dolly very firmly put the matter out of her mind. What did it matter who her father was, so long as it wasn't Nifty Jack? It took some weeks but eventually Dolly plucked up the courage to ask Nifty Jack how much the debt had been reduced by her working for him. He got out his book, sucked the end of his pencil and began making calculations.

'Sad to say not very much! If you'd worked for me longer, it might've been better. As it is, what with the added interest while I was laid up – which we'll call compensation for injuries sustained – I'd say you've probably increased what you owe me by about five pounds, sixteen shillings and sixpence.'

'*What?*' Dolly gasped.

'You surely didn't think you'd get off scot-free, just running off like that over an innocent little cuddle.'

'Innocent?'

'We'll call it a straight five quid. Does that sound fair? Just keep up with your regular payments and we can discuss the matter another time. There's allus ways and means of settling.' Then he gave one of his leering winks and waddled off to make someone else's life a misery.

Dolly and Sam were married in September 1928, the moment she turned eighteen. She made herself a dress in white embroidered muslin, which showed off her neat figure to perfection and after a short ceremony at the chapel they invited a few friends in for tea. After the expense of the celebrations and buying a bed for them to share, they'd run out of money entirely. They'd moved in with Maisie, as agreed, and, six months later, were still living with her mother in Tully Court.

Not that it mattered to Dolly, not one bit. They'd done their bit of courting on walks down by the canal, or in Seedley Park, spending as little money as possible. As the nights had drawn in and it became too cold to be out, Sam had come round to Tully Court on the pretext of doing the place up a bit, in preparation. They'd given the kitchen and bedrooms several coats of lime wash but managed to find plenty of time for a bit of canoodling in between. He'd sometimes got a bit carried away and asked for more than she was prepared to give, much as she might want to. Then they'd both end up panting like they'd run a mile but Dolly always managed to call a halt before matters got entirely out of hand.

Now that they were happily married there were no restraints on that score but nothing else about their lives had changed. They were still stuck fast in the poverty trap, scraping by on bread and dripping half the time, not forgetting the familiar stewpot. They were still pawning their Sunday coats every Monday morning and getting them back again on a Friday, if they were lucky, still with no furniture in the back bedroom they occupied, other than their bed. Oh, but they were happy as larks so what did anything matter so long as they had each other?

Dolly was utterly content. How could she not be, married to her beloved Sam? He was a good, loving husband and they spent every precious moment they could together. They went to bed early, just so they could be on their own, and on Sundays, the only day of the week they could have a lie in, they would stay in their lovely bed till dinner time if they felt like it.

'Best day's work I ever did was to marry you, Dolly Tomkins. If I'd known you were such a hot little number I'd 've done it years ago.'

Dolly giggled. 'It's hard to imagine that you once professed to be so awkward and shy over this love stuff between us, isn't it?' she giggled.

'I was never shy, you're mixing me up with Matt Thornton.' He was concentrating on peeling off her nightgown so didn't see the troubled expression that came over her face. Matt had been conspicuous by his absence for months, had only agreed to come to their wedding at the very last moment, leaving it to Davey to act as best man. 'Though I hope you never got up to these sort of tricks with him.'

'Course not, the very idea.' And they both burst out laughing.

'Can't imagine Matt with a fast piece like you, Dolly Tomkins – er Clayton, sorry.' And he tucked her into the crook of his arm all the better to kiss her.

'Never. He wouldn't know what to do,' Dolly agreed, though even as she succumbed to Sam's greedy kisses, a part of her felt guilty that they were making fun of an old friend, even one with whom she seemed to be at odds for some reason she couldn't quite fathom. Why Matt didn't approve of her marriage she couldn't imagine, but he didn't, and that was that. So far as Dolly was concerned it was really none of his business. But now wasn't the moment to be thinking about Matt Thornton, not when she was lying naked in her husband's arms, and he such an eager lover.

Excitement was mounting in her and Dolly was drifting into ecstasy when Maisie called up the stairs, her tone irritable. 'Are you two not up yet? I've made yer porridge, it's all ready and waiting.'

Dolly groaned but managed, through her giggles, to shout back that they'd be down in a minute before Sam pulled her under the blankets, and started to make love to her all over again. In the end, as so often before, they forgot to go down at all.

Later in the day when they did finally emerge, Maisie complained that the porridge was ruined, that it was a waste of good food, which they could ill afford.

'Since we've not enough money to go anywhere, nor coal to warm the kitchen, staying in bed saves us, doesn't it?' Dolly said. 'And we can enjoy ourselves at the same time.'

Maisie clammed shut at this, not wishing to consider the implications.

Every other day of the week the house was filled with washing, great piles of it waiting to be pummelled and scrubbed and bleached, then hung steaming on the rack, or on the clothes maiden set up by the fire, taking days to dry.

'I can't feel any warmth from that fire,' Sam would grumble. 'Can't even see it. What sort of place is this for a chap to come home to? Why can't you hang it in the yard?'

'Where it gets speckled with soot, or splattered by kids' footballs? What would my customers have to say if I took their sheets back worse than they were before,' Maisie would tartly respond. 'I have my living to earn same as you, lad. Keeping house, minding childer and doing other folk's washing is all I know.'

That was another thing, which began to grate on Sam's nerves. Most days she would have one or more of her grandchildren to mind, either because they were too young for school, too sick, or she'd picked them up at the end of their school day and was minding them until their mothers collected them. They would screech and fight, demand bread and jam, or for someone to play a game with them or tell them a story. Sometimes Dolly had to agree when Sam said he felt as if he'd come to live in bedlam. There never seemed to be a moment's peace in the little house.

On Fridays, when they all wanted a bath, Dolly and Maisie would have to sit upstairs while Sam took his turn in the tin bathtub in front of the fire. Dolly would much rather have been in the kitchen with her husband, scrubbing his back, pouring hot water over his head, and up to other sorts of mischief, but how could she do that in her mother's house?

And if having her mam around all the time wasn't bad enough, there was also Willy. Dolly would be acutely aware of her brother reading in his room, on the other side of their bedroom wall. And because of his bad health he was such a homebody, forever staying in. On the nights Maisie went out, which was admittedly increasing in number, they'd be breathing a sigh of relief that they were alone at last, when the front door would swing open and Willy would saunter in, cheerfully whistling, to settle with his paper in front of the fire, perfectly oblivious to the agonised glances the two newly-weds exchanged.

Maisie had once walked in and discovered them making love on her peg rug. Dolly didn't think she'd ever live down the embarrassment of that awful moment. And the worst of it was that Mam hadn't batted an eyelid, just headed for the kettle and told them to go and finish whatever they were doing upstairs.

Relations between mother and daughter were growing ever more difficult. Gone were the days of sharing a pot of tea and happily exchanging news and household tips. More often than not the pair didn't speak to each other for days. They took to spending more time in their bedroom, and Dolly would only venture downstairs to make a meal for her husband when she heard the front door slam and knew that Maisie had gone out. She never asked where her mother went, but was simply glad to be free of the sight of her tightly set face and be on their own at last.

Chapter Sixteen

After several months of this, Sam was complaining bitterly over the lack of privacy, the restrictions and embarrassments and how he hated being confined to one back bedroom. 'We need a place of our own. Why are we always so short of money? I turn it over to you regular as clockwork every week, and you're supposed to be saving it up in the Post Office, so why can't we rent our own little house? Where does it all go?'

Dolly too dreamed of having their own place where they'd be free to please themselves, and was equally frustrated and dismayed by the problems of sharing a home with her mother. 'One day,' she'd say. 'We'll have enough next year maybe, only we'll need a deal of money and lots of patience before we can achieve that particular dream.'

'It's not good enough, Dolly.'

'You know I want us to be on our own as much as you do, love. But I have to pay something to Mam every week, quite a bit in actual fact. We'll be rid of all that soon, I'm sure of it.'

'I'm beginning to wonder.' And he'd slam out of the house and go off to the pub for a pint. Later, he'd come home contrite and they'd make love with a new fierceness, Dolly determined to make it up to him after their quarrel.

This then was the crux of the problem. Not only did she not have regular employment but there was still the matter of the debt to settle. She'd explained the problem briefly to Sam, without actually giving figures or amounts. Dolly liked to hold on to some of her pride, and really it was her mam's private business, not his. It hadn't come as any great surprise to Sam as it was a familiar situation in this neighbourhood. Few people in Castlefield didn't owe Nifty Jack money.

Despite their differences, Dolly remained firmly committed to helping Maisie pay it off. She still handed over every spare penny she could to Nifty Jack, tried not to complain about the problems of living in a tiny house with her mother but sometimes, like Sam, she too would be filled with frustration. Dolly still struggled to find decent work, which made it harder for them to save. Yet her mother refused, absolutely, to come clean and tell the truth. Neither Cyril nor any of her mother's other alleged lovers were ever mentioned, so the question of Dolly's unknown father remained unresolved.

–

Harold was proving to be a good husband, cosseting and indulging Aggie's every whim, rubbing her feet if she was tired after a long day at the mill, scrubbing her back in the bath, even going to the expense of having a bathroom installed when she complained about using the old tin bath in front of the fire. On a Sunday, he would bring her breakfast in bed before they went off to chapel, arm in arm. And in Aggie's opinion, she was one of the best dressed women in the congregation.

Although Harold was undoubtedly prudent where money was concerned, expecting her to contribute to the household income, he often gave her a little extra to buy herself something special: a new hat for the Sunday School anniversary, a damask tablecloth, a plant stand or some other item for the house. Oh, indeed, she was surely the most cherished of wives.

She would generously give leftovers from her table, or clothes she no longer had any use for, to Dolly and Maisie, seeing herself as some sort of Lady Bountiful. Today it was a pair of boots but Dolly showed not the slightest bit of gratitude.

'Don't dump yer rubbish on me. I'll buy me own boots, ta very much.'

'Oh, and how will you manage that? Are you working at present?'

'Not right now, no, but I've heard there's chance of a job at the raincoat factory. I'm going round this afternoon.'

'Then wear the boots. If you're properly shod, you will at least *look* respectable.'

'Meaning I'm not?'

Aggie gave a delicate shrug. 'If there's any doubt on the subject, the boots might help. And I don't need them as Harold has bought me a lovely new pair.'

She also took great pleasure in exploiting the difficulties between Maisie and Dolly. She was like a dog worrying a bone, seeming to take pleasure in Dolly's discomfort. 'Have you told Sam yet, about what you got up to in that dreadful place?'

'You know I haven't. And I didn't get up to anything.'

Dolly had meant to tell Sam long before this, of course she had, but somehow the longer she'd left it, the harder it was to pluck up the courage to do so. They had enough on their plate right now, settling into married life. Besides, he'd be sure to ask why she hadn't mentioned it before they were wed, and Dolly knew she'd let herself be easily put off because she was fearful of losing him, too afraid that he wouldn't believe in her innocence, any more than she could believe in Maisie's. Not that she dare admit as much to her sister.

Aggie persisted. 'I don't want any gossip being bruited about. He's going places, is my Harold, climbing the ladder of success and I'm going up with him. We've been looking at houses out in the suburbs, so I'm certainly not having our lives ruined by you. Not at any price. I always knew Mam was no better than she should be. Why else would poor Dad have been so miserable? It breaks my heart to think how she betrayed him.'

'Oh, for goodness sake, Aggie, stop making him out to be some sort of plaster saint.'

'And you're no better. Like mother, like daughter, eh? Folk might start thinking that I'm tarred with the same brush. I shudder to think what Harold would say. He has his reputation to think of, you know.'

'I did nothing. I'm innocent. My situation was nothing like Mam's.'

'I still think it's fishy that the pair of you are being accused of the self-same thing. Bothering with men. I shudder to think of it,' she said, gimlet eyes bright with curiosity. 'Whatever did they ask you to do?'

'Aggie, will you let it drop. I did *nothing*.'

'It's all right for *you*, but what about how it affects *me*? And Sam. It's time you told your own husband what went on, at least. That would be a start.'

'I've told you, Aggie, I'll tell Sam when I'm good and ready and not before.'

The only problem with her own life, so far as Aggie was concerned, was that she still had to work. In her opinion the spinning room was now an uncomfortable place, full of nasty little gossips only too keen to poke fun at the overlooker's wife. They'd switch her machine off when she wasn't looking, give her the worst cotton which was always breaking, fetch hot water for her tea that smelled as if someone had boiled black puddings in it. They really weren't at all nice to her.

And look at what had happened to Betty Deurden, obviously attacked by somebody from that mill. The same thing could happen to her. There were times when Aggie felt extremely vulnerable, which was really quite unfair for a woman in her position. As the overlooker's wife she should be above all of such worries.

'Why can't we move away?' she would ask Harold, as they sat down together at the dining table each evening, right under the front window where they could be observed in all their splendour by anyone passing by as they ate the smoked haddock she'd prepared, or the tasty shepherd's pie.

'Because, my love, we can't quite afford to move, not just yet. But we will soon, I promise, and then we shall start a family and you will be the best of mothers.'

Much to her surprise, Aggie was growing desperate for a child and was tired of taking precautions. She watched mothers in the street with something like envy. Harold had made her go to the Mothers' Clinic and get herself fixed up with the necessary device, unsavoury though it might be, insisting that it was a necessity. They needed to save up a bit longer for the kind of house they both dreamed of. Aggie getting pregnant, he warned, was the last thing they wanted right now. Such folly could condemn her to life in the mill as a working mother forever, as it had so many of her contemporaries.

'So how long will it take? When will we move? How much longer must I wait?' she would constantly ask. 'How long before we try for a child?'

'Very soon,' he'd tell her. 'A year or two, three at the most.'

'What? I'll be old by then.'

'Nonsense, you're only in your early twenties.'

But you will be, she thought, keeping that traitorous calculation silent in her head.

Aggie tried to be patient, and it was true that she enjoyed having money in her purse to spend, food on the table, a bright future to look forward to, and she certainly had no intention of putting any of that at risk. And she wanted Harold to do well so they'd have even more. Moreover, she'd certainly no intention of denying him his rights. That was the best part of their relationship, though lately he'd seemed a bit lacklustre, not quite up to his usual performance or level of enthusiasm. The poor dear was overworked and overtired.

'Are you tired, dear? If so, I blame Nathan Barker. He's turning into a proper slave driver, growing increasingly short tempered, snapping heads off left, right and centre. Have you noticed?'

Harold chewed on the haddock with a meditative expression on his sombre face. 'I reckon we'll pull out of this little dip in trade very soon. Mark my words.'

'But he's changed the pay system from one penny to half-penny a yard, which means we have to work twice as fast to earn the same amount of money. Penalising us for being good workers, that's what he's doing.'

'You can leave the worry of all that to me, Aggie love. Don't let your fish go cold.'

Aggie had the sudden, traitorous thought that it was all right for Harold, swanning around doing a bit of piecing here and there, but for her, working twice as hard was exhausting.

In her view, Nathan Barker's bad mood had something to do with that daughter of his, who'd been nothing but trouble ever since she arrived. If so, then he'd no right to take out his displeasure on innocent folk. Evie Barker was a lazy tart, sneaking off work every five minute and spoiling the record of the entire floor. Aggie resolved to give the girl a piece of her mind if she didn't mend her ways soon. Surely, as the overlooker's wife, she had the right to deal with such matters.

–

Evie had had more than enough. She was thoroughly bored with having to get up early every morning. She hated the cotton dust that choked her lungs, the steaming heat in the spinning room and having to knock off cones, change slubbings or rovings, names and tasks which thoroughly confused and infuriated her. Evie knew that she would never learn to be a spinner, nor did she wish to. The cones or spindles, or whatever they were called, went far too fast and she never wanted to piece another broken thread as long as she lived. Her head felt as if it were bursting, exhausted by the noise and smell, and by the demand upon her to work, work, work. The sooner she was out of the mill, the better. Anything would be better than this.

As if the work wasn't bad enough, the other girls cackled and giggled behind her back, and were always playing tricks on her, sending her for a 'sky hook' or 'a long wait'. She'd thought at first that they meant *weight* and had stood about for ages in the rain in the mill yard while Ned, the tenter, had pretended to look for one, before realising she'd been had. She hadn't gone back inside though. Soaking wet through, she'd stormed off home and sent the maids rushing to run her a hot bath. Clara had been most sympathetic.

'Poor darling, I can't imagine what has got into Nathan to make you work like a common mill girl. He really isn't himself at the moment. But do try and pander to him, sweetie, just for a little while. Perhaps, if you make a show of learning these mysterious tasks which the mill girls perform so easily, he'll move you into the office, then at least you could wear a pretty skirt and blouse.'

'Oh, Mumsie, will you shut up!' Evie had felt so tired and wet and frustrated that she'd actually burst into tears, which wasn't like her at all.

Her father, when he'd got home from work that night, had taken her to task for running out on the job. 'If you do that again, you'll be sacked, same as anyone else would be.'

'Good!'

'You won't think so when you've no money left in your pocket. No work, no allowance. It's as simple as that.' And he'd stalked back to his study, without even giving her the opportunity to flounce off upstairs in a huff.

If she'd managed to save any money of her own, or found a place to go, she'd have left long before this. But she was trapped, for the moment at least. And then one morning, just a few days later, something happened which was to change everything. She bumped into an old acquaintance.

'Why, Sam Clayton, fancy seeing you again.'

'I work here.'

'Well, of course you do. I'd quite forgotten.'

'I must say I was surprised to hear you'd joined the work force, Evie. No doubt it's only temporary, and you'll be off on your travels again soon.'

'Oh, no,' Evie lied, offering her most bewitching smile. 'I intend to learn the ropes from Pops, as is only right and proper, from the factory floor right up to the gaffer's office. Isn't that what you call it? The mill will be mine one day, after all, so I need to understand everything about it. No doubt we'll be seeing quite a lot of each other in the future, wouldn't you say, Sam?'

Things could be looking up, Evie thought. Leaning against the wall she folded her arms, nicely lifting her breasts as she did so, and smiled up at Sam. 'I was thinking of calling in Dot's cafe for a cuppa before I went home. Care to join me?'

Sam was trying not to stare at her cleavage, easily visible as several buttons of her blouse were open at the neck. Unlike the other girls, Evie always took off her work overall before leaving the premises and he could see the slender line of her throat and the ripe fullness of her pert breasts. Her lovely face seemed to glow, her fair hair in its chic bob enticingly ruffled by a playful breeze, and those pale, blue eyes seemed to contrive an innocent fragility, somehow imploring protection and promising unexplored pleasures, all at the same time.

'You're looking tired,' she told him, as later they sipped their tea in the cafe. 'Married life not agreeing with you then, or are you not sleeping much?' She chuckled, and took great pleasure in seeing him flinch.

'Dolly and me are having a few problems at the moment. Nothing we can't sort out though.' His mind turned to their latest row the previous night. He'd wanted to make love and she had refused because he stank of beer and had woken her mother up when he'd stumbled upstairs.

'How will we ever get a place of our own if you waste good money on booze,' she'd flung the accusation at him and he'd flung one back. 'It might help if we weren't saddled with your bloody mother's debts.'

That had done it. Despite the two women hardly exchanging a civil word between them, Dolly wouldn't hear a word against Maisie from anyone, not even Aggie. She'd spent the night curled up on the clippy rug in front of the fire and had been even more furious with him this morning because he'd let her.

'Why didn't you come downstairs and ask me to come back to bed?'

'Because you'd left it of your own free will, and I assumed you would return under your own steam.'

'Why won't men ever apologise?'

'Because we're never wrong,' he'd laughed, and she'd thrown something at him as he went out the door, something that smashed against the cracked wood, but he'd made good his escape, not even pausing to find out what it was.

But the argument had upset him. Some of his misery must have been evident in his face now for Evie put out a hand and gave his a little squeeze. 'Oh dear, I'm sorry to hear that. Well, if there's anything I can do, you've only to say the word.'

'Aye, thanks.' He stared down at her hand, one finger rubbing gently against his thumb. He couldn't remember the last time Dolly had caressed him so softly.

Evie cast him a sultry glance from beneath her lashes but Sam didn't notice as he was staring gloomily into his tea, which he'd quite forgotten to drink. 'I can't invite you home, I'm afraid, as I'm currently living with Papa and Mumsie, although that is a situation which might change, in time. I mean to get a place of my own soon.' She allowed a moment's pause; sufficient to be sure that she had his full attention. 'But I still have my little car, of course.'

Sam looked up then and met the open invitation in her eyes. 'Aye,' he said, after a moment. 'I remember.'

He felt so randy after she'd gone that when he saw Myra Johnson swinging along the road with her undulating walk, plainly aware of his gaze following her, he fell into step beside her. 'How are you then, Myra?'

'All the better for seeing you, Sam boy.' She batted her eyelashes up at him. 'Fancy a swift half in the Navigation?'

'Why not?' They followed this with several chasers and afterwards she was more than willing to satisfy the craving that Evie had ignited, and if Myra Johnson wasn't quite in Evie Barker's league, well, thought Sam, all cats are grey in the dark, are they not?

–

How to deal with the talleyman and stop that crippling debt from utterly ruining their lives occupied Dolly's every waking thought. She'd failed to get the job in the raincoat factory, despite wearing her sister's boots, and came home to find her mother in tears. 'What is it? What's wrong now?'

'Nifty Jack came round. He says you've one week left to get the rest of the money or he'll throw us out of the house. He says he'll take me to court and see us both in jail for debt.'

'Huh, don't listen to his threats. People don't get incarcerated for debt, not these days. At least I hope not. I've certainly no intention of pandering to his nasty little perversions, even if you do. Not while I live and breathe.'

'Oh, our Dolly, we have to talk, you and me. I'm sorry about all of this, but it isn't what you think. Let me try to explain.'

'Will you tell me who my father is?'

'No, love, I can't do that. But I want to explain that I'm not what you think I am, not a – a loose woman as Nifty claims.'

Dolly shook her head. 'If you won't tell me who my father is then I don't want to hear. There have been too many lies told already. You should have come up with some explanations before this. You should have told me the *whole truth*!'

Dolly managed to hold him off by paying him every brass farthing she possessed, even the bit of money she'd saved up in the post office for her and Sam to put down on a place of their own. She strived to eat less, living on starvation rations, tried to appeal to his better nature but he didn't have one, and the debt continued to grow. Time and again Nifty would offer her an alternative way to wipe the slate clean.

'Yer husband'll never know. I'll not tell him.'

'Leave me alone, you dirty old man.'

Willy finally left home, getting himself wed to a lovely girl called Joan, every bit as quiet as himself. They'd got to know each other at the mill, since he never went out anywhere. They'd not a penny between them but he happily moved in with Joan and her widowed mother. This meant that there was even less money coming in to Tully Court, which put more of a strain on Sam.

Dolly knew that he was reaching the end of his tether. He worked every hour God sent and was exhausted by the worry of it all, as was she. They'd spend hours talking over the problem, desperately seeking a way out. Sadly, it was true what the old wives said: 'When money goes out the door, love flies out the window.' The old intimacy they'd once enjoyed, now seemed to be a thing of the past. There were too many nights when Sam simply turned his back on her, claiming he was too tired. Or he'd stop off at the pub and not come home till she was fast asleep, or at least pretending to be.

When one evening she begged him not to go out, he turned on her, his face dark with anger. 'What am I supposed to do, spend my life cooped up in this bedroom, or sitting listening to the silence between you and your mam? No thank you. I never imagined I was taking on such a burden when I wed you, Dolly Tomkins.'

'I know, love, and we must try to find some way to be rid of it, to get that flipping talleyman off our backs.'

'It isn't even your problem, not really. It's your mam's, left over from Calvin, who wasn't even your proper dad. It doesn't seem fair.'

'Are you saying I should leave her to pay it off? Because despite our differences, I'm not prepared to simply walk away and leave her at the mercy of Nifty Jack. She's still my mam, after all.'

The difficult situation with Sam didn't help relations between herself and Maisie either, which remained cool and distant. It broke Dolly's heart that they should have come to this. She still loved her mother, with all her heart, even if she couldn't quite bring herself to forgive her for this pickle they were in.

'I'm off to the pub, where at least the company is more cheerful.'

And off he went, leaving Dolly to worry over the disastrous affect the debt was having upon her marriage. When would they ever be able to afford a home of their own, let alone children?

The minute Sam stormed off Dolly went straight downstairs and accused Maisie of driving them apart. 'He's gone off to the pub again, so this is another man you've driven to drink, as you did Calvin.' Tears were spurting, running down her face.

'Nay lass, don't say such things. I never did anything of the sort.'

'I don't know what to believe any more, or who to trust.' Dolly longed to throw herself in her mother's arms and be comforted, as she had as a child. But she wasn't a child any more, and Maisie wasn't the mother she'd imagined her to be.

'If you want to think badly of me and believe Nifty Jack's lies, that I've slept with half of Castlefield, there's no way I can stop you.'

'All you have to do is tell me who my father is. That's not too much to ask, surely?'

'You deserve an answer, love, and I'm sorry that I can't give you one. I promised I'd never tell, and I've kept me word.'

'And keeping your word to this man, whoever he is, is more important than your own daughter's needs, is it?'

'It's not like that. He's not an easy man to cross.'

Dolly began to feel sick. Oh, God, then it must be Nifty Jack, after all. *If the talleyman was her father and yet he'd tried to...* Why would he do such a thing with his own daughter? Unless he knew and didn't care, being more corrupt than she had appreciated! Lord she was going to throw up.

'Can't we at least be friends?' Maisie sobbed.

But Dolly had fled upstairs.

Later, after she'd allowed herself a quiet sob into her pillow, had washed her face in cold water and was calmer, she remembered that Nifty had once said that Maisie had actually refused him. Now why would he say such a thing if it weren't true? There was nothing Nifty Jack loved better than to brag about his conquests. He wanted Dolly *because* Maisie had refused him. It was his way of taking revenge. A tide of relief flooded through her. If that was true, then she was getting herself into a state over nothing. She'd been fretting unnecessarily. It wasn't him. She was safe. But if Nifty Jack wasn't her father, then who was? And why wouldn't her mother tell?

–

That night Maisie sat up in bed scribbling a note and, despite it being short, it took her hours to work out just what to say, then even longer to rewrite it in the kind of careful, round letters a child might write. When she was finally done, she suffered a sleepless night trying to decide whether she had the courage to deliver it. She certainly dare not risk entrusting it to the post. But how could she ignore her own child's suffering? Maisie had never expected Dolly to even find out. She'd never forgive Aggie for that piece of mischief. But something had to be done. Her entire life seemed to be unravelling before her eyes.

She slid the envelope through the letterbox in the green painted front door just as the factory hooter sounded, calling the operatives to a new day's work.

Clara spotted the envelope on the mat as she came down to breakfast early that morning and placed it on the silver tray kept on the hall table where Nathan would look for his letters when he came down later.

But something about the round childish handwriting arrested her attention. Could it be from one of those young, uneducated mill girls? She was in no way ignorant of her husband's philandering over the years, for all she'd studiously turned a blind eye in order to avoid humiliation. But a letter from one of those flighty little madams being delivered to her house was rather too much to bear. Quite outrageous! What would he ask of her next?

She was still staring at the envelope in her hand, wondering who it was from and what she should do when she heard his step upon the stair. Without making any conscious decision to do so, Clara slid the missive into her pocket and turned to greet her husband, her face a wreath of smiles.

'Shall I pour you a cup of coffee darling? Kippers this morning, your favourite.'

Chapter Seventeen

A day or two later, Dolly arrived home following yet another fruitless day pounding the pavements seeking work, to find her mam standing on the pavement weeping. Their goods and chattels were all being carried out and put on a handcart by two disreputable looking men.

'Here, what's going on? What's all this?'

'Nothing to do with us, ask Nifty Jack.' They went back inside and brought out the big bed, hers and Sam's, the one thing they possessed in the entire world and which had taken them months to save up for.

'You can't take that,' Dolly cried.

'Watch us.'

Dolly ran straight round to Nifty Jack's and hammered on his door. He took his time opening it but finally stood solid and foursquare on his doorstep, arms folded, and smiled his sickly smile at her. 'What can I do for you, lass? Is there a problem?'

'Yes, there's a problem. You've put the screws on us again, haven't you? First bumping up our debt by five whole pounds, and then giving us no time to pay the extra off. We've not even anything worth pinching.'

'Then you'll not miss it much, will you? I hope you haven't come armed. I don't care for clients setting about me with shovels or any other household goods for that matter, which you Tomkins lot seem fond of doing.'

'I'd like to—'

'Don't say it lass. Don't say anything you might regret later. I'm sure we can find some way for you to settle this loan which has become such a burden to you.' He cocked one bushy eyebrow at her. 'Have you given the matter any thought?'

'You're the nastiest piece of work that ever drew breath. When you were born, the midwife should've thrown you away with the bathwater, you evil—'

'Careful, young Dolly, I've warned you before to watch that sharp wit of yours. It's a dangerous weapon.'

'I understand your little game but you're wasting your time. I'll do nothing of that sort with the likes of you, no matter what pressures you bring to bear. Besides the fact I want to vomit just at the thought of it, I'm a married woman, in case you've forgotten.'

'There are ways and means of keeping a husband in ignorance. The housekeeper's job is still open, for instance. Or I could call at yours when he's at work or in the pub. What do you reckon?'

'That you put your fat head in a bucket and forget to take it out.'

'Dear me, that's not very friendly, nor very constructive. I'll give you a month to come up with a more sensible solution. All you have to do to wipe the slate clean is to be nice to me, Dolly, as I've been at pains to explain. In the meantime, if you want your stuff back – like I say – yer old job is still available. Take it or leave it, it's up to you.' Then he shut the door in her face.

–

'Are we supposed to sleep without a bed now?' Dolly had never seen Sam so angry. Gone was the placid, easy-going man that she loved. Maisie hadn't moved from the orange box where she'd parked herself after all her furniture had been carted away. She hadn't shed a tear either, just sat staring numbly into space. Dolly was feeling pretty numb herself and Sam ranting on at her didn't help. 'Why is he doing this? We're already paying him every penny we can spare, and plenty we can't, so why has he got it in for you?'

'You know why! I wouldn't let him play his nasty games on me and I belted him and ran away. He hates to lose but I wouldn't let that scumbag anywhere near me.'

'Aye, well, you'd better not. Things are different now,' Sam reminded her, pacing the floor of the empty kitchen like a caged lion, his face dark as thunder. 'He'd surely not try and make a cuckold out of me. If that's what he's threatening, I'll go and sort him out right now.' He set off for the door but Dolly grabbed his arm, dragging him to a halt.

'I've already spoken to him and he's agreed to return all our stuff. Only there's a condition.'

'Which is?'

Dolly swallowed then attempted a careless shrug. 'He's still in need of a housekeeper, so he wants me to go on working for him.'

'Not bloody likely.'

'It would only be for a few hours a week and I wouldn't be living in, not like before. You're right; things are different now that we're wed. He'd not be so stupid as to risk trying it on again, not knowing how you'd beat him to a pulp if he did.' She cast Sam a sideways glance, hoping it had been jealousy that had created that violent reaction, and not hurt pride. 'It would be one way of paying off this dratted loan. What do you say?'

'Every instinct tells me that I don't want you anywhere near that nasty piece of work, only...' They both looked across at Maisie, still seated on the orange box, arms wrapped about herself, rocking back and forth. 'We can't go on like this. You have to persuade him to loosen this vice-like grip he has on us, or we'll not survive. I didn't expect to have to deal with this.'

'Oh, Sam, I'm really sorry and know what I'm asking.' She gave a little sob and fell into his arms, then he was nuzzling into her neck and the next minute half carried her upstairs. Pushing her down onto the clippy rug where the bed should be, he made love to her with an urgency she hadn't known for a long time, as if he needed to reclaim her and prove that she still belonged to him. It was particularly romantic and felt so good that he still wanted her. Everything would be fine if Sam did love her as he surely did. This whole business had just upset him as much as it had her. But he was right, a solution had to be found to make Nifty Jack back off.

—

Matt offered to lend Dolly money. She could hardly believe it since they hadn't spoken in an age. The memory of his disapproving words about her imminent marriage was still a nasty taste in her mouth. 'I don't need any charity, ta very much,' she told him, holding on to her pride.

'And I'm not offering any. I don't have much to give in any case, but I heard you were in trouble and thought maybe I could help. I'm working in the timber yard, doing well.'

He looked different somehow, as if he'd filled out, grown more muscle. The fact he wasn't wearing a suit half a size too small might have improved his looks considerably. Dressed in slacks and an open-necked blue shirt with the sleeves rolled up, for once Matt Thornton looked almost presentable, a strong man to be reckoned with. He ran his fingers through dark brown curls, ruffling them more than the brisk breeze, which came off the canal as they stood watching the timber being loaded onto barges. Dolly had a sudden urge to tidy them for him and turned quickly away, pressing her lips tightly together for a moment while she sought the right words.

'We might be in a bit of bother at the moment but it's only temporary. I'm in the process of sorting it all out, so you don't need to worry.'

'*You're* sorting it all out. Sam not being much help then? Why does that not surprise me?'

'Of course he's helping. I've no complaints.'

'I'm relieved to hear it.' He sounded far from convinced.

'He is, I tell you.'

'It can't be much fun having no furniture. Your poor mam must be going demented.'

'I've told you we're coping. I've been to see Nifty and he's agreed to let us have our stuff back, giving us a bit more time to pay.' She made no mention of the conditions attached.

They stood for a while staring out into space, not seeing the derricks as they swung containers on board, not hearing the shouts of the men. She felt oddly comforted by his quiet concern. Dolly realised that she'd missed having him around as a friend to turn to, even to chat to in a gossipy way, or share a bag of chips with. They'd always been friends for as long as she could remember. It had hurt that he'd turned away from her for no reason.

Yet she could kick herself for giving the impression Sam wasn't helping, even if there was some truth in that. He never seemed prepared to talk the matter through with her, always going off in a temper, escaping to the pub, saying it was her fault they were in this pickle, which was true in a way. It was her mam's debt, Maisie's responsibility really. But how could she walk away and leave her mother with this burden round her neck? It would kill her.

Matt stirred himself, almost with reluctance. 'Right then, I'd best be getting back to work. Just remember that I offered, Dolly. You know where to find me, if you ever need me.'

'I don't imagine I will, but thanks anyway.' She kept her voice deliberately cool, although not unfriendly. Really Matt had no right to imply that Sam wasn't looking after her properly. None of this was Sam's fault, and wasn't he the best husband in the world? He absolutely adored her, as she knew.

By the end of the month Dolly was back working for Nifty Jack. She went two mornings a week to clean house for him, and took him round a meal each evening, which she prepared in her own home. In addition, Maisie did all his washing and ironing, on top of all she did for her own family. And neither of them were paid a penny for the work they did, beyond the cost of the food or washing soda. They were his slaves. Dolly kept reassuring herself that it was only temporary, till they'd worked off the debt, and at least they had their bits and pieces back: the table and chairs, pots and pans, their precious beds and blankets, so they could at least live in a modicum of comfort.

But somehow or other she had to get rid of that debt completely.

A change of job was the answer but how to find one, that was the problem. Whenever Aggie came to visit, and entertained them with the latest tidbits of mill gossip, Dolly couldn't help being smitten with jealousy, not for her sister's comfortable marriage with dull old Harold Entwistle, but the fact that she had a good job, as did Nathan Barker's daughter, apparently. Dolly would have given her eye teeth to change places with Evie Barker yet, perversely, neither of these two girls actually wanted or truly needed the work, while she ached for the chance. Sadly she saw little hope of getting her old job back. Her days as a spinner were over.

Never had she felt so low. Depression swamped her and for days she barely left her bed, let alone her bedroom, much to Sam's annoyance.

'It's no good feeling sorry for yourself. A sickly, moping wife on top of everything else is no use to me.'

He was right, Dolly thought. She really didn't know why he put up with her.

–

Sam was sitting in Evie's car wondering if he'd strike lucky this time. It was true that things had grown a little easier between himself and Dolly since she'd gone back to work for Nifty Jack. At least their furniture had been returned and Nifty didn't come knocking on the door quite so often. But the situation was still difficult, not a satisfactory start to married life, and the last thing he'd expected. Despite the fact he was fond of Dolly, he felt resentful of her obsession with this debt. He felt cheated in a way.

Sam had only taken her on to get his own back on Aggie, then somehow he'd found himself offering to wed her. He hadn't minded at first as they seemed to be getting on all right, and she was a nice bit of stuff was Dolly. But he'd never expected anything of this sort. He enjoyed a bet now and then, had suffered a few close shaves with bookies himself, but preferred not to get involved with nasty money sharks of the Nifty Jack variety. Too dangerous by far. Now look at him, up to his neck in trouble of someone else's making. It was damned unfair.

Their chance of a good life together had been ruined by the legacy of Calvin Tomkins, and, sorry as he was for Maisie, a part of him believed that if Dolly could bring herself to walk away from it, then Nifty Jack would stop his malicious campaign and leave well alone. Perhaps for no other reason than a widow like Maisie had no means of paying off such a debt herself, so how could he get it off her? Anyroad, why should Dolly make herself responsible? She wasn't even getting on with her mother and Calvin wasn't her real father. Nor had he been a good stepfather to her. Dolly was too soft and sensitive for her own good, and at what cost? He was the one suffering the most, the one she was neglecting: her own husband. She never gave a thought to him.

'What can I do to make you smile?'

Sam looked into a pair of glistening blue eyes, a sultry mouth smiling wryly up at him, and couldn't help but smile in response. Evie Barker was a tease, but irresistible all the same. It was such a relief to be with a woman who had time to pay him some attention. She was running her fingers through his hair, pulling his hand down over the curve of her breast and Sam felt a surge of hot desire. Seconds later he was kissing her, her mouth warm and eager beneath his, opening for his pleasure. His hands tightened on the slender waist, drawing that slender body close.

Sam didn't usually care for this latest fad for flat-chested beauties but Evie's body had a beauty that owed nothing to fashion.

He began fiddling with the buttons on the back of her frock, dragging it down over her bare shoulders, wanting more. His hand was on her knee, now caressing the inside of her thigh. He'd never felt quite like this before, so powerful, as if he could soar into the clouds and conquer the world. Could this be love? Whatever it was, he scented danger, excitement, a fiery intensity and the indefinable aura of sexual arousal. Nipping, biting, tongues entwined, kissing the beat of a pulse on that glorious sweep of white throat. Her body seemed to flow beneath his, rippling and shuddering to his touch. Groping, grabbing, fondling. He couldn't get enough of her. It shook him how much he wanted her, the pain of his need overwhelming. She pushed him away.

'Sam Clayton, what are you thinking of? A respectable married man shouldn't have his hand up another girl's skirt.'

His breathing was rapid and shallow, as was Evie's, as needy as himself. He was dazed by desire, a shaming movement he couldn't control in his trousers but she was pulling away from him, curling up in the corner of the back seat.

'Evie, I'm sorry, have I hurt you? What have I done?'

'Never apologise for wanting a girl, sweetie. But before we go any further, you should be absolutely certain that this is what you want. It's certainly what *I* want. I adore you, you must know that.' Her arms were back about his neck and she was kissing his chin, his mouth and eyes. 'I can't stop thinking about you. Why do you imagine I stay in this god-forsaken place? You don't imagine that I want to work in my father's mill, do you? I don't leave because I can't resist being near to you. But I want to see you beg for it. Would you do that, sweetie?'

His heart was beating like a hammer in his chest and Sam ached to take her, a quick bang wallop, like he'd done with Myra the previous night, just to slake his lust. He needed her very, very badly. But Evie Barker was different to Myra Johnson and all the other girls who obliged his needs from time to time, and he was suddenly afraid. Her words had sobered him, reminding him who she was, the gaffer's daughter.

If Nathan Barker ever heard about these goings-on he'd be out on his ear, without a job, money, anything. He'd be mincemeat. If he didn't get out of this dratted car soon, he might just slam himself into her and ruin everything. Sam thrust open the door and felt a welcoming blast of cold night air.

'I have to go.' He was out of the car in a trice and Evie made no attempt to stop him, simply sat watching him, a smile playing about that wide, sensual mouth.

'You'll be back, sweetie. And I'll be waiting.'

–

Dolly realised she must put all hope of going back to work at the mill out of her mind for good, and think of something else. All she possessed in the world were a few clothes hanging in her wardrobe and whatever was in her old carpet bag. She'd shoved it under the bed when she'd arrived back home that spring, and there it still was, evidence of her shame. No wonder she hadn't even unpacked it.

Short of something better to do, she did so now, pulling out the tatty frock she'd worn for weeks on end. How she had come to hate it. A faint aroma of stale perfume, dirt and human sweat came with it, a painful reminder of the back streets of Salford, and of Cabbage Lil and her girls. She took out her apron and old boots, now with more holes than a sieve, a brown woollen shawl and a much-darned pair of warm stockings. The stockings were rolled up, as she'd always kept them, but they felt more solid than usual, as if there was something inside. Dolly carefully unrolled them so that she could investigate. There was something tucked within the folds. Dolly stared, unable to believe her eyes. It was a roll of notes, fastened with a clip, and a note from Cabbage Lil.

These are your wages love, for all that cooking and cleaning you did for my girls, and you deserve every penny. We're going to miss you Dolly but don't let me see you back here. Use the money wisely to follow your dreams.

Tears spilled from her eyes and Dolly could hardly see as she counted out the notes. There were six. Large and white, rather grubby and torn, but clearly genuine with the watermark and the King's head and 'pay the bearer Five Pounds' written on each. It felt like a fortune. It *was* a fortune. She was sorely tempted to keep it. However Lil had come by it, Dolly herself had done nothing wrong, nothing to be ashamed of. And this money, this small fortune, represented a new beginning for them all.

But Dolly knew that she couldn't possibly accept it. Even though this wasn't money for favours but for hard graft, for cleaning and cooking, Aggie would almost certainly imply that it was. Oh, but it was so tempting. What should she do?

She ran to the bedroom door, anxious to find Sam and ask for his advice but then slithered to a halt half way down the stairs as a new thought struck her. How could she explain where the money had come from, without running the risk of too many questions about what sort of business, exactly, Cabbage Lil was running which enabled her to pay such excellent wages.

Details of what Lil really was would all come out, details that she'd kept from him and he'd be bound to think the worst. With the way things were between them these days, with him so prickly and tense over this debt, he wouldn't have the patience to listen to the truth. Anyroad, how could he believe in her innocence with this kind of money as evidence?

Dolly crept back to sit on her bed cross-legged, gazing at the notes spread out in a fan on the eiderdown before her while tears ran unchecked down her cheeks. How unfair life was. She'd prayed for a bit of spare cash. Now that she had more money than she'd ever dreamed of, she daren't use it.

Should she risk giving it to Nifty Jack off what they owed? That seemed to be the obvious solution. Except that it would clear little more than half the debt, in no way give them a clean slate. It would of course reduce the weekly payments and cut down on the relentless growth of interest but he too might be curious about where she'd got it from and start asking awkward questions.

Oh, what a tangle! If only she'd listened to Aggie and not Lil, she would have confessed everything to Sam right at the start, and wouldn't be in this terrible muddle. She'd believed there were some secrets, which ought to be kept. Now she wasn't so sure. Dolly realised that she'd made herself look guilty just by keeping quiet.

She folded the notes carefully away and then worried about where to hide them. No one must find them until she'd found the opportunity to return them. Certainly not Sam. She was forced to maintain her silence now. What alternative did she have? Dolly put the roll of notes in the only safe place she could think of, back where she'd found them in the rolled up stockings, tucked these under a loose floor board and hoped for the best. She'd go looking for Cabbage Lil first thing tomorrow.

Chapter Eighteen

Evie was delighted with the progress she'd made. She believed Sam Clayton might make an interesting lover, given the right encouragement. And she deserved some excitement in her life, otherwise, how would she survive? She'd never realised before how very grim life could be and found working at the factory a nightmare. Above all else, Evie hated the lavatory in the mill yard. She'd been utterly shocked the first time she'd set eyes on the building, a row of only three privies for sixty women. She'd refused, at first, to even contemplate using it. Aware of Elsie Crabtree sniggering behind her hand, she'd stormed off to her father's office and insisted she use his, a beautifully appointed, mahogany-panelled cloakroom. Her father refused to allow it, was adamant that she must be treated exactly the same as everyone else. Evie had stamped her foot and screamed at him.

'This is an outrage! Have you any idea how much they smell? So revolting, something should be done.'

'A woman comes in to clean them twice a week, what more can I do?'

'Have her come in twice a day. Or build new ones, inside the mill, and at least twice as many.'

Nathan had grunted with annoyance. 'And what do you propose I use for money? Will building extra privies improve my profits? I doubt it. Cross your legs, lass, like the rest, or find yourself a job elsewhere.'

Evie was furious. The way the girls had to wait their turn was a scandal. Some of them, she was quite sure, deliberately took their time, either reading a newspaper in there, smoking a ciggy – as she did too, of course – or up to God knows what mischief. Some of them took so long over this natural function; Harold had started setting his stopwatch on them, counting the minutes they took to relieve themselves. It was all dreadfully undignified. Ever since then, and quite against her father's instructions, whenever he wasn't around she would sneak into his cloakroom and avail herself of these palatial facilities, which surely, as his daughter, she had the right to do?

As she was today, seated on the linen basket where he put soiled towels, happily reading a magazine, smoking her Turkish and devising little plans of escape in her head.

Sam was a sweetie, if not the most exciting lover she'd ever had. But then anyone would be better than nothing in this dull, boring existence, so predictable and so incredibly *tiring*. It flattered her to have him want her, and she loved the smell of grease and oil on him, of his 'muck and sweat' as he called it, which she found titillating. Would she allow him to 'go all the way' soon? She rather thought she might.

Evie was beginning to harbour the dreadful suspicion that she'd missed the boat so far as chances of a good marriage were concerned. She certainly wouldn't find a husband here, in this godforsaken hell-hole, and she'd need to do some fairly radical thinking if she was ever to make good her escape. Even Evie appreciated that her father's benevolence was finally over. He'd pretty well washed his hands of her. Money, that was key. It really didn't matter how she got it but it was a necessity of life. She'd never get away from this dreadful mill otherwise.

In the meantime, there was Sam Clayton to keep her amused. He was clearly nervous of the fact that she was the boss's daughter. But Evie had every hope of him overcoming that particular worry and start to revel in her high status, once his need became too much to bear. The only other problem was that little wife of his. She could tell that he was tempted, but remained loyal and the ties needed to be severed, or at least untangled somewhat. Evie drew hard on her cigarette then flushed the stub down her father's toilet. She needed some sort of wedge to drive the two apart. She knew where Dolly Tomkins, or rather, Dolly Clayton lived, so it shouldn't be too difficult to watch and listen, and see if she could find one.

–

Dolly found Cabbage Lil without any difficulty at all, and her one-time friend was delighted, yet surprised to see her. She gave Dolly a hug and a kiss, her one good eye all bright and merry, then insisted on buying her an Italian ice cream from Luigi's stand. They sat on a wall by the market, each with a licking dish, enjoying this treat in the late summer sunshine.

'So what you doing in this neck of the woods? You should be with that lovely husband of yours. I assume you did manage to drag him down the aisle?'

'Oh yes, though he didn't take much persuading.'

Her face became suddenly quite serious. 'You didn't tell him then, about – you know? Me and my girls?'

Dolly shook her head, but she wasn't smiling either. 'No, I didn't tell him but I almost wish that I had. It doesn't seem right to keep secrets from him.'

'Like I said, some secrets are best not told. You keep mum, girl. Mark my words, honesty is not always the best policy. You shouldn't even be here. Wouldn't do for anyone to spot us together.'

Dolly glanced about, but there was no one around that she recognised. An old woman haggling over the price of some wool, a woman with a child in a pram and a young, smartly dressed girl fingering some lace handkerchiefs on another stall. She shrugged and pulled a small packet from her bag. 'I wanted to return this.'

Cabbage Lil stared at the brown envelope, recognising at once what it was. 'But those are your wages.'

'I worked only to earn my keep, for which I was truly grateful.'

'You did much more than that, chuck.'

'I can't take this money.'

'Why, because they're wages of sin?' Lil's tone was bitter and Dolly felt a sting of shame, as if she were throwing her one-time friend's goodness back in her face.

'No, that's not it at all, at least, not entirely. What I mean is, there's far too much, and how can I accept this money if I can't tell Sam where it came from? He'll never believe I earned this amount of cash honestly. It's too much.'

'It's what you deserve. You were good to my girls and came to be like a daughter to me. No, you keep it lass. Don't tell Sam and use it to some good purpose, like getting that nasty talleyman off your back.'

'Sadly, it's not quite enough for that. He keeps adding interest faster than I can ever repay it.'

'I could get you more. I like a lass with guts and stamina, and you have both in plenty.'

'*No!* For heaven's sake Lil, that's not why I came. I want to give you the money back. It'll create too many problems as it is, and I can manage quite well without it.'

'I don't think you can, love, and no I won't take it back. I want you to use this money to set yourself up in something worthwhile, a little business of your own happen. When you've done that, and been married to that bloke of yours for twenty-five years, with a gaggle of kids at your knee, then you can tell him where it came from, and all about me and my girls. Right? Is that a deal?'

Tears were sliding from the corners of her eyes, stealing down her cheeks. 'Oh, Lil, what can I say?' And then Lil put her arms about her and hugged her like a mother, enveloping Dolly in cheap scent and sweat, not necessarily of the honest sort.

'Now no crying, or you'll set me off too. Just see that you do something good with yer life. That's all I ask. It'd be grand for me to know that. Now get off home and start looking forward, not back. And don't ever come round here again, or I'll give you what for.'

—

When Dolly had gone, after more hugs and kisses and with effusive thanks and protestations of undying gratitude, Cabbage Lil stayed sitting on the wall, drew a great big handkerchief from her skirt pocket and blew her nose hard. She was growing soft in her old age but it felt good to help, particularly someone as lovely and kind as Dolly. She wished her well and the money offset her own sense of guilt for very nearly drawing that innocent little lass into a trade which would have done her no good at all.

'Excuse me, I believe you're Cabbage Lil, and I'm told that you offer accommodation to homeless girls.'

Lil glanced up, startled out of her reverie, quickly swiped the last of the tears from her eyes then narrowed her gaze to study this stranger more closely. 'Who says so?'

'I don't mean to intrude on your private thoughts, but I asked the stallholder over there. I need a bed for the night. Can you offer me one?'

Lil frowned as she regarded the pretty blue costume and neat ankle boots, the navy cloche hat with a flirty feather. 'You don't look the sort to be in desperate need of the kind of bed I can offer. If Stan told you my name, I dare say he made no bones about what I do.'

Evie raised her carefully plucked brows in a parody of shocked surprise. 'Actually, he didn't say a word.' She was deeply intrigued that Dolly should have got herself embroiled with a madam, which was clearly Cabbage Lil's trade. What absolutely spiffing fun! She was almost tempted to join the little harem and try it out for herself. But no, she had other fish to fry, for the moment anyway. Still, it was worth keeping in mind for the future. Evie struggled to sound all contrite and sincere.

'Oh dear, perhaps I've made a mistake. I didn't realise. Thanks anyway. Sorry to have troubled you.' And turning on her well-shod heels, she hunched up her shoulders as if dreadfully upset, and started to walk away.

Lil watched her go with a troubled frown. Something didn't smell right. Why would this woman suddenly appear just as Dolly had departed? Had she made a big mistake in letting on about what she did? No, Stan would have told her anyway, made no bones about the matter. The girl knew right enough. But then why pretend she didn't know, and what did she intend to do with the information? If she meant to hurt Dolly… Unfortunately, Cabbage Lil had no real idea where Dolly lived, or how to contact her. So the poor girl would have to deal with this little problem on her own.

–

Evie was tempted to rush to Sam and tell him what she'd discovered. Wasn't that the perfect solution? He'd fall into her arms once he knew his wife was on the game, which would certainly liven up her rather dull life. He hadn't been near her since their last little fumble in the car, and she was already regretting allowing him to escape so easily. Perhaps she'd teased him for long enough and it was time to reap her reward. She missed him, well, not Sam Clayton himself, exactly, but she was certainly missing the thrill of the chase, the sensual excitement of having a man rampant for her. And sex, of course. Evie couldn't remember the last time she'd shared her bed with a man. It must be months. Life was too boring for words!

But really she needed to be sure of her facts before she told him. Sam Clayton wasn't proving quite so easy to hook as Evie had hoped. He was playing hard to get, perhaps overawed by her status, or else stubbornly loyal to his little Dolly, and she'd no wish to look a fool. What if the woman, this Cabbage Lil, were an aunt or cousin, or some such; what if there was some good reason why Dolly was talking to her. Who knew what sort of riff-raff she was related to, the dregs of society, no doubt. She needed to check that out first.

The next time the threads broke on her frame and she called upon Aggie, who was always ready to fix them for her, which saved her the bother, Evie took the opportunity to have a quick word.

'I saw your Dolly when I was out shopping yesterday afternoon,' she mildly commented.

'Oh, where was that then? Down the market, lazing about?'

'As a matter of fact she was talking to a very odd looking woman. I asked a stallholder about her, and she's apparently called Cabbage Lil. Do you know anything about her? Not a relative, is she?'

The expression on Aggie's face was enough. She went deathly pale and then uncharacteristically snapped at Evie. 'Of course she isn't. The very idea. Anyroad, it's none of your business who our Dolly talks to. She can surely chat to folk if she wants to. There you are, the thread is mended. Time you learned to do this job yourself.' And she stalked off, chin high.

Well, well, well, so the stallholder was right, Evie thought. Aggie's prickly attitude said everything. She was, quite plainly, worried about gossip. But then who'd want a sister for a tart? These people had no idea how to conduct themselves. Class was everything.

–

Aggie was feeling somewhat disillusioned. Her marriage hadn't turned out quite as she'd expected. Harold's spirit of generosity had begun to wane. It all started when she'd ordered new furniture for the second bedroom, secretly tired of waiting to move to the suburbs and hoping to at least be starting a family soon. She'd bought a single bed, wash stand and a pretty flowered rug for the floor. Aggie would have bought a cot but decided that might be tempting fate. She hadn't paid for any of it, of course but when she'd asked Harold to go round to the Co-op and sign the necessary papers so that it could be delivered in the plain van the company used for hire purchase goods, he completely lost his temper.

'Haven't you bought enough new furniture? When are you ever going to be satisfied? You think I'm made of brass?' And much more in the same vein. Harold, Aggie discovered, was turning out to have a mean streak, to be over-cautious and nurture a strong desire to remain close to home and vegetate. She was beginning to fear that Dolly's description of him as an old stick-in-the-mud might be chillingly accurate.

Now that the novelty had worn off, Aggie had discovered that his efforts at love making were nearly always rather clumsy affairs, and quickly over. Before she'd even got warmed up, he'd be spent and lying back on the bed exhausted, like a beached whale. He was certainly nowhere near as exciting as the much-lamented Sam, the man she'd turned down. And where were the promised compensations for her sacrifice? Even the planned move to the suburb had been put off yet again.

'You keep saying we mustn't touch our savings because of the move. When are we moving then? Give me a date to look forward to.'

'How can I move out to the suburbs when my work is here in Castlefield? It doesn't make sense. Be patient, dear. In a few years time it will all be different. We'll be able to afford to take the risk.'

There was a lump of bitter disappointment lodged in her throat. What had she condemned herself to by marrying this man? 'You mean when I'm old and grey. Oh, Harold, don't be such a spoilsport.' She kissed his round, flushed cheek, rubbed herself against him like a cat. 'Clever chap like you could always change his job.'

A bit of wheedling and flattery had generally done the trick in the past, certainly before they were married. Unfortunately, her charms didn't seem to have quite the same appeal now he could enjoy them any night of the week. On this occasion he did take her up to bed where they spent a most satisfactory hour, well, more like half an hour perhaps and Harold got very excited, almost like old times. Even so, he held out for a long time against allowing her to take delivery of the goods.

'Our house is beautifully furnished as it is, the best in the street, so we don't need another thing. We never use the second bedroom anyway.'

'But we might, if it looked decent. We could have guests to stay.'

'I don't want to have strangers staying in my house, Aggie.'

Aggie wriggled closer against him, licking the curl of his ear. 'We might have someone come to stay who isn't a little stranger. Someone permanent.'

'If you mean a baby, I've told you it's too soon. Not yet, Aggie.' And then a moment of panic. 'I hope you are wearing your device, as you should.' It troubled him that he wasn't in control of this aspect of their lives.

'Of course I am, Harold, what do you take me for? Aren't I a good wife to you? Don't I work hard and deserve a few treats now and then? I mean, I'd love an electric washing machine, Harold, and a vacuum cleaner. Doing the housework would be so much easier then, and I wouldn't get too tired for – other things. Wouldn't that be nice? And you know, deep down, that we need a better house, Harold. Come on, love, give us another kiss. Or shall I kiss your little soldier?'

He was shaking with need by the time she was done with him. 'All right, my love, on this occasion I'll go round to the Co-op and sign the papers, let you have what you want. But it's got to stop. Do you understand? We can't go on like this.'

She'd won, this time, but it was getting so much more difficult.

–

Evie decided to wait for Sam at the mill gates and the moment she saw him, fell into step beside him. Armed with this new information, she felt in a strong position, yet still something held her back, an uncertainty about his likely reaction. One minute he had looked as if he was panting for her then backed off remembering his wife. Evie decided that she must judge that possibility with care. And despite Aggie's reaction, did she have sufficient proof about Dolly's connection with this Cabbage Lil woman? Sam Clayton was unlikely to be impressed by the tales of Stan the stallholder, so would it be enough that she'd seen his wife talking to this woman? Evie decided that she must judge her moment with care.

She tucked her arm into his. 'Long time no see. Anyone would think you'd been avoiding me.'

He pushed her arm away, glancing nervously about. 'Behave yourself, Evie. Someone might see.'

'Do you care?'

'Aye, I care. They might tell Dolly, or worse, your dad. Let's just be a bit more discreet, shall we?'

Evie screwed up her delightful nose and giggled. 'Discreet isn't a word I recognise in my vocabulary. Besides, nothing has happened between us yet. Unfortunately! Aren't we simply good friends? Anyway, what makes you imagine I'd go with a chap like you? Maybe you think too highly of yourself, Sam Clayton.' And casting him a withering glance, she swivelled on her heel and walked away. She'd win him round in the end, if she teased and tempted him for long enough. Had she ever failed with a man yet? Never! And even Sam Clayton would be easy meat when he wanted her enough.

Sam stood and watched her go, feeling furious with himself for messing it up yet again, and oddly bereft and wounded. Every time he saw her, he wanted her more. He'd be sorry to upset Dolly but she wasn't his main concern. If he touched her, and Nathan Barker found out, what then? Was he prepared to risk everything to get her, even his own livelihood?

Instead, he headed down Rice Street and knocked on Myra's door. She was out with her fella, her mother explained with a coy glance. This wasn't his day. He treated himself to a consoling pint at the Crown and soon caught the attention of the barmaid. In no time at all they were having it off in the back yard, among the beer barrels. There was always compensation to be found somewhere.

—

Dolly couldn't get Cabbage Lil's suggestion out of her head. Could she do something with this money? Did she have the confidence to set up a business of her own, and what sort would it be? She still hadn't worked out how she would explain the money to Sam but the idea persisted, growing in her mind into all manner of crazy notions. Perhaps it would be best to make some decisions first, get things underway and deal with explanations later. By then Sam might be in a more amenable mood to listen, but what sort of business? If only she could decide what to do for the best.

The very next time she spotted Matt on the quay, she asked him what he thought about her setting herself up in a business of some sort. 'Do you reckon I have the confidence and capability to do something on my own, Matt?' She looked up into those soft brown eyes, patiently waiting for his comments, knowing that she trusted his opinion implicitly.

'Of course you can. No question. I've told you before, Dolly, you can do anything you put your mind to.' He cleared his throat. 'What does Sam think?'

She glanced away, hiding her face beneath the swing of her dark hair. 'Sam doesn't know yet.'

'I see.' A short pause, and then, 'Do you mind my asking you something, Dolly?'

Half fearfully she cast him a sideways glance. 'Depends what it is.'

'Why would you want my opinion? Why ask me?'

'Why shouldn't I ask you? You're one of my oldest friends, aren't you?'

'I hope I always will be your friend. But by rights Sam's the one you should be talking to about setting up in business, not me. I'm not your husband, more's the pity.' Matt gave his self-deprecating smile, not quite so shy as it had once been but every bit as beguiling. Dolly took the full impact of it and felt a strange sort of lurch somewhere deep inside as if a part of her had shifted. She had a sudden urge to reach out and touch him, to lean her head against his shoulder and have him wrap his arms tight about her. The experience shook her, entirely robbing her of speech.

'You are happy with Sam, aren't you, Dolly? I mean, he is good to you, isn't he? I'd be really cut up, if he wasn't.'

'He's wonderful.' Her response was sharp, her eyes filling with a rush of tears so that again she had to turn away to avoid him seeing her distress and confusion.

Matt said, 'I always felt I lost my chance with you by being so awkward and slow. I must have been a bit backward at coming forward when I was a scrap of a lad but you always seemed out of my league. Far too gorgeous to look my way.'

She was flustered now, startled by what he was saying and by her response to it, but then why shouldn't she feel some sort of attraction towards Matt Thornton? He was an attractive man, he had changed and matured quite a lot over the years. But Sam was the man she loved and always would be. She must never forget that. She'd made her bed, as her mam would say, and she must lie in it.

'I've got to go,' she said, and fled.

–

Dolly went next to the corner shop and began to pick Edna's brains about how she'd got started, if it had proved profitable to open and run a shop.

'Profitable? You must joking. I put all me savings into this place when my Bill died,' Edna said. 'It's only rented but I had to pay for the good will and stock. But the chap I bought it off cheated me good and proper.'

'How?'

'He made out there was more stock than there actually was, when half of it were nothing more than dummy packets. I were the dummy, for believing him. I've rent and light and heating to pay, fresh food and stock to buy and what with another mill closing down last week, I'll have even fewer customers coming through t'door to buy sandwiches and pies at dinner time.

'And them what do come in might buy nothing more than half a loaf, ha'p'orth of tea or two ounces of cheese. Not that they have any money to pay for it even then. They pay for everything on t'tick. Worst of it is, if they ever do have any spare cash, they'll spend it at the Co-op, in order to get their divvy. Nay lass, there's no profit in shopkeeping, I can tell you that for nothing. They don't seem to realise that even shopkeepers have to eat. We have money troubles too.'

Dolly decided against running a shop. Instead, she tried her hand at door to door selling.

She set herself up with a display box of cotton reels, darning wool, safety pins, tape and elastic and went round the streets knocking on doors. She didn't sell very many so decided to try standing the market. But then an old soldier came up and accused her of stealing his patch, saying he'd already lost his leg, and was she going to steal his income as well? Dolly fled, gave the box to her mother and vowed to look for some other form of employment.

It was so frustrating. Not the mill, not a shop, not the market. She was running out of ideas. She had all this money and not the first notion how to make good use of it. And then she remembered something Edna had said, about even a shopkeeper having money troubles, and the answer came to her, clear as day. She'd set herself up as a moneylender. She'd take on Nifty Jack at his own game.

Chapter Nineteen

The first thing Dolly did was to use half the money to pay something off the vast sum they owed him. 'Here's fifteen pounds on account,' she told Nifty Jack. 'I'll give you the rest as soon as I have it.'

It was a huge risk to part with such a large amount all at one go, but surely worth it just to see his jaw slacken and his mouth drop open. 'Where'd you get this sort of money from?'

'None of your business! It's honestly come by, which is more than can be said for most of your income.'

'I'll be keeping a closer eye on you in future, girl. You're up to something.'

'Nothing illegal, unlike some folk, so you keep your nose out of my affairs.' Looking at him, Dolly couldn't bear to think that this man had put his grubby hands all over her. The very idea made her want to vomit. She could hardly tolerate being near him and the sooner she no longer needed to act as his housekeeper, the better, even if it was only part-time and he was currently behaving himself.

'I'll be expecting to see a drop in the amount of interest you add on every week. What's more, I'd appreciate it if you'd tot up exactly what remains on the book, since I must have worked quite a bit of it off, as has Mam, with all the washing and ironing she's done for you. You can let me have the details next week.'

Oh, it felt good to be in control at last.

She went back to Edna. 'If you're tight Edna, or if you hear of anyone else who is, I might be able to help out with the odd few bob.'

'Oh, aye, and pigs might fly.'

'No, I'm serious. I've come by a windfall, you might say, and I'd like to use it to set myself up in opposition to Nifty Jack, as a moneylender. An honest one, mind! Is that a crazy idea, do you reckon?'

Now it was Edna's turn to gaze, slack-mouthed, at Dolly. 'I'd say that's the best news I've heard since our Albert left home and got someone else to wash his dirty socks. How can you do that? Where would you come by a stack of money? No, don't tell me, love, as I don't want to know.'

'It was honestly got, Edna, believe me. That's all I can say.'

Edna nodded. 'Fair enough. Well then, if you're serious, I could do with thirty bob to pay one of my suppliers, just to the end of the month. What's yer rate of interest?'

'Oh, I hadn't thought. No, you can have it for nothing, you've been so good to me.'

'No lass, that's no way to do business. It should be a penny in the shilling at least. Nifty Jack charges a penny-halfpenny, two pence if he doesn't like the look of you. If you're going to do it at all, lass, do it right. I'm certainly willing to pay a proper whack for a loan, so long as it's all honest and above board.'

'I promise you that it will be. And if you fall behind with your payments because of problems with the shop, Nifty won't be chasing after your daughter for favours, nor any of his cronies coming round to remove your furniture or stock. We'll just renegotiate the time you need to pay, or the sum you pay each week. How does that sound?'

'Champion.'

–

Edna Crawshaw paid off the thirty bob within the agreed timescale, but then borrowed it again the following month, and the one after that. She said it was making a big difference to her cash flow, just to get her through this sticky patch. Edna also spread the word to those on her tick book, the ones she trusted to pay regular, and Dolly gradually acquired several more clients. In some cases she settled what they owed to Nifty, thereby taking over the debt herself. This did not please him in the slightest.

'What's going on?' he growled, the first time it happened, but Dolly simply smiled and warned him to mind his manners in future, or he'd find himself running out of clients altogether.

'Like hell, I will.'

'I'm giving you a bit of competition, Nifty, and there's not a thing you can do about it.'

'You stay off my patch, if you know what's good for you.'

'Who's going to stop me? Not those scraggy little men you call your henchmen. They'd best not touch me, or I'll be forced to call on all my big brothers. And they won't bother with the monkeys, they'll take it out on the organ grinder. So lay off.'

Nifty Jack was left spluttering with rage. Nobody had ever dared to stand up to him before, not like this, let alone set up in opposition. It was bare-faced cheek. He couldn't believe what was happening, the last thing he'd expected.

He'd thought he was wearing her down, believing that if he piled on enough interest she'd finally cave in and climb into his bed, just for a bit of peace and quiet. It certainly wasn't worth her while trying to save that shaky marriage of hers. He'd seen Sam Clayton in the pub night after night, and once, he could have sworn he saw him in the passenger seat of that fancy car which belonged to Nathan Barker's daughter. Things obviously weren't going well for the two lovebirds, which he'd taken to indicate that he was winning.

Now he jabbed Dolly's shoulder with the stub of one nicotine-stained finger, pushing her back against the wall. 'I'll not have some slip of a girl telling me what to do. I don't know where you've come by this money, but don't think that'll let you off the hook. You still owe me a tidy sum, and would do well to remember that.'

'I paid you extra last week. I'll pay you extra next, and every one after that. I've a nice little income coming in now, so I can afford to. You were quite right Nifty. Money makes money. You and me will have settled our differences in no time, mark my words.'

–

Dolly finally broached the subject of the money with Sam one evening, explaining it away by telling a story as near to the truth as she dare; that she'd been working as maid-companion for an old woman during those months she'd been away. 'I thought she was mean and I was only earning my keep, but then I opened that old bag for the first time since I got home and there it was, all the wages she owed me, all rolled up neat in a clip. Can you believe it?'

He didn't believe it, not entirely. Sam frowned and considered the matter for some long moments in silence. 'This isn't one of your convoluted ways of telling me you did something wrong, is it, Dolly?'

'What, like I pinched it? Do you take me for a thief? Well, ta very much. That's a nice thing for your husband to accuse of, I must say.'

'I didn't accuse you of anything, I was only wondering if you were embroidering the tale, as you so often do. It just seems a bit odd, that this woman, whoever she is, should pay you like that. How much was it?'

This was something Dolly had no wish to tell him. 'A few quid that I earned is all legal and above board. Enough to give me a start.'

'It sounds a bit fishy to me. Was she the one I spoke to? Lily, was it?'

What a memory he had. 'No, that was someone else entirely. Look, aren't you pleased I'm doing well? We're on our way out of this mire, at last. Isn't that something to be happy about?'

'Aye, course it is.'

'Well, give us a kiss then, you daft ha'p'orth.' She always had to ask for a kiss these days, and he somehow lacked enthusiasm when he complied. She'd win him round though, once he saw that things were improving for them.

–

Following her conversation with Evie, Aggie made a few enquiries and soon got wind of her sister's changed fortunes. She came bustling round to check if the rumours were correct. Dolly groaned the moment she saw her. It was obvious Aggie was bursting to have her say about something.

'Go on then,' Dolly said. 'Get it off your chest, why don't you.'

'I reckon you'd best tell me what's going on, our Dolly.' Aggie took off her coat, hanging it with care on the hooks at the bottom of the stairs, set her kid gloves and bag on the table but left her hat in place. It was blue felt with a bunch of purple grapes stuck on the side. 'What are you up to? I've heard you've got a job. Who'd employ you after what you did?'

Dolly was glad that Maisie was out at Nifty Jack's collecting his laundry, and the two sisters could have the kitchen to themselves. 'It's not a job, not as such. I've started my own business.'

Aggie's mouth fell open. 'What sort of business?'

'You'll just have to wait and see, won't you, like everyone else. Or ask your gossipy friends. They seem to keep you well informed.'

Aggie settled herself on one of the stand chairs, fidgeting a little as if to show that she wasn't used to such stark discomfort. 'It's got something to do with that woman, Cabbage Lil, hasn't it? Don't try any of your fancy fairy stories on me because you were seen talking to her on the market the other day. What have you been up to now?'

Dolly felt herself go cold. 'I've not been up to anything. Who's been making up nasty tales about me?'

Aggie gave a disdainful sniff. 'Don't I get a pot of tea? It is customary to offer refreshments to a visitor, or have you lost all your manners?'

Dolly got up and banged the kettle on to the hob, began to clatter about the sink, searching for two clean mugs. 'Go on get on with it. Who saw me?'

'As a matter of fact the information came from an impeccable source,' Aggie said, purring with satisfaction. 'Miss Barker herself saw you, the gaffer's daughter no less.'

'Miss…? Oh, Evie Barker, the girl with the fancy motor who started all our troubles in the first place.' Dolly came back to the table and sank down on to a chair, feeling slightly bemused. What on earth had Evie Barker been doing in that neck of the woods? Surely not her sort of territory at all. 'So you'd believe her, rather than me, your own sister?'

'How would I know what to believe, and isn't our family famous for keeping secrets? Have you told Sam yet? Have you told your husband about this Cabbage Lil, and what you got up to?'

'Oh, put a sock in it, Aggie, why don't you? How many times do I have to tell you that I didn't get up to anything.' Dolly turned away, glad now of the distraction of making tea, which at least kept her hands occupied and stopped them from strangling her sister.

'Mark my words, if you don't tell him soon, someone else will. Happen this Evie Barker.'

'Why would she? She doesn't even know my Sam.'

'Oh, she knows him right enough. Don't they both work at the mill, so how can she not know him? And Sam is never backward at coming forward when there's a pretty woman around. I'd keep an eye on that husband of yours, if I were you.'

'If you've only come to stir up trouble…'

'You should have wed someone nice and safe, and well placed, like my Harold. He never gives me a moment's concern. And he's going up in the world, is Harold.' This no longer seemed to be true, but not for a moment would Aggie admit as much to Dolly.

'So you've told me a thousand times. Pity it isn't with a bang. Well, you may not believe this, Aggie, but I'm on the up and up too, so put that in your pipe and smoke it.'

'And how could you manage to do that with not a penny to call your own?'

'That's where you're wrong. I do have a bit of money, and all honestly earned. So I've set myself up in competition to Nifty Jack as a money lender.'

Aggie's mouth fell open. 'Moneylender? I don't believe it. How can you lend money when you can't pay off your own debts?'

'Not *my* debts but our father's debts, or rather *your* father as you frequently remind me he was.'

Aggie had the grace the flush, since she'd done nothing to help clear them.

'I pay off other folk's smaller debts and then they pay me, week by week and, because of the interest I charge, fair and less than Nifty Jack charges, I make a profit which helps pay more off Mam's. I've cleared quite a bit already and feel confident of being rid of the lot within a couple of years, if I'm lucky.'

Aggie could hardly believe her ears. Having her little sister go up in the world was not part of the plan at all. And the worst of it was, it was so clever. She would never have thought of it herself. She scoured her mind for some way to fight back. 'So what is Sam's reaction to all of this?'

Dolly turned away to warm the teapot, aware that her cheeks were flushing as she recalled the suspicious questions he'd asked when she'd tried to explain, and the many more since, all indicating complete lack of trust. 'He's coming round to the idea,' was all she said, and heard Aggie's grunt of satisfaction.

'Ah, so he smells a rat too, which doesn't surprise me. He'll have his own *private* source of information about what you're really up to: that you're very likely keeping Nifty Jack's bed warm as well as Cabbage Lil's clients. You watch him with that Evie Barker. They're up to no good, mark my words.'

Dolly whirled upon her sister. 'Shut that nasty trap of yours before I shut it for you. If you've nothing decent to say, don't bother coming round here again. I'm sick of your spite and vicious tittle-tattle.'

Whereupon Aggie departed before even the kettle boiled, slamming the door shut behind her.

'I've done it,' Dolly announced to Matt. It was a day or two later and she was on her way back from Martin's Bank where she'd set up an account, strictly for business, and there he was on Potato Wharf, just as if he'd known she'd come by and was waiting for her. 'I've set up in competition to Nifty Jack. I expect you've heard.'

'I have and I'm proud of you. But then I always was. I hope Sam is too.'

She gave a self-conscious little laugh. 'Oh, you know men, he's a bit miffed that I've done something off me own bat. He wanted to know how I came by the money but I'm afraid he didn't believe me when I tried to explain.' She was smiling brightly but the shimmer of light and the way his face blurred told her that her eyes were filling with a rush of tears again. 'He wouldn't properly listen but I earned it honestly. I swear it. I've done nothing – *nothing* wrong, or to be ashamed of.'

Matt nodded, his expression grim. 'I'm sure you haven't. You never would. Not our Dolly.' He put a hand in his pocket, drew out a clean white handkerchief and handed it to her. 'Don't worry, with luck he'll come round. It's his pride, I expect.'

Dolly dried her eyes and blew her nose, feeling foolish now, embarrassed by this show of emotion. 'What a sorry sight I must look.'

'You look wonderful, Dolly, as always.'

She glanced up then and met the full impact of his gaze. His eyes were moving over her face and yet seeming to be riveted on hers, gazing right into the heart of her. He wasn't smiling, didn't say a word, just stood there as if memorising every feature. Deep in the pit of her stomach was a beat of what she could only call excitement. What was happening to her? How could she feel so anguished about Sam's lack of trust, and yet so disturbed and flustered simply from looking at Matt? Always, in the past, she'd felt quite comfortable with him, now she felt anything but. She felt exhilarated, yes that was the word, as if something had changed between them but Dolly wasn't quite sure what, or why. Oh, what a muddle she was in, and what of Sam? Aggie's comments had been typically blunt and cruel, but were they true? 'Do you know if he's...'

'If he's what, Dolly?'

She was going to say, if he's seeing anyone, if he's having an affair, but how could she involve Matt in this mess? Sam was her problem and nobody else's. Besides, why listen to Aggie's nasty gossip? It was all jealousy, retaliation against her success in making some money at last. Aggie had ever been so and Dolly knew that she really shouldn't take her sister's malice so much to heart.

'Nothing. It's not important.' She began to back slowly away, her feet dragging as if reluctant to leave. 'I'd best be off. I'm in a bit of a muddle this morning. As you say, there's nothing to worry about. He'll come round. Thanks for listening.'

'I'm always ready to listen, Dolly. You know that. And Dolly...' He took a step towards her, rested a hand on her shoulder and she felt the reassuring warmth of it flow through her veins.

'What?'

'I'm really pleased you've started something of your own. It's a good thing for a woman to have a bit of independence, and money of her own. You never know when it might come in handy, and if...' He paused, as if considering what more he might say, but apparently thought better of it, thrust both hands back in his pockets and nodded. 'I just wanted to say that.'

'Right, well, thank you. Bye for now, Matt. Nice talking to you.'

'And you, Dolly. Mind how you go.'

She was aware of his eyes following her the full length of the wharf but she didn't turn and wave as she reached the corner and headed off towards Dawson Street Bridge. For some reason she didn't dare.

–

Dolly collected two more clients the following week, both of whom seemed likely to be good payers but despite Matt's consoling words, she was deeply worried about Sam. Could Aggie be right for once? It was true that he had been behaving oddly of late. Did he really know this girl, this Evie Barker? If so, how well did he know her? Dolly struggled to damp down the sour taste of jealousy, telling herself Aggie was feeding her foul gossip simply to upset her. Even so, she had to find out for sure. She couldn't seem to help herself.

The next night when Sam turned to her, clearly in the mood for a bit of a kiss and cuddle, Dolly instinctively turned away.

Sam let out a heavy sigh. 'What is it now?'

'I don't feel like it.'

'You never do these days.'

'That's not true, only I think it's time we had a little chat.' Dolly pushed him off and sat up in bed, a pool of moonlight that should have been romantic but somehow wasn't, encompassing the pair of them.

'I'm surprised you've time to even notice I'm around, you're that busy dashing here, there and everywhere.'

'Oh, Sam, don't start. At least I'm working and making money at last. I think this little business might be our salvation. I'm being careful, going slowly and taking advice.'

'You didn't take my advice not to work for Nifty Jack, so how do I know what you're up to? Everyone is talking about how you've taken over their debts. They seem to think you've won this money on the horses or something but you and me know different, don't we? We know you don't approve of gambling, and that you can't afford to borrow any more money, not with that great big debt hanging round your necks. All this talk of a money roll, wages from some old dear you once worked for is a load of codswallop, isn't it? I don't believe a word.'

'It is not codswallop. And I suppose by *everyone*, you mean Evie Barker. Word is you know her *very* well.' Dolly saw him flinch, an expression of surprise and guilt on his face that he hastily tried to disguise. A wave of sickness hit her. 'So Aggie *was* right. She says you and she are getting quite cosy. Is that the way of it?'

Face flushed scarlet, Sam wagged a furious finger at her. 'Your Aggie is the biggest troublemaker on earth. If you believe her, rather than me, then I reckon you're just trying to offload your own guilty conscience.'

'What?'

'Aye, I know what you're up to. You're working in cahoots with Nifty Jack. Not just as his housekeeper or go-between, but sharing his bed too. It's him what's funded this enterprise, isn't it?'

Dolly gave him a look that should have nailed him to the ground for even entertaining such a thought. 'You think I'd sleep with that nasty piece of work?'

'I don't know what to think, Dolly, or who to trust, except this is not how I imagined it would be between us. You and me started off well, now it's all ruined by money.' Reaching for his clothes he pulled them hastily on, grabbed his cap and scarf and headed for the door. Dolly tried to stop him, leapt out of bed and ran after him, begging him not to go.

'Don't go out, love, not tonight. Let's talk this through sensibly and calmly instead of just shouting at each other and making stupid accusations. Can we do that please?'

'It's too late for talk. You don't need me. You only want my flipping wage packet.' The sound of the door slamming reverberated in her heart.

–

Nifty Jack hadn't taken her threat too seriously, not at first. But it gradually dawned on him what she was up to, and the cheek of it quite robbed him of breath. He'd make that little madam rue the day she'd ever dared to cross swords with the talleyman.

His chance came when he discovered that she'd taken over the debt of the Shuttleworths, a feckless crew if ever there was one. But they had two plump daughters. Pretty and round, sweet and rosy, like cherries ripe for the picking. He'd been encouraging daft Annie Shuttleworth to spend, and not to worry her empty head about interest rates, or ever paying the debt off.

'I'll see you right,' he'd always assured her, whenever she'd whined about the amount she still owed him, which naturally never got any less, rather the reverse. 'Why doesn't your Cherry – sorry, young Sally here – come and do a few jobs for me now and then. I'm short of a housekeeper at the moment, since my last one upped and left.'

Annie Shuttleworth wasn't half so stupid as he imagined, well aware of who that housekeeper had been, and the goings on which had taken place at his house in the past. She was also most protective of her precious daughters. She went at once to see Dolly and asked for her help.

'You must do something or that nasty piece of shite will do to our Sal what he tried to do to you.'

'Nay, Annie, we'll not let happen, I promise you.' Dolly went round to Nifty's that very night and paid the woman's debt off with a crisp, new five pound note. 'Keep the change but stay away from Annie's house in future. She's not of the brightest, but she's pure gold and loves them daughters of hers to bits, so you can keep your mucky hands of them. Do I make myself clear?'

Dolly thought she'd won because he made no comment, simply looked at her calmly, unmoved and unprotesting. Two nights later, a frantic Annie Shuttleworth came hammering on her door. 'He's done it, he has. He grabbed her on her way home from work, like that other girl, Betty Deurden. It was dark but I swear it was him, it must have been, the nasty, no good…'

The rest of her words were lost in an incoherent babble of tears and recriminations but Dolly got the message, loud and clear. Nifty was making it perfectly clear by this latest assault that he was still in charge. He was still the one with the power and she'd best watch her step.

Chapter Twenty

Sam was waiting for Evie, not at the mill gates where he might be seen by Aggie or Harold, or any of the other girls who knew Dolly, but round the corner in the ginnel. He couldn't help himself. Didn't he deserve a warm, loving woman? Not that he had ever been short of women before he married, but this one was a cut above the rest and a challenge he had to conquer. He'd no idea whether the accusations he'd thrown at Dolly were justified or not. He might have been a touch hasty accusing her of sleeping with Nifty Jack, when he knew she loathed him with a venom, but she must be working hand in glove with him to have all that money. Anyroad, he was angry with her. She'd scarcely been in the house lately and there was something she wasn't telling him, he could sense it, smell it on her.

She'd started this money lending business and he was the last to know. Now why was that, if it was all perfectly innocent? He'd handed over his share of the housekeeping regular as clockwork, most of it going to pay the flaming talleyman. What did she do with the rest? Could he trust her, or did she want his blood as well, not to mention shaming him in front of his mates? She'd not get another penny out of him. He had his pride and his feelings, and all she could think of these days was money.

'Were you waiting for me?'

And Evie was looking as beautiful and tempting as ever. Sam cleared his throat, lost for words now that she was actually standing before him. She took hold of his arm and the warmth of her body pressed up close against him. She didn't smell of oily cotton waste as many of the other girls did, but of some flowery perfume Sam couldn't identify.

'I'm glad you came,' she whispered. 'I've been so lonely without you this last week. Where shall we go, Seedley Park or a spin in my trusty motor? Oh, do say yes, Sam. I'm desperate for you, sweetie.'

Just the pressure of her slender thigh against his was making him ache with need. He lifted the hem of her frock, sliding his fingers under the lacy edge of her cami-knickers and she didn't protest. He could take her here and now in this back alley if he'd a mind. Then, as luck would have it, he spotted Aggie walking by with a crowd of girls on the opposite side of the street and he quickly ducked into a doorway, pulling Evie with him, fearful they might be seen.

Evie snuggled up against him, wrapping her arms about his waist beneath his rough fustian coat, tugging at his shirt and seeking the warmth of his flesh. 'This is more like it. I've never done it in a back alley before but why not? I'm all for a little originality. Could we balance on a dustbin do you reckon?'

'Be serious, Evie, this isn't the moment for jokes, nor the place for a girl like you.' Just seeing Aggie walk by had set his mind in a whirl. She'd been his girlfriend for as long as he could remember, the one he'd fully expected to marry one day. Yet she'd gone and chosen po-faced Harold instead, no doubt for his money. So why did he still fancy her when he was about to have his wicked way with sexy Evie Barker, the gaffer's daughter? If he had any choice in the matter he'd much rather be up an alley with Aggie, not this little tart, classy though she may be.

'I understand that you loved your little wife. Poor Sam. She doesn't at all appreciate you, or why would she go with other men?'

Sam blinked, dragging his attention away from Aggie's swaying hips and pert backside as she vanished down the road, scenting something not quite right in Evie's last remark. 'Other men, what are you talking about?'

Evie smiled with false sympathy trying to judge his reaction. 'Oh dear, what have I done? Forget I spoke. Of course, she may have stopped and I shouldn't have said anything. I could be entirely wrong now.' She began to walk away, quite slowly so that he had no trouble at all in catching her up.

He grabbed hold of her arm and yanked her round to face him. 'What *other men*? For God's sake, Evie, you can't say such a thing and simply walk away. Tell me what's going on.'

She told the whole sordid tale, or at least her version of it. All about how she'd happened to be close, quite by chance, and saw Dolly talking to that strange looking woman she was apparently working with, who made women available for men's needs. 'It was perfectly obvious who she was talking to just by looking at her. But once Dolly was safely out of the way, to make sure I checked with a nearby stallholder I then approached that woman. We had a small chat and I asked for a bed for the night, feeling the need to check up on her. She said that she didn't have the kind of beds on offer that would be suitable for a decent girl like me.'

'You're lying! If you're making this up just to get your own back on me in some way, I'll have none of it. Dolly may be obstinately independent but she'd never sink so low.' Like most men who casually took their pleasure with many women, Sam was not in favour of his wife enjoying similar freedom.

Her revelation, rather than making him hate a betraying wife and decide he might as well do likewise, didn't seem to be having that effect. He was practically defending her, insisting Dolly was a decent girl that he'd known all his life and she would never do anything so cheap and nasty.

Evie pressed her hand to her lips and attempted a whimper. 'It's very hurtful to accuse me of telling lies. It's true that I do fancy you like crazy, and I'll admit that I can't get you out of my head. But if you love Dolly more I'd give you up, I swear I would.' She squeezed a tear, slanted a sideways glance up at him, hoping he would be convinced by this show of her contrition.

But Evie was beginning to wonder if he was worth the winning. These facts were meant to excite him, not put him off. 'I'm sorry, Sam, but I'd say that was where Dolly spent those missing months, doing tricks for Cabbage Lil, which was apparently her name. If you don't believe me, ask her and see what she has to say.'

—

'Who is Cabbage Lil?'

Dolly felt the blood drain from her cheeks and a wave of nausea hit the pit of her stomach. She'd been boiling some milk for their bedtime drink when Sam burst in upon them like a whirlwind, eyes blazing, every fibre of his being poised for a fight. For an instant, Dolly had felt cold fear, and then remembered that this wasn't Calvin, this was her Sam who, for all his faults, would never hurt her. But he might leave her, and then where would she be? Hadn't Aggie warned her that this moment would come? Shouldn't she have been prepared for it, have avoided it by coming clean from the start?

'Here's your Ovaltine, Mam, take it up to bed, if you please. I think Sam and me need to talk.'

Maisie cast a sympathetic glance across at her son-in-law, and reaching out, gently squeezed his hand. 'While you're talking, lad, put in a word for me, will you? Evenings with my daughter are getting so quiet I might as well not be here for all the notice she takes of me.'

'Mam, not now, please. Sam and me need some privacy. Go to bed.'

'Aye, course you do. Good night, lad. Good night, love. God bless.'

Dolly did not respond. She sat at the table, all her emotions buttoned up tight, but the moment her mother had gone, words began to bubble out of her. She started with how she had run away following Nifty Jack's attack. She told Sam of the nights in flea-bitten, cockroach-infested lodgings, how she'd been footsore and hungry on the streets, eating out of rubbish bins. She spoke about the old folk and starving families she'd met along the way, many of them screwed by Nifty Jack too, sparing him none of the details. And finally how Cabbage Lil had found and saved her.

'She was my salvation. I'd have starved, otherwise, or been frozen to death with the cold.'

Dolly glanced up at Sam through her lashes and waited for him to say how glad he was that she had survived. But he didn't say a word. He wasn't even looking at her. She hoped and prayed that perhaps he was too moved by her tale to know how to react, appalled, as she had been, by the evidence of human misery she was confronted with on a daily basis. 'Isn't it dreadful that some people have to live like that all the time? Makes you realise how lucky we really are, doesn't it?' she prompted.

When still he made no comment, she hurried on and told him the rest, how she had worked as a maid and general dogs-body for the working girls, and then told how, in the depths of her misery over her mam, she'd almost become one of them. 'Only I couldn't go through with it, of course. I ran, like the devil was on my heels.' She gave a half-laugh. 'Such a pickle I'd got myself in, you'd think I'd have more sense, wouldn't you?'

He looked at her then, his eyes cold and distant. 'I don't know what to think, Dolly. I'm speechless. I can't imagine why you would willingly join a brothel.'

'I didn't join a brothel, willingly or otherwise. I'd no idea what sort of place Lil would take me to, not when she first found me. Once I realised, I just worked in the kitchen, but I'd no place else to go. Nifty *attacked* me, don't forget, and I thought I'd killed him. How do you reckon that made me feel?'

'So if you're innocent, why have you never told me any of this before?'

'You said that you didn't need to know what had happened to me, or where I'd been that winter. You said we should put the past behind us, and that you trusted me.'

'But I didn't realise things would turn out this bad.' He was pacing the room again in that wild way he had, not knowing where to put himself. 'You stayed in that *brothel* for God's sake! Became a *prostitute*!'

Dolly was on her feet in a second, following him back and forth, desperate to stop him and make him listen. 'No, no, I didn't become anything of the sort. I've just explained that I couldn't go through with it.'

'So you imply.'

'It's true, I swear it.' Her knees gave way and Dolly had to sit down to catch her breath as she went over it all again, answering the questions he fired at her, describing in painful, sordid detail, the embarrassing episode with her first and only client.

She told of how afraid and sickened she'd been, how she'd tried to do what was expected by taking off her stockings, but then had fled in fear and trembling. Stony-faced, Sam appeared unimpressed by her answers, unmoved by her halting tale. This was turning out to be even worse than she'd feared. Dolly had a strange, hollow feeling deep inside as she remembered Cabbage Lil warning her not to say a word, not till they'd been wed twenty-five years with a gaggle of kids at her knee. They'd not manage twenty-five months now.

Sam's tone was clipped and hard. 'You must have been willing to go through with it, for you to be alone with a man, in a bed, and him with his trousers down. I've only your word that nothing more happened.' His face had gone all tight, as if the skin was being stretched over the bones. 'Why did you agree to it in the first place?'

'I don't know why. Because I was angry with Mam, I suppose. I didn't realise what it would be like, what I would be letting myself in for. It had been so frightening, so awful living rough on the streets, and terrifying what Nifty Jack tried to do to me. I just wanted some money, to set everything right, to pay for the food Lil was putting in my belly, and to give me a fresh start.'

'Don't make me laugh.' There was bitter anger in his voice now, a cold, hard-edged fury, and he was backing away as if he might catch something nasty off her just by standing too near. 'No, I'm sorry, Dolly. I can't get me head round this. It's too much. I can't believe you'd make a fool of me in this way.'

'I didn't mean to make a fool of you. I hoped you'd trust me, take my word for it. Can't you believe me when I say nothing happened? I'm guilty only of being stupidly naïve.'

'I'm not sure I can, not right now. I'll need time to think about that.'

'I see. For how long, exactly, do you reckon you'll need to think?' Fear was hot in her now, like a fever clawing at her brain, screaming out that she was losing him, that it was all over, and yet outwardly she remained cool and deceptively calm.

Sam was far from calm. He was shouting at her loud enough to rouse half the street, striding up and down, waving his arms about. 'I don't know, do I? I can't take it all in. I thought she was making it up.'

Dolly's head snapped up at this. 'She? Who's *she*? You thought *who* was making it up? Was it our Aggie who told you?'

He shook his head. 'Oh no, you can't blame Aggie, not this time. It was – someone at the mill. Another girl.'

'Who? Which girl?' From burning up with fever, Dolly's blood chilled, froze in her veins. This was turning into a night-mare.

Sam slammed his fist on the table. 'What difference does it make which bloody girl it was? I'm not the one at fault here, you are. *You!* How could you, Dolly? How *could* you? You'll make me a laughing stock.'

'Never mind about what it will do to *you*, what about *me*? And what about this girl? It was Evie Barker, wasn't it? Aggie warned me that you and she were seeing each other. You denied it when I asked you before, but this is proof. Oh, Sam, how could you?'

'Don't you dare look at me like that, Dolly. I've done nothing!' Not with Evie he hadn't, not yet anyway.

'I wish I could believe that.'

'It's true, though God knows why. Being married obviously hasn't stopped you from warming Nifty Jack's bed. All your pathetic protests about how you hate him are laughable now. No wonder you always have so much bloody money. You don't care who you sleep with. You're a bloody tart, you.'

Dolly couldn't speak for several long minutes. Finally, she said, 'It would seem that there is no trust left between us. So why should I believe in you, if you don't believe me?'

He jabbed a furious finger in the air, inches from her face. 'Don't try to wriggle out of this by tying me in knots as you so like to do. I'll tell you something for nothing. You're not the girl I thought you were, Dolly Tomkins. Not for a minute did I imagine you'd be the sort to put yourself about like any cheap hussy. And I certainly don't want a *prossy* for a wife. I should have believed it about your mam an' all. You're both at it.'

'Sam, stop it. You don't understand. You're not listening to me.'

'Oh, I understand right enough. More than you think. I'm not stupid. I know when I've been made a fool of.'

Then he walked out without a single backward glance, and this time Dolly made no attempt to stop him. What was the point? She'd lost him for good. Sam Clayton wasn't ever going to be interested in her now because she was beneath contempt. In his eyes she was a prostitute, the lowest of the low. Dolly sat at the kitchen table and let the tears of utter misery slide down her face.

Chapter Twenty-One

Cabbage Lil noticed the girl quite by chance. She was leaning on the wall quietly weeping, looking as if she might collapse at any moment.

'Don't cry lass. What's up?'

'I'm fine, don't worry about me.'

'You don't look fine. Haven't I seen you round here before? I'd recognise that posh accent anywhere.'

'I once asked you for a bed for the night, and you refused. This is the result.'

Evie turned to face Cabbage Lil, revealing a livid purple bruise on her cheek. It had hurt more than she'd expected to inflict this upon herself by banging the cupboard door in her face, but still, it was all in a good cause. 'I might not look as if I'm in need, but I do assure you that I am. My father is so cruel. He's cut me off without a penny and I swear if I went home tonight, he might do even worse.' With consummate skill, she let the tears flow. 'Oh, I don't know what to do or where to go. Staying with friends would be no good, he'd find me too easily.'

Cabbage Lil's soft heart was easily moved by a woman perse-cuted by a man, in view of the memories she held of her own bully of a father, but on this occasion she remained cautious. This was the girl who had coincidentally appeared shortly after she'd been talking to Dolly. 'Why would he hit you? What have you done? Are you in the pudding club?'

'Pudding...?'

'You know – up the spout?'

'Oh, I see.' Evie shook her head, and then realised that if she would win over this woman's confidence, she'd need to offer a bit more information about herself, some real life drama. Well, she had plenty of those, didn't she? 'The truth is that I was pregnant but got rid of it, ages ago. Now he's found out, and he's furious. Says I've ruined my chances of matrimony.'

'Hoping for an heir, was he?'

'That's all he cares about. Money, position, power. I don't care a jot about such things.' She was weeping into her hand-kerchief with some conviction now, huge hiccupping sobs that were beginning to feel almost genuine. 'I just need to be loved. Perhaps that's why – why I like men. Can't resist them. I need to know someone cares, to be loved. Is it any wonder after the way he treats me? It's my father's entire fault for neglecting and bullying me, don't you think?' she sobbed. 'Can you understand what I'm saying?'

Evie hoped she was making some sort of sense, because she was making much of this up as she went along. Then she lifted those lovely pale blue eyes, swimming with tears, to meet Cabbage Lil's probing gaze, which did the trick, as always. Who could deny such irresistible appeal?

'Ah, girls who like men is summat I do understand. You'd best come with me, love. I'll see you right.'

Evie was treated with the same consideration as Dolly. She was provided with a substantial meal, a hot bath and a clean nightgown, plus a shared room in the attic well away from the working area.

The other girls, Gladys, who came from Deansgate, and Joan, who was popular with the swells took to her right away, mesmerised by her beauty. Joan's brightly rouged cheeks glowed ever more scarlet when Evie commented that she admired her mysterious black eyes and slender, boy-like figure. 'And your outfit is the absolute tops, truly wondrous, wherever did you buy it?'

Plain, round, pancake-faced Joan was dressed in a short, scarlet and gold striped dress, and on her head a purple and gold, much beribboned hat. The whole ensemble gave her every appearance of a joker in a pack of cards, but she believed the compliment to be sincerely meant.

Sylvie and Fran, on the other hand, were less enchanted, recognising nouveau riche masquerading as so-called class when they saw it, and being very wary of it. They'd had their own experiences at the hands of those who thought themselves grand, what with factory overlookers and rich men's sons in posh houses where they'd been in service once. Would their daughters be any better? They very much doubted it.

'You're welcome to stay as long as you need,' Cabbage Lil assured her, 'although I should point out that we're not a refuge for battered daughters, so you'll have to pay your way, one way or another.'

'One way or… oh, I see. Cash or kind, you mean?'

'That's the way of it. Which is it to be in your case?' Lil lifted one brow in mild enquiry. She'd already made a shrewd assessment about this particular little filly, and had a small bet on the result with Sylvie.

'Money is so hard to come by these days. Besides, life is for living so why would I not have some fun along the way?'

Evie stayed for several days and found no trouble at all in fitting in with the routine. The work was pleasant, the clients appreciative and the other girls, with the exception of one or two, were reasonably respectful. But she saw this as a mere interlude, a fillip to brighten up the dullness of her existence. After four days, she mildly informed Lil that she intended returning home.

'What if he knocks you about again?'

'Who?' Forgetting, for a moment, the story she'd fabricated.

'Your pa.'

'Oh, he'll be utterly contrite, completely remorseful, at least for a while. But don't worry, Lil, I'll be back. This is the most fun I've had in an age. You certainly haven't seen the last of me.'

'I'll look forward to it. I like a girl who takes pleasure in her work.'

Dolly was finding it hard living without Sam. After he'd left that night it took several days to convince herself that he'd actually gone for good. She kept expecting him to walk in through the door, calling to her with that loving tone in his voice which told her that he couldn't wait to see her. That first day after he left, she'd prepared his tea, as usual, and set it on the table at exactly the moment she would expect him to come home from the mill. The front door remained fast shut.

Maisie watched all of this with sadness in her eyes. 'He's not coming, is he?'

Not trusting herself to speak, Dolly blinked hard and shook her head.

'Have you had a falling-out? Or is it because he hates living here with me?'

'This has got nothing to do with you, Mother.'

'Mam. You used to call me Mam.'

'Well, perhaps it has got something to do with you after all, with Calvin anyway, and that flaming debt. It's all got on top of him and he just can't cope any more.'

Maisie gazed at her daughter in silence for a long, thoughtful moment. 'It wouldn't have anything to do with that woman you took up with when you ran away that time, then?'

'How did you…? Who told you…?'

'Who do you think? Gabby-mouth Aggie, who else? Took great pleasure in describing it all to me in intimate detail. Like mother, like daughter, she said.'

'Oh, Mam, what a thing to say! I don't understand why our Aggie is so mean-mouthed. Anyroad, she's got it all wrong. But you know our Aggie, once she has an idea in her head, she won't let go.' Dolly sighed, pushed her plate away untouched and leaned back in her chair, eyes closed. 'It was all a bad mistake but nothing happened. I did nothing wrong.'

'I can understand that feeling well enough. I did nothing wrong either, 'cept fall in love with the wrong man. I did drop him a note, after our last little chat, hoping as how he'd release me from my promise.'

Dolly stared at her mother, wide-eyed. 'Did you? What did he say?'

'Nothing. I never even got a reply.'

Dolly turned away, bitterly disappointed. 'Why wouldn't he reply, if you loved each other? You could marry now surely, now that Calvin is dead. Assuming you actually did write to him, that is.'

'Dolly, don't start accusing me of lying again.'

'I'm not starting anything. I just can't handle anything more today. I've other worries on my mind. Sam heard about Cabbage Lil from some girl at the mill, and so I had to tell him the whole story and of course he believes her, and not me.' She'd no wish to go into too much detail about this latest disagreement with her husband. It was too personal, too raw. The thought that at this moment he might be with her, with Evie Barker, brought a pain to Dolly's chest that near ripped her in half. She could hardly bear it. Allowing her mother to witness that pain would only make matters worse.

Maisie was toying with the strips of bacon and mashed potato on her plate, which she too had hardly touched, hunger having become so much a part of her, she barely noticed it any more. 'Funny old world, eh? You're upset with Aggie because she won't believe in your innocence. And I'm upset with you, because you won't believe in mine.'

'That's entirely different.'

'Is it?'

Dolly fidgeted in her seat, feeling slightly uncomfortable. 'Well, she's saying I did sex for money, which is a dreadful thing to accuse a person of, particularly your own sister. You only did it for pleasure, presumably because you liked it. Though a proper pickle you've made of all our lives as a result.'

'Eeh, our Dolly, you can be a hard-hearted little madam at times.'

Dolly blinked back tears, knowing her heart was breaking, yet realising that the criticism was largely justified. It was certainly true that she did always seem to blame her mother for everything these days but who else could she blame? The solution was surely in Maisie's own hands. She simply had to tell her the truth, to name the man who had fathered her. Dolly picked up Sam's plate and divided the bacon between the two of them. 'Waste not want not. We might as well eat this ourselves. I'll fry up the leftover potato for breakfast.'

'But—'

'Don't argue, Mam. Do as you're told for once. And don't ask any more questions. Sam has gone and he's not coming back.'

'You're not going to give it another try then?'

'No, I'm not.'

'Pity. Still, it depends how you feel about him in your heart, and whether he's worth the effort or not. If he is, then you need to swallow your pride and ask him to come home. But if he's betrayed you, then you might decide to let him go. It's up to you.'

'Eat your dinner for God's sake, Mam. When I want your advice, I'll ask for it.'

Dolly didn't know what she wanted. Was Sam worth the effort? Their marriage had not been quite the unmitigated success that she'd hoped for. The rumours about him and that Barker girl had upset Dolly but were they true or just Aggie's nasty gossip? She longed to run to Matt and ask for his help and advice, as she had done so often in the past, but instinct told her it would be wrong to involve Matt in all this. He had feelings for her, there was no doubt about that, so how could she expect him to give her an unbiased opinion on whether she should give Sam another chance?

And Sam was still her husband. They were still man and wife, and things had been stacked against them from the start, what with the debt and having to live with Mam. Even that had been difficult, relations between them not quite what they should be. If it was only money that was keeping them apart, then surely these problems could be resolved. Mam was right in one respect. It was up to her to decide. Was Sam Clayton worth one more try, or not?

Maisie had been disappointed not to get a response to her letter. She hadn't expected to be ignored, in view of what they'd once been to each other. Then it occurred to her that he might not even have received it. Perhaps it had gone astray, or a servant not handed to him. Maisie didn't understand how such big houses operated but she was quite certain that he wouldn't collect his own post. She made up her mind to follow it up in person. She'd never asked anything of him before now, and this was important. Her poor lass was suffering, and needed help.

When she said the words out loud to him though, Maisie felt a trifle less confident. Nathan Barker looked at her as if she were some sort of madwoman dropped in off the streets, whom he didn't even know.

She'd waited till everyone else had left before sneaking into his office via the back door, as she had used to do all those years ago. He'd looked stunned, as well he might at this unexpected intrusion. Maisie had almost giggled.

'I know what you're thinking, the Ghost of Christmas Past.'

When he didn't say anything to this, she'd quickly gone on to explain what she wanted, how she'd never asked anything of him before, wanted nothing for herself at all, only for Dolly. She needs to know the truth.

'She's a good lass,' Maisie finished. 'But she's having a hard time of it right now and she deserves a chance. You don't have to answer right away. Think about it and let me know. You know where to find me. I do assure you that I'm not here to make any bother. I'll stay out of your life, as I always have. But if you ever loved me, were ever fond of me at all, you'll do this for our girl. She's bright as a button. A real chip off the old block.' And without giving him time to say a word by way of response, Maisie slipped quietly away into the night the same as she'd come, not wanting to be a trouble to anyone.

Sam was waiting outside the mill gates as Evie made her way home. She wasn't particularly pleased to see him, was really quite bored with the man, wondering what on earth she'd ever seen in him, and had been doing her best to avoid him for some time. Unfortunately, he didn't seem able to take no for an answer. She'd spotted him on several occasions lingering by the mill gates and taken to slipping out the back way to avoid him.

'Evie, I'm glad I've caught you at last.'

'Were you wanting something, Sam? It's quite a surprise to see you here.'

'Course there's something I'm wanting. I was waiting to see you. I can't get you out of my mind. You know I'm crazy about you.'

'Oh, I thought you were no longer interested, too concerned about losing your job, or your wife finding out.'

'Dolly and me have separated. It didn't work out.'

Evie began to walk away. 'I'm sorry to hear that, Sam, but I really don't think it would work out with us either, do you?'

'Why not? We could at least give it a try.' Sam grabbed hold of her arm and dragged her to a halt. 'Listen to me when I'm talking to you. Me and Dolly is finished, all washed up. I never should've married her.'

'Why did you then?'

'I was on the rebound, from her sister.'

'Aggie?' Evie trilled with laughter. 'What taste you do have.'

'She's all right is Aggie, bit full of herself, but she was no more than a childhood sweetheart. I need to start afresh with a real woman, with you. Why don't we give it a go? You know I fancy you rotten. We could happen go to the flicks or something.'

'To the flicks?' Evie gurgled with laughter. 'You think I'm the sort of girl who'd be happy with a quick fumble on the back seat of the one and nines? I don't think so. You were just a teeny-tiny part of my life, sweetie, and not of the least importance. Merely a tumble in the hay, as it were.'

260

'Tumble in the hay?' Sam was confused.

'Metaphorically speaking, darling, as I'm trying to delicately explain that it was merely a little dalliance, and not even a full blown affair. We didn't *do* anything, not properly. You were always too distracted, and ran away at the last moment, coward that you are.'

'I'm not a coward,' Sam burst out. He could feel himself growing hot with embarrassment, and angry in his desperation. He'd had enough of her teasing, could bear it no longer. 'More often than not it was you what pulled back, a right little tease you were. Though it's true I didn't want to risk losing my job. And I was confused, about Aggie, and maybe because Dolly and me were having problems and she was still my wife. And yet—'

'You still fancied me like mad.'

'Aye, and I still do.'

'Women are your weakness, sweetie, I can see that.'

'But you're different. I haven't been able to get you out of my head. Still can't. I reckon you and me have something special, something serious.'

'*Serious?*' Evie put back her head and laughed out loud. 'Don't be ridiculous. I wouldn't walk out with a man of your sort in a serious way, not if you paid me. Well no, perhaps I might if you *paid* me.' She laughed again, a trilling, musical sound as if she'd said something highly amusing. 'Go home to your sweet little wife, Sam, and forget you ever knew me.'

A tide of scarlet rose from Sam's neck and flushed right up his face. Evie Barker was making a fool of him and he didn't much care for that, not one bit. He no longer seemed to be in control, not of his women who'd always been easy meat, nor of his own life. Sam felt as if he was shrinking beneath her scornful gaze. Why did she no longer want him? If only he could've loved Dolly as she deserved, and not be hankering after this fancy madam?

'I dare say you think I'm a right daft lummock but Dolly and me were having a hard time of it, so I didn't want to hurt her.

I kept hoping it might work out between us. She's pure gold is my Dolly.'

It was true, he thought. Had he thrown everything good in his life out the window by leaving her?

'*Your* Dolly is she now? What a touching little speech, utterly heart-rending and loyal. Then why are you here, dearest heart? Because you're still rampant for me, poor boy, simply panting for it. Can't get me out of your mind, as you said yourself. Dear me, don't look so downcast and disappointed, I really can't bear it.' She glanced at her watch and let out a resigned sigh. 'You can have a quickie if you like, why not? I've got a few minutes to kill and it might be quite amusing.'

Sam went cold, his pride cut to ribbons. 'No thanks! I'm not begging for it. I've changed me mind and I wouldn't touch you with a barge pole.'

'Goodness, don't say you're refusing my offer?'

'Aye, I am. I weren't thinking straight. Happen your patronising, toffee-nosed attitude has cleared my head.' He turned away, pleased with himself for holding on to his pride, even if he could feel himself still shaking from the fever that consumed him.

Evie did not care to be denied or ignored, and have someone turn his back upon her. Perversely she now became determined to have him and grabbing hold of his jacket, pulled him to her. 'Do stop these petty sulks and come here, you silly boy. I can't bear to see a man deprived.'

The smell of her perfume was intoxicating, filling his nostrils and, in an instant, the fire in him exploded. He thrust her back against the wall, kissing her long and hard, lifting her skirt, eager to take her.

The voice he knew came out of nowhere. 'So, our Aggie was right that this woman is the real reason you left me, Sam Clayton, and nothing to do with the talleyman or debts at all.'

Sam whirled about as if he'd been struck. 'Dolly, it's not how it looks. I can explain.'

'I'm sure you can but I don't need any explanation. There's nothing wrong with my eyesight, even if I have been a bit soft in the head for believing in you all this time. I was going to ask if we could try again, explain what I'm doing to try to set things right, but I won't waste my time any more. Don't *ever* come back home as I'm better off without you messing up my life, Sam Clayton.'

–

Dolly strode swiftly along Liverpool Road, her boots ringing on the pavement, echoing the fury of her temper. Nothing had quite turned out as she'd hoped. How could she have been so naïve as to trust Sam Clayton? Why had she ever loved him, ever been daft enough as to marry him? What an utter and complete fool she'd been and all the time he'd been knocking off Evie Barker, probably since before they were wed.

How dare he accuse *her* of being cheap, of doing unspeakable things and going with men for money, when he was no innocent. *How dare he?* By the time she reached Potato Wharf the anger had dissipated and she was stumbling along, half blinded by tears and wretched in her misery. She might well have fallen, had not Aggie suddenly appeared out of nowhere and hooked on to her arm.

'Hey, what's this? Not been on the booze, have you Dolly, lass?'

'Oh, Aggie, I'm that glad to see you. It's all so awful.' And the tears began to flow as if a tap had been opened. Aggie helped her sister the length of the wharf, up through Tully Court and in their front door. Thankfully, the house was empty, Maisie nowhere in sight, probably collecting or returning either children or washing.

Once the tears had been dried and the usual healing cuppa had been put into Dolly's hands, Aggie folded her arms across her plump breasts and demanded to know what was going on. Dolly told her what she had just witnessed, making no bones about her discovery that Sam had left her not because of the debt, but because he was indeed having an affair with Evie Barker, the gaffer's daughter. Once again the tears flowed so that Aggie had to rescue the mug and find a clean handkerchief for Dolly to blow her nose.

'Well, it's no surprise to me.'

Were Dolly willing to credit her sister with such nastiness, she'd have thought the expression on her face was one of pure satisfaction that she found herself in this dreadful situation. But surely even Aggie couldn't be so unkind as to take pleasure in her own sister's misery?

Aggie was secretly delighted that Dolly's marriage with Sam appeared to be failing, if irritated over the reason. She had no more liking to see him carrying on with Evie Barker than had Dolly. Men were so weak, so bloody useless. But there was some satisfaction in seeing her sister brought low, and quite a struggle not to show it.

'I wouldn't trust that little madam as far as our back yard gate. She's a right nasty piece of work. And didn't I warn you that Sam Clayton would be a lousy husband? You should've listened to me in the first place. And if you'd confessed to Sam what you got up to with that Cabbage Lil person, then he might never have turned against you. That's always been your trouble, Dolly, you never will take advice.'

'But I did, I told him in the end, like you said, and look what happened. He left me.'

'Too late! You told him far too late. You can't expect me to pull you out of these holes you get yourself into. I can't keep on slipping you the odd shilling, or pair of boots. We're saving for a new house, so you'll have to find every penny yourself from now on. I'm sorry, Dolly, but there it is.'

She didn't know whether to laugh or cry, and couldn't remember a time when Aggie had actually got her out of a hole, let alone slip her a shilling. And her worn out boots she could well do without. She rather hoped her sister didn't try offering her cast-off hats as well. The one she had on today was a sickly green colour that just about cleared her eyebrows and had a great bow on the side.

'I'll get by, don't you worry about me. I have my little round of clients who pay me regular as clockwork every week, plus a bit of interest.'

'And what sort of clients might they be?' Aggie smirked.

'I'm a moneylender. I told you, and an honest one at that.'

Aggie looked as if she'd been slapped in the face. She'd quite forgotten about this little show of enterprise on Dolly's behalf, had put it firmly out of her mind, not liking to see her younger sister, or rather half-sister, so independent and successful. She looked at her now with loathing in her heart, seeing the pretty elfin face, the ebony curls and feeling the familiar twist of jealousy. 'Moneylender? Don't talk daft. You surely can't depend upon that for a living? I never took that nonsense seriously.'

'Aye, you did. You were jealous as hell, and I'm doing very nicely thank you.'

Dolly was smiling but the casual way she dismissed Aggie's opinion on the subject, made her want to gag. So much so that she found difficulty speaking in a normal voice, probably because her teeth were clenched together so hard her jaw hurt. It was quite an effort to release them.

'It's perfectly obvious to me how you earned the money on your back, to set yourself up in business. And you'd probably earn more if you'd stayed in that position.'

'You nasty minded cow! Every penny I earned was honest and above board, as I've explained more than once.'

Aggie snorted her derision. 'Go on, tell the truth that it was for services rendered.' She hated to think that this little cuckoo in the nest who Mam thought the sun shone out of, might be making money when Aggie herself seemed to be increasingly hard up. It really wasn't fair. Maybe her flaming sister would be the one to move out to a posh new house in the suburbs. Serve her right if she had lost Sam, at least she wouldn't be starting a family. Aggie couldn't be more delighted.

Life wasn't going according to plan for her either. She was not enjoying her work at all, not one little bit. The atmosphere at the mill had changed since she married and she hated it. The other girls didn't seem to care for working with the overlooker's wife and she felt increasingly isolated, alone and without friends.

She'd once been quite friendly with Lizzie Bramley and Myra Johnson, now they both turned their noses up at her. So desperate did she feel at times that she'd looked back with fond nostalgia upon the times she and Dolly had squabbled over who was to take their dinner break first. Nowadays, Aggie felt fortunate to get a break at all. No one was willing to watch her frame while she ate, so she was forced to stop her machine altogether, which meant she was losing money she really couldn't afford to lose.

What was worse, Harold had come home from his shift the other night looking thoroughly shaken. Nathan Barker had informed him that his wages were to be cut. And when he'd objected to this kind of cavalier treatment, citing his years of loyalty to the firm, he'd been curtly informed that times were hard and he was fortunate to have a job at all.

Aggie had listened to his tale in stark horror, fear cutting into her like a cold knife. 'But what about our dream of moving to the suburbs?'

Asking Harold this innocent question, he'd turned on her, eyes blazing. 'Never mind the suburbs, how are we going to make all the payments on all this bloody new furniture?'

Never, in all their time together had she heard Harold swear. It was this, rather than the way he'd stomped off to bed in a foul mood, which had convinced her that matters were dire indeed. So she had little patience with her stupid sister's troubles.

Dolly was dabbing at her eyes, reaching for a brush to drag through her tousled hair, and still defending herself.

'As I told you before, I earned that money fair and square. For cooking and cleaning, but nothing more. I didn't peel off

266

any stockings or undo a single button to earn it, so don't imply that I did. Though I wonder sometimes if that would be any worse than what you do with your Harold. Don't tell me you married him for his good looks or his charm. You wed Harold Entwistle for the size of his bank balance and a house in the suburbs. And much good may it do for you. As for me, I'm doing nicely on me own now, ta very much. I'll cope with or without Sam Clayton, you can bet your sweet life on that. Now I have work to do, so you can see yourself out.'

The conversation between the two sisters ended as usual with the banging of the door, only this time it was Dolly who grabbed her coat, picked up her money bag and left. Aggie remained exactly where she was, seething with fury.

She was still sitting there, head in hands, feeling sorry for herself when the door opened and Sam staggered in, very much the worse for drink. He peered at Aggie, bleary-eyed.

'Where's Dolly? I need to speak to her.'

'She's not here. By heck lad, you've had a skinful.'

'It's not my fault Aggie. I never meant this to happen.'

'Course you didn't, love.' She could see that he'd turned maudlin in his drunken state and her heart went out to him. Oh, how she wanted him. This was the man who should be warming her bed at night. If only he'd had a bit more go about him they might have made a pair, then everything could have been so different. Dolly wouldn't now be feeling betrayed, and she wouldn't be endlessly waiting for Harold to deliver on his promises.

Aggie had been reasonably content with her marriage to begin with, Harold fulfilling her needs in many ways even though he didn't quite have Sam's charm or good looks. Now he always seemed to be tired, concerned about money, constantly checking his accounts and complaining about how much things cost. He was turning into a right old skinflint. Aggie could see nothing but years of hard work ahead of her. She might just as well have married Sam Clayton.

She looked with an expression of bitter regret. 'Our Dolly doesn't deserve you. She's the one to blame, fussing over that debt, as if paying the talleyman is all that matters in life.'

'You're right there, lass. It's all Dolly's fault.' He gave a loud hiccup, seemed about to keel over, and Aggie put her shoulder under his arm, grabbing him round the waist.

'Come on lad, we'd best get you upstairs to bed.' She started to push him up the stairs, which took all her strength leaving her exhausted and breathless by the time they reached the top. Sam was clearly on his last legs. She just managed to reach the bed before he collapsed. Within seconds he was snoring his head off.

Aggie shook him. 'Sam, don't you dare go to sleep on me. What were you doing with that Evie Barker?'

'Nothing. Toffee-nosed bitch.'

Aggie smiled to herself. So his advances had been refused. She gazed down at him spread-eagled on the bed, his long legs with those powerful muscled thighs, the tantalising bulge in his trousers. He was quite a man. She unpinned her hair, shook out the chestnut curls then began to unbutton her blouse.

'So what are you going to do about our Dolly? She spends half her time with that Nifty Jack. God knows what she gets up to while she's supposedly cleaning his house.' Aggie peeled off her blouse, stepped out of her skirt. Sam's gaze wasn't entirely focused but he was interested, she could tell. 'And she undoubtedly made that money she lends out by lying on her back for some chap or other. Doesn't that bother you?'

'Course it bloody bothers me. Oh, Aggie, why didn't I wed you?'

She quickly rolled off her stockings, followed by her petticoat and slid into bed beside him. 'That doesn't mean we can't have a bit of fun like we used to, does it?'

Chapter Twenty-Two

Nathan Barker was a worried man. He sat at the breakfast table, reading *The Times*, feeling as if his blood was turning to ice in his veins. This terrible business in America with the Wall Street Crash seemed to be going from bad to worse. The market was plummeting and starting to badly affect his investments.

'A car in every garage, a chicken in every pot,' had been the cry. The Americans had played the stock market as if it were a casino for years, believing prices would continue to rise. Spend, spend, spend, had been their creed but then the clever investors had bailed out and left the rest floundering. The crash had happened back in October '29, when the bottom had dropped out of the market. At first it was assumed that there would be a recovery yet now, only a few months into the new year, it was clear that wasn't going to happen. People were actually committing suicide, taking their own lives, jumping out of skyscraper windows. Even banks were going bust, for God's sake.

This morning's paper claimed that Britain too could also be affected. So far as Nathan was concerned, it was affecting him *now*. He'd speculated in the American market to help get him out of a hole, and to keep the business competitive. His losses were great. How he would recover from this latest blow he hadn't the first idea. Should he close the mill right away and have done with it, throwing a hundred or so workers out on to the scrapheap, or hang on till the bitter end? His head ached he felt so tired, couldn't even think clearly, and he hadn't slept well.

Nothing had quite gone right for him in a long while, what with that dreadful accident at the mill, the cancelled wedding and Evie failing to find herself a husband. Not to mention wasting a fortune idling her way around Europe. Nathan would have considered it money well spent if she'd come home with a rich son-in-law eager to invest in the business. But whatever opportunities she'd had, she'd ruined them by her profligate selfishness and greed. There wasn't going to be a good marriage. The foolish child had missed the boat and would continue to be a burden to him, probably for the rest of his life.

Nathan had to admit that he too had missed many chances of happiness in life, all too frequently making the wrong decisions. His marriage to feeble Clara, what a let down she had been. Even to quarrel with his oh-so-agreeable wife was well nigh impossible, as it felt like batting against a soft, squashy pillow. He could walk all over her and she would never even notice.

What had happened to him over the years? Why had he made such a mess of his life? Driven by ambition and greed, no doubt, and a constant dissatisfaction that niggled away at him, as if just around the corner he might find something better. No, he really shouldn't be too hard on himself. He'd stayed in his marriage, no matter how unsatisfactory, if only out of loyalty rather than love? For all her insipid charms, Clara's devotion was beyond question. She would never say a word against him, which was partly why she was so unutterably boring. Evie certainly didn't inherit her wild streak from her mother. He'd put up a show of being a good husband because he had a position to maintain in the community.

But he felt so alone, so bone weary.

He spent his days struggling to make the figures tally, as well as trying to knock some sense into his colleagues at the Exchange. A vain task as the industry continued to flounder and lose orders to cheaper competitors. His nights were spent drinking too much brandy alone in his study while his wife dabbled in art, or gossiped with her old school chums. And what his daughter did with her time he hadn't the first idea, and cared even less, so long as she behaved herself and brought not a whiff of scandal to his door.

But with no son to follow him, there were times when he asked himself what was the point of it all?

He thought of that other girl, the daughter he might have had: the one with the lovely, elfin beauty and jet-black hair, exactly the colour his own had used to be when he was young. He'd made mistakes over her too, one of the few he regretted. Could he have made things better for her? Would he have done so had he known of her existence earlier? Take the risk of scandal? He suspected not. He should have paid off her mother in order to keep her quiet, but Maisie had never spoken of her, or asked for a penny. Until now!

He shook his head in despair. It was surely too late, too big a risk on top of all his other worries. He was too old now to stir up past problems and create yet more havoc in his life. If only he could exchange irritating, lazy, heedless Evie for the fiery and enchanting Dolly. It was a tempting but traitorous thought.

–

Dolly's brave words to Aggie about her successful career as a moneylender had sounded hollow and over-optimistic. Following the incident of Nifty Jack attacking the Shuttleworth girl, despite every effort to protect the family, she had become increasingly concerned over recent weeks. She'd wanted to do some good but all she'd really achieved was to bring more trouble upon folk. Furthermore, many of her regulars were coming to her, somewhat shamefaced, and saying they wouldn't need her services any longer. They were settling their debts with incredible swiftness, but when she asked where they'd got the money from to pay her off, folk would mumble excuses about a windfall, or a relative leaving them some unlikely legacy, and hastily hurry away.

Then one day, Elsie Crabtree's mother came with a wad of notes in her hand. Everyone knew the family didn't have two pennies to rub together, and Dolly took her to task, insisting on knowing what was going on. The woman finally admitted that Nifty Jack had been round 'for a chat', and made her see the error of her ways.

'I have to use him, d'you see, not you, Dolly. Nifty don't take kindly to you queering his pitch. Best for all of us if we don't upset him any more than necessary.'

Dolly decided that future clients must be chosen with greater care. She hoped this might resolve the problem. Sadly, it hardly mattered as before the month was out she had no clients left at all, save for one old man who'd refused to be bullied, and Edna, of course. She'd have to think of some way to deal with the problem, but no solution came to mind at the moment.

It seemed that Nifty Jack still held the upper hand.

This evening, not having any rounds to do, no payments to collect, no loans outstanding, she'd spent a whole hour carefully preparing a beef stew which she'd put on to simmer, even though she had no appetite. She wished Sam would walk in through the door just one more time. Where was he and why wouldn't he at least talk to her? Could she ever persuade him to come back home and try again? Did she even want him to?

Maisie came marching in having no doubt delivered the latest clean washing, with more than her usual vigour. She hung her shawl on the nail behind the door, tugged off her old boots, and sat down with a happy sigh. 'Have you had a nice day, chuck?' she asked, sounding surprisingly cheerful.

'Not particularly, why?'

'Well, I've a bit of news that might cheer you up. I know I've been a burden to you, lass, so I've made up me mind to do something about it. I'm leaving. Cyril and I have decided to get wed. There, what d'you think of that?' She sat back, her arms wrapped about herself as if for protection.

'Getting married to Cyril?' At one time Dolly would have been delighted over such news. She'd have hugged her mother and wished her well. But because of the way things stood between them she couldn't quite decide how to react, couldn't work out how she felt about it.

'Like I told you, Cyril fancied me once-over, when I was a girl, and he's remained fond, so I thought, why not? We get on grand so I reckon we'll make a go of it.'

'You mean he's going to make an honest woman of you at last?'

Maisie sighed.

They were interrupted by the bang of the door as Aggie strolled in. She'd called to gloat over some news of her own, but instantly sensed something brewing. Looking from one to the other, she asked, 'What's going on here?'

'Mam is getting wed, isn't that wonderful?' Dolly attempted to inject some enthusiasm into her voice because, deep down, she was truly pleased for her. It was just difficult to understand why now, and why she still wouldn't admit Cyril was her father.

'Aye, Cyril and me have named the day. What do you say to that?'

Aggie's brow rose in surprise. 'I hope he knows what he's taking on. You don't have a good record with men, Mam. I hope he appreciates that fact.'

'Oh, Cyril understands more than you think.'

'I dare say.'

'Don't underestimate him.'

Aggie was having difficulty in keeping her expression bland and not looking too pleased, but now looked Dolly straight in the eye. 'I've a bit of news of my own. I'm pregnant.'

'Pregnant? Oh, Aggie, that's wonderful. You must be thrilled. I bet Harold is pleased too, isn't he?'

Aggie's smile slipped just a little. 'Course he is, pleased as punch.' Harold had sternly taken her to task for forgetting to wear the device, reminding her how difficult it had been to save what they had so far, how hard it was for them to manage now that his wages had been cut. And how they'd be in a worse state when Aggie gave up work. She'd been upset by his attitude but had every hope she could win him round and he'd get used to the idea. All men were a bit indifferent about fatherhood at first.

The important thing was for him to go on thinking she'd forgotten to put in the device one night, instead of the truth, that the baby wasn't even his. It was Sam's. How could it not be? The timing was right and she certainly hadn't been thinking of contraception on that particular afternoon. She and Sam had enjoyed several more encounters since that day, finding the pleasure in each other every bit as good as in the old days. It gave Aggie enormous satisfaction to get one over on her sister. Common sense had prevailed on those occasions and she'd been better prepared, nevertheless, there seemed little doubt in her mind about the father of her child.

Aggie blithely continued, 'Course we'll have to put on hold our move out to the suburbs.' Just as if they'd very nearly started packing. 'Although I'm sure once business picks up at the mill, things will be different. I certainly have no intention of bringing up a child of mine in these streets.'

'It never did you two any harm,' Maisie stoutly responded. 'They've hearts of gold, folk what live round here, a fact you'd do well to appreciate, girl.'

'You'll be moving out and living with Cyril on Gartside Street?' And when her mother agreed that she would, Aggie turned to Dolly with a smirk. 'Pity your husband has left you, as the pair of you would've had the place to yourselves at last.'

Dolly flinched. 'Who says he's left me? We're just giving each other a bit of space, that's all. He's thinking things through.'

'He's having a randy old time with any girl in a skirt.'

Maisie jumped to her feet to wag a finger in Aggie's face. 'I'll have none of your squabbling today. This is a day for celebrating my good fortune, not starting another family feud. We'll have a fresh pot of tea, and then Cyril thought we might all go to the Co-operative tearooms for steak pudding and chips. His treat. What do you say to that?'

Evie had become a regular, and a popular one at that, coming to be known as the Duchess, a title she rather approved of. She visited Cabbage Lil's on her days off from the mill and at weekends, or whenever she had a few hours to kill. Apart from the money, and she was quickly able to save a considerable sum, she found the work thoroughly entertaining and enjoyable – surprisingly so.

The clients came from all walks of life, doctors, lawyers, dockers, builders, sailors, market traders, all with varied interests and tastes. It was most educational. Dressed in harness for one client, she let him 'ride' her to hounds. For another she played a nurse and 'mended' his strained back by pounding it with a carpet beater. Yet another enjoyed sucking a dummy and then more delectable parts of her anatomy. She would scrub, tickle, touch, rub, caress, soothe, smack, or do whatever was required of her, without the slightest reservation. In fact, as her many satisfied clients all confessed, her enthusiasm and imagination were exciting, titillating, and sometimes quite exhausting.

What's more, she and Lil were growing comfortable enough with each other for them to enjoy a regular glass of port together. One evening Evie said, 'Might I ask how you got into this business?'

Lil filled the glass with the rich ruby port and handed it to her. 'Same as everyone else, on me back.'

'And was your first time with anyone in particular?'

'Oh, my father was very particular. He liked to keep it in the family, and made life simpler, in his opinion. Instead of walking the streets at night looking for a woman, he could just pop upstairs and have me. My mother died when I was born and there was just him and me.'

Evie was shaken by this insight into her new friend's early life. 'Oh, Lil, that's appalling. How old were you when it started?'

'About seven I reckon, then fifteen before I finally found the courage to leave. By then I considered myself an expert on men, and hated them all enough to use them and take their money without blinking an eye. I served my apprenticeship on the streets, same as all the other girls I got ambitious, saved hard and started up on me own. Happen you should do the same, though not in competition to me, ta very much.' Cabbage Lil chuckled. 'Somewhere that won't damage my trade, but you'll do well being classic at your job. With the right girls you could probably entice some real swells who'd pay a bit more than the scrubbers who come in here.'

'I hadn't thought that, but what an interesting idea.'

'Think about it, why don't you?' Cabbage Lil laughed. 'I wasn't too sure about you at first, but I've warmed to you and you certainly give value for money.'

'Oh, my father has always taught me the value of money.' Evie chuckled softly. 'But in his opinion, work and me are complete strangers.'

'It depends what sort of work we're talking about, don't it?'

'It certainly does.'

–

Breakfast in the Barker household was generally a silent, difficult meal. Only Clara remained cheerful these days, remarkably so, this morning brightly informing her husband and daughter that she intended to spend the day with her old school chum. 'We might drive into the Peak District and stay overnight in a charming little inn we found. Would that be a problem for you, dear?' she asked Nathan, refilling his coffee cup.

Nathan scarcely glanced at his wife as he swallowed it down in one gulp, folded up his paper and got quickly to his feet. 'I've more serious matters on my mind than the whereabouts of useless women, or what you do with your copious spare time, Clara.'

She beamed happily at him. 'Of course you do, dear.' And she went to collect his hat and coat, as usual.

Evie accompanied him to the mill, like the obedient daughter she was pretending to be. She stood at her frame all morning with the other girls and made a show, at least, of doing some work while knowing that her heart wasn't in it.

Oh, but she'd tolerated this dreadful life for long enough, and it really was time to move on. She would have liked to return to France or Italy and take up her travels again, but money would be a problem. Besides, she seemed to have found something to engage her interest much closer to home, a pastime which was both titillating and profitable, and that fed her appetite for excitement. Cabbage Lil's idea was intriguing, so why not? She always enjoyed a new challenge. Evie sneaked out of the mill for a longer lunch break than usual and began to make plans.

–

Cabbage Lil was taken aback by the suggestion that she and Evie form a partnership. 'You've quite knocked me sideways. I didn't expect this.'

'But it was your idea.'

'I thought you'd be setting up on your own, all gloss and polish like?'

'I'm not against a little gloss but thought we'd do much better as a team. You have the experience, and I have the contacts, which might prove useful. We'd need to find suitable girls for the quality clients, those who are fastidious in their tastes. My own tastes, as you are well aware, are far more egalitarian.'

'You like a bit of rough.'

Evie chortled with laughter. 'I like a man to be a man, certainly, and not some over-stuffed dandy trumped up on self-pride and smelling of cologne. I have some ideas, which might be worth trying and I'd be quite happy to put money into the enterprise. Apart from the fees I've saved, for services rendered,

I also have some jewellery I could sell. Pardon me for saying so, Lil, but I think we would need to improve our premises.'

'One that doesn't have a leaky roof would be a good place to start,' she agreed, and soon they were fully engrossed in writing a list of essential needs.

The house they found was ideal for their purpose, near enough to London Road Station to be of benefit to commercial travellers and other passing trade, and large enough to accommodate a dozen girls without overcrowding. No more unseemly goings-on in the back kitchen.

Evie sold a sapphire ring and one of her pearl necklaces and paid for the entire place to be redecorated with impeccable taste in classic style. The drawing room was refurbished in white and gold with lots of elegant sofas and armoires in pastel shades; Italian chests and bronze nymphs; Turkish rugs and green satin curtains with vases of white lilies and mirrors everywhere. In the large entrance hall a fountain played, water lilies in the pool at its base, and there were crystal chandeliers in every room. The whole place glittered but did not outshine the clientele.

Here would gather the men of Manchester: commercial travellers, business men; cotton magnates; judges; members of parliament and men who had made their mark on the world. Word would quickly spread that this was not only the most enthralling and exciting place to savour those intimate delights enjoyed by men of taste, but also the most fashionable. A telephone was installed, and prospective clients were required to ring first for an 'invitation'.

Guests would then be entertained to a champagne breakfast, lunch or dinner, prepared by a young chef Evie poached from a Parisian pension where she'd once stayed. A small gramophone supplied endless music. The food was of the highest standard as Evie's aim was to invoke a sense of café society. She tolerated only impeccable manners, proper introductions between guests and absolutely no loutish behaviour or indiscretions at dinner. She would rap her long, sharp finger nails on the table and call everyone to join with her in a toast to the King. Should one or more couples choose to leave the table before the meal was finished, nothing was said, no comments made. Privacy and discretion were guaranteed.

Evie was the star, sometimes bright and sparkling, at others coldly sensual. Pale blue eyes glowing with curiosity she would watch events unfold and quietly smile with satisfaction. Her chief passion was her need for money, although there were occasions, should she take a fancy to a young man herself, when she would softly whisper in her deep, throaty voice. Ever the attentive hostess, she made it her business to ensure that visits to Regency House, as it became known, never failed to delight. The object was that clients would not only remember their visit with awe and affection, but be eager to return week after week for more.

'You could have me instead, if you wish.' They never refused. Evie was the crème de la crème, and no client she accepted went away disappointed.

Chapter Twenty-Three

Maisie married Cyril in a short and simple ceremony at the chapel, and afterwards the wedding party, largely consisting of choir members and family, enjoyed a cold collation in the vestry. Dolly was delighted for her and it was the closest she'd felt to her mam in ages.

'I wish you every happiness,' she said, kissing her on the cheek, then she shook Cyril's hand and said the same to him.

Cyril gravely thanked her before adding, 'Happen I can be a sort of dad to you, Dolly.'

'Yes,' she said, trying to smile. 'Perhaps you can.'

To her surprise, Sam was also present, since Maisie had insisted on inviting him. She could see him at the far side of the room talking to Aggie. The pair of them looked quite animated as if they were having words. Then Harold appeared at her side and Dolly saw Sam turn away and head in her direction. 'Oh, bother,' she muttered to herself. Did she have the strength to deal with him today? Well, he had to be faced some time.

'Hello Dolly.'

'Hello Sam.'

He asked if she was keeping well, spoke of the weather being kind on Maisie's special day and other useless small talk till Dolly could bear it no longer. 'If there's something you want to say to me, Sam, will you get on and say it.'

'All right, I just wanted to apologise for ruining everything. I know I made a complete mess of our marriage. I should have had more patience, more loyalty.'

'Yes, you should.'

'But you need to know that nothing happened between me and Evie Barker.' Not for the want of trying, he thought, but the statement was nonetheless true.

'It didn't appear that way to me.'

'We didn't – you know – go all the way. It was just a bit of harmless flirtation, and it's over now. She'd been chasing me for months and I nearly succumbed, I'll admit that, but I didn't in the end, and I wondered if you'd give me another chance. Please, Dolly?'

The question took her by surprise. It was so unexpected and she'd given the matter no thought, was almost growing used to being without him. Dolly had even begun to look forward to having the house to herself, now that her mam was married and would be moving in with Cyril. She was also busy trying to rebuild her money lending business. She'd spent quite a bit of time lately calling on all her old clients, reminding them she was still around and offering lower interest than Nifty Jack. She'd also sought out new ones and been fortunate enough to pick up a few. But then it made her heart sore to see the little waifs and strays hanging about the yards in their rags and tatters, with empty bellies and their little faces pinched with hunger. Something had to be done.

Why couldn't Sam Clayton see how fortunate he was to have a job and a loving wife?

'I can't give you an answer right off,' she told him. 'I'd need to think about it.'

'I understand. But I dare say you've paid off your mam's debt by now. No more worries over the talleyman.'

'Not quite, but I don't trouble my head about Nifty Jack any more.' Yes, she did, Nifty was very much still a force to be reckoned with, and she worried a great deal about the daughters of her new clients. But Dolly had no wish to go into all of that with Sam. 'Where are you living at the moment? With Matt?'

Sam eased a finger round the inside of his collar, suddenly looking uncomfortable. 'No, Matt and I don't see much of each other these days. We've grown apart, like.'

'I always thought you two were inseparable.'

'I'm staying with Davey Lee. He's wed and has a couple of childer, so it's only temporary. I'm looking for a place of me own.'

'So you thought why not move back in with the good little wife, is that it? Particularly since she has the house to herself now.'

'Nay, that's not it at all, Dolly. You're being unkind.'

'It's been nice talking to you, Sam.' As she turned away, he grabbed her wrist and pulled her to a halt.

'You'll think about it though, eh? We could still make a go of it, I'm sure. I am fond of you, Dolly.'

'Fond?'

He hastily corrected himself. 'I love you. I just don't find it easy to express my feelings.'

'I wonder why.'

'If you'll only give me another chance, love, I'll not let you down again.'

She shook his hand free and walked away, surprised to find that her heart wasn't racing, feeling surprisingly calm. Now what did that mean?

–

Dolly couldn't make up her mind what to do about Sam, and as always when in a quandary, went to talk to Matt Thornton.

'I don't know why you bother with him. Didn't you see him with Evie Barker? I don't understand, Dolly, that you might want him back?'

Dolly shook her head, not knowing what she wanted. They stood staring bleakly out at the derricks, the tugs loading and unloading and were silent for some long minutes. 'It's all a muddle, a bit of a mess to be honest. I don't want him back, not now I've seen with my own eyes how he's betrayed me. The problem is I do still love him, d'you see. At least I think I do.'

'Oh, Dolly.' Matt took a step closer, held her gently by the shoulders as he turned her towards him. 'Look at me, and tell me honestly. Are you saying that if he came knocking on your door, you'd let him in?'

Matt's brown eyes were filled with sadness and something she could only describe as raw pain. He looked so dreadfully hurt she could hardly bear to look him in the eye. 'Sam swears he's innocent, that nothing has actually happened between them. That she was kissing him, not the other way around.'

Matt pursed his lips. 'If you believe that, you're a bigger fool than I took you for, Dolly Tomkins. Wake up and see the light. Have you not considered that there could be other women, besides Evie Barker?'

'Don't say such dreadful things. Why would there be?'

'I'm saying what if there was someone you hadn't thought about. Have you spoken to your Aggie about it?'

'Why would I need to talk to my her?'

He held up his hands by way of apology, aware that he was treading on dangerous ground, yet how could he stand by and say nothing when he loved her? But to tell her that Sam had boasted he was enjoying Aggie's favours, as in the old days, was perhaps a step too far. Or that he claimed Aggie being his sister-in-law made it even more exciting.

'A bit naughty, if you know what I mean,' had been his exact words.

Matt had asked him about Evie Barker and Sam had nonchalantly declared that she'd take a bit longer to get into his bed but he still held every hope of success. 'Who needs prim little Dolly with two women chasing me?'

He'd given Sam a piece of his mind and walked away. They hadn't spoken since.

But he couldn't bring himself to relay any of this to Dolly. 'I just thought if anyone knew anything, she would. Your Aggie always seems to have her ear to the ground. I didn't mean to upset you, Dolly, but you really have to face facts. Sam hasn't been fair to you. He's played around with this other woman and may do so again. You shouldn't believe everything he tells you. Don't let him take you for a fool.'

'And I'd be obliged if you didn't call me one.' Anger was rising in her, and regret, for she'd thought they were friends.

'I'm only saying it's time you thought of yourself for a change, found some sort of contentment and happiness. He'd only let you down, wouldn't be able to help himself. Then you'd be badly hurt all over again.' His tone hardened as Matt spoke with fervour, anxious to make his point. 'If he truly loved you and properly appreciated his good fortune at having you for a wife, as any normal man would, I'd encourage you to take him back, despite the loss to myself. But he really doesn't deserve you, and it's time you got over this infatuation you have with him.'

'Infatuation?'

'If you want my honest opinion, I don't think you ever did love him. You don't even know what love is.'

'I most certainly do.'

'No, Dolly, you don't, and I'll prove it.' And before she'd guessed what he was about to do, he pulled her into his arms and kissed her. It was a kiss like no other. His mouth was warm and soft against hers, yet compulsively demanding. She found herself leaning into him, wanting it to go on. His tongue caressed and teased hers, setting up a need in her that she'd never thought to feel for any man other than her husband. And in a way this was more real, more exciting than anything she'd experienced with Sam. It felt so right, as if she belonged in Matt's arms. When the kiss was finally over, Dolly sagged against him with a regretful sigh.

Matt spoke to her softly. 'You don't know how long I've ached to do that. I envy Sam. Always have. I wanted you to notice me, to love me, but I was too awkward and shy, too stupid to say anything.'

She put a hand up to his tender lips, knowing her own must be rosy with his kisses. 'Don't say such things. You aren't in the least bit stupid. Things just turned out wrong, that's all. You're right though, I was young and daft, potty over Sam, while he was always crazy about our Aggie.'

'He still is.'

Dolly was startled that he should still insist upon making this point. 'No, you're wrong. Sam did love me, in his way. And our Aggie is a married woman, mad about Harold and about to have a baby. So don't say such stupid things.' She was concentrating on his mouth and impulsively kissed him again, her lips curled upwards into the most beguiling smile. This couldn't be happening to her. She really ought to be ashamed of herself, yet she wasn't in the least. His arms pulled her tighter against his chest and Dolly felt that kick of emotion somewhere deep inside. She teased the curls on his brow, kissing the tip of his nose. He was a lovely man, kind but wise, gentle and so strong. Why had she never given him the attention he deserved? She could no longer hear the sounds of the timber yard all around them, the shouts of the men, the whirr of the saw. Dolly felt as if she was cocooned in a magic bubble within the circle of Matt's arms.

Matt frowned in a short pause then his next words burst out. 'I can't *not* say it, Dolly, because it's true. He's still seeing your Aggie and they are at it like rabbits. He's also seeing that Barker girl. You can't trust a word he says, he's a liar, as is your loving sister.'

Dolly stared at him in cold fury, then pulling herself from his arms began to back away, her tears starting. 'You're saying he's sleeping with my sister, Aggie? No, no, that was over long before we were married. Sam isn't a liar, just a bit misguided, easily led by that Evie Barker who's been after him for ages.'

Matt let out a heavy sigh. Oh lord, the damage was done now, so why not stick with it? 'Sorry love, but that's exactly what I'm saying.'

Red-hot anger soared through her veins, although whether that was because of the possible depth of her husband's betrayal, or the fact Matt had known about it and she hadn't, Dolly couldn't rightly say at that moment. But Matt was handy to take the brunt of her ire, and Sam wasn't. 'I'll not have you say such terrible things about my husband. Sam swears he's done nothing with Evie Barker, and I've no reason not to believe him. People tend to make harsh judgements far too quickly, as they did with me. It's all my fault, is this, for becoming obsessed with Nifty Jack.'

'Oh, Dolly, don't blame yourself, not again.'

She was crying now, hot, furious tears that rolled unchecked down her pale cheeks. '*At it like rabbits?* That's a *lie*! You're only saying all of this because you fancy me yourself. You're every bit as bad as Sam, Matt Thornton. Marriage is sacred and behaving no better myself, maybe I *should* give him another try. Maybe I *will*.'

Turning on her heel she began to walk away, as fast as her trembling legs would take her. Matt hurried after her. 'I'm sorry I've hurt you but think what you're saying, as I would *never* lie to you. The last thing I want is to turn you against me.'

'Then you should keep your nose out of my affairs, Matt Thornton.' And since he was obliged to return to his work, she left him kicking himself with frustration at the timber yard.

Dolly considered going straight to Aggie and tackling her on the subject there and then. She could ask her straight out if there was anything going on between her and Sam, then carefully watch her sister's expression for any sign of a lie. But since Aggie was proving to be curiously besotted with the wonderful Harold, why would she even look in Sam's direction?

Matt Thornton had said all of that about Sam in order to win her round, as all men did when they needed to satisfy their lust. It could be just his opinion and not at all true. She did care for Matt and had been absorbed by the kiss he gave her, but his comments were surely entirely wrong. Could she trust him any more than she could Sam? But having come to this conclusion, why did she feel as if her whole world had collapsed?

First thing the next morning, Matt was knocking at her door. 'I've come to apologise for overstepping the mark. I haven't slept for worrying about it.'

Dolly looked at his dear face. Despite her best efforts she too had suffered a sleepless night, unable to get Matt Thornton out of her head. 'You most certainly did overstep the mark. You shouldn't have said all that about Sam and our Aggie. I'll not believe a word of it.' She paused a moment while she wondered if that was true, whether there may not be a grain of truth in what Matt had said, then catching his anxious expression found herself smiling.

'However, since you and I are old friends, I'll forgive you and put the matter out of my mind. It was probably only jealousy talking.'

Matt let out a sigh of relief. 'Thank goodness for that. You're my best friend, Dolly, and I hope always will be.'

'I'm sure I will,' she murmured. But were they already more than that, despite her protests? That kiss seemed to have awakened some hidden emotions deep inside.

'Since it's Saturday, I wondered if maybe we could go for a walk down by the canal, or take a tram out into the country. I promise to behave.'

'I should hope so. I'm still a respectable married woman, don't forget, and I haven't yet made up my mind about Sam. I'm still a bit mixed up. I do like you, Matt, but I can't just throw my husband away like a used dish cloth. I shouldn't fancy you at all, so it's a bit difficult, do you see?'

He was grinning at her now, almost laughing. 'I'm glad to hear you fancy me. That's encouraging.'

Then she was laughing too. 'All right, I've said too much.'

'No, you haven't, Dolly, nowhere near enough.'

'Matt had actually planned a picnic, even brought food: sandwiches, buttered scones, a bottle of lemonade and a few boiled sweets. You can't have a day in the country without fizzy pop and toffees. I hope that's all right.'

Dolly was thrilled and deeply touched. It was a glorious sunny day in early July and a picnic would be such fun. 'It all sounds marvellous. Mam used to take us out on picnics when we were little. We'd have jam butties, lemonade or cold tea in a bottle, and take a jam jar and a net to catch tiddlers. My brothers were experts at fishing but I was hopeless.'

'Oh, me too,' he laughed. 'I never caught many and whatever fish I did catch I put back again. Can't bear to think of anything being trapped.'

Travelling on the tram to Worsley made Dolly feel as if they were going to the end of the world. They said little during the journey, swaying rhythmically together on the slatted wooden seat, watching the tram gradually empty of people. When they got off, the conductor got out too so he could swing the big pole round, ready for the return journey, while the driver walked through the tram to the other end.

'I hope they remember to come back for us,' Dolly laughed. 'We mustn't miss the last tram or we'll be stranded here all night.'

'Now there's a tempting thought.'

As the empty tram rattled away back into the city, they set off walking, carefully not touching, although Dolly was acutely conscious that they were truly alone for the first time. At the timber yard or on the wharf, where they'd met up before for a chat, often while Matt took his dinner break there were always other men around. There would also be the noise of the tugs, the sawmill and machinery. Here, there was nothing but a long track winding away over a patch of scrub land and the sound of the wind sighing in the trees. They went through a kissing gate, and Dolly was relieved that Matt made no attempt to take advantage of it. She felt shy suddenly, unsure of herself.

Passing by a churchyard they walked on across the moor, through other gates, across a railway line and by a row of small cottages each with a long vegetable garden. It seemed marvellous that these fingers of green could stretch right into the heart of the city.

They set out their picnic under an old elm tree and Matt smiled at her enthusiasm as she sipped the lemonade and tucked into a sandwich, the sun glistening on her hair so that it shone like satin velvet.

After a moment, he said, 'You do know what's happening, don't you, Dolly? At least, I assume you feel the same way. It certainly felt that way when we kissed yesterday.'

Dolly set down the sandwich, answering in her smallest voice. 'I do, but I feel so guilty. I never expected this to happen. Sam was the only man for me and all I can think about now is you, the only face I see when I close me eyes is yours. It's a sin, dreadfully wrong.'

'No it isn't, love. How can it be when he's treated you so badly? You were too young when you got wed, hadn't had time to find out who you were, let alone who you wanted to marry. Oh, but I can't bear to just sit here and not touch you.'

She gazed at him with longing in her eyes. 'Me neither.'

When he kissed her this time, she was ready for him. The kiss went on a long time and Dolly wasn't aware when they sank down into the sweet smelling long grass, but she made no protest when he lifted her blouse to caress her breast.

Matt made love to her in a way she'd never experienced before. He took her to heights of happiness Dolly had never known existed. He was tender and patient with her, sometimes too patient as she became ever more eager to have him inside her, to fill her, envelope her with his love. Yet he was eager and passionate, exciting her with his need. She'd meant to call a halt at an appropriate moment but her need was equal to his, a desire that demanded fulfilment. She was overwhelmed by passion, could barely think let alone put up any resistance. Dolly knew now that she loved Matt Thornton, and somehow it seemed right to show him just how much.

Afterwards, they lay on their backs gazing up into a clear blue sky streaked with pink and white clouds. 'You've forgotten your sandwich,' he said.

'So have you.'

'I don't seem to be hungry, not for food anyway.' He turned on his side so that he could look at her, and for a long time they were content just to gaze into each other's eyes, as lovers do, drinking in the joy of the moment, the miracle of this new-found love. He tucked back a stray curl, stroked a cheek warmed by loving as much as the sun then pulled her gently into the curve of his arm and kissed her again.

'I wish we could stay like this forever, not let the tram come back for us. We could live in one of those little cottages with our children around our feet and be happy as larks.'

Perhaps it was the mention of children, or this idyll of togetherness he'd described which brought her to her senses. Dolly sat up and picked up her abandoned sandwich, now curling slightly in the heat. 'I think we'd best eat our picnic and try to come back down to earth, don't you?'

'I don't ever want to come down to earth if it means losing you, Dolly. I want you to be my wife. I want to marry you.'

'Oh, Matt!' Her eyes were bleak, raw with longing as she looked at him. 'What are we going to do?'

'I don't know love, but I mean it to happen, come what may. You're my woman now, Dolly, and my future wife. Make no mistake about that.'

Chapter Twenty-Four

Later, back home in the solitude of her little house, Dolly was swamped by guilt, almost overwhelmed by it. It gnawed at her, consumed her, had her pacing the bedroom floor before dawn. One minute she wished Mam was still at home so she could talk her worries through with her and share the tumult of these emotions, the next she'd feel relieved that she wasn't.

Hadn't she tormented Maisie for doing this self-same thing, going with another man while she was still married? Hadn't she blamed Sam too? She was no better than either of them. Dolly saw herself as a hypocrite. Loving Matt as she did was no excuse at all, not in her eyes. She'd allowed him to make love to her, a man other than her husband. Never mind that it had been wonderful and glorious, what had she been thinking of to let it happen?

It was time to take stock and come to her senses. Sam was still her husband, but had made mistakes and was not perfect.

'We're all weak because we're human,' she told herself sternly as the first rays of sunlight prodded away the dusky shadows of her room. Marriage was sacred, so if for nothing else he surely deserved another chance. It surely wouldn't be right to lead a double life, one of secrecy and furtive meetings? Could she afford a divorce, now that she was as guilty as him?

Dolly stood at her bedroom window for a long time with the image of Matt's face before her, seeming to be imprinted on the rose-tinted glass as the sun grew in strength and filtered through the grime, tears rolling down her cheeks. Oh, but how could she ever manage to give Matt up, now that she'd found him? They needed to talk, and hopefully he'd call by later.

–

Matt fully intended calling on Dolly, just to check that she was all right, and reassure her about how he felt after what had taken place between them yesterday. He certainly didn't want her to feel guilty, or to think that was all he'd been after. He was getting ready to go when his boss called at his door to ask if he'd pop to the yard for an hour or two, even though it was a Sunday, as a load of timber had just been delivered that needed shifting and sorting. Matt agreed. He liked his gaffer and needed the work.

In the event it was nearly three o'clock by the time he'd finished but Matt decided to go anyway. He desperately wanted to see her, and it was important to tell her again how much he loved her, how much their special day together had meant to him. He hurried home to sluice himself down with hot, soapy water and quickly change into his smart Sunday suit.

Moments later he was striding along Potato Wharf, all slick and smart, when he spotted Sam leaning on a lamp post talking to Lizzie Bramley, one of the mill girls. Matt didn't pause he merely nodded by way of recognition and continued on his way. Seconds later, Sam was at his elbow, playfully punching his shoulder, almost dancing along beside him.

'Are you still not speaking? Too stuck up to talk to an old mate?'

'You seemed busy, more interested in your new girlfriend.'

Sam punched him harder, bringing him to a halt. 'Hey, what you implying? She's not my girlfriend, just a bit light relief as you might say. What about you? Where are you off to in such a hurry? Still trying to catch a bit of skirt for yourself, eh?'

Matt shrugged him off and kept on walking. 'None of your damned business! You and me haven't been mates in a long while, Sam. I don't like your style any more.'

'It's my style that gets me any likely lass I set my cap at.'

'So I've heard.'

'Who from? Who's been gossiping about me?' Sam was hurrying now, his shorter stride finding it hard to keep up with Matt's cracking pace. 'It wouldn't be my wife, would it?'

'Dolly never says a word against you. Far too trusting, more's the pity.'

Sam chuckled, preening himself with delight. 'Aye, that lass thinks the sun shines out of my bleedin' backside! I regret having left her and will ask her to take me back. She's a right little cracker in bed, and never minded how much I went out of an evening. Not the nagging sort, our Dolly.'

Matt abruptly stopped, his expression livid and grabbed Sam by the collar and pulled him up sharp. 'I hope that doesn't mean what I think.'

'What's it to you?'

'You know how I feel about Dolly; always have, and I won't see her badly treated. If you do wrong for her again, you'll have me to deal with.'

'Who are you to tell me how to treat me own wife?' Sam's expression changed to one of open curiosity. 'Hey, have you been having it off with my missus?'

'Don't be stupid.' Try as he might, Matt could not prevent the tide of colour from flooding his cheekbones.

'You bloody have.'

'Who are you to cast judgement? You walked out on Dolly months ago. We've become much more friendly, but don't try to make it out as something dirty, because it isn't. I love Dolly and she's falling in love with me.'

Matt knew, the instant he said these words, that he'd made a bad mistake. If there was one thing Sam Clayton couldn't abide, it was competition. He'd always been that way, in sport, in lessons at school, and particularly with girls. He always had to be top dog, the one who won all the prizes, scored the most goals and, now, slept with the most women.

His eyes had narrowed, his tone hardened. 'Clearly I'm not the only one who enjoys playing away from home. Always makes for a better match and more goals, don't you reckon?'

Matt turned from him in disgust, eager now to put some distance between them. The fist that connected with the side of his jaw came out of nowhere, taking him completely by surprise, instantly followed by a punch in the stomach, which brought him to his knees.

'Serve you right, you bleeding scumbag. Nobody else enjoys my wife's favours, do you understand?'

Matt managed to say, 'I'll not fight you. I refuse to lower myself to your standards. Just leave Dolly alone and—'

His words were cut off as he was kicked with the toe of Sam's boot. He managed to grab hold of his leg and pull Sam down with him. Then the two men were grappling and rolling about in the filth of the wharf, Sam aiming wild blows, punching and kicking. Matt did his best to hold him off, to stop the fight before too much damage was done. That was a bad mistake. He never knew what hit him but he was knocked out cold, flat on his face on the hard stone setts. Nor was he aware that Sam went on kicking him for some long time.

–

Dolly was warming herself a dish of soup in an effort to rekindle a failing appetite when the knock came. She ran to the door, guessing it must be Matt come to see if she was all right. Then stopped, her hand on the knob, paralysed by indecision. How could she let him in? They could never be together as he had described yesterday. How could she ever be his wife? It was an impossible dream.

And yet...

The knocking came again and her heart began to thud, whether with excitement or blind panic she couldn't be sure. It was all very well to talk herself into giving Sam another chance but what if it didn't work? And how could she give Matt up now that she knew how she felt about him? She opened the door but it wasn't Matt standing on the doorstep, it was Sam.

'Can I come in? There's something I need to say.'

Dolly gave him the dish of soup and sat and watched while he ate it, smacking his lips with gusto. 'Nobody makes a good Scotch broth like you, Dolly. You're a wonder in the kitchen. I must say I've missed your cooking. Is there any more bread? I've worked up quite an appetite for some reason.' Silently, she spread a dab of marg on another slice and handed it to him.

Dolly couldn't think of a thing to say. She was too heartsore, too utterly miserable. Where was Matt? Why hadn't he come to see her today? If he'd really cared about her, as he claimed, surely he would have called by now. Perhaps it was true what people said, that once a man has enjoyed your favours he's no longer interested. Or perhaps he thought her cheap and of no account. She could feel her eyes burning with tears and quickly brushed them away, afraid Sam might notice.

But he wasn't even looking at her as all his attention was fixed on scraping up the last of his soup before setting the dish aside with a satisfied sigh.

'I wondered if you'd had time to think over what I said the other week. I've tried to be patient, not force you into a quick decision but I feel we should get things straight between us. We can't go on like this. I miss you, Dolly. You know I'm crackers about you really, never realised how much till we split up. Like that time when you ran away, I missed you something shocking. Never know what I've got till I lose it.'

'Perhaps we should stay apart more, then you might really start to love me,' Dolly said, a touch of asperity in her tone. She was still secretly hoping for a second knock to come to the door. It didn't happen.

He laughed, as if she'd made a joke. 'Don't be like that. We're good together, you and me. I've told you already how sorry I am for hurting your feelings. What more can I say?' Sam was desperate to move out of that overcrowded little house with Davey and his wife constantly carping at each other, and their noisy screaming kids. They nearly drove him mad. He'd promise anything for a decent billet and he'd nothing to lose and everything to gain for a little peace.

Dolly could hear the anxiety in his voice and a part of her began to soften. There was a pleading in his eyes, that little-boy-lost expression she'd once loved so much; a sulky droop to the sensual mouth, which always undid her. If he really did love her, perhaps she should give him another chance. They'd both made mistakes but with good will on both sides, it might work. Surely that was the right thing to do, and the sensible answer? And Matt hadn't called again, as she'd hoped.

Sam was growing anxious. He'd expected her to fall on his neck and for some reason she was proving obstinate. He had to get round her somehow. Not only did he miss the creature comforts Dolly had to offer but Aggie had revealed to him her suspicions over her pregnancy, which had alarmed him greatly. The last thing he needed was for Harold to find out it was his. It wasn't that he was a violent man or anything of that sort, but what if he dumped Aggie on to him and said; it's your child so you must keep her and bring it up? What the hell would he do then? A bit of fun was all very well, everyone enjoyed a bit of slap and sex, but he really didn't want the responsibility of bringing up a kid.

In any case, how could he be sure it was his? He didn't know how active she still was with Harold. For all he knew, the pair of them could still be going at it hammer and tongs. How could he be sure since she's a married woman? Much safer to move back in with Dolly and write it off as a bit of a lark. Sam was very good at shutting such difficulties out of his head, as more than one girl had discovered to her cost. Dumping Aggie would also give him more time to pursue Evie. He'd quite neglected her recently.

'So what do you say, Dolly? You're me own sweet, lovely wife, after all, and I need you. I'm asking for your forgiveness so won't let you down again. I've learned me lesson.' He was fast running out of patience, and certainly had no intention of begging. That would be too much, though he could always pretend. 'Do you want me to go down on one knee and declare my undying passion?' He wondered if he'd pushed it too far but she was blushing prettily, and even gave a little chuckle. He hoped he might be winning her round.

Dolly glanced across at the front door, which remained obstinately closed and silent. 'All right,' she said wearily, coming to a sudden decision. 'We'll give it one more try. But you sleep in the spare room, right?'

Sam eagerly agreed. 'That'll be grand. Dolly. You won't regret giving me another chance, and I'm sure you'll soon change your mind about our sleeping arrangements, in time.' Being back before his own fireside would make the point to Aggie that their past was over and done with, and she'd best get used to her baby having Harold for a dad and not him. As for the back bedroom, well, he'd be out of there in no time, given his skill with women. Dolly would be putty in his hands before the week was out.

Something inside her gave a silent cry of denial. She really didn't want him in her bed ever again, yet gave no indication of this as she valiantly smiled her agreement. 'We'll see how things go, shall we? Take things slowly. You can fetch your things round tomorrow and come home to that spare room.' That gave Matt one last evening to call and say that he still loved her, and she hadn't shamed herself by giving in to his charms. Maybe then she'd change her mind allowing Sam to stay.

Matt didn't call. Dolly waited up quite late, hoping and praying that he would, that he'd have some reason for leaving it so late and would finally arrive to reassure her that his feelings for her were as strong as ever, that he still respected and loved her. But she sat alone, largely in tears, all evening.

–

Sam moved in the following day and Dolly suffered a second night of torment, worrying over whether she'd done the right thing. Why had Matt let her down so cruelly? After that on the next day, she went early to the timber yard, long before any of the men had arrived for work and left a note for him with the night watchman. It stated that she couldn't ever see him again. It explained that Sam had moved back in, and she closed by saying that, however much she cared for Matt, she believed their time together had been a mistake, as perhaps he did too. She hoped he wouldn't think too badly of her. Making her marriage work seemed to be the best solution all round. She signed the letter in friendship, tears blotching the words.

On Tuesday, when Matt finally received the letter, following his return from hospital where he had spent the last two days, he screwed the paper up into a furious ball and flung it into the canal.

If only he hadn't met Sam on Saturday afternoon! If he'd kept his mouth shut and not given the impression he loved Dolly and she was growing fond of him, Sam might not have goaded him into acting like a fool. That had cost him dear and Dolly was now persuaded to take her husband back. In despair and fury Matt punched the wall with his fist, damaging his knuckles. Then he kicked several big stones into the canal that sank along with the note and all his hopes and dreams. His agony was so unbearable he didn't speak to another soul for the rest of that day. Even his workmates recognised distress when they saw it in his face, guessing it had something to do with the cuts and bruises he'd recently acquired and judiciously kept a respectful distance.

Chapter Twenty-Five

Aggie was bitterly disappointed when she heard that Sam had moved back into Tully Court with Dolly. It wasn't that she had any intention of leaving Harold for him, far from it. Nor did she have the slightest wish of eliciting scandal by carrying on the affair for too long. Her nerves had been a wreck during those few short weeks while she and Sam had been having their little fling. Oh, but it had been so exciting, so thrilling, and such a boost to her morale that it had even livened up her flagging sex life with Harold.

But what she'd enjoyed most of all was getting one over on Dolly, the sister who'd inveigled her way into the Tomkins family under false pretences. A cuckoo in the nest! A bastard, no less, however much she might claim otherwise.

Filled with her own self-righteous view of life, and obsessed by petty jealousy and malice, Aggie didn't make the connection that she was about to do the very same thing as Maisie. She was about to present her husband with a child that wasn't his.

This baby was special and must have the very best. For that reason she asked Harold for money to buy the layette, cot, baby carriage and other essentials.

'We'll wait till it's safely born, shall we?' Harold cautioned. 'By then we'll happen have found some second-hand equipment we could buy.'

'Second-hand?' Aggie was appalled. 'I'm not having second-hand for any child of mine.'

'Why on earth not? How long does a baby use a cot or a bath? Hardly any time at all. We have to be prudent with our savings, Aggie, now that I'm not earning as much as I used to.

Aggie paid no heed to this but called at Kendal Milne's baby department and ordered not only a complete layette, since she certainly had no time to knit while working at the mill, but also every item of furniture and baby equipment which she might conceivably need for baby's nursery. From bottles to a baby bath, from a cot to a high chair, bibs to pram suits, baby Entwistle would be the smartest child on the street, as was only right and proper.

They promised to store the items for her, until they were needed, handed over the necessary forms for her husband to sign and a club card so that weekly payments could be made. Aggie walked away perfectly happy, and with only the slightest reservation about the actual filling in of the form. She put off telling Harold that evening as he was in a sour mood, complaining about a fist fight that had broken out in the mill yard, which he'd had to deal with. He was tired and snored loudly in his chair for hours before waking up with a start and ordering her to bed.

Days later Harold received a letter from his bank manager concerning payments on the hire purchase loan they'd taken out for the spare room furniture some time ago. So when he issued a further lecture on the value of money and the necessity for prudence and no more buying, as he had instructed her, Aggie found it was not appropriate to mention the latest hire purchase she'd made. Not yet! But all done and dusted, Harold would have to stop being selfish with his savings and dig deeper into his pockets to provide for her precious son or daughter.

Later, when he'd gone off to bed early, claiming to be exhausted, she signed it herself using his name. Who would know?

It proved to be perfectly correct in that the cashier at the department store did not blink an eye when she handed it over the next day, merely wished Aggie well with her coming confinement and said they were happy to be of assistance. So, there we are, Aggie thought happily. All settled and arranged, and Harold will simply have to stop being so selfish with his savings and dig deeper into his pockets to provide for our precious son or daughter. As for Sam Clayton, Dolly was welcome to him. Aggie fully intended to take the first opportunity to tell her so.

–

When Sam called, asking for an appointment or an invitation, Evie almost laughed out loud but did at least agree to see him. She even instructed her little maid to bring them tea, which they took in her private boudoir. 'Was it something in particular you wished to say to me?'

Sam was looking about him with interest, noting the fancy décor, the gilt, the pastel colours. He'd heard the rumours and been eager to check them out for himself. Since he had personal acquaintance with the owner of this fine establishment, he was quite certain he'd be able to procure special rates. 'You seem to be doing very well for yourself, lass.'

'Don't call me that,' she sweetly corrected him. 'Earl Grey or Indian?'

Sam glanced at her, bemused by the question until he saw her holding the teapot. 'As it comes.'

'If you were considering requesting my services, I don't think you can afford me,' she told him, handing him a china cup of the finest Earl Grey.

Sam sniffed it and set it down with a grimace of distaste. 'I'll have a drop of milk, if you can spare it. And how would you know what I could afford? Anyroad, you can't pick and choose, can you, not in your line of business.' He smirked, giving her a big wink.

'Oh, I most certainly can. Unlike your poor wife, I don't have to put up with you.'

'What's that supposed to mean?'

'I heard you'd moved back in with your silly girl. Why ever did she agree? No doubt you spun her a load of lies, promising to be faithful. Did she welcome you with open arms?'

Contrary to his optimistic belief, Dolly had not succumbed to his charms within the week. Over a month later he was still in the back bedroom and not enjoying it one little bit. Of course, he had his usual compensations, although Myra had got herself a new chap and was no longer available. Even so, he missed Dolly, and since she was near at hand it seemed a shame to waste the opportunity. Unfortunately, she was proving to be remarkably obstinate. No matter how much he argued that they were still man and wife and he was entitled to her, she absolutely refused to allow him to move back into her bed. 'Dolly and me are having a trial reunion,' he admitted. 'To see if it'll work.'

'Oh dear! I must say, Sam darling, you are feeling rather neglected but were quite fun once. I've moved on to richer, more exciting fish. You're just a little tiddler in a big pond, and of no account at all. Didn't you realise?'

Still hankering after Evie Barker, and ready to get her, Sam could feel his face start to burn, almost cracking the fragile cup and saucer as he slammed it down. He was on his feet in a second. 'I've not come here to be insulted. I just thought it might be interesting to—'

'Give me a good seeing for old time's sake?' She laughed, and put back her head chortled with delight. 'I don't think so, sweetie. You never were the stud you imagined yourself to be, so I hardly think you can be now. Close the door on your way out, there's a dear.'

—

Dolly had never been more miserable in all her life. She felt utterly wretched. It had been a terrible mistake letting Sam move back in. She'd come so close to real happiness with Matt yet somehow it had all unravelled and gone sour. She avoided going anywhere near the timber yard now, unable to bear the thought of running into him by pure chance.

To be fair, Sam was doing his best and behaving himself in his way, being polite and considerate, rarely going out and not trying anything on. But relations between them could best be described as awkward. He did ask once or twice if he might move out of the back bedroom. She'd said no, and he seemed to accept that. But they really had nothing left to say to each other and were more like strangers than man and wife. Whatever spark there'd once been between them was now dead.

Dolly made his tea, did his washing, ironed his shirts, carried out all those wifely duties in addition to her normal routine of house calls to her clients, collecting their weekly payments and trying to find a few more customers. At least Nifty Jack seemed to be keeping his distance, which was a huge relief.

Each evening the pair of them would sit at either side of the hearth, not speaking or even looking at each other, and keeping up the façade of a happy marriage while Dolly darned his socks.

Sam would keep sighing, pretend to listen to the wireless and glance at his pocket watch every five minutes. 'Have you not done yet? And what about supper?' he'd complain.

'You've had your supper. I made hotpot. What more do you want?'

'I meant a snack before I go to bed. A sandwich or something.'

'Make one for yourself, if you're still hungry.'

'You're my wife, you should make it.'

In the end, she could stand it no longer. 'Oh, for goodness sake, I've fed you well, so go to the pub, why don't you? I can't bear to see you sitting there with a face as long as a wet fortnight. Get from under my feet then I can have a bit of peace.'

He was out of the door like a shot from a gun, which was such a relief. When he'd gone, she kicked off her shoes, tucked her feet under her and thought of Matt.

When Sam returned later that night very much to worse for drink, Dolly heard him come stumbling up the stairs. He rapped on her bedroom door and called her name. But she'd wedged a chair under the door handle so paid no attention, blotting out his pleading by stuffing her fingers in her ears. Turning over in her lonely bed she wondered how she could live like this for the rest of her life, hating her husband, nor wanting him to touch her. She could hardly bear to have him in the same house, let alone her bed. Her last thought as she wept silent tears into her pillow, was for Matt. If only he wasn't avoiding her, like everyone else in her life.

—

It took no time at all for Aggie to get into financial difficulties. In a frighteningly short space of time she discovered that her housekeeping money did not stretch to the normal weekly payments for all the items she had ordered, let alone pay off any extra. She tried wheedling a little extra out of Harold, but he was stubbornly resistant to her pleas, constantly reminding her how generous her allowance was already, which was true. Normally she'd had plenty left over from her housekeeping after food had been bought and paid for, and he'd sometimes given her a bit extra for treats or the odd frock she'd a fancy to buy. All that had stopped when his wages had been cut. It was most vexing.

'You don't seem to understand that I need new clothes, since my old ones no longer fit,' she tried to explain.

'I bought you a larger overall for work, and a smock to wear at home with that special sort of skirt with the drop down apron front. What more do you need? It's not as if we can afford to go out much these days, so no one sees you but me, and I think you look lovely whatever you wear, love.'

His soft words, even his teasing kisses didn't waken the usual response in her and she'd flounced off to bed in a huff, leaving Harold even more worried and concerned about her condition.

Later, he brought her up a cup of hot cocoa and gently suggested that if she was feeling below par, perhaps it was time, after all, for her to give up work. Fear shot through her like liquid fire. The last thing Aggie wanted was to lose her wages. How would she manage then?

'No, I'm fine, really I am. Just a bit tired. I can do another month at least.' Hopefully, by then she'd have coaxed some of those blasted savings out of him.

She tried cutting down on grocery and butcher bills by giving him meat less frequently, and trying cheaper cuts. But Harold had a healthy appetite, loved his meat and two veg and considered that he worked hard enough to deserve it. He also enjoyed home-made cakes and puddings and so economies on that front did not go down well either.

'Complain to the fishmonger next time you go, dear. This piece of cod is dreadful.'

'Yes dear, I will.' It wasn't cod at all but some unknown species Aggie had never heard of but the fishmonger had assured her, when she'd pointed out that she must be a little more economical with the baby coming along, that her husband would never notice the difference. Clearly he didn't know Harold.

It gave her some satisfaction that life seemed to be no easier for Dolly. 'Sam behaving himself, is he?' she would blithely enquire, whenever she decided to pop round and do a bit of nosing.

Dolly generally said little, merely asking if she was having an easy pregnancy, but Aggie could tell that things weren't going well between them. 'I'm fine and dandy, thank you. So, is Sam still seeing Evie Barker? She never comes into work now. Rumour has it she's set up as a madam.'

'A what?'

'With Cabbage Lil, that friend of yours! Don't pretend you know nowt about it. You probably introduced them.'

'I didn't!' Dolly said, appalled. This was news to her and surely couldn't be a coincidence. 'How on earth did they meet?'

Aggie stood up and began to button on her gloves. 'Don't play the innocent. It's you what moves in those sort of circles, not me. But I doubt Mr Barker will be too chuffed to hear how you brought his precious daughter into contact with that nasty piece of merchandise, so yet again you've brought shame on our family, Dolly. What Harold will say when he hears, I cannot imagine.'

—

On his way to bed a night or two later, Nathan tapped on Evie's door. There was no reply. It occurred to him that he hadn't seen her around for a day or two. She was frequently absent from the mill, constantly sneaking days off, and he'd been forced to take her to task on the matter on more than one occasion recently. He'd made it clear that anyone else would have got the sack. What was the little madam up to? He couldn't even recall if she'd been at her frame any day this last week, but he certainly hadn't noticed her car parked in the yard. At least, it hadn't been there today when that big delivery of cotton bales had been made. He would have noticed.

'Evie, are you here?' No answer. 'If you're not asleep please open the door. I want to talk to you.' Still receiving no response, he gave up and went to bed, deciding that perhaps she was asleep, and decided to ask Clara about her in the morning.

But at breakfast he became once more absorbed in the falling value of his shares, a far more serious matter than a troublesome daughter. They would need to get into profit soon or he'd be in deep trouble.

'You haven't eaten your toast, darling,' Clara gently reminded him. 'It's gone quite cold. Shall I ring for some fresh?'

Nathan crumpled up his newspaper. 'No, dammit, I'm not hungry. Even toast will soon become a luxury in this house and that stupid maid will have to go,' he said, speaking his thoughts out loud.

'Dear me! Whatever has poor Mabel done?'

'Nothing at all, except cost me a small fortune in bed and board, as is the case with all the women in this household. And where is Evie, dammit? What's the girl up to? She never seems to come down to breakfast these days.'

'Ah, she's not at her best early morning, dear, that's all it is. She'll be down later I expect, dashing off to the mill at the last minute as usual.' Clara was sweetly evasive, neatly avoiding his gaze as she spread marmalade on her toast. She was well aware that Evie had not slept in her bed for at least a week and she hoped to avoid bringing this information to her husband's attention, at least until she'd discovered what her darling child was up to. Asking questions never seemed to bear fruit. She'd tried once or twice already only to be stonewalled. But then interrogation had never worked with her husband either. The only way she'd ever learned what was going on in Nathan's life was to unearth the information in an underhand way, such as by reading his post. She still possessed the letter that revealed the presence of one of his fancy women. Though it wasn't clear who the letter had come from, as it hadn't been signed but judging by the bad scribble it must be some uneducated mill girl. Clara had decided not to confront him on the issue, for the present at least. Where was the point? His taste with women was truly diabolical.

As was Evie's taste in men. Clara secretly hoped she might have found a lovely new man who would solve all her problems and theirs too, if he had sufficient funds. Though no doubt that was wishful thinking on her part. What the girl was doing with her life she really didn't care to think of.

Her own life had certainly taken a turn for the better recently. Her old school chum, darling Jeffrey, her beau as she privately called him, had brought joy back to her life. How marvellous they'd met up again after all these years. One might go so far as to say that he'd actually saved her sanity. Yet somehow, as a result, she'd rather less patience with Nathan's sulks and felt less inclined to tolerate his neglect. Jeffrey was urging her to abandon ship and move in with him, insisting that Nathan did not appreciate her. Quite an interesting notion!

'Hadn't you better be going, dear? Don't want you to be late.' She guessed there was a problem at the mill with finance but Nathan refused to discuss this with her, claiming she wouldn't understand. She'd stopped asking as why should she care? Hadn't he wasted a small fortune on his women over the years? Was she prepared to continue to play the role of the obedient, compliant little wife, or was it time for the worm to turn?

Clara went to fetch Nathan's hat and gloves from the hall. 'I shall be going out this afternoon with my old school chum, and might be late back this evening. You don't mind dining at eight instead of seven for once, do you dear?'

Nathan mumbled something to the effect that he really couldn't care less what time she got back from seeing Dorothy or Daisy or whoever her old school chum was, so long as he got his dinner at some point during the evening.

Clara smilingly agreed, content as she saw him off to the mill, handing him his hat and gloves and giving him a little peck on the cheek. After he'd gone, instead of hurrying upstairs to the sanctuary of her studio as she usually did, she put on her coat and hat, picked up her handbag, and went out.

Chapter Twenty-Six

When Nathan arrived home from the mill looking even more tired and strained than usual, he demanded to know if Evie had returned home. 'What if she's taken it into her head to do something silly, like that time during the strike.'

Clara was forced to confess that she had, in fact, spent hours searching, and visiting all of Evie's friends, trying to discover the whereabouts of her darling daughter. Even dear Jeffrey had helped, not that she wished to mention him. The day had seemed endless, and their personal plans completely ruined. In the end she'd been forced to admit defeat and return home. But what if her precious girl had been involved in an accident? Clara felt swamped in utter misery and consumed by guilt. If she hadn't been so engrossed with herself these last weeks, in discovering this new love in her life, she might have paid more attention to what her daughter was up to. Clara said none of this to Nathan, who appeared largely unmoved, except for the muscles of his jaw drawing ever tighter.

'Don't worry your head about her. The girl is a survivor and utterly selfish into the bargain, with not the slightest consideration for anyone but herself.'

Evie sauntered in just as they were about to sit down to dinner and Clara went weak with relief. So grateful was she to see her daughter fit and well that she made no comment about her strange apparel: a gold and crimson velvet jacket and skirt with matching hat, far too loud for Clara's taste. Not to mention the sparkling embroidery on the piping, probably of Nabob origin, really rather too exotic for words.

Nathan demanded that Evie be at the mill first thing in the morning, ordering her to present herself at his office with a suitable explanation about her conduct. A visit to the bank manager had not improved his temper today and his patience was running dangerously thin. He privately hoped that by morning he might have better control of things, once the bank had put his demands into effect. Right now, he insisted she sit down and dine with them in a civilised fashion, not even allowing her time to freshen up or change.

Following a dinner in which neither the food nor the atmosphere got above chilled, Clara paid a visit to Evie's room. She was already tucked up in bed reading a magazine, her fair hair neatly pinned into tight little waves so they wouldn't be too disturbed in sleep. Sitting on the side of her bed, she adopted a suitably cross expression and demanded to know where it was she went on these regular absences of hers, only to be blandly informed that she'd been staying with a friend. No names were offered and Clara baulked at asking. The poor girl would probably be made to suffer enough from Nathan's irascible temper so she decided against probing further. Besides, any interference on her part may well spoil a blossoming romance, for Clara suspected she may be staying with a man.

'How lovely for you, sweetie, but you might have said where you were! We were worried about you. Even your dear father has expressed concern about your whereabouts which is why he is so angry with you, although I refrained from telling him how often your bed hasn't been slept in lately.' And she gave a conspiratorial wink.

Evie visibly relaxed, laughed out loud and kissed her mother's cheek. 'Well done, Mumsie, I can always rely on you. He's ranting and raving because he thinks I'm not pulling my weight at the mill, or some such nonsense. Why would I? Running a factory is a task best suited to the male of the species. I certainly have no intention of 'learning the ropes' as he calls it, despite my having once promised that I might. I have other plans.'

'Oh, do tell, darling. Have you met someone utterly divine? Are you going to do something absolutely thrilling and exciting?'

Evie was quite beside herself with laughter by this time. 'One day, dearest Mumsie, when you are quite grown up and strong enough, I might tell you.'

—

Clara had gone happily away, perfectly satisfied with this fabricated tale, much to Evie's amusement. Her father, however, was less easily fooled, and called her to his study straight after breakfast the next morning.

'Well, madam, where have you been? What tricks have you been up to this time?' he roared when she stood placidly before him.

Evie nearly laughed out loud at his choice of words, but judged it wise to say nothing. Sadly, even her silence seemed to annoy him.

'Speak, girl. If you're up to some mischief or other, dragging my name in the mud, then I'll turn you out of the house faster than you can say ninepence.'

Evie smiled at him. 'Do as you wish, Pops.'

'Drat you madam, don't you patronise me. I'll not be disobeyed. You can start by not taking days off work whenever you've a mind to, or I'll start docking your wages.' Her father seemed to be preaching his favourite theme, rattling out the old clichés about how the whole caboodle would be hers one day, how she needed to 'learn the ropes' to 'set a good example to the work force' of which she was only a small cog in a very big wheel. 'You need to remember, madam, that you'll be in charge one day when I am gone. You should be the mistress of the mill. How will you cope if you don't learn the trade?'

Half stifling a yawn, she gave a smile. 'I haven't the first idea and think it would be best if I handed in my notice. I'm really rather bored with the mill and have better things to do with my time.'

'What did you say?' Nathan went quite red in the face. 'What are you involved with? You can't just hand in your notice.'

'Yes, I can. I've just done so.' She turned to leave.

'But this is your heritage, and you must stay and work if I tell you to. It's long past time you started to take life more seriously, girl. You'll damn well behave yourself while you're living in my house, under my roof.'

'Oh, and that's another thing, I'm leaving.'

'Leaving?'

'The fact of the matter is, dear Pops, that I don't have to live under your roof. Nor do I want to inherit the mill. So why don't you sell it, or disinherit me. I really don't care. Do whatever you please. There are plenty of other ways I can make a living, and places I could stay.' It flickered through her mind that it would serve him right for all his cruel treatment of her over the years, for ruining her wedding and keeping her short of money, especially now she was involved with Cabbage Lil and doing well financially. Not that she would tell him such truths!

He was shouting now, wagging a furious finger in her face, his face a gargoyle of fury. 'There would be no necessity for you to earn a living if you'd made an effort to find a husband. Since you can't manage to do that simple task, you'll stop at home like any decent unmarried daughter should, and earn your keep for as long as I damned!'

'Like hell I will.'

'Don't you swear at me!'

'Why not? You've ruined my *life*!' Evie shouted back, beginning to lose control. 'You stopped me from marrying Freddie, ordered me back home from my travels, which I was *so* enjoying, then deprived me of my allowance. Now I have no hope of a future that appeals to me.'

'*And whose fault is that?* You were costing me a fortune and I'm not made of brass. Have you any idea what's happening to my shares at this precise moment? Are you aware that there's been a stock market crash in New York?' His fury was escalating and he pounded on the desk with his fist, as if he'd like to be hammering the message into her skull.

Evie leaned over the desk and calmly stated, 'You're so damned mean with your money, all you do is keep me working at the dratted mill, a virtual prisoner.'

'That is necessary as you are a stupid, ignorant, selfish child.'

Her pale blue eyes were like pebbles in ice cool water, and Evie furiously shook her head. 'Oh, no, father dear, I am twenty-three, a grown woman who needs money and can do as I wish! I've found a good way to earn it. *On my back!*'

The silence that followed this shouted declaration was long and deathly.

Nathan's voice, when it finally came, was a low snarl. 'I hope you don't mean what I imagine.'

Evie flicked back her peek-a-boo bobbed hair, her amused gaze glittering with triumph. 'Oh, I enjoy every minute of it. It's such fun! I love it when strange men run their grubby little fingers over my creamy soft flesh, when they knead and paw at me. It makes me feel wanted.'

Evie saw his hand lash out, and realised a slap was coming, almost as if it were taking place in slow motion. He knocked her backwards and she staggered, jarring her hip on the corner of the desk. She didn't fall to the ground, nor did she sob or cry, although her head was drumming with pain, nearly blinding her.

She spat her next words with cruel venom. '*I hate you!* At least the men I met in Italy and France, all handsome and rich, had compassion and warm feelings! I slept with most of them. God knows how many. And is it any wonder? You've constantly found fault with me, telling me how useless I am, never showing the slightest sign of approval or love for me. At least I was enjoying myself abroad, making a new life for myself until you stopped my money and ordered me home. So

I thought, why not carry on doing what I'm good at? Why not get paid for having a good time? You can hardly complain about that now, since you instructed me to find useful, paid employment? I needed to find some way to live because *you're the worst father in the world*!'

She was screaming at him now, inches from his face, which was turning a desperate shade of scarlet and purple and then a strange blue. Nathan made an odd gurgling sound in his throat, clutched frantically at his chest, gasping for breath before sinking to his knees and falling face down on the floor.

—

Aggie knew that Harold was hoping for a rise soon, and lived in hope it would come sooner rather than later. Mr Nathan Barker was tight-fisted, rather grand and full of himself as all the nobs are, and bitter about the way things had turned out in the industry. Her husband thought he'd have it easy but was now having to work twice as hard to earn only half whatever his father did before him, or so he said.

Harold had still not agreed to withdraw a single penny from his savings to pay for baby goods and Aggie was in despair. More often than not her purse was empty, her larder drained of its choicest items and she'd already missed one payment at the department store. Nor could she see any way of making up the missing sum, or even manage the full amount due for this week because she'd been forced to buy a new brassiere as her old one would no longer fasten over her burgeoning breasts. In addition, Harold had reminded her that she must stock up with a ton of coal at summer prices, before the price went up in the autumn.

'We don't want our baby to be cold, now do we, dear?'

'Couldn't you manage to take just a little out of your Post Office savings account, to help?' she tentatively enquired.

He looked shocked by the very suggestion. 'Indeed not, it is earning good interest and is earmarked for other things. Haven't you been saving up for the coal in the little tin box I gave you, dear?'

'Um, yes, of course I have. Only with the baby due soon, I do need to buy one or two things like a cot and...'

'I've already told you that we'll buy second-hand when the time comes.'

'I don't want second-hand, Harold. I want all new.'

'Now don't be foolish. Nobody buys new. I've already been offered a fine black carriage, which I'm sure will do splendidly. Now don't you worry your little head any more about the matter, but leave it to me. The baby and your health are all that matter at the moment, not the age of a cot or whether it has been used before or not.' And he smiled condescendingly at her, as if the pregnancy prevented her from thinking too clearly.

Aggie gazed back at him appalled. Should she tell him about the stuff she'd ordered and partly paid for? But she had no wish to mention the form she'd signed on his behalf, as he would be furious. On no account could she afford for the store to start sending reminders to their home address. Forging a husband's signature might well prove to be illegal and then she would be arrested for fraud. Besides, they were a major customer of Barker's Mill, so what would they think of an overlooker's wife being in debt to them over a few baby items? It was unthinkable. She must find some other way to pay these last few instalments left, then she could pretend that she'd saved up for the equipment secretly and Harold never would discover the truth. But the question was, how could she achieve it?

There seemed only one obvious answer. She needed to call on Nifty Jack and negotiate a temporary loan.

–

'Well, there's a turn up for the book. Back in business with the Tomkins family, am I?'

'My name is now Mrs Entwistle, and this is but a temporary arrangement until my baby is born. My husband, Harold, the overlooker at Barkers if you remember, has suffered a temporary setback at the mill but it will be rectified soon.'

Nifty Jack chortled with glee. 'Aye, had his wages cut like the rest of 'em. But it's an ill wind. Done me a power of good, old Barker cutting back like that. They've been queuing up for loans. So, you need a bit of help too, do you?' Smoothing his baldpate with the flat of his hand, he considered her carefully. 'What is it you want exactly?'

'Enough to pay off what I owe for baby equipment at Kendal Milne.'

'And you prefer to owe me instead of them, is that it? I'm flattered.'

Aggie could feel herself blushing but the last thing she wanted was for Nifty Jack to learn that Harold was unaware of the hire purchase agreement, or that she'd forged his signature in order to acquire the goods. Unfortunately, before she could devise some other excuse quickly enough, he guessed.

'Ah, the lord and master is unaware of this little transaction? Now where have I heard that tale before? Common enough round here. I'm sure I can oblige, but I won't have no falling behind with payments, you understand. T'ain't allowed as you should know from past experience with your mam.'

Aggie was perfectly certain that she could cope with Nifty Jack far better than her own mother ever had. Didn't she have good wages coming in and Harold all those savings he was rather selfishly hanging on to.

'It's purely temporary, as I say. Once the baby is born then my husband will settle the loan in full. He has means.'

'But not the will, eh? Right then, not for me to question why. How much do you want?'

A sum was agreed and handed over, a rate interest fixed, which was meaningless to Aggie. Nevertheless, she gratefully took the bundle of notes and hurried straight round to Kendal Milne, graciously handing over the somewhat grubby notes to the shop assistant with the instruction that the store would be informed when they needed the equipment delivered. Having concluded this delicate bit of business, Aggie departed, perfectly satisfied. She even celebrated her small success by treating herself to a pot of tea and a cream cake in their café. Problem solved.

—

'Morning, Dolly!' her mother said, popping in to see her one morning. 'Cyril says it's long past time for you and I to have a talk.'

'Not now, Mam, I've enough on my plate at the moment. In any case, I can't say I'm interested in raking up the past, not with Sam being difficult at the moment. The pair of us are hardly speaking.' Dolly didn't care about anything, not Aggie preening herself because she was pregnant and insufferably content in her comfortable life, nor her mother's lies. Although a part of her still ached to know who her father might be, she certainly had no intention of asking her again. That was over and done with, best left buried. There was only work keeping Dolly sane. Deep down in the ball of pain where her heart used to be, she knew that all she really needed to make her happy was Matt.

Maisie didn't seem to be listening. 'I can see you're not happy and I'm cut up about that. There's nothing I want more than to see my girl happy. You deserve that much at least. Cyril wants you to be happy, an' all.'

Dolly sighed. 'I don't I think I care what Cyril wants.'

'I admit I gave you the impression we'd been lovers when I told you all that stuff about me running away, but it wasn't strictly true. I admit I stretched the truth.'

'You mean you lied. When did you ever do anything else, Mam?' Dolly thought her mother had called in to offer warmth and comfort but found herself suffering yet another lecture so got briskly to her feet. 'Sorry, I'm a bit busy right now. I've work to do,' she said, hoping her mam would get the message that she wasn't welcome and leave.

Maisie put out a hand and made her sit down again. 'Just hear me out.'

The door banged open and Aggie came running in, her face beetroot red with exertion. Maisie looked up, startled. 'Here, what's up with you? You shouldn't be running in your condition.'

'Have you heard the news? Mr Barker has had a heart attack. They've rushed him to hospital in an ambulance and say he might not live.'

Maisie was on her feet in a second, her face ashen. 'Oh, my God! Nat? Oh, no!' And she fainted clean away.

—

'Are you going to tell me your problem now? It's about time.' Dolly was sitting by her bed in which her mother lay. Maisie had finally come round, dazed and weeping, aided by a hefty dose of smelling salts, and she and Aggie had helped her upstairs. Now she was lying between the sheets with a hot water bottle and a comforting mug of tea. Some colour had returned to her cheeks but her hands, Dolly noticed, were trembling and making the tea spill over the rim. Once she'd drunk a little, Aggie took the mug from her and set it on the bedside table.

'Will you promise to go to the hospital and ask how Nat is?' Maisie implored, looking from one to the other of her daughters.

Aggie and Dolly exchanged glances. Dolly said, 'I think you'd best carry on with what you were telling me before our Aggie came in. Though I reckon I can guess what it is now.'

Maisie dabbed at her eyes with a handkerchief then braced herself for the confession. 'The chap what got me into trouble, your proper dad, wasn't Cyril Duckett but another man.'

Aggie let out a sigh of impatience. 'We've gathered that, Mam. Get on with it, will you?'

'How can I if you keep interrupting me, girl. If you remember, Dolly, it was you who suggested that it might be

Cyril, so I let you go on thinking that way to stop you finding out the truth. But I never meant for it to cause such friction between us, love. Many is the time I've tried to find the right words to pluck up the courage to say something but I couldn't bring myself to do it, because I knew you'd ask questions and might get hurt.'

'And why shouldn't I when I need to know who my father is? I deserve that, surely?'

'Course you do, but I'd promised not to say anything about our little dalliance, no matter what the consequences. However, Cyril objects to my reputation being sullied as he calls it. He's insisted that I must face the devil and brave the world. Is that what you would say, Aggie?'

'Oh for pity's sake, Mam, why don't you—'

Maisie put up a hand to silence her elder daughter. 'Cyril insists that I make it clear once and for all, that I haven't been spreading my favours around half of Castlefield. I'm innocent as charged and so is he. We want to put things on a proper footing, now that we're wed. The fact is him and me were never intimate in the past, despite my staying in his house. Not till we were legally married.' Maisie was smiling as if at the memory of this happy time. 'So Cyril can't be your father. He feels you should know that.'

A tiny pulse was beating hard in Dolly's throat. 'Then who is?'

'I'm sure you've worked that out yourself by this time. All I will say in my own defence is that Nathan Barker was the love of my life and being told how a scandal could ruin him I had to keep quiet about our affair, telling no one. I pretended the baby was Cyril's because I knew Calvin would have made a lot of bother if he'd learned the truth. He might have got himself sacked and all our boys with him. We'd have been penniless, packed off to the workhouse. Cyril never objected to being held responsible, only to spare my reputation and be fair to you. It all worked out in the end and Calvin agreed to have me back. You had a father, albeit not a perfect one.'

Dolly gave a short laugh. 'That's putting it mildly. Calvin hated the sight of me.'

'Life can be difficult, eh? But I couldn't regret that I had you, my love. You were safe and well, so what did anything else matter?'

Aggie said, 'Oh, now I've heard everything.'

But Dolly's eyes were awash with tears, quite moved by this story. 'Oh Mam, I love you too. Why have we been so at odds with each other? I'm so sorry, can you ever forgive me for accusing you of sleeping with half of Castlefield?'

Maisie was holding out her arms and Dolly wrapped her own about her frail body, tears rolling freely down her cheeks. 'I wish you and Cyril all the happiness in the world. I'm almost sorry he isn't my dad as he's a grand chap.'

'If I might intrude on this touching little scene may I remind you that nothing has changed. You're still a bastard, Dolly, and always will be.'

Maisie jerked as if she'd been slapped. 'You should wash your mouth out with soap and water, Aggie. Where you learn such filthy words I wouldn't care to imagine.'

'And don't think,' Aggie continued, her arms folded atop her blossoming stomach, lips pressed tightly together and looking as if she'd been sucking a lemon, 'that having the master of the mill for a father will gain you anything. He's a hard man is Mr Barker, he'll stand no nonsense from spongers.'

Dolly got quietly to her feet. 'Is that what you expect me to be, Aggie – a sponger? I suppose you would go and ask him for money. Well, don't judge me by your standards.' Turning to her mother, she said, 'I'll go and see him at the hospital for you, Mam, to find out how he is. But I want you to know that I'm entirely content now that I know the truth, I want nothing from him and I never will.'

Chapter Twenty-Seven

Sitting by the hospital bed, Dolly kept her thoughtful gaze on the patient lying within it. This near stranger, the gaffer himself, was her father and she felt nothing for him. No, that wasn't quite right. She felt a burning resentment that for all these years he'd ignored her existence, not only that but forced her mother to keep it a secret, one that had driven a huge wedge between them. Dolly hated the idea that she'd been lied to and not told who her true father was. Something inside her shifted and changed as a result of this new information. When he'd grown tired of his affair with Maisie he'd clearly ignored her, which made Dolly angry on her mother's behalf. It meant that he'd rejected them both.

A nurse approached, lifted the patient's limp wrist to check his pulse. 'Oh dear, is he asleep again? He's doing quite a bit of sleeping bless him. Are you his daughter?'

'No, I am,' said Evie Barker, marching in.

Dolly swung about to find her standing behind her chair, a frosty glaze in her pale blue eyes. Dolly jumped to her feet. 'Oh, I was told no visitors were expected this evening. I used to work for your father at the mill.' Her heart was pounding, as here was the woman who had stolen her husband yet this wasn't the moment to confront her on that issue, not with Nathan Barker lying sick beside them. But she didn't look in the least embarrassed, merely offered a wintry smile.

Addressing Dolly in cool, distant tones, she said, 'I know who you are. I seem to remember that we met years ago, during that strike. I'm sure I would have managed to extricate myself from those ruffians, but thank you for your assistance. Might I ask why you're here?'

'I'm sorry, I didn't mean to intrude.'

'Leave us, Evie.' The voice from the man in bed took them both by surprise.

'Pops, you're awake.' Evie leaned over the bed and kissed the air inches from her father's brow.

The nurse too was startled and rushing to his side began taking his pulse, attempting to stick a thermometer under his tongue and warning him not to get too excited. Nathan was having none of it and spat the thing out. 'You can get out as well.'

'You really must keep very calm, Mr Barker.'

'I will if you go away. I certainly don't want any damned fuss just because I had a funny turn.' The doctor had carefully explained to him that he'd suffered a mild stroke in addition to the heart attack; that it would take some time for him to recover and he was fortunate to have any movement at all, despite a useless left arm and legs which refused to do his bidding. His speech was slightly slurred but not incomprehensible. 'Leave now, I wish to have a few words in private with this young woman.'

Evie let out a sigh of exasperation. 'I shall wait outside in the lobby. Call, if you need me, Pops.' Then firing a furious glance at Dolly, she followed the nurse out of the room.

There was a small silence, which stretched out so long Dolly had no notion how to fill it. The anger that burned deep inside her had not properly subsided and now she felt awkward and nervous, anxious not to say the wrong thing that might upset him. He was seriously ill, after all, and she'd no idea how he would react to the news that she was his illegitimate daughter. The last thing she wanted was to cause another heart attack by giving him the shock of his life. Yet despite all of this confused emotion Dolly longed to talk to him and find out more about this man who was her father, and perhaps allow him to learn more about herself. But she couldn't seem to find the right words, fearing rejection.

'Why did you come? Did you have something to say to me?' His expression was penetrating, quietly summing up the situation. 'Sit down as you make me tired hovering about like that.'

'I'll stand, Mr Barker, if you don't mind. I'm not stopping long.'

He gave a snarl as if he didn't care to be thwarted. 'There's no excuse for rudeness. *Sit!*' He flapped an impatient hand at the chair and Dolly sat, as it was an order she dare not disobey, although he didn't seem to recognise that he was the one being rude.

In truth, Dolly was quite glad of the chair, as her knees no longer felt strong enough to support her. 'I don't know where to start.'

His thin lips twisted into a wry smile, the expression in the grey-blue eyes coolly assessing. 'For pity's sake Dolly, get on with it. We've known each other a long time?'

She took a deep breath. 'All right then, here goes. Are you my father?'

'Yes, I am. Not that I was aware you would know I was until these last few years, since that time in the boiler room when you had your dinner stolen, do you remember?'

She was stunned. Dolly had expected him to be shocked by her question. 'You're right, Mam never told me about you until now. I assume you didn't allow me to know?'

'It would not have been a good thing for you to know. She was wary of causing trouble in case I sacked all those blasted sons of hers. Doesn't say much for my reputation, does it, that my own mistress was afraid of me?' He paused for a moment to catch his breath. 'She was a sweet girl, your mother, but cautious and far too loyal to that damned husband of hers. I thought her lovely.'

'But you never loved her.'

Another silence and a sigh followed by a sad shake of the head. 'I'll admit she was one among many, not exactly a love match. We met at the chapel, cared for each other and had fun. You must understand that I never meant her any harm. I didn't get the feeling that she was the flighty sort. She was no seductive vamp just a decent, honest woman. I reckon she was in need of love during a difficult period of her life.'

Dolly's cheeks fired bright red. It didn't seem decent to hear such things about her mother and yet she was avid to know and understand. 'She loved you.'

He sighed. 'I dare say she did. She read too much into our relationship, I'm afraid.'

'Happen that's why she kept my existence a secret all these years because of her love for you. I always wondered why I was different from the rest of my family. I felt like the cuckoo in the nest and when our Aggie blurted it all out after that accident at the mill when Calvin died, everything became clear. But Mam still wouldn't say who my father was. She made up all sorts of lies rather than tell me the truth. I resented that. Now I forgive her.'

'I'm sure you do.' He gave a small laugh that invoked a cough and it was some moments before he could speak again as he spluttered into a coughing fit.

Dolly was on her feet in a second, all concern. 'Hush now, I'm tiring you out.'

The door flew open and Evie marched in followed by a flustered nurse. 'I think you'd best go. I don't want him upset.'

'I'm sorry.'

Nathan Barker lifted one hand, striving to catch his breath yet anxious to attract Dolly's attention. 'You'll come again tomorrow?'

'I'm not sure that it would be best if—'

'There are still things I want to say.'

And despite the blazing fury on Evie's face, Dolly agreed to his request. 'All right, I'll pop in for ten minutes before the end of visiting time.'

Back home she assured Maisie that he was making a good recovery. 'There's no need for you to worry about him as he'll be fine.'

'I feared he was about to peg out. Did you two get on all right or did it feel a bit queer?' her mother anxiously enquired.

Eager to keep her happy, Dolly agreed that they had got along tolerably well although she'd felt a bit odd at first. 'He's asked me to call again tomorrow.'

'There, didn't I say he was a special person? That's why I had to keep my promise to him. I might never have told you had Cyril not insisted I do right for you. Did he ask about me? Did he explain how we couldn't stay together because of his wife and my children and that he had to give me up? Did he explain how I was the love of his life?'

Dolly looked at her mother, her heart was filled with pity and love. 'Yes Mam, he did.'

–

Not entirely sure how she felt about having this man as a father let alone Evie as a half-sister, Dolly called to see Nathan Barker the next day, as he'd requested. Her disappointment in her so-called father was acute. There was pain in her heart, her throat constricting with emotion and it instantly became clear that he was only truly concerned about himself and the mill. Even his attitude to his family was one of casual dismissal, complaining about his situation and expressing a need for his daughter to work at the mill for him.

'I'm going to be below par for a long while. They're sending me to a convalescent home, which Evie is not likely to agree to. It's a pity you couldn't help either.'

'Are you planning to tell her about me?'

Nathan shook his head. 'I'll maybe get around to it eventually, once I'm on the mend and can summon up the strength.'

'Don't, as she won't like it.'

'You're probably right. What happened between your mother and me, I decided for selfish reasons that our affair must end. I couldn't abandon Clara and Evie, and how could Maisie leave Calvin and risk losing your brothers? I think not. We did what seemed right at the time. Maisie decided for equally good reasons to keep you a secret. It was, at first, awkward for us, but we're not strangers, still good friends. I don't know about you, Dolly, but to me it's as if there's an invisible cord binding us together.'

Emotion welled up in her, tightening her throat and for a moment Dolly couldn't speak. She hadn't expected this, or to feel vulnerable. It was true that she'd always felt as if a part of her was missing. She had wanted to go on being angry with him, which was far easier, but couldn't. The prospect of accepting this man as her father would at least feel appropriate for her mam. But she was determined to stick to her own life. 'You need to understand that my mother and I are much closer now that she has told me the truth. But I want nothing from you at all. I've only come to make that absolutely clear. I'm not asking for a job, as I have one of my own now. Nor do I require any compensation for the years in which you ignored the fact that I existed. I accept that you are my father but I can manage perfectly well on my own.'

'Good for you, dear,' he quietly said, giving her a smile.

She gave her head a little shake. 'You imagine I could now meekly set aside all those lost years: the fact that you left me in the hands of a neglectful, cruel stepfather. That you watched my mother, the woman you once professed to be fond of, even if you didn't truly love her, reach the point of near starvation at times and did nothing to help? You even let Harold sack me when Calvin died, and still you did nothing. I don't see how you and I *could* be friends. I'm not sure I want to see you again. *Ever!*'

Her disappointment in her so-called father was acute, and there was no respite for Dolly even at home – no one to open her heart to and help her to make some difficult decisions. Thankfully, relations with Maisie had improved but, having satisfied herself that she'd finally cleansed her soul and told the truth, Maisie devoted her attention entirely to her new husband. She and Cyril were inseparable, utterly besotted, like a pair of lovebirds, and, not wishing to intrude, Dolly couldn't help feeling neglected and left out, very much on the fringes.

As for Sam, he rarely spoke a civil word to her. They lived like strangers in the same house. Dolly had come to bitterly regret her weakness in allowing him to move back in. On several occasions she'd tried to talk to him, to point out in a sensible, calm fashion how hopeless their situation was, that it was time for them to call it a day, that he should leave and start a new life on his own somewhere. But he absolutely refused to do so.

'I like it here, Dolly. Give us a chance. Have you made more of those scones for tea? Grand!'

If only she could talk to Matt, he would surely help her. But he never had called again. He'd taken what he wanted and left her too. She tried not to think of the day of the picnic, or a terrible pain would fill her heart. Only when she lay alone in her bed, did she allow herself to conjure up his face and think of him.

One night Sam came to her room, easily gaining entrance because she'd carelessly forgotten to wedge the chair under the door handle. Dolly told him to leave at once but he refused.

'We're still man and wife, if you haven't noticed, and should be together.' He put out a hand to stroke her neck and the swell of her breast.

Dolly slapped it away. 'I said you would have to wait till I was ready, and I'm not. I might never be.'

'And you expect me to put up with this chaste existence?'

'I don't expect you to put up with anything. You asked to come back, but I didn't invite you. The door is open for you to leave whenever you choose.'

Sam felt a spurt of irritation, annoyed by her casual attitude. He hadn't expected the once loving Dolly to be so unresponsive, as if she didn't care whether he was there or not. He was beginning to think that it was all a waste of time that he'd made a bad mistake in coming back. But where else could he go? He'd had enough of Davey and his screaming kids, and it was vitally important that he didn't appear available to Aggie. Nor did he fancy moving into a tenement room and cooking for himself. At least Dolly was a good cook so he got well fed and watered.

He wasn't even having much luck with the magnificent Evie. He'd visited her seedy palace on a couple of occasions and on neither visit had he been allowed through the door, let alone granted an audience with the Duchess. He certainly wasn't prepared to pay for it with one of the other tarts. Even so, the experience had damaged his self-esteem. Surely he couldn't be losing his charms altogether. He came closer and flung back the covers, as if he was about to climb in the bed with her.

Dolly jerked away as if she'd been scalded. 'Get away from me. I've told you, I'm not ready.' For a long moment she thought he might be about to get in anyway, but then he snatched hold of her nightdress and yanked it up high to view her naked body. 'Just reminding meself of what I'm missing. Not much, I'd say. There's plenty better.'

Dolly flew at him like an alley cat, pushing and shoving him towards the door. '*Get out*, you dirty little man! Go and find someone else and leave me alone!' She was shouting at him, overwhelmed by the desperation that her life never would be happy, her dream of being with Matt not resolved. 'Get out of my house *now*!'

'Oh no,' he said, in an infuriatingly calm voice. 'I don't think so, Dolly. I'm most comfortable here. Very content indeed.'

–

Following several dull weeks in a nursing home in the care of nurses he dubbed as 'dragons', Nathan was to be discharged into the tender care of his family to continue his recuperation at home. Although his speech had improved considerably, he was still confined to a wheelchair, had limited movement in one arm and was still unable to move his legs. His frustration was palpable. Under strict instructions not to excite himself, he'd said nothing thus far about Dolly. Clara had come to see him only once a week, a short duty-visit with little conversation attached to it. Evie had refused to visit at all, clearly still nursing a grievance following the spat, which had led to his heart attack in the first place. But now she was ready to drive him home. In view of this coolness towards him, Nathan determined to approach the subject on his mind, with caution.

'I bear you no grudge, Evie, over that little contretemps we had which set all of this off.'

Evie said nothing as she settled him into the back seat of her motor and tucked the blanket about his knees.

'But I would like to know, is it true, what you told me?' When she did not reply, he answered his own question. 'I dare say it is. I should have guessed. There's already been tittle-tattle. I sensed it at the Exchange, though had not understood the reason. Well, you'll have to give it up now, get back to work and help me with the mill.'

Evie laughed as she climbed into the driver's seat. 'Not on your sweet life.'

'*Your* life may depend upon it, let alone mine. The doctors say it might take another month, at least, before I'm fit to return to the mill, so someone needs to keep an eye on the place, to see that orders are properly fulfilled, work kept up to scratch and new shipments of cotton dealt with. A factory can't run itself, and who better to take charge than my own daughter who will inherit it one day?'

'You have employees to deal with all of that boring stuff. I've already told you, I've better things to do with my time.'

Nathan strived to control his worsening temper. 'As for this other business, I'll not have you make a laughing stock of me. We'll talk more later but mark my words, it's got to stop. Do you understand?'

'Who says so?'

'I do. Let that be an end to the matter.'

Evie fired up the engine and drove off at speed, itching to retaliate but mindful of bringing on another attack. 'I'll speak to Harold, if you like, get him to call a meeting of those in a position of authority so everyone fully comprehends how they must simply get on with things as if you were still in the office. Which I'm sure they're doing already. That will have to do.'

Nathan began to splutter with rage, all his good intentions to stay calm vanishing in a blood-red mist of fury. 'If you choose not to help, Evie, I'll find someone else who will have other options.'

'I'm sure you do, so use them. This is all too boring, so can we change the subject? Ah look, here we are, home at last. Now do be a brave old chap and don't make a fuss.'

With a sigh of relief, Evie drew the motor to a halt on the gravelled drive and Clara came rushing out of the house, pushing a wheelchair before her, ready to sweep him inside and start fussing over his recuperation.

Nathan resisted, refusing to get out of the car, and waving his fist at Evie who made no move to assist while Clara struggled with the wheelchair down the steps. 'Mark my words I'll have my way in this matter. I shall expect you to have done something about closing that nasty place down by the time we speak again. Do you understand? You will stop behaving like a floozy, at once, do you hear?'

'I think Mumsie is here with your invalid carriage, Pops dear.' And having dismissed both the mill and her father as being of trifling concern, Evie left him to Clara's tender care and returned her attention to her more important concerns.

Chapter Twenty-Eight

Aggie's son was born without any problems one morning in early December. Rather fancifully she opted to call him Noel, since Christmas was approaching.

'Isn't he just the perfect little man?' she gushed, and even Harold looked thoroughly pleased with himself, as if he'd carried out the entire task: pregnancy, labour and delivery, all by himself, without any help whatsoever.

'He's a way to go before he's a man but he's certainly perfect, and with my nose, I think.'

'Most definitely,' Aggie agreed, relieved that her indiscretion remained undetected. 'I can't wait to get home and start to look after him. Nursing and feeding him will be lovely. Now, Harold, about the cot and pram and such like—'

'I've told you already, dear, that there's no need for you to worry your head over such things. Lizzie Bramley's cousin can supply everything we need. She's done with babies now, apparently, and will be glad to have the stuff taken off her hands.'

Aggie could feel her face going all stiff and cold, even as she attempted to smile. 'But love, I've given you a fine, healthy son. Surely he deserves the best? I thought we'd agreed that we'd get all new for our first child.'

'Of course.' And his smile grew increasingly fixed as Aggie attempted to appear enticing.

'There will be others, two or three I hope, so think of it as an investment for the future. Besides...' Aggie drew in a hasty breath. She'd gone this far, and there was no turning back. 'I've been keeping it as a surprise but I've already bought and paid for all the baby equipment we might possibly need: pram, high chair, cot, complete layette, everything.'

Harold's eyebrows shot up. 'Everything?'

'Everything.' It hadn't come out quite as she'd intended but it was too late now.

'But how did you find the money?' He was giving her a quizzical, sideways look, which made her feel decidedly uncomfortable.

'I saved hard,' Aggie lied, hurrying on before he followed this up with too many probing questions. She needed Harold to not only be proud of her, but to show sympathy for her sacrifice and generously offer to refund the cost. 'Oh, but it was hard, I freely confess. Pinching a bit from the housekeeping here, there and everywhere. Some weeks I never knew how I was going to manage from one day to the next.'

'Were those the weeks we had tough beef and stringy lamb?'

'Well, it did leave me a bit short but this is our wonderful boy. I wanted him to have the best, and wanted *you* to have the best when you take him out for an airing on Sunday afternoons in his fine new baby carriage.'

Harold was taking it really rather well, she thought, not showing any sign of being cross with her. He looked almost jovial. 'My word, Aggie but you're a likely lass. Who'd have thought you could have managed to save all that money with me still on short rations at the mill. You're a wonder! And the best of it is we still have my savings, all tucked away nice and safe for a rainy day.' Kissing her on the cheek, he lifted his son proudly in his arms. 'And that's where they can stay, son, isn't it, since you've got such a clever mam?'

Aggie stared at him aghast. It had all gone wrong, as he wasn't going to give her any money. But the real problem was that Nifty Jack was never off her doorstep.

He was waiting for Aggie, lurking in an alleyway, as she strolled by one morning a week or two later. She was going nowhere in particular but the sun was shining and she was determined to show off her son in his fine new baby carriage. Aggie was feeling quite perky, planning what to make for Harold's dinner when he suddenly stepped out in front of her.

Grabbing the handle of the pram he tugged it from her grasp and sent it rolling away down the alley. Aggie screamed, watching horrified as the baby carriage bounced over the cobbles, little Noel screaming at the top of his small lungs. Aggie started to run after him but Nifty slammed her up against a wall and held her firm, one hand grasping her chin in a tight grip, the other shoving an arm up her back.

'Your fancy pram has crashed into that back yard wall so don't fret about the babby, it's only given him a shaking up. What you need to fix your mind on is that come Monday morning, at nine sharp, I'll be round for the balance, which by my reckoning comes to just short of seven pounds.'

'What? But I only borrowed three pounds ten shillings from you in the first place. Where's the rest come from?'

'Interest. Nothing is cheap.'

'But that's criminal. You must be charging me a hundred per cent.'

He gave her what might pass for a sympathetic smile. 'That's life, *Mrs* Entwistle. Fair reward for the bother you gave me by missing some payments. And remember, if you don't settle soon, there'll be even more interest added. Monday morning, at nine sharp. We wouldn't want anything worse to happen to your son and heir, now would we?'

Aggie couldn't get to her baby fast enough, snatching him up and holding him to her breast almost faint with relief. He was all hot and bothered, in a lather of sweat from his crying, his nappy sopping wet, but he didn't seem to have come to any harm. This time. Dear God, but how much worse of a state might he be in if she failed to comply with Nifty Jack's orders? But she didn't have seven pounds, not even half or a quarter of that sum. Aggie no longer had two wages coming in, and she had a baby to feed and clothe and care for.

'Oh, what on earth am I going to do, Noel? How can we persuade your daddy to hand over his savings?'

Aggie had never been more frightened in all her life. Everywhere she walked she felt certain Nifty Jack was watching and following her. She half expected him to appear at every corner to snatch the pram off her again and run off with her precious darling. She could hardly sleep or eat for the fear growing in her like a canker. Finally, she gathered together all her courage and asked Harold for more money.

He looked at her askance and then smiled benevolently. 'I know, it's hard for you with Christmas coming, and you not earning any money of your own these days. Don't worry my love, it's your task to take care of our little Noel and of course I'll provide you with a bit extra for Christmas puddings, mince tarts and the like. I'm not Scrooge, you know.'

'I didn't suggest that you were.'

'The girls at the mill are planning their Christmas party, their "footings" as they call it and they've told me to invite you, so you've something to look forward to. It's going to be a good do that they've been saving up for weeks, a shilling at a time. They must have a tidy sum saved.'

'Who's organising it?' Aggie asked, looking thoughtful.

'Lizzie Bramley, not the most level headed lass, although she's tucked it away safe in the boiler room under Ned's eagle eye, I believe.' Harold chuckled. 'I reckon they're all planning to dress up and have a right old time of it.'

'Well of course, I'd love to come,' Aggie said, her interest sharpening. 'And I must call in and show off our little Noel soon, don't you think?'

She called the very next day, allowing all her old mates, even those who'd teased and played tricks on her, to hold Noel and pass him around like a parcel. They kissed and tickled the baby and then Aggie retrieved her son, wrapped him in his blanket, and holding him close promised she'd see them all at the party and went on her way. She'd spotted old Ned, through the grimy window. He was in the mill yard, playing football with one or two of the lads on his morning tea break. It was easy enough to slip into the boiler room, and it took no time at all to find the tin box, secreted in Ned's locker where he kept his tools. What a very silly place to put all that money.

There were one or two of the girls' bags left with him for safe keeping, and she quickly rifled through them, finding the odd sixpence or shilling tucked away. Aggie felt not a trace of guilt. What had they ever done for her except plagued the life out of her, making fun because she was the overlooker's wife. Well, her need was greater than theirs. Noel's welfare was far more important than some silly party.

When she got her little hoard safely home, Aggie was disappointed to discover that the total sum was far less than she'd hoped for. Little more than a couple of pounds had been saved towards the party. And not even that from the girls' bags. Nowhere near enough to get her off the hook with Nifty Jack, although it might pacify him for a week or two. She also had the problem of disposing of the tin box. She quickly bundled Noel back into his pram and hurried down to the canal where she threw it in, standing on the tow path till it had sunk quite out of sight.

On her way home she was surprised to bump into Matt Thornton.

'Hello Aggie, I thought it was you. Hey up, does this young 'un belong to you? He's a bobby dazzler, isn't he?'

Her first sensation on seeing Matt was one of pure panic, worrying he might have seen what she was up to. Now, flattered by his comments she stood back for him to admire her child.

After a moment, Matt said, 'How's Dolly? I never seem to see her these days.'

'Oh, she's busy trying to patch up her marriage.'

A small silence, then he gave a sigh. 'Well, next time you see her, give her my regards, will you, Aggie?'

'Of course, if I remember, but I don't see much of her these days, what with my new baby and Harold working hard on the new orders.'

As she turned to walk home, Nifty Jack appeared at her elbow, like a ghost out of nowhere. Aggie almost jumped out of her skin. 'Have you got the money I asked for, *Mrs* Entwistle?' She glanced quickly back over her shoulder to check that Matt had gone, then handed over three of the pounds she'd stolen. She needed the other few shillings to get her through the week.

'This isn't enough, I'm afraid. The whole sum should have been paid by now or I'll have to increase the interest. Have you spoken to your husband yet?'

Aggie could feel herself start to shake. 'I'll have the rest next week, I promise. I'll get you the money as soon as I can. Please give me time Nifty, will you? I'm doing my best but I have my baby to think of.'

'Course you do,' said Nifty, picking a thread off the lapel of his fine tweed jacket. 'But I'd recommend you walk him some place safer in future, eh lass? The canal is a damp, dangerous place for babbies.'

–

The theft was soon spotted and poor Ned was devastated.

'Who would steal the party money? Someone must have slipped in from outside when my back was turned. No one from this mill would ever consider taking it. I'd trust everyone here with me life, so I would.'

'What a sad thing to happen,' Aggie softly said.

When Harold sat down to their meal of boiled ham and tomatoes, he gave a sad shake of his head. 'The party has been called off, as no one can afford to pay for it twice. Lizzie suggested that we could maybe all of us take in a bit of food, instead. I told her you would certainly make a contribution.'

Aggie flared up instantly, all pink-cheeked and flustered outrage. 'You'd no right to say such a thing. Aren't things

336

difficult enough with a new baby and down to one wage? I can't afford to pay for no fancy party food.'

Harold frowned at her. 'But I thought you were managing so well, and it doesn't have to be fancy. A few sandwiches or some of your home made scones would go down a treat.'

'I'd manage much better if you dipped a bit deeper into those savings of yours.'

Harold smiled kindly at her. 'They are for our dream, Aggie, as you well know. Our projected move to the suburbs.'

'Which won't happen till I'm old and grey, at this rate.'

'Well then, it will be a good place to retire to,' said Harold placidly. 'Is there any more ham, dear, I'm a bit peckish this evening?'

—

'You've got to help me, I'm in desperate trouble.' Aggie would rather have cut off her right arm than ask her sister for help, but she knew now that she had no choice.

Dolly regarded her with a somewhat jaundiced eye. 'What sort of trouble? You've got a fine baby, a loving husband, so what have you got to complain about?'

'Money, what else?'

'Overspent on baby stuff? This is certainly an expensive looking pram. Fit for a prince.' Dolly jiggled it, smiling down at baby Noel.

'Maybe I have overspent a bit, so I need to make use of your facilities as a money lender.'

Dolly gave a brittle little laugh. 'No doubt at a special rate of interest.'

Aggie looked affronted. 'I wasn't expecting to pay any interest at all. You're my sister.'

'Oh, you've remembered at last, have you? Now that it suits you. Although I don't remember you helping to pay off Mam's debts when she was in hock up to her eyeballs. Considering I'm the cuckoo in the nest, a bastard as you insist on calling me, I

337

really feel I've done more than my share. Nobody ever thinks to ask what *I* might need, or feel about the way things have turned out. You were the one who started all of this upset in the first place, with your mean mouth and nasty jealousy. I'm the one who had to fight to regain my job and damaged reputation, I then lost my husband, thanks to your interference.'

'You can't blame me for everything.'

'Why can't I? Not satisfied with happily informing me I didn't belong in your family, you were the one who ruined my marriage.'

'What makes you say that?' Aggie stammered, her cheeks flushing bright pink.

'Didn't you talk me into telling Sam about Cabbage Lil? Quite unnecessarily.'

'Oh, that's all. What else could it be?'

Dolly frowned. 'Now I've lost a man I love and find myself stuck with a no-good lump who refuses to leave my home and treats the place like a flipping hotel, expecting to be fed like a lord and waited on hand, foot and finger. You should have married Sam Clayton, Aggie, you and him were made for each other.'

'Oh, stop complaining. I'm the one with real problems, having got the talleyman on my tail.'

Dolly's jaw dropped open and she stared at her sister, aghast. 'Oh, Aggie no, after everything that's happened to us in the past, why on earth would you be so stupid as to involve yourself with Nifty Jack?'

Desperate for some sympathy, Aggie told the tale from start to finish, carefully omitting any mention of the missing party money, and how she'd nicked it.

Dolly didn't interrupt once, not until she was done, then asked the obvious question. 'Have you told Harold?'

Aggie's voice rose on a familiar note of hysteria. 'No I haven't. He insisted we buy second-hand, which I couldn't tolerate. He's not nearly so generous as you might imagine.'

Neither did she make any mention of forging his signature, cheating the store or lying to him by pretending that she'd saved every penny. 'How can I admit to him that in trying to sort myself out, I've got into debt with Nifty Jack? He'll hit the roof.'

'I'm not surprised. Have you no sense, Aggie? No, of course you haven't, you're too full of venom and selfishness to allow your brain the opportunity to think clearly.'

'I never meant this to happen, so you must help me.'

'Where were you when I tried to do the right thing and pay off Mam's debt? Handing out second-hand boots, that's all you ever did. You should've made do with second-hand stuff for the baby, like everybody else. No, Aggie, there's only one solution and that's to own up to Harold, hope he forgives you and digs deep into his pocket, or at least into his savings account.'

'Are you saying you don't intend to help?'

'That's exactly what I'm saying. It may have escaped your notice but I've enough problems of my own striving to keep clients Nifty Jack is constantly trying to pinch off me. And look what taking over Calvin and Mam's debt did to my marriage, having ruined my life. So getting myself tangled up in yours wouldn't do me any good at all would it? No more debt for me, love. Sorry, but you're on your own.'

–

Furious with the need for revenge against her sister for taking this attitude, the very next day Aggie called on Mrs Barker. She sat in the fine drawing room jigging baby Noel on her lap to keep him quiet and faced her employer's wife with a face like granite.

'Is there was some problem I can help you with, Mrs Entwistle?' Clara politely enquired.

'I think the reverse is the case, Mrs Barker. I'm the one who can help you. Did you know that Dolly Clayton, my half-sister, is actually your husband's bastard?'

Clara Barker's face went bright pink and then ash pale. For a second, Aggie thought she might be about to faint. Perhaps she should have put it a bit more tactfully but anger and resentment were still hot in her. Why should Dolly, a bastard in anyone's eyes, treat her with such utter contempt? It made Aggie sick to think of how callously she'd refused to help. 'I'm sorry to be so blunt, Mrs Barker, but there's no easy way of saying these things and I thought you'd a right to know.'

'I'm most grateful for your consideration.'

Her tone of voice caused Aggie to cast the woman a piercing glance. Was she being sarcastic? Aggie settled the baby more comfortably on her lap, feeling she very much had the upper hand as the poor wronged sister. 'She's been a cuckoo in our nest for as long as I can remember, and you know that she was responsible for the death of my father, Calvin Tomkins. What's more, she clobbered Nifty Jack on the head, nearly doing for him an' all, when he'd been generous enough to offer her employment as his housekeeper. She then pinched the man I'd hoped to marry.'

'That's quite a story,' said Clara, after a slight pause.

Aggie didn't worry over twisting the truth, not mentioning that she'd already chosen Harold as the better provider, or so she had believed. 'Now things aren't working out between them, which is hardly surprising since Sam discovered Dolly spent several months living as a prossy with a woman called Cabbage Lil. And she's probably had an affair with another man. I thought you should know that she seems to be trying to wheedle her way into your husband's good books. Who knows what she's got her eyes on?'

'Well,' said Clara. 'She does seem to have quite a history.' A moment of tense silence and then Clara got swiftly to her feet. 'Thank you for taking the trouble to tell me this, Aggie, before it becomes common gossip! I am not unaware of my husband's peccadillo's, although he has always been most discreet. Men will be men, as they say. I didn't realise, however, that Dolly was...'

Leaving the sentence unfinished, Clara was ringing the bell for the maid to show her out. When her visitor was gone she stood unmoving for some time, sunk in deep thought.

Chapter Twenty-Nine

Nathan was not a good patient. His frustration at still being tied to a wheelchair with no date set for his return to the mill, or 'back in harness' as he termed it, was making him increasingly grumpy and bad tempered, more demanding than usual. But then neither Clara, nor his long-suffering servants would have expected anything different. He kept loudly proclaiming that he really had no time to be ill, that he had work to do, then would promptly fall asleep.

He would declare himself ravenous and then refuse to eat whatever was cooked and set before him, demanding something else entirely. He would have no truck with invalid food: milk sops, as he called them. When presented with cook's special beef tea he fed it to the dog. 'Now bring me roast beef and Yorkshire pudding, if you please.'

Clara bore all of this with her usual saint-like patience. But he dreaded her reaction when finally he revealed the existence of an illegitimate daughter. He was, as always, direct to the point of callousness, sparing her feelings not one jot, almost making himself out to be a hero for keeping the facts from her for so long. Clara said nothing, which puzzled him.

He looked at his wife keenly. 'You don't seem too shocked or surprised by what I've just told you.'

She might have responded by saying that she'd already been informed by Dolly's malicious sister, or that her sensibilities had long ago been blunted by his casual disregard of her feelings, but it was easier to make no comment whatsoever.

'I wouldn't have mentioned it had Maisie, that's the girl's mother, not let the cat out of the bag. Then the lass herself came to see me and asked me straight out.'

When Clara still said nothing, he expanded the tale by saying how he'd guessed Dolly was his daughter some time ago, when he'd come across her once in the boiler room. 'She's the spitting image of my dear Mama. You'd never believe the resemblance if you hadn't seen her with your own eyes. Not that I ever expect you to see her, Clara, and won't insist that you receive her. I've no intention of doing anything daft, like accept her as a daughter in place of Evie.'

Clara, who had sat in silence throughout this long explanation, her hands neatly folded on her lap, finally lifted her gaze to his. 'Have you told Evie that she has a half-sister?'

Nathan shuffled with discomfort, wishing he could jump out of his chair and get back to the mill where life was much less complicated. 'Not yet! I thought you'd be the best one to break it to her.'

Clara decisively shook her head. 'Oh no, I think that is your responsibility, not mine. Be gentle with her, please, as she'll need to get used to the idea.'

'She's hard as nails, that lass, more's the pity.'

'Nonsense, she's sensitive underneath all of that rebellious streak.'

He regarded his wife with pity in his eyes. 'Have you any idea what she's up to these days, how she's making a living? My friends have been sniggering behind their hands for months.' He could feel himself growing hot and agitated just at the thought.

If Clara had heard rumours she'd chosen to ignore them, as she did most things that were unpleasant or disagreeable. She really had no wish to know how her darling daughter spent her days, or more to the point, her nights. The very notion brought a chill of foreboding to her heart.

But why did no one ever bother to tell her what was going on in her family? Why did her darling daughter largely ignore her, as if she were of no more consequence than a piece of furniture? No one ever paid her the slightest attention, or asked how she felt about anything. Even now it hadn't crossed Nathan's mind to apologise for his betrayal. As these thoughts raced through her mind, Clara became aware that Nathan was bluntly informing her that Evie had set herself up as a madam in a house of ill repute.

'One thing I will say for our Evie, she's very selective in who she allows through the door. Only the very best, the crème de la crème, are granted admission, apparently. They have to ring and ask for an invitation. But then that's Evie, being a proper snob.'

Clara was staring at him, bemused, as he continued to rant and rave about what he would like to do to the girl, while she attempted to take in the full import of his words. Even so, her first instinct was to pacify a sick husband. 'Please stay calm, Nathan. Remember the doctor has advised no undue excitement or you'll bring on another attack. You really mustn't get yourself into a state.'

Nathan wagged a furious finger at her. 'I dare say you'll turn a blind eye, Clara, as you generally do. If it comforts you to do so, then go ahead, but mark my words that no good will come of this business.'

Could it be true, and if so how did she feel about it? Was she shocked, disappointed, resigned? Clara was surprised to discover that it was none of these things. She simply felt as if it was happening to someone else entirely, and really shouldn't concern her at all. Could she, at last, be growing very slightly selfish and even independent of them both?

'Are you listening to a word I'm saying, woman?'

Clara merely smiled.

—

Evie was appalled by the news. 'I can't believe this. How dare he preach to me about moral behaviour when he's misbehaved just as badly, worse if he cavorts with mill girls and expects me to accept that creature as a *sister*? Never!'

Clara had kept well clear while Nathan told his sorry tale, but had come running when the furious shouts of outrage and fury from father and daughter lashing out at each other became too much for her to bear. Desperate to calm them both down, Clara attempted to act as pacifier. Sadly, to no avail, Evie stormed from the room and since Nathan could not charge after her, Clara had followed her daughter, and was now attempting to smooth things over.

'You really shouldn't allow this matter to bother you. It was *me* he betrayed, after all, not *you*, darling.'

'Mumsie, listen to yourself. You surely aren't taking his side?'

'No, dear, but if what he tells me about you is only half true, are *you* in any position to criticise?'

Evie turned on her, spitting like an alley cat. 'I'll have you know that I'm not the one who has ruined my life. *He* did that by not allowing me to marry Freddie.'

'Rubbish! Absolute stuff and nonsense,' said Clara, and felt a surge of something very like power race through her veins. 'You've always been a wilful child, and entirely selfish, just like your father. You could have waited and postponed the wedding, or found another young man to marry. You could even, God forbid, have done some good work and learnt something useful about the mill and your inheritance. But no, you were always far too hedonistic, too hell-bent on having a good time and enjoying yourself, spending all our hard owned money. Perhaps I spoiled you, but was it any wonder that your father finally pulled the plug? I don't blame him for that, not one bit. But the way you choose to make your living now is not his fault, nor mine. It's *yours*! We did the best we could for you, now you are a young woman responsible for yourself.'

Evie was staring at her mother as if she'd run mad. 'I never thought to hear you say such things, to me of all people.'

'Perhaps I should have said this sooner. I've indulged every-body's whims, come to think of it. It may be that Dolly will have no wish to acknowledge you either. But no one can be thrilled to have a brothel keeper for a sister, can they?'

What Evie's response might have been to this damning indictment, Clara was never to discover as the chamber maid came running along the landing at precisely that moment calling for someone to fetch the doctor. Nathan was having a second heart attack.

—

Some days later Clara informed Nathan, as tactfully as she was able, but with resolute firmness, that she had hired a nurse to care for him. She was brisk and businesslike, uncharacteristically decisive, not a sign of the agreeable, complaisant doormat Nathan had come to expect.

'The doctor has advised that you should either retire, or hire someone to run the mill for you, in order to reduce the risk of further attacks. You were fortunate that this was not a serious one, but they could become worse and more frequent if you don't take care.'

Nathan was puffing and blowing, his face going all shades of red and purple. 'You think you can put me out to grass, do you?'

'The choice is entirely yours, I am simply informing you of medical advice.'

He gave a low growl but mindful of his condition he managed not to erupt into temper, as he once might have done.

'Now I really must be on my way as Jeffrey is picking me up in half an hour and I must finish my packing.'

'Packing? Jeffrey?'

'Yes, Nathan, I'm leaving you, I'm afraid. Jeffrey, my old school friend and I think we might settle in Portugal. I rather liked it there. If you need anything, just ring the bell and Nurse Jocelyn will look after you.'

She then pecked him on the cheek and smilingly departed. Nathan watched her go, looking shockingly open-mouthed.

Aggie wasted no time in informing her sister of what she'd done. They met just as Dolly was coming out of the house to go on her rounds, and she took great pleasure in describing all she had told Mrs Barker.

Dolly stared at her sister, speechless for several minutes. 'So you took it into your nasty head to further ruin my reputation by making out I'm after Nathan Barker's money, when I'm nothing of the sort?'

Aggie smirked. 'Why not, as you refused to help me? If you think you can boss me about, you can think again. I'll not have you dictate what I say to my husband.'

Dolly carefully locked the front door and stood waiting for Aggie to move out of her path so that she could get on her way. 'So you haven't told Harold the truth yet? Well, don't come running to me when he finds out you've lied and have Nifty Jack on your tail.'

'You bastard!' And quite out of the blue, Aggie socked Dolly with her fist, right on the chin. In seconds the two sisters were rolling about in the gutter, Aggie snatching and tearing at her hair, trying to claw her face with her nails while Dolly desperately tried to fend her off. Doors opened, lace curtains twitched and soon they had half the street as an audience, laughing and cheering them on.

'Come on, Dolly girl, thump her and grab her hair!'

'Nay Aggie, can't you do better than that?' said another.

Dolly was dodging blows left, right and centre, and couldn't believe what was happening. 'For God's sake, stop it! What are you so excited about?'

Aggie was sitting astride Dolly's prostrate form, holding her pinned to the ground as she stuck her face close to hers, almost nose to nose, hissing out her next words like venom from a snake. 'You think Sam's behaving himself, do you? You imagine he isn't going round to that fancy palace where Evie Barker hangs out and does exactly what he pleases with her? How do you feel about your husband hanging out with prostitutes? Though since you were one yourself, it probably doesn't trouble you.'

Dolly gave Aggie a hefty shove to push her off. 'I've told you before that nothing happened. What will convince you that I'm innocent?' It still bothered her that her own sister should think the worst of her in that way. As Aggie came for her again Dolly stood her ground and punched her back, bringing a roar of approval from the assembled audience.

But Aggie was back on her feet in seconds, if a bit groggy and surprised, prodding Dolly in the chest. 'And don't think it's only Evie Barker he's got his eye on. He has women all over the place. I'd need only to crook my little finger and Sam would come running back to me like a shot.' She tossed back her chestnut curls, which looked somewhat lank at that moment, not half so glossy and bouncy as they'd once been.

Dolly bent to pick up her bag, which had rolled into the road, hating being the source of entertainment to half the street and itching to escape. Even so, she couldn't let Aggie's malice stir up any more mischief. She'd done enough. 'Don't flatter yourself, girl. You've let yourself go: put on weight, even your hair needs washing. Sam wouldn't be attracted to you looking like that, even if you weren't a married woman with a child.'

This was too much and Aggie launched herself at Dolly again. Eventually, it was Edna Crawshaw who bore down upon the pair of them, like the avenging witch from the north and tore them bodily apart. 'What's got into you two? Looks like blue murder is going on here. If you were nobbut nippers, I'd tell you to kiss and make up but you're grown women, so shake hands and behave yourself.' Turning her attention to the gathered audience. 'And you lot can get off home. Show's over.'

Edna made Dolly unlock the front door and packed them both inside with instructions to put on the kettle. 'And don't come out till your sorted.'

They sat, either side of the kitchen table where many of their rows had taken place in the past and carefully avoided eye contact. In the end it was Dolly who spoke first. 'If it's true what you say, that Sam has women all over the place, then why does he come back here every night? Why isn't he interested in leaving?' Dolly might have added that she wished he would go, but not for the world was she prepared to let Aggie know how bad things were between them,

She'd tackled him about Evie once, demanding to know if he was seeing her again but he'd denied it with such a pained expression that Dolly had believed him. Each and every day she asked herself why she put up with him: his regular and prolonged trips to the pub, coming home drunk more often than not; the fact they had nothing left to say to each other, not even interested in arguing any more; his demands upon her were gone. She'd believed that marriage was sacred, that if they both put in the necessary effort they could make it work. But Sam put no effort into anything. She was the one doing all the giving and he simply took. She almost hoped it was true that he was seeing Evie again, for that would change everything.

Aggie was saying, 'I expect because he feels sorry for you, I was the one he wanted to marry, not you. Potty about me, he was. You were only second choice. Still are, even now. You stole him from me.'

'Oh Aggie, don't talk daft. You'd already made up your mind to marry Harold before ever Sam looked my way. You wanted security and comfort, talked of little else. Perhaps you thought you could have them both, Harold to pay the bills and Sam for a bit on the side.'

'I did not. I have my decency.'

'Have you indeed? Well, you decided he wasn't good enough for you, but what you hated most was to think that *I* had him. That really hurt, didn't it? That's the reason you showed no sympathy when I caught him kissing Evie Barker and foolishly came to you, my own sister, for support. You thought he'd betrayed me but you were wrong. He might have wanted to have his wicked way with Evie Barker but he never actually did. She refused him. Didn't you realise that? Despite everything he's actually stayed faithful, which is why I gave him another chance.'

'Stayed faithful? Like hell he has. Whose child do you think that is?'

The words burst out of her mouth without thought, as she indicated the pram still parked under the front window, and the innocent Noel happily sleeping through it all. Too late, Aggie realised that she'd gone too far and couldn't take the words back.

'What did you say?'

Fear cascaded through her, as things seemed to be slipping out of her control. But if she'd foolishly said too much, was it any wonder? She'd needed to lash out at someone and who better than this bastard half-sister who'd been a thorn in her side for years, who'd basically killed her father and robbed her of the man she'd wanted for herself. Somehow, the facts had become twisted in her demented brain and Aggie no longer recognised the truth.

Nor had she managed to pay off Nifty Jack, who was haunting her doorstep pretty well every day. She never had a minute's peace, terrified he might snatch little Noel, hold her baby to ransom, or drown him in the canal like a cat. If only they could move to the suburbs, as Harold had once promised, but with the gaffer sick things were going from bad to worse at the mill. She couldn't even squeeze any of her husband's savings out of him to pay off the talleyman for good. Harold was determined to hang on to every penny.

As ever, Aggie took refuge in self-pity. 'What have you ever done to help me? Not even prepared to lend me money to get myself out of debt, so why shouldn't I have a bit of fun?'

Dolly regarded her out of narrowed eyes. 'You didn't ask for a loan until *after* you got pregnant, when you needed baby stuff so don't use that as an excuse. You had it in for me, Aggie, and were always jealous, malicious, conniving and manipulating. You used to play nasty little tricks on me when we were growing up, always wanting to be Calvin's favourite, shutting me out and making me feel unwanted! You were determined to blame me for his accident. Is that the reason you slept with my husband? Because you did, didn't you? How many times?'

'It was your own fault for stupidly getting yourself embroiled with Evie Barker and her strike breaking. If you'd never done that she'd've married her rich husband, never come to work at the mill and taken up with Sam. It might all have been different.'

Dolly was thinking fast. 'You have a strange knack of twisting the truth to suit yourself. You rejected Sam and chose Harold, only wanting him out of spite for money. After I'd caught Sam with Evie Barker and rejected him, did he come looking for you instead?'

'Aye, he was drunk and yes, he couldn't keep his hands off me, just like the old days. He never did love you!'

The flush on Aggie's cheeks proved she'd guessed correctly. 'So you took your revenge by sleeping with my husband. Well, you're welcome to him.'

'You adored Sam Clayton, always did, always will.'

'Oh, I think I'm cured of that particular sickness.' Dolly was fighting to keep control, to steady the tremor in her voice, patience having disappeared. This silly woman had deliberately set out to hurt and ruin her life and her marriage. How much easier it would all have been if they'd supported each other, as sisters should; and Aggie had helped to pay off the debt her own father had left. Instead she'd been eaten up with jealousy because of the good relationship she and Maisie had enjoyed. She'd successfully ruined that too for a while.

'Pity you didn't marry Sam, as you and he would make a good pair. And what does Harold think of this little fling of yours?'

Dolly watched with interest as every ounce of colour drained from Aggie's face. 'Oh dear, didn't you stop to consider how your own husband might react if he found out Noel wasn't his son? You were always quick to condemn Mam, now you're the one who has brought a little cuckoo into the nest. How would you like it if someone addressed your child with the kind of words you've used on me? I doubt you'd care for it much. At least Mam loved Nathan Barker, difficult and selfish though he undoubtedly was. What's your excuse, revenge and jealousy? Is that a good reason for betraying a faithful husband?'

'You aren't going to tell him? You must never mention this to Harold.'

A short pause before Dolly answered. Long enough to see Aggie start to sweat. 'No, I'm not going to mention this most enlightening conversation. You are the telltale, the one with a rotten egg where your heart should be, not me. I seem to remember once saying that some secrets are best kept. I still believe that.'

Aggie didn't offer any thanks for this generosity of spirit on Dolly's behalf. Instead, she sharply remarked, 'He'd never believe you in any case. Harold adores me, and Noel too.'

Dolly could see that she was shaking, her small eyes darting frantically about as if seeking escape and finding none. It was plain she could see her whole life collapsing about her like a house of cards, and looked as if she was about to burst into tears.

Dolly said, 'How much do you owe?'

Aggie was startled by the question but wearily gave the answer, proving this was in the forefront of her mind. 'About five pounds, or maybe six! I paid some off but—'

'He keeps changing the interest rate, putting it up and up. If I settle this debt for you, Aggie, I want you to promise never to borrow money again. Ever! And you mustn't sleep with anyone other than your own husband, nor accuse me, or anyone else for the matter of being a bastard, or blame them for a situation that is none of their making. Do I make myself clear? You are going to try, Aggie, against all the odds, to turn yourself into

352

the type of mother that your son deserves. That way, you and I can put all this nasty mess behind us.'

'That's blackmail!' Aggie was staring at her wide-eyed, her expression a mixture of shock and relief.

'So it is. And I shall be watching to see that you keep to our bargain. I wouldn't wish to find myself obliged to call upon Harold's assistance in the matter. Do we have a deal?'

'What are you going to do about Sam?'

'That's my business. Do we have a deal, or not, sister dear? Your future good behaviour in return for me wiping your slate clean is essential.'

'All right, we have,' agreed a strangely subdued Aggie.

Chapter Thirty

Sam left the house without a word of argument, seeming to be almost relieved that the battle was over, even if he had lost his comfy billet. Finding another wasn't proving easy. Dave refused to let him move back in with them as there was another baby on the way, and when Sam told his one-time friend, Matt, that Dolly had thrown him out and he was in need of new quarters, instead of the anticipated sympathy, Matt simply stared at him then turned his back and hurried away.

Fortunately, later that day, Sam spotted a likely new barmaid in the Navigation. In no time at all, on hearing of his plight, she'd invited him round to her house, which she shared with her twin sister. Two for the price of one, thought Sam, pulling off his boots by a blazing fire while the girls fussed about him. This would do nicely.

Dolly kept her word and paid off Nifty Jack. Even gave him a piece of her mind about harassing nursing mothers and small babies. 'I'll have you arrested for the attempted murder of my nephew if you come anywhere near me and mine ever again,' she told him.

Her remarks bounced off him like water off a tar baby, having no effect whatsoever. Nifty Jack carefully counted the coins she gave him, slid them into his pocket, expressed his pleasure at doing business with her and swaggered off.

''Til next time,' he called. He even had the cheek to graciously tip his bowler hat at her, before vanishing round the corner looking mighty pleased with himself.

'I don't think so,' Dolly murmured to herself.

This time when she asked her brothers for help, they readily agreed. Being a nuisance to an adult in debt was one thing, threatening a baby was quite another. Later that same evening as the talleyman was going about his nefarious business, making his calls and creating havoc in every household, as was his wont, several figures suddenly emerged from the shadows and before he'd had time to see who they were, a gag had been stuffed in his mouth and a sack pulled over his head. Even as he tried to kick them off, he found himself being trussed up like a chicken and lifted from the ground by several pairs of strong hands. Then all went black as something hit him over the head.

'We dumped him deep in the hold of a ship bound for Ireland via Liverpool,' Josh told her the next day.

Eli said, 'Aye, by the time they find him and let him out, he'll be far from these shores. It might even go all the way to America, and he'll not have a penny to his name since we gave his collecting tin to the orphanage.

'Oh, well done! Excellent, but what if he does get out at Ireland and takes the next ship back?'

'We made it very clear that if he ever came home he'd get worse next time,' Abel put in. 'He knew who we were, right enough, and that we meant business.'

'Don't you fret, Dolly,' Willy comforted her. 'We're rid of him for good this time.'

'Bless you!' Dolly said, kissing all her brothers with relief.

–

Two weeks later Dolly was seated by her fire in the comfy chair she'd bought herself, feeling very much alone with nothing to do, nowhere to go, no one to talk to, and far too much time on her hands to think.

Mam and Cyril were happily playing the role of lovebirds, singing their hearts out at the chapel and busily practising for the next *Messiah*. Her brothers and sisters-in-law were now making alternative arrangements for baby-minders, even doing their own washing these days. Young Willy was happily married and about to become a father for the first time.

Aggie and Harold were increasingly absorbed in their son, and now renting a house in the suburbs. The last time she'd seen her sister, Aggie had complained that she was finding life a bit quiet and Harold didn't get home till much later, which was highly inconvenient. Dolly had merely given her a firm remark. 'As Mam always used to say, Aggie, you make your bed and you lie in it.'

At least Aggie had a husband who would remain in blissful ignorance of his wife's infidelity. And there was no one in Dolly's bed at all.

When the knock came, she didn't hear it. She'd had a tiring day doing her rounds, and must have drifted off to sleep in this deliciously comfy new chair. Dolly woke with a start and for a moment her mind took her back to the time when she'd worked as housekeeper for Nifty Jack, and he'd come home to find her still up and had attacked her. What a chain of events that had led to. It took a moment before her heart stopped racing and remembered that she didn't need to watch for the talleyman any more. She was safe. They all were.

The knock came again, louder this time, and she shook herself awake. That was all in the past, over and done with. She hadn't killed Nifty Jack, hadn't killed anyone. Nor had she done anything wrong for Cabbage Lil, unlike some, and even Aggie had learned a valuable lesson.

She went to the door knowing that it wasn't bad news, as it couldn't be Sam coming home drunk from the pub. The last she'd heard he'd moved out Droylsden way with the barmaid from the Navigation. The divorce would go through in the fullness of time, using his desertion as grounds. She opened the door and blinked in surprise. 'Matt?'

'I kept hoping you'd come by the timber yard. Sam told me as how you'd called it a day at last, but I couldn't quite pluck up the courage to call.'

'Oh!' She stared at him, not quite able to believe her eyes, or find anything more sensible to say.

'I kept hoping you'd call and tell me yourself. You haven't been avoiding me by any chance have you Dolly? Because, if so, I'd be upset, being a chap who doesn't like to think that the girl I love has turned against me for no reason. You are still my girl, aren't you Dolly? Or have you got too grand, now that you're running your own business?'

A bubble of laughter started somewhere deep in her throat. 'Don't you start, I've enough with our Aggie.'

'Well, are you going you ask me in, or keep me standing on the doorstep till Edna Crawshaw has everyone out on the street to have a good dander at me. No doubt they'll all be saying that soon-to-be-divorced, Dolly Clayton, is seeing her fancy man again. What do you reckon?'

'I think you'd best come in, Matt Thornton. I have my reputation to consider, after all.'

Blue eyes twinkling, she pushed wide the door and he had her in his arms before ever she'd managed to get it closed, which was most satisfying for all the matrons of Tully Court who sighed with pleasure behind their lace curtains at the sight of this pair of reunited lovers, and wiped a tear from their eye with the corner of a pinny.

Acknowledgements

I would first like to thank Bella Tweedale, whose Lancashire folk songs gave me the idea for the original title, *Watch for the Talleyman*. Thanks also to May Stothard, Bessie Jones, Alice Brook and Irene Baxter, who all gave up hours of their time to talk to me about life in the mill. A particular mention to Dolly Fitton, who allowed me to borrow her name, and although my story is entirely fictitious, I hope my character borrows some of this ninety-year-old's get-up-and-go. My greatest thanks must go to librarian Dorothy Taylor, who found all these delightful people for me.

A Salford Saga

Ruby McBride
The Favourite Child
The Castlefield Collector
Dancing on Deansgate